GW01463980

SUB ROSA

SUB ROSA

by

Robert Aickman

Tartarus Press

Sub Rosa
by Robert Aickman

First published Gollancz (London), 1968.

This edition is published by Tartarus Press, 2010 at
Coverley House, Carlton-in-Coverdale, Leyburn,
North Yorkshire, DL8 4AY, UK.

Sub Rosa © the Estate of Robert Aickman, 2010, c/o Artellus Limited,
30 Dorset House, Gloucester Place, London NW1 5AD, England.

'Introduction' © R.B. Russell, 2010.

'Notes by the Author' used by permission, Rare Books and
Special Collections, Center for Archival Collections,
University Libraries, Bowling Green State University.

Cover illustration © Stephen J. Clark/
The Singing Garden, 2010.

ISBN 978-1-905784-28-8

The publishers would like to thank Jim Rockhill,
Douglas A. Anderson, Gary W. Crawford, Lee N. McLaird and
Richard Dalby for their help in the preparation of this volume.

Printed in Great Britain by the MPG Books Group,
Bodmin and King's Lynn.

Sub Rosa by Robert Aickman
is limited to 350 copies.

For Miranda

CONTENTS

The highest State that man can achieve is that of astonishment; and when a primary phenomenon astonishes him, he should be satisfied. It cannot give him anything higher, and he must not look for anything more beyond it; this is the frontier.

Goethe

INTRODUCTION
R.B. Russell

DURING HIS literary career Robert Aickman worked as a successful editor and reviewer, wrote non-fiction, and attempted several novels, but he excelled at the composition of 'strange' short stories. In these he offers a world in which the inexplicable, the ghostly and the macabre are manifested, but the source and meaning of such intrusions are not at all clear. Very often the explanation of events would seem to be super-natural, but this alone will not account for everything that has happened. It would appear that we should look at the mental state of Aickman's protagonists if we are to fully understand the implications of his stories. An examination of their unconscious minds would seem to be the way forward, but neither does this approach entirely suffice. It is reasonable to assume that these two driving forces, the supernatural and the psychological, could be brought together, but the results of this are often contradictory. Aickman seems to have given us more than enough clues to the puzzles he offers in his tales, and yet they do not quite account for all that happens in them.

It is not entirely surprising that Robert Aickman should have written such unconventional stories, for his life was itself unconventional. He was born in London on 27th June 1914, and originally followed his eccentric and awkward father into the architectural profession. Until the Second World War, Aickman lived a bohemian life with few friends and little money. He helped his father in his ailing business, and had hopes of becoming an author. The theatre appears to have been his main interest at this time, along with meeting unusual women.

Aickman opposed the approaching war. As a pacifist and a conscientious objector he was interviewed by a tribunal which not only granted him immunity from fighting, but freed him from war work of any kind. When his father died in 1941, Aickman inherited the family house and a small allowance, married Edith Ray Gregorson, and attempted to publish a long philosophical work called *Panacea*, without success.

Aickman and Ray set themselves up as literary agents, calling their business the Richard Marsh Agency after Aickman's grandfather, who had written the famous horror novel, *The Beetle*. Aickman wrote drama and film reviews, and was drawn to research into the paranormal. Late in the war he read *Narrow Boat* by L.T.C. Rolt and became interested in the canals of Britain. His subsequent meeting with Rolt led to their founding of the Inland Waterways Association, devoted to the restoration and preservation of England's canals. For several years it was Aickman's work for the Association that brought him into the public eye.

The Inland Waterways Association had unforeseen literary benefits for both co-founders. The Richard Marsh Agency was able to find a publisher for Rolt's volume of ghost stories, *Sleep No More*, and Aickman became fascinated by the Association's beautiful new secretary, Elizabeth Jane Howard. The Marsh Agency also found a publisher for her first book, *The Beautiful Visit*, and Aickman and Howard became lovers. Together they wrote the six stories which made up his first book, *We Are For the Dark*.

Introduction

We Are For the Dark was published in 1951 and the strange tales therein set the tone for his subsequent stories, although he did not start writing and publishing these in earnest until the 1960s. The Inland Waterways Association was Aickman's main interest through the 1950s and in that decade he published two popular books on the subject. He also became the chairman of both the London Opera Society and Ballets Minerva.

Aickman's career as an author of 'strange' stories took off in the early 1960s when 'Ringing the Changes' came to the notice of the agent, publishing executive and editor, Herbert van Thal. The result was the publication of Aickman's novel *The Late Breakfasters* and the volume of short stories, *Dark Entries*, published in 1964. He also began to edit the well-received Fontana series of 'Great Ghost Stories'.

Powers of Darkness followed in 1966 and this collection, *Sub Rosa*, was published in 1968. *Sub Rosa* represents the author at the height of his powers. There are traditional ghost stories; in 'The Houses of the Russians' and 'The Unsettled Dust' we see just how different and strange they can be in Aickman's hands. In the latter the dust that continually and excessively falls is a surreal counterpart to the more traditional ghost with which it is associated. The story is as much about the relationship between all of the characters, and the sad sexual tension, as it is about ghosts. A rather more heightened sexuality is a fundamental part of 'Ravissante', but in this story the relationships between the characters on and off stage are all called into question. In 'The Cicerones' the connection between the various young people and the terrifying figure glimpsed at the beginning of the story is even harder to define.

In *Sub Rosa* Aickman included stories that are concerned with the plight of the individual. 'No Stronger Than a Flower' is a classic 'Aickmanesque' story in that it is not obvious exactly what Nesta is fighting against with her beauty regime. 'The Inner Room' is another tale of personal terror and it is open to various readings.

Further original collections were published in the 1970s; *Cold Hand in Mine* and *Tales of Love and Death*. Aickman's writing garnered some popular and critical success, and by the end of his career he was the recipient of two awards. In 1975 he won the World Fantasy Award for 'Pages from a Young Girl's Journal', and in 1981 the British Fantasy Award for 'The Stains'. The last collection that Aickman saw in print was *Intrusions: Strange Tales*, in 1980.

1980 was also the year that Robert Aickman was diagnosed with cancer. He refused conventional medical treatment and was nursed at home, mainly by friends. He finally died in hospital on 26th February 1981.

Aickman's publisher, Victor Gollancz, issued a posthumous collection of short stories, *Night Voices*, in 1985. Further reprints have appeared over the following three decades. During this time Aickman's work has been periodically out of print and many of his books have become prohibitively expensive collectors' items. Interest in his writing has continued and in the last ten years he has been receiving serious attention from critics and fans alike.

Not every commentator has been convinced by Aickman's work. There can be no doubt that Aickman's stories succeed in causing uncertainty and unease in the mind of the reader. There are some literal-minded observers, though, who prefer a story to be brought to a neat conclusion, a comfort that Aickman steadfastly refused to offer. That which is left imperfectly explained haunts the more imaginative reader, who will go over the story for clues and hints. We will ultimately try to find answers 'off the page'. We attempt to imagine what has happened to the characters both before and after the few scenes offered to us by Aickman. We are left with the idea that something has occurred off stage which may be the key to proceedings.

It must not be thought, though, that Aickman leaves his stories 'open-ended', uncompleted, or that they do not satisfy on a technical level. The development of each story leaves the reader in no doubt that the tale has come to an inevitable conclusion.

Robert Aickman writes of the 'strange', but as a believer in the supernatural himself, perhaps he would have considered himself a realist, recognising that in life there are some occurrences for which there are no comfortable explanations. For example, nobody has ever satisfactorily accounted for why ghosts seem to manifest themselves to one person and not another. Perhaps ghosts, if they exist, do so in our unconscious mind, but, like Aickman's stories, this approach does not give us a full answer.

Robert Aickman would have been aware of the work of Arthur Machen, but not, perhaps, of the Latin inscription on Machen's grave. In death that venerable Welsh author accepts that *Omnia Exeunt in Mysterium*; everything ends in mystery. It's a dictum that Aickman seems to have endorsed in his strange stories.

RAVISSANTE

I HAD an acquaintance who had begun, before I knew him, as a painter but who took to 'compiling and editing' those costly, glossy books about art which are said to sell in surprising numbers but which no person one knows ever buys and no person one sees ever opens.

I first met this man at a party. The very modern room was illuminated only in patches by dazzling standard lamps beneath metal frames. The man stood in one of the dark corners, looking shy and out of it. He wore a light blue suit, a darker blue shirt, and a tie that was pretty well blue-black. He looked very malleable and slender. I walked towards him. I saw that he had a high, narrow head and smooth dark hair, cut off in a sharp, horizontal line at the back. I saw also that with him was a woman, previously invisible, though, as a matter of fact, and when she had come into focus, rather oddly dressed. None the less, I spoke.

It seemed that I was welcome after all. The man said something customary about knowing almost none of the guests, and introduced the nearly invisible woman to me as his wife. He proceeded to chat away eagerly but a little anxiously, as if to extenuate his presence among so many dark strangers. He told me then and there about his abandonment of painting for

1

editorship: 'I soon realised I could not expect my pictures to sell,' he said, or words to that effect. 'Too far-fetched.' About that particular epithet of his I am certain. It stuck in my mind immediately. He offered no particulars, but talked about the terms he got for his gaudy pictorial caravanserais. I have, of course, written a little myself from time to time, and the sums he named, struck me as pretty good. I avoided all comment to the effect that it is the unread book which brings in the royalty (after all, modern translations of the *Iliad* and the *Odyssey* are said to sell by the hundred thousand, and the Bible to be more decisively the best seller of all with every year that passes); and observed instead that his life must be an interesting one, with much travel, and, after all, much beauty to behold. He agreed warmly and, taking another Martini from a passing tray, described in some detail his latest business excursion, which had been to somewhere in Central America where there were strange things painted on walls, perfect for colour photography. He said he hoped he hadn't been boring me. 'Oh, no,' I said. All the time, the man's wife had said nothing. I remark on this simply as a fact. I do not imply that she *was* bored. She might indeed have been enthralled. Silence can, after all, mean either thing. In her case, I never found out which it meant. She was even slenderer than he was, with hair the colour (as far as I could see) of old wheat, collected into a bun low on the neck, a pale face, long like her husband's, and these slightly odd, dark garments I've mentioned. I noticed now that the man had a rather weak, undeveloped nose. In the end, the man said would I visit their flat in Battersea and have dinner? and I gave my promise.

It will be noticed that I am being discreet with names. I think it is best because the man himself was so discreet in that way, as will be apparent later. Moreover, at no time did I become a close friend of the pair. One thing, however, must have had importance.

The Battersea flat (not quite overlooking the Park) did exhibit some of the man's paintings. I might compare them, though a little distantly, with the once controversial last works of the late Charles Sims: apparently confused on the surface, even demented, they made one doubt while one continued to gaze, as upon Sims's pictures, whether the painter had not in truth broken through to a deep and terrible order. Titles of the Sims species, 'Behold I Am Graven on the Palm of Thy Hand' or 'Am I Not The Light in the Abyss?', would have served with this man's pictures also. In fact, with him there was no question of titles, not, I thought, only out of compliance with the contemporary attitude, but more because the man did not appear to see his works as separate and possibly saleable objets d'art. 'I found that I couldn't paint what people might want to buy,' he said, smiling beneath his weak nose. His wife, seated on a hard chair and again oddly dressed, said nothing. As a matter of fact, I could imagine quite well these strange pictures being ingathered for a time by fashion's flapping feelers, though, obviously for entirely wrong reasons. I remarked to the two of them that the pictures were among the most powerful and exciting I had ever seen, and what I said was sincere, despite a certain non-professionalism in the execution. I am not sure that I should have cared to live surrounded by such pictures, as they did, but that is another matter. Perhaps I exaggerate the number: there were, I think, three of these mystical works in the living room, all quite large; four in the matrimonial bedroom, into which I was conducted to look at them; and one each in the small bedroom for visitors and in the bathroom. They were framed very casually, because the painter did not take them seriously enough; and mingled them on his walls with framed proofs from the art books, all perpetrated at the fullest stretch of modern reproductive processes.

I went there several times to dinner, perhaps six or seven times in all; and I reciprocated by entertaining the two of them at the Royal Automobile Club, which at that time I found convenient for such purposes, as I was living alone in Richmond. The Battersea dinners were very much of a pattern: my host did most of the talking; his wife, in her odd clothes, seemed to say less and less; the food, cooked by her, was perfectly good though a trifle earnest; I was treated very consciously as a guest. From this last, and from other things, I deduced that guests were infrequent. Perhaps the trouble was that the establishment lacked magic. The painter of those pictures should, one felt, have had something to say, but everything he brought out, much though there was of it, was faintly disappointing. He seemed eager to welcome me and reluctant to let me go, but entirely unable to make a hole in the wall that presumably enclosed him, however long he punched. Nor, as will be gathered, can his wife be said to have been much help. Or, at least, as far as one could see. Human relationships are so fantastically oblique that one can never be sure.

Anyway I fear that the acquaintanceship slowly died, or almost died. The near-death was slow because I made it so. I felt, almost at the beginning, that anything quicker would have meant a painfulness, conceivably even a dispute. Knowing what I was doing (within the inevitable—exceedingly narrow—limits), I fear that I very slowly strangled the connection. I was sad about it in a general sort of way, but neither the man nor his wife had truly touched anything about me or within me, and associations that are not alive are best amputated as skilfully as possible before the rot infects too much of one's total tissue and unnecessarily lowers the tone of life. If one goes to parties or meets many new people in any other way, one has to take protective action quite frequently, however much one hates oneself in the process; just as human beings are compelled to massacre animals unceasingly, because human beings are simply unable to survive, for the most part, on apples and nuts.

Total death of the connection, however, it never was. The next thing that happened, was a letter from a firm of solicitors. It arrived more than four years after I had last seen the Battersea couple, as I discovered from looking through my old engagement books after I had read it; and two years, I believed, after the last Christmas card had passed between us. I had moved during that latter period from Richmond to Highgate. The letter told me that my Battersea acquaintance had died ('after a long illness', the solicitors added) and that he had appointed me joint executor of his Will. The other executor was his wife. Needless to say, it was the first I had heard of it. There was a legacy which the testator 'hoped I would accept': the amount was £100, which, I regret to say, struck me at once as having been arrived at during an earlier period of Britain's financial history. Finally, the letter requested me to communicate as soon as possible with the writers or directly with their client's wife.

I groaned a little, but when I had reached the office where I worked before my marriage, I composed a letter of sympathy and in a postscript suggested, as tactfully as I could, that an evening be named for a first meeting of the executors. The reply came instantly. In the smallest number of words possible, it thanked me for my sympathy and proposed the evening of the next day. I put off an engagement to meet my fiancée and drove once more to Battersea.

I noticed that my co-executor had abandoned the unusual style of costume she had previously favoured, and wore an unremarkable, even commonplace, dress from a multiple store.

Perhaps it was her response to the inner drive that until recently swept the bereaved into black. In no other respect could I observe a change in her.

She did not seem broken, or even ruffled, with grief, and she had little more to say than before. I did try to discover the cause of death, but could get no clear answer, and took for granted that it had been one of the usual bitter maladies. I was told that there was no need for me to put myself to trouble. She would do all there was to be done, and I could just come in at the end.

I did remark that as an executor I should have to see a copy of the Will. She at once handed the original to me in silence: it had been lying about the room. It was simple enough. The body was to be cremated, and the entire estate was left to the testator's wife, except for my £100, and except for the fact that all the testator's pictures were to be offered to the National Gallery of British Art; if refused, to a long list of other public galleries, ten or twelve of them; and if still refused, to be burnt. I saw at once why I had been brought into the settlement of the estate. I had been apprehensive ever since I had heard from the solicitors. Now I was terrified.

'Don't worry,' said my co-executor, smiling faintly. 'I dealt with that part myself while he was still alive. None of the places would touch the pictures with a bargepole.'

'But,' I said, 'as an executor I can't just leave it at that.'

'See their letters.' She produced a heap of paper and passed it over to me. 'Sit down and read them.'

She herself drew back her normal hard chair, and sat half watching me, half not; but without taking up any other occupation.

I thought that I might as well settle the matter, if it really were possible, there and then. I checked the letters against the list in the Will. Every named gallery was accounted for. All the letters were negative: some courteously and apologetically negative; some not. The correspondence covered rather more than the previous twelve months. Many public servants are slow to make up their minds and slower to commit themselves.

'Did he know?' I asked.

That was another question to which I failed to get a clear answer, because she merely smiled, and even that only slightly. It seemed difficult to persist.

'Don't worry,' she said again. 'I'll look after the bonfire.'

'But don't *you* want to keep the pictures?' I cried. 'Perhaps you've lived with them so long that they've become over-familiar, but they really are rather remarkable.'

'Surely as executors we have to obey the Will?'

'I am certain you can keep the pictures, as far as the law is concerned.'

'Would *you* like to take them? Bearing in mind,' she added, 'that there's about a hundred more of them stored in Kingston.'

'I simply haven't room, much though I regret it.'

'Nor, in the future, shall I.'

'I'd like to take *one* of them, if I may.'

'As many as you wish. Would you like the manuscripts also? They're all in that suitcase.' It was a battered green object, standing against the wall. I think it was largely her rather unpleasant indifference that made me accept. It was quite apparent what would happen to the manuscripts if I did not take them, and one did not like to think of a man's life disappearing in a few flames, as his body.

'When's the funeral?' I asked.

'Tomorrow, but it will be quite private.'

I wondered where the body *was*. In the matrimonial bedroom? In the small room for guests? In some mortuary?

'We neither of us believed in God.' In my experience of her, it was the first time she had taken the initiative in making such a general pronouncement, negative though it had proved to be.

I looked at the pictures, including the one I had mentally selected for myself. She said nothing more. Of course, the pictures had been painted a number of years earlier: perhaps before the painter had first met her.

She offered me neither a cup of coffee nor a helping hand with the picture and the heavy suitcase down the many flights of stairs in a Battersea block of flats. Driving home, it occurred to me that for the amount of work involved, my executor's legacy was not so inadequate after all.

The picture has travelled round with me ever since. It is now in the room next to the one which used to be the nursery. I often go in and look at it for perhaps five or six minutes when the light is good.

The suitcase contained the tumbled typescripts of the art books, apparently composed straight on to the machine. They were heavily gashed with corrections in different coloured inks, but this did not matter to me, because it had never been in my mind to read them. All the same, I have never thrown them away. They are in the attic now, still in the green suitcase, with labels stuck on it from Mussolini's Italy. To that small extent, my poor acquaintance lives still. He must presumably have felt that I, more than most, had something in common with him, or he would not have made me his executor.

But the suitcase contained something else: a shorter, more personal narrative, typed out on large sheets of undulating foreign paper, and rolled up within a thick rubber band, now rotten. It is to introduce this narrative, so strange and so intimate, to explain how it came my way and how it comes to be published, that I have written the foregoing. The sheer oddity of life seems to me of more and more importance, because more and more the pretence is that life is charted, predictable, and controllable. And for oddity, of course, one could well write mystery.

Under the Will, a publication fee belongs to the widow, who plainly holds the copyright. I give notice that she has but to apply. Remembering that last evening, on the day before the funeral, I am not sure that she will. But we shall see. The rest I leave to the words of my poor acquaintance.

ʘ

Yesterday I returned from three weeks in Belgium. While there, I had an experience which made a great impression on me. I think it may even have changed my entire way of looking at things; troubled my soul, as people say. Anyway, I feel that I am unlikely ever to forget it. On the other hand, I have learned that what one remembers is always far from what took place. So I am taking this first opportunity of writing down as many of the details as I can remember and as seem important. Only six days have passed since it happened, but I am aware that already there are certain to be gaps bridged by imagination, and unconscious distortions in the interests of consistency and effect. It is possibly unfortunate that I could not make this record while I was still in Brussels, but I found it impossible. I lacked the time, or, more probably, the application, as people always say of me. I also felt that I was under a spell. I felt that something terrible and alarming might happen as I sat by myself in my bedroom writing it all down. The English Channel proves to have loosened this spell considerably, though I can still feel all those textures on my hands and face, still see those queer creatures, and still hear Madame A.'s croaking voice. I find that, when I think about it, I am frightened still, but attracted overwhelmingly also, as at the time. This, I believe, is what is properly meant by the word fascination.

As others may read this, even if only in the distant future, I set forth a few basic facts. I am a painter, and twenty-six years old: the age when Bonnington died. I have about £300 a year of my own, so can paint what interests me; at least I can while I remain on my own. Until now I have been quite happy on my own, though this fact seems to upset almost everyone I know. So far I have had very little to do with women, mainly because I cannot see that I have anything to offer that is likely to appeal to them, and because I detest the competitive aspect of the relations between the sexes. I should hate it for a woman to pity me, and, on the other hand, I should hate to be involved with a woman whom I had to pity; a woman, in fact, who was not attractive enough to be in the full sex war, and who might, therefore, be available for such as me. I should not care to be involved with a woman who was anything less than very beautiful. Perhaps that is the artist in me. I do not really know. I feel that I should want only the kind of woman who could not conceivably want me. I cannot say that the whole problem does not trouble me, but, by the standard of what I have read and heard, I am surprised that it does not trouble me more.

I find also that I have no difficulty in writing these things down. On the contrary, I find that I like it. I fancy that I could produce a quite long narrative about my own inner feelings, though this is obviously not the occasion, for I think I have already said all that is necessary. I have to strike a balance between clearing my own mind and imparting facts to strangers. I conceive of this narrative, if I finish it, as being read only by myself and by strangers. I should not care for someone intimately in my life to read it—if there ever is such a person. I doubt whether there ever will be. Sometimes this frightens me, but sometimes it reassures me.

At this point, I remember to mention, for the strangers who may read, that both my parents died seven years ago in an aeroplane accident. It was my Mother who insisted on their going to Paris by air. I was present when my Father argued with her. It was the usual situation between them. All the same, I loved my Mother very much, even though she was as bossy towards me as she was towards my Father. No doubt this has affected me too. I fear that a woman would steal my independence—perhaps even kill me. Nor, from what I have seen, do I think these particularly unreal fears.

On the whole, I do not like people. I seem incapable of approaching them, but I find that when they approach me, I am often quite successful with them—more so, indeed, than many of those who have no trouble with bustling in and making the first gesture. When once I am started, I can talk on fluently and even amusingly (though I believe inwardly that I have no sense of humour at all), and frequently, usually indeed, seem to make a strong impression. I suppose I must get some pleasure out of this, but I do not think I ever exert any real influence. It is almost as if someone else were talking through me—wound up by an outsider, my interlocutor. It is not I who talk, and certainly not I who please. I seriously suspect that I myself never speak, and I am certain that if I did, I should never please. This is, of course, another reason why I could not sensibly think of living with anyone.

Similarly with my art. My pictures are visionary and symbolical, and, from first to last, have seemed to be painted by someone other than myself. Indeed, I have the greatest difficulty in painting anything to command. I am useless at portraits, incapable of painting at all in the open air, and quite indifferent to the various kinds of abstract painting that have followed the invention of the camera. Also I am weak on drawing, which, of course, should be a hopeless handicap. I have to be alone in a room in order to paint, though then I can sometimes paint day and night, twenty hours at a stretch. My Father, who was quite sympathetic to my talent, arranged for me to attend a London school of art. It was quite pointless. I could achieve nothing, and was unhappier than at any other period of my life. It was the only time when I felt really lonely—though worse may, of course, lie ahead. I am thus almost entirely self-taught, or taught by that other within me. I am aware that my pictures lack serious technique (if there is a technique that can be distinguished from inspiration and invention). I should have given up painting them some time ago, were it not that a certain number of people have seemed to find something remarkable in them, and have thus identified me with them and made me feel mildly important. If I were to give up, I should have to give up altogether. I could not possibly paint, as so many do, just as a hobby or on Sundays only. I am sure that soon I *shall* give up—or be given up. When I read about the mediumship of Willi and Rudi Schneider, and of how the gift departed first from one brother and then from the other, and when both were quite young, I felt at once that something of the same kind will happen to me, and that I shall settle down, like Willi Schneider, as a hairdresser or other tradesman. Not that I wish to suggest any kind of mediumistic element in my works. It is simply that they contain a glory which is assuredly not in the painter, as the few who know him will confirm. It is a commonplace that there is often more than one soul in a single body.

I must admit also to certain 'influences'. This sounds pretentious, but it has to be said because it explains what I have been doing in Belgium and how I came to visit Madame A. I find that certain works, or the works of certain painters, affect me strongly, almost agonisingly on occasion, but only *certain* pictures and *certain* painters, really very few. Art in general leaves me rather cold, I regret to say, especially when put on public display to crowds, most of them, inevitably, insensitive. I am sure that pictures should always belong to single individuals. I even believe that pictures suffer death when shared among too many. I also dislike books about art, with their dreadful 'reproductions', repellent when in colour, boring when not. On the other hand, in the painters who *do* affect me, I become almost completely absorbed: in their lives and thoughts, to the extent that I can find out about these things or divine them, as well as in their works. The look of a painter and the look of the places where he painted, can, I think, be very important. I have no use for the theory that it is the picture only that matters and the way the paint has been stuck on it. That idea seems to me both lazy and soulless. Perhaps 'my' painters are my true intimates, and them only. I cannot believe I shall ever be so close to any living person as I was to Magnasco when first I sought him out. But there again, I should emphasise that these 'influences' seem to me far from direct. I can see little sign of other people's mannerisms in my own pictures. The influence is far deeper than that. The 'only the picture' people would not understand at all.

It has been possible for me to travel a little in search of my particular pictures because at all times I live simply and spend hardly anything. It was to look at pictures that I have been to Belgium: not, needless to say, the Memlings and Rubenses, fine though I daresay they once were, but the works of the symbolists and their kind, painters such as William Degouve de Nuncques, Fernand Khnopff, Xavier Mellery, who said (and who else has ever said it?) that he painted 'silence' and the 'soul of things', above all, of course, James Ensor, the charming

Baron. I had worked for months before I left, to equip myself with a list of addresses, many of the finest paintings of the school being happily still in private hands. Almost everyone was kind to me, though I can speak very little French, and for the first fortnight I was totally lost and absolutely happy. Not all the owners gave signs of appreciating their various properties, but, naturally, I did not expect that. At least they were prepared, most of them, to leave me alone and in peace, which was something I had seldom found among the private owners who survive in Italy. Of them many seemed to think they might sell me something; most made a great noise; and all refused me privacy.

One of the Belgian authorities with whom I exchanged letters, told me that the widow of a certain painter of the symbolist school still survived in Brussels. Not even to myself, in the light of what has happened, do I wish to write the name of this painter. I shall simply call him A., the late A. The informed may succeed in identifying him. Even if they do, it will not matter so much by the time they are likely to read this report. If strangers read sooner than I expect, it will only be because I am dead, so that the burden of discretion will be upon them and not upon me.

The Belgian authority, without comment, gave me an address in Brussels to which I wrote from England in my basic French, not seriously expecting any kind of reply. My habitual concern with the lives and personalities of 'my' painters may, however, have made me write more urgently and persuasively than I supposed. It seemed a considerable opportunity for me. Despite my great interest, I had never met one of my particular painters nor even a widow or relative. Many of the painters, in any case, had lived too long ago for such a thing. If now I received no reply, I was quite prepared to stand about outside the house, and consider in the light of what I observed, how best to get in. That proved unnecessary. Within three days, I heard from Madame A.

She wrote in a loose, curving hand, and confined herself to the centre of a large sheet of dark blue paper. Her letter looked like the springs bursting out of a watch in a nineteenth-century comic drawing. It would have been difficult to read even if it had been in English, but in the end I deciphered most of it. Madame A. said she was extremely old, had not left the house for years or received any visitors, but was enchanted that anyone should go out of his way to see her, and would receive me at six o'clock on an evening she named with exactitude. I had given her the dates of my proposed stay in Belgium, but none the less was surprised by her decisiveness, because it was without precedent. People with pictures had always left to me the time of a visit, and an embarrassing responsibility I had often found it. Madame A. ended by asking how old *I* was?

When the time came, I spent the afternoon at the Musée Wiertz, because it seemed to be in much the same part of the city as the abode of Madame A. 'Wiertz's work is noted rather for the sensational character of his subjects than for artistic merit', states, in true Beckmesser fashion, the English guide book I had borrowed from my public library. Possibly it is true in a way. It was not true for me. I was enthralled by Wiertz's living burials and imminent decapitations; by his livid, gory vision of that 'real' world which surely is livid and gory, though boring and monotonous also, which Wiertz omits. Wiertz's way of painting reality seems to me most apt to the character of reality. I was delighted also by the silence and emptiness of Wiertz's enormous, exciting studio. His official lack of merit keeps out the conducted art-lover.

All the same, anxiety was rising in me about my commitment with Madame A. I had remained fairly confident through most of my visits to picture owners, even in Italy, but these had been accepted as business transactions, and I had had no difficulty in concealing that for me they were stations on a spiritual ascent. With Madame A. I might have to disclose much more of myself and find words, even French words, for comments that were not purely conventional. She might be very infirm and intractable. It was probable that she was. It was September, and I sat on a bench before 'The Fight for the Body of Patroclus', all alone in the high studio, except for the attendant, who was mumbling to himself round the corner, while evening fell and the many clocks chimed and boomed me forward to my ambiguous assignation.

The power of solitude, not least in the Musée Wiertz, delayed me, in fact, too long. I found that I had underestimated the distance from the Rue Wiertz to the street in the direction of the Boulevard de Waterloo where Madame A. lived. They are beautiful streets through which I walked, though unostentatious; quiet, well-proportioned, and warmly alive with the feel of history. I have seen no other part of Brussels that I like so much. I loved the big opening windows, filling so much of every façade, and so unlike England. I even thought that this would be a perfect district in which to spend my life. One never really doubts that one will feel always what one feels at any given moment, good or bad; or, when the moment is good, at least that one *could* always feel it if one might only preserve the attendant framework and circumstances. The activity of walking through these unobtrusively beautiful streets quietened me. Also I commonly notice that for the *very* last stretch, I cease to be anxious.

Madame A. lived in just another such house: only two storeys high, white and elegant, with rococo twirls in the fanlight above the handsome front door, a properly sized front door for a house, wide enough for a crinoline, tall enough for an admiral, not a mere vertical slit for little men to steal through on the way to work. The houses to left and right repeated the pattern with subtle minor variations. I am glad to have been born soon enough to see such houses before either demolition or preservation: so far all was well.

There was a light in an upper window. It was of the colour known as old gold.

There was a bell and I heard it ring. I expected some kind of retainer or relative, since I visualised Madame A. as almost bed-ridden. But the door opened, and it was obvious that this was Madame A. herself. She looked very short and very square, almost gnomelike in shape; but the outline of her was all I could see because it was now almost dark, the street lighting was dim (thank goodness), and there was no light at all in the hall.

'*Entrez*,' said Madame A. in her distinctive croak. '*Entrez, monsieur. Fermez la porte, s'il vous plait.*' Though she croaked, she croaked as one accustomed, if she spoke at all, to speak only in terms of command. Nothing less, I felt at once, interested her in the context of human discourse.

Up from the hall led a straight, uncarpeted staircase, much wider than in an English house of that size, and with a heavy wooden baluster, just visible by a light from the landing above.

'*Suivez, monsieur.*'

Madame A. went clambering upwards. It is the only word. She was perfectly agile, but curiously uncouth in her movements. In the dim light, she went up those stairs almost like an old man of the woods, but I believe that age not infrequently has this effect on the gait of all but the tallest. I should say that Madame A.'s height was rather under than over five feet.

The light on the landing proved to hang by a thick golden chain in an art nouveau lantern of lumpy old gold glass speckled

with irregular dabs of crimson. I followed Madame A. into a
room which traversed the whole depth of the house, with one
window on to the street and, opposite it, another at the back of
the building. The door of the room was already open. Standing
ahead of me in the big doorway, Madame A. looked squatter
than ever.

The room was lighted by lanterns similar to that on the
landing. They were larger than the lantern outside, but the old
gold effulgence of the room remained distinctly dim, and the
crimson dabs cast irregular red splashes on the shiny, golden
wallpaper. The furnishings were art nouveau also. Everything,
even the common objects of use, tended to stop and start at
unexpected places; to spring upwards in ecstasy, to sag in
melancholia, or simply to overhang and break away. One felt
that every object was in tension. The colours of the room
coalesced into strikingly individual harmony. Almost as soon as I
entered, it struck me that the general colouration had something
in common with that of my own works. It was most curious. The
golden walls bore many pictures, mostly in golden frames: mainly,
I could see, the work of the late A., as was to be expected, and
about which I must not further particularise; but also some
esoteric drawings manifestly by Felicien Rops, and stranger than
his strangest, I thought as I sat amongst them. In the substantial,
art nouveau fireplace blazed a fire, making the room considerably too hot, as so often on the Continent. None the less, I
again shut the door. As I did so, I saw that behind it was a life-
size marble figure of a woman in the moment of maternity. I
identified it at once as the work of a symbolist sculptor well
known for figures of this type, but, again, I had better not name
him because about this particular figure was something very
odd—odd even to me who knew about childbirth only from
works of art, not least the works of this particular man.

'*Mais oui,*' said Madame A., as I could not withdraw my gaze from the figure. '*C'est la naissance d'un succube.*'

But at this point I think I had better stop trying to remember what was said in French by Madame A. In the first place, I cannot succeed in doing so, though her very first words, those that I have set down, remain clearly with me. In the second place, Madame A. soon disclosed that she could speak English perfectly well—or rather, perhaps, and as I oddly felt, as well as she could speak French. There was something about her which suggested, even to an unsophisticate like me, that she was no more a native of Belgium or France than she was of Britain. I am trying to set down events and my feelings exactly as they were, or as nearly as possible, and I am not going to pretend that I did not sense something queer about Madame A. from the very start, because there is nothing in the whole story of which I am more certain than of that.

And now there she was standing dumpily before the big, bright fire with her long bare arms extended, almost as if to embrace me.

Yes, despite the impending autumn, despite the blazing fire, her arms were bare; and not only her arms. Her hairy legs were bare also, and her dull red dress was cut startlingly low for a woman of her years, making her creased bosom all too visible. My absurd impression was that this plain red scrap of a garment was all she was wearing, apart from the golden slippers on her small, square feet.

And yet old she certainly was; very old, as she had said in her letter. Her face was deeply grooved and grained. Her neck had lost all shape. Her stance was hunched and bowed under the weight of time. Her voice, though masterful, was senile. I imagined that her black hair, somewhat scant, but wiry and upstanding, could only be dyed. Her head was like an old, brown egg.

She made me sit and sweat before the fire, constantly urging me nearer to it, and plied me with cognac and water. She herself remained on her feet, though, even so, her corrugated brown cheekbones and oddly vague black eyes were almost on a level with mine. The chair in which she had put me, had wings at the level of the sitter's head, thus making me even hotter, and, every now and then, as she spoke, she leant forward, put a hand on each of these wings, and, for emphasis or to indicate a confidence, spoke right at my face, coming almost near enough to kiss me. She appeared to drink very little herself, but she made me drink far more than I wanted, praising the quality of the brandy and also (little did she know, I thought) the power and strength of my youth. Her very first question when we had settled ourselves was: How old had I said I was? And, she continued, born in Scorpio? Yes, I replied, impressed but not astonished, because many people have this particular divination, even though the materialists say otherwise. And how do you interpret that? I went on; because different people emphasise different aspects. Secrecy and sensuality, she croaked back. Only the first, I smiled. Then I must direct myself to awakening the second, she replied rather horribly.

And yet, I thought, how hard I am, how unsympathetic, after all; and, at the same time, how weak.

She did soon begin to talk about art, and the painters she had known long, long before. Perhaps she thought that this was the topic which would awaken me. She tended to lose the way in her long, ancient chronicles, and to fill or overfill my glass while she recovered direction.

It was noticeable that she seemed neither to admire nor to have liked any of the men she spoke of, many of whom were and are objects of my particular regard. At least I hope they still are: an object of admiration is impaired by hostile criticism of any kind, however ill judged, and there is nothing the admirer can do to mend the wound, even though his full reason may tell him that the critic has no case. Madame A.'s comments were hardly reasoned at all and thus all the more upsetting. They were jeers and insinuations and flat rejections.

'X.,' she would say, 'was an absurd man, always very dapper and with a voice like a goat.' 'Y!' she exclaimed. 'I had a very close friendship with Y.—as long as I could stand him.' 'Z.'s pictures are supposed to be philosophical but really they're not even successfully pornographic.' All the time she implied that my own enthusiastic assessments were grotesquely immature, and, when I argued back, sometimes with success, because she was not much of a hand with logic and not too accurate with her facts either, she flattened me with personal reminiscences of the comic or shady circumstances in which particular works had come to be painted, or with anecdotes which, as she claimed, showed the painter in his true colours.

'J.,' she asserted, 'was madly in love with me for years, but I wouldn't have used him as a pocket handkerchief when I had the grippe, and nor would any other woman.' Madame A. had a fine turn of phrase, but as I knew (though we did not mention) that J., painter of the most exquisite oriental fantasies, had hanged himself in poverty and despair, her line of talk depressed and disconcerted me very much. I felt that in too many cases, even though, I was sure, not in all, her harsh comments were true, even though doubtless not the whole truth. I felt that, true or not by my standards, so many people (among the few interested at all) would agree with these comments as thereby to give them a kind of truth by majority vote. I felt, most sadly of all, that what I have called harshness in Madame A. was simply a blast of life's essential quality as it drags us all over the stones; artists—these selected divinities of mine among them—included.

As so often, it would have been better not to know.

'K.!' croaked Madame A. 'K. worked for three years as a police spy and it was the happiest period of his life. He told me so himself. He was drunk at the time—or perhaps drugged—but it was the truth. And you can see it in his pictures if you only look. They are the pictures of a self-abuser. Do you know why K.'s wife left him? It was because he was impotent with a real woman, and always had been. He knew it perfectly well when he married her. He did it because she had inherited a little money and he was on cocaine already and the good God knows what else. When I read about K.'s pictures being bought for the Musée Royal des Beaux-Arts, I laugh. I laugh and I spit.' And Madame A. did both. She had a habit of snatching at the neck-line of her red dress as she spoke, and dragging it yet further down. It seemed by now to have become an unconscious reflex with her, or tic.

'L.,' she said, 'started as a painter of enormous landscapes. That was what he really liked to paint. He liked to spend days and weeks entirely by himself in Norway or Scotland just paint-ing exactly what lay before him, bigger all the time. The trouble was that no one would buy such pictures. They were competent enough but dull, dull. When you saw them lined up against the walls of his studio, you could do nothing but yawn. And that's the way people saw them when he hoped they might buy them. You couldn't imagine anyone ever buying one. You wanted only to get out of the studio and forget about such dull pictures. All those pictures of L. that you talk about, the "Salomés" and "Whores of Babylon", weren't what he liked at all. He turned to them because two things happened at once: L.'s money ran out and at about the same time he met Maeterlinck. He met

Maeterlinck only once, but it did something to him. Maeterlinck seemed fashionable and successful, and L. couldn't see why he shouldn't be too. But it really wasn't in the little man, and before long he gave it all up and became a *fonctionnaire*, as you know, though it was a bit late in the day for that.'

'No, madame, I didn't know.'

'Why, he's alive still! He's got the jumps, some kind of disease that gives you the jumps. The "Whore of Babylon" might have given it to him, but he never got near enough to her to make it possible. L.'s alive all right—just. I used to go and see him when I still went out. He liked to borrow my old art papers. I've got hundreds of them, all from before the war. *Ah, les sales Boches*,' added Madame A. irrelevantly, but as many people do in Belgium and France from force of habit.

Despite everything, I suppose my eyes must have lighted up at the mention of the pre-war art journals. In such publications is often information not to be found anywhere else and information of just the sort that I find most valuable and absorbing.

'Ah,' croaked Madame A. almost jubilantly. 'That's better. You are getting accustomed to me, *hein?*' She grasped my hands.

By now, she was flowing on in English. It was a relief. At one moment, she had spoken several sentences in a language I could not even identify. She had doubtless forgotten about me, or was confusing me with someone else.

'But you look hot,' cried Madame A., releasing me. 'Why do you not remove your jacket?'

'Perhaps,' I replied, 'I could walk round the room and look at the pictures.'

'But certainly. If you wish.' She spoke as if it were a remarkably ridiculous wish, and perhaps discourteous also.

I struggled away from her, and proceeded from picture to picture. She said nothing while I promenaded, but remained standing with her back to the fire, and her short legs well apart; gnomic in more than one sense. I cannot say that her eyes followed me with ironical glances, because her eyes were too vague for such a thing. The light in the room, though pictur-esque was quite unsuited to the inspection of pictures. I could see hardly anything. At the end of the room away from the street and away from the fire, it was almost dark. It was absurd for me to persist, though I was exceedingly disappointed.

'It is a pity my adopted daughter is not here,' said Madame A. from the brightness. 'She could entertain you better than I can. You would prefer her to me.'

She spoke in a tone of dreadful coyness. I could think of no convincing reply. 'Where is your adopted daughter?' I asked lamely and tamely.

'Away. Abroad. With some creature, of course. Who knows where?' She cackled. 'Who knows with whom?'

'I am sorry to have missed her,' I said, not very convinc-ingly, I am sure. I was indignant that I had not been invited for some hour when I could see the pictures by daylight.

'Come back over here, monsieur,' cried Madame A., point-ing with her right forefinger to my hot armchair and then slapping her knee with the palm of her hand, all as if she were summoning a small, unruly dog. It was *exactly* like that, I thought. I have often seen it, though I have never owned a dog myself. I forebore from comment and returned reluctantly to the hot fire. Madame A., as I have said, was commanding as well as coy.

And then an extraordinary thing happened. A real dog was there in the room. At least, I suppose I am now not sure how real it was. Let me just say a dog. It was like a small black poodle, clipped, glossy, and spry. It appeared from the shadowy corner to the right of the door as one entered. It pattered perkily up to the fire, then round several times in a circle in front of Madame A. and to my right as I sat, then off into the shadow to my left and where I had just been standing. It seemed to me, as I looked at it, to have very big eyes and very long legs, perhaps more like a spider than a poodle, but no doubt this was merely an effect of the firelight.

At that moment, there was much to take in fairly quickly, but one thing was that Madame A., as I clearly realised, seemed not to see the dog. She was staring ahead, her black eyes expressionless as ever. Even while I was watching the dog, I divined that she was still thinking of her adopted daughter, and was entranced by her thoughts. It did not seem particularly remarkable that she had missed the dog, because the dog had been quite silent, and she might well have been so accustomed to seeing it around the house that often she no longer noticed it. What puzzled me at that stage was where the dog had hidden itself all the time I had been in the room with the door shut.

'Nice poodle,' I said to Madame A., because I had to break the silence, and because Englishmen are supposed to be fond of dogs (though I am, comparatively, an exception).

'*Comment, monsieur?*' I can see and hear her still, exactly as she looked and spoke.

'Nicely kept poodle,' I said, firmly sticking to English.

She turned and stared at me, but came no nearer, as at such moments she usually did.

'So you have seen a poodle?'

'Yes,' I said, and still not thinking there was anything really wrong, 'this moment. If it's not yours, it must have got in from the darkness outside.' The darkness was still on my mind, because of the pictures, but immediately I spoke, I felt a chill, despite the blazing fire. I wanted to get up and look for the dog, which, after all, must still have been in the room; but at the same time I feared to do any such thing. I feared to move at all.

'Animals often appear in here,' said Madame A. huskily. 'Dogs, cats, toads, monkeys. And occasionally less commonplace species. I expect it will have gone by now.'

I think I only stared back at her.

'Sometimes my husband painted them.' It was the only reference she had made to her husband, and it was one which I found difficult to follow up. She dragged down the front of her dress in her compulsive way.

'I will talk to you,' said Madame A., 'about Chrysothème, my adopted daughter. Do you know that Chrysothème is the most beautiful girl in Europe? Not like me. Oh, not at all.'

'What a pity I cannot have the pleasure of meeting her!' I said, again trying to enter into the spirit of it, but wondering how I could escape, especially in view of what had just happened. On the instant, and for the second time, I regretted what I had said.

But Madame A. merely croaked dreamily, staring straight ahead. 'She appears here. She stays quite often. For a quite long time, you understand. She cannot be expected to remain longer. After all, I am far from being her mother.'

I nodded, though it was obscure to what I was assenting.

'Chrysothème!' cried Madame A. rapturously clasping her hands. 'My Chrysothème!' She paused, her face illumined, though not her eyes. Then she turned back to me. 'If you could see her naked, monsieur, you would understand everything.'

I giggled uneasily, as one does.

'I repeat, monsieur, that you would understand everything.'

It dawned on me that in some way she meant more than one would at first have thought.

One trouble was that I most certainly did not *want* to understand everything. I had once even told a fortune teller as much; a big-nosed but beautiful woman in a tent when I was a schoolboy.

'Would you like to see her clothes?' said Madame A., quite softly. 'She keeps some of them here, to wear when she comes to stay.'

'Yes,' I said. 'I should.' I cannot fully analyse why I said it, but I said it. Madame A. being what she was, I could claim that I was given very little voice in the matter. Perhaps I wasn't. But that time it didn't arise. I undoubtedly chose.

Madame A. took me lightly by the wrist and drew me out of the chair. I opened the big door for her, and then another big door which she indicated. There were two on the opposite side of the landing, and she pointed to the one on the right.

'I myself sleep in the next room,' said Madame A. on the threshold, making the very wall sound like an invitation. 'When I can sleep at all.'

The room within was darkly panelled, almost to the ceiling. The corner on the left behind the door was filled by a panelled bed, with a coverlet of dark red brocade. It seemed to fill more space than a single bed, but not as much space as a double bed. From the foot of it, the plain, dark panelling of the wall continued undecorated to the end of the room. In the centre of the far wall stood a red brocaded dressing table, looking very much like an altar, especially as no chair stood before it. On the right was a window, now covered by dark red curtains, of the heavy kind which my Mother used to say collected the dust. Against the wall on each side of this window, stood a big dark chest. There were several of the usual art nouveau lanterns hanging high on the walls, but the glass in them was so heavily obscured that the room seemed scarcely brighter than the dim landing outside. The only picture hung over the head of the bed in the corner behind the door.

'What a beautiful room!' I exclaimed politely.

But I was looking over my shoulder to see if the black dog had emerged through the open door on the other side of the landing.

'That is because many people have died in it,' said Madame A. 'The two beautiful things are love and death.'

I went right into the room.

'Shut the door,' said Madame A.

I shut it. There was still no sign of the dog. I tried to postpone further thought on the subject.

'Most of her clothes are in here,' said Madame A. She pulled at the panelling by the foot of the bed, and two doors opened; then another pair; then a third. All that part of the bedroom panelling fronted deep cupboards.

'Come and look,' said Madame A.

Feeling foolish, I went over to her. All three cupboards were filled with dresses, hanging from a central rail, as in a shop. If they had been antiquarian rags or expectant shrouds, I should hardly have been surprised, but they were quite normal women's clothes of today; as far as I could tell, of very high quality. There were garments for all purposes: winter dresses, summer dresses, and a great number of those long evening dresses which one sees less and less frequently. All the dresses appeared to be carefully looked after, as if they were waiting to be sold. It struck me that in that direction might lie the truth: that the dresses might never have been worn. Certainly the room looked extremely unoccupied. Apart from the dresses, it looked more like a chapel than a bedroom. More like a mortuary chapel, it suddenly struck me; with a sequence of corpses at rest and beflowered on the bier-like bed behind the door, as Madame A. had so depressingly hinted.

'Touch the clothes,' said Madame A., reading my mind.

'Take them out and see the marks of Chrysothème's body.'

I hesitated. Unless one is a tailor, one instinctively dislikes the touch of other people's clothes, whoever they may be; and of unknown strangers' clothes not least.

'Take them out,' repeated Madame A. in her commanding way.

I gingerly detached a random dress on its hanger. It was a workaday, woollen garment. Even in the poor light, the signs of wear were evident.

That point made silently between us, Madame A. showed impatience with my timid choice. She herself drew out an evening gown in pale satin.

'Marvellous, exquisite, incomparable,' she exclaimed stridently. I think that if she had been tall enough, she would have held the dress against her own body, as the saleswomen so curiously do in shops; but, as it was, she could only hold it out at the end of her long arms, so that most of it flowed across the dark red carpet like a train. 'Kneel down and examine it.' I hesitated. 'Kneel,' cried Madame A. more peremptorily.

I knelt and picked up the bottom hem of the dress. Now I was down on the floor, I noticed a big dark patch which the dark carpet was not dark enough to hide.

'Lift the dress to your face,' ordered Madame A. I did so. It was a wonderful sensation. I felt myself enveloped in a complex silky nebula. The owner, the wearer of that elegant garment, began, even though entirely without definition, to be much more present to me than Madame A.

Madame A. dropped the dress and on the instant was holding out another in the same way. It also was a long dress. It was made of what I believe is called georgette, and was in some kind of mottled orange and red.

The pale satin dress lay on the floor between us.

'Kneel on it. Tread on it,' directed Madame A., seeing me about to circumvent it. 'Chrysothème would approve.'

I was unable to do such a thing, and crawled round the edges of the satin dress to the georgette dress. Immediately I reached the georgette dress, Madame A. threw it adroitly over my head, so that I had a ridiculous minute or two extricating myself. I could not but notice, and more than just notice, that the georgette retained a most enchanting scent. Her scent made the wearer of the dress more real to me than ever.

Away to my left, Madame A. now extended a third long dress; this time in dark blue taffeta, very slender and skimpy.

'You could almost wear it yourself,' cackled Madame A. 'You like wearing blue and you are thin enough.' I had, of course, not told her that I liked wearing blue, but I suppose it was obvious.

Madame A. twisted round a chair with her foot and laid the dress on it, with the low top hanging abandonedly over the back of it.

'Why don't you kiss it?' asked Madame A., jeering slightly.

Kneeling at the foot of the chair, I realised that my lips were only slightly above the edge of the seat. To refuse would be more foolish than to comply. I lowered my face and pressed my lips against the dress. Madame A. might be ridiculing me, but I felt now that my true concern was with that other who wore the dresses.

When I looked up, Madame A. was actually standing on another chair (there were only two in the room, both originally in the corners, both heavy, dark, and elaborate). She was holding up a short dress in black velvet. She said nothing, and I admit that, without bidding, I darted towards her and pressed the wonderful fabric against my face.

'The moon,' gurgled Madame A., pointing to the pale satin

dress on the floor. 'And the night.' She flapped the black velvet up and down and from side to side. It too smelt adorably. I clutched at it to keep it still and found that it was quite limp, inert in my grasp.

Madame A. had leapt off the chair with one flop, like a leprechaun.

'Do you like my adopted daughter's clothes?'

'They are beautiful.'

'Chrysothème has perfect taste.' Madame A.'s tone was entirely conventional. I was still sniffing the velvet dress. 'You must see the lingerie,' Madame A. added, merely as if to confirm the claim she had just made.

She crossed to the chest at the left of the curtained window and lifted the unlocked lid. 'Come,' said Madame A.

The big chest was full of soft underclothes in various colours; not ordered like the dresses, but tangled and clinging apparently at random.

I suppose I just stood and stared. And the same scent was rising hypnotically from the chest.

'Take off your blue jacket,' said Madame A., almost with solemnity. 'Roll up your blue sleeves, and plunge in your white arms.'

Without question, I did what she said.

'Sink your face in them.'

I hardly needed to be instructed. The scent was intoxicating in itself.

'Love them, tear them, possess them,' admonished Madame A.

All of which I daresay I did to the best of my ability. Certainly time passed.

I began to shiver. After all, I had left a very over-heated room.

I found that all my muscles were stiff with kneeling; and I

suppose with concentration too. I could hardly rise to my feet in order to rescue my jacket. As I rolled down my shirt-sleeves, I became aware that the hairs on my forearms really were standing on end. They seemed quite barbed and sharp.

'Blue boy!' exclaimed Madame A., waiting for me to make the next move.

I made it. I shut the lid of the chest.

'The other chest contains souvenirs,' said Madame A., dragging at the neckline of her dress.

I shook my head. I was still shaking all over, and could no longer smell that wonderful scent. When one is very cold, the sense of smell departs.

And at that moment, for the first time, I really apprehended the one picture, which hung above the wide bed in the corner. Despite the bad light, it seemed familiar. I went over to it, and putting one knee on the bed, leant towards it. Now I was certain. The picture was by me.

But there were two especially strange things. Though I was quite certain that the picture could only be mine (my talent may be circumscribed, but it is distinctive), I could not remember ever having painted it, and there were things about it which could at no time have been put there by me. Artists, in their later years, do sometimes forget their own works, but I was, and am, sure that this could never happen in my case. My pictures are not of a kind to be forgotten by the painter. Much worse was the fact that, for example, the central figure which I might have painted as an angel, had somehow become more like a clown. It was hard to say why this was, but, as I looked at it, I felt it irresistibly.

My attack of shivering was turning to nausea, as one often finds. I felt that I was in danger of making a final fool of myself by being actually sick on the floor.

'Quite right,' said Madame A., regarding the picture with her vague eyes, and speaking as she had spoken in the other room. 'Not a painter at all. Would have done better as a sweeper out of cabinets, wouldn't you agree, or as fetcher and carrier in a horse-meat market? It is kept in here because Chrysothème has no time for pictures, no time at all.'

It would have been absurd and undignified to argue. Nor could I be sure that she was clear in her mind as to who I was.

'Thank you, madame,' I said, 'for receiving me. I must detain you no longer.'

'A souvenir,' she cried. 'At least leave me a souvenir.'

I saw that she held a quite large pair of silvery scissors.

I did not feel at all like leaving even a lock of my hair in Madame A.'s keeping.

I opened the bedroom door, and began to retreat. I was trying to think of a phrase or two that would cover my precipitancy with a glaze of convention, but then I saw that, squatted on the single golden light that hung by a golden chain from the golden ceiling of the landing, was a tiny fluffy animal; so very small, that it might almost have been a dark furry insect with unusually distinct pale eyes. Moreover, the door into the big, hot room on my left was, of course, still open. I was overcome. I merely took to my heels; clattering idiotically down the bare, slippery staircase. I was lucky not to slide headlong.

'*Mais, monsieur!*'

I was struggling in the dark with the many handles, chains, and catches of the front door. It seemed likely that I should be unable to open it.

'*Mais, monsieur!*' Madame A. was lumbering down after me. But suddenly the door was open. Now that I could be sure I was not trapped, a small concession to good manners was possible.

'Good-night, madame,' I said in English. 'And thank you again.'

She made a vague snatch in my direction with the big, silvery scissors. They positively flashed in the light from the street lamp outside. She was like a squat granny seeing off a child with a gesture of mock aggression. 'Begone,' she might have said; or, alternatively, 'Come back at once': but I did not wait to hear Madame A. say anything more. Soon I found that I was walking down the populous Chausée d'Ixelles, still vibrating, and every now and then looking over one shoulder or the other.

Within twenty-four hours I perceived clearly enough that there could have been no dog, no little animal squatted on the lantern, no picture over the bed, and probably no adopted daughter. That hardly needed saying. The trouble was, and is, that this obvious truth only makes things worse. Indeed, it is precisely where the real trouble begins. What is to become of me? What will happen to me next? What can I do? What am I?

THE INNER ROOM

IT WAS never less than half an hour after the engine stopped running that my Father deigned to signal for succour. If in the process of breaking down, we had climbed, or descended, a bank, then first we must all exhaust ourselves pushing. If we had collided, there was, of course, a row. If, as had happened that day, it was simply that, while we coasted along, the machinery had ceased to churn and rattle, then my Father tried his hand as a mechanic. That was the worst contingency of all: at least, it was the worst one connected with motoring.

I had learned by experience that neither rain nor snow made much difference, and certainly not fog; but that afternoon it was hotter than any day I could remember. I realised later that it was the famous Long Summer of 1921, when the water at the bottom of cottage wells turned salt, and when eels were found baked and edible in their mud. But to know this at the time, I should have had to read the papers, and though, through my Mother's devotion, I had the trick of reading before my third birthday, I mostly left the practice to my younger brother, Constantin. He was reading now from a pudgy volume, as thick as it was broad, and resembling his own head in size and pro-portion. As always, he had resumed his studies immediately the bumping of our almost springless car permitted, and even before motion had ceased. My Mother sat in the front seat inevitably correcting pupils' exercises. By teaching her native German in five schools at once, three of them distant, one of them fashionable, she surprisingly managed to maintain the four of us, and even our car. The front offside door of the car leaned dangerously open into the seething highway.

'I say,' cried my Father.

The young man in the big yellow racer shook his head as he tore by. My Father had addressed the least appropriate car on the road.

'I say.'

I cannot recall what the next car looked like, but it did not stop.

My Father was facing the direction from which we had come, and sawing the air with his left arm, like a very inexperienced policeman. Perhaps no one stopped because all thought him eccentric. Then a car going in the opposite direction came to a standstill behind my Father's back. My Father perceived nothing. The motorist sounded his horn. In those days, horns squealed, and I covered my ears with my hands. Between my hands and my head my long fair hair was like brittle flax in the sun.

My Father darted through the traffic. I think it was the Portsmouth Road. The man in the other car got out and came to us. I noticed his companion, much younger and in a cherry-coloured cloche, begin to deal with her nails.

'Broken down?' asked the man. To me it seemed obvious, as the road was strewn with bits of the engine and oozy blobs of oil. Moreover, surely my Father had explained?

'I can't quite locate the seat of the trouble,' said my Father.

The man took off one of his driving gauntlets, big and dirty.

'Catch hold for a moment.' My Father caught hold.

The man put his hand into the engine and made a casual movement. Something snapped loudly.

'Done right in. If you ask me, I'm not sure she'll ever go again.'

'Then I don't think I'll ask you,' said my Father affably. 'Hot, isn't it?' My Father began to mop his tall corrugated brow, and front-to-back ridges of grey hair.

'Want a tow?'

'Just to the nearest garage.' My Father always spoke the word in perfect French.

'Where to?'

'To the nearest car repair workshop. If it would not be troubling you too much.'

'Can't help myself now, can I?'

From under the back seat in the other car, the owner got out a thick, frayed rope, black and greasy as the hangman's. The owner's friend simply said 'Pleased to meet you,' and began to replace her scalpels and enamels in their cabinet. We jolted towards the town we had traversed an hour or two before; and were then untied outside a garage on the outskirts.

'Surely it is closed for the holiday?' said my Mother. Hers is a voice I can always recall upon an instant: guttural, of course, but beautiful, truly golden.

' 'Spect he'll be back,' said our benefactor, drawing in his rope like a fisherman. 'Give him a bang.' He kicked three times very loudly upon the dropped iron shutter. Then without another word he drove away.

It was my birthday, I had been promised the sea, and I began to weep. Constantin, with a fretful little wriggle, closed further into himself and his book; but my Mother leaned over the front seat of the car and opened her arms to me. I went to her and sobbed on the shoulder of her bright red dress.

'*Kleine Lene, wir stecken schön in der Tinte.*'

My Father, who could pronounce six languages perfectly but speak only one of them, never liked my Mother to use her native tongue within the family. He rapped more sharply on the shutter. My Mother knew his ways, but, where our welfare was at stake, ignored them.

'Edgar,' said my Mother, 'let us give the children presents. Especially my little Lene.' My tears, though childish, and less viscous than those shed in later life, had turned the scarlet shoulder of her dress to purple. She squinted smilingly sideways at the damage.

My Father was delighted to defer the decision about what next to do with the car. But, as pillage was possible, my Mother took with her the exercises, and Constantin his fat little book.

We straggled along the main road, torrid, raucous, adequate only for a gentler period of history. The grit and dust stung my face and arms and knees, like granulated glass. My Mother and I went first, she holding my hand. My Father struggled to walk at her other side, but for most of the way, the path was too narrow. Constantin mused along in the rear, abstracted as usual.

'It is true what the papers say,' exclaimed my Father. 'British roads were never built for motor traffic. Beyond the odd car, of course.'

My Mother nodded and slightly smiled. Even in the lineless hopsacks of the twenties, she could not ever but look magnificent, with her rolling, turbulent, honey hair, and Hellenic proportions. Ultimately we reached the High Street. The very first shop had one of its windows stuffed with toys; the other being stacked with groceries and draperies and coal-hods, all dingy. The name 'Popular Bazaar', in wooden relief as if glued on in building blocks, stretched across the whole front, not quite centre.

It was not merely an out of fashion shop, but a shop that at the best sold too much of what no one wanted. My Father comprehended the contents of the Toy Department window with a single, anxious glance, and said 'Choose whatever you like. Both of you. But look very carefully first. Don't hurry.' Then he turned away and began to hum a fragment from 'The Lady of the Rose'.

But Constantin spoke at once. 'I choose those telegraph wires.' They ranged beside a line of tin railway that stretched right across the window, long undusted and tending to buckle. There were seven or eight posts, with six wires on each side of the post. Though I could not think why Constantin wanted them, and though in the event he did not get them, the appearance of them, and of the rusty track beneath them, is all that remains clear in my memory of that window.

'I doubt whether they're for sale,' said my Father. 'Look again. There's a good boy. No hurry.'

'They're all I want,' said Constantin, and turned his back on the uninspiring display.

'Well, we'll see,' said my Father. 'I'll make a special point of it with the man . . .' He turned to me. 'And what about you? Very few dolls, I'm afraid.'

'I don't like dolls any more.' As a matter of fact, I had never owned a proper one, although I suffered from this fact only when competing with other girls, which meant very seldom, for our friends were few and occasional. The dolls in the window were flyblown and detestable.

'I think we could find a better shop from which to give Lene a birthday present,' said my Mother, in her correct, dignified English.

'We must not be unjust,' said my Father, 'when we have not even looked inside.'

The inferiority of the goods implied cheapness, which unfortunately always mattered; although, as it happened, none of the articles seemed actually to be priced.

'I do not like this shop,' said my Mother. 'It is a shop that has died.'

Her regal manner when she said such things was, I think, too Germanic for my Father's Englishness. That, and the prospect of unexpected economy, perhaps led him to be firm.

'We have Constantin's present to consider as well as Lene's. Let us go in.'

By contrast with the blazing highway, the main impression of the interior was darkness. After a few moments, I also became aware of a smell. Everything in the shop smelt of that smell, and, one felt, always would do so; the mixed odour of any General Store, but at once enhanced and passé. I can smell it now.

'We do not necessarily want to buy anything,' said my Father, 'but, if we may, should like to look round?'

Since the days of Mr Selfridge the proposition is supposed to be taken for granted, but at that time the message had yet to spread. The bazaar keeper seemed hardly to welcome it. He was younger than I had expected (an unusual thing for a child, but I had probably been awaiting a white-bearded gnome); though pale, nearly bald, and perceptibly grimy. He wore an untidy grey suit and bedroom slippers.

'Look about you, children,' said my Father. 'Take your time. We can't buy presents every day.'

I noticed that my Mother still stood in the doorway.

'I want those wires,' said Constantin.

'Make quite sure by looking at the other things first.'

Constantin turned aside bored, his book held behind his

back. He began to scrape his feet. It was up to me to uphold my Father's position. Rather timidly, I began to peer about, not going far from him. The bazaar keeper silently watched me with eyes colourless in the twilight.

'Those toy telegraph poles in your window,' said my Father after a pause, fraught for me with anxiety and responsibility. 'How much would you take for them?'

'They are not for sale,' said the bazaar keeper, and said no more.

'Then why do you display them in the window?'

'They are a kind of decoration, I suppose.' Did he not know? I wondered.

'Even if they're not normally for sale, perhaps you'll sell them to me,' said my vagabond Father, smiling like Rothschild. 'My son, you see, has taken a special fancy to them.'

'Sorry,' said the man in the shop.

'Are you the principal here?'

'I am.'

'Then surely as a reasonable man,' said my Father, switching from superiority to ingratiation—

'They are to dress the window,' said the bazaar man. 'They are not for sale.'

This dialogue entered through the back of my head as, diligently and unobtrusively, I conned the musty stock. At the back of the shop was a window, curtained all over in grey lace: to judge by the weak light it offered, it gave on to the living quarters. Through this much filtered illumination glimmered the façade of an enormous dolls' house. I wanted it at once. Dolls had never been central to my happiness, but this abode of theirs was the most grown-up thing in the shop.

It had battlements, and long straight walls, and a variety of pointed windows. A gothic revival house, no doubt; or even mansion. It was painted the colour of stone; a grey stone darker than the grey light, which flickered round it. There was a two-leaved front door, with a small classical portico. It was impossible to see the whole house at once, as it stood grimed and neglected on the corner of the wide trestle-shelf. Very slowly I walked along two of the sides; the other two being dark against the walls of the shop. From a first floor window in the side not immediately visible as one approached, leaned a doll, droopy and unkempt. It was unlike any real house I had seen, and, as for dolls' houses, they were always after the style of the villa near Gerrard's Cross belonging to my Father's successful brother. My uncle's house itself looked much more like a toy than this austere structure before me.

'Wake up,' said my Mother's voice. She was standing just behind me.

'What about some light on the subject?' enquired my Father.

A switch clicked.

The house really was magnificent. Obviously, beyond all financial reach.

'Looks like a model for Pentonville Gaol,' observed my Father.

'It is beautiful,' I said. 'It's what I want.'

'It's the most depressing looking plaything I ever saw.'

'I want to pretend I live in it,' I said, 'and give masked balls.' My social history was eager but indiscriminate.

'How much is it?' asked my Mother. The bazaar keeper stood resentfully in the background, sliding each hand between the thumb and fingers of the other.

'It's only second-hand,' he said. 'Tenth-hand, more like. A lady brought it in and said she needed to get rid of it. I don't want to sell you something you don't want.'

'But suppose we *do* want it?' said my Father truculently. 'Is nothing in this shop for sale?'

'You can take it away for a quid,' said the bazaar keeper. 'And glad to have the space.'

'There's someone looking out,' said Constantin. He seemed to be assessing the house, like a surveyor or valuer.

'It's full of dolls,' said the bazaar keeper. 'They're thrown in. Sure you can transport it?'

'Not at the moment,' said my Father, 'but I'll send someone down.' This, I knew, would be Moon the seedman, who owned a large canvas-topped lorry, and with whom my Father used to fraternise on the putting green.

'Are you quite sure?' my Mother asked me.

'Will it take up too much room?'

My Mother shook her head. Indeed, our home, though out of date and out at elbows, was considerably too large for us.

'Then, please.'

Poor Constantin got nothing.

Mercifully, all our rooms had wide doors; so that Moon's driver, assisted by the youth out of the shop, lent specially for the purpose, could ease my birthday present to its new resting place, without tilting it or inflicting a wound upon my Mother's new and self-applied paint. I noticed that the doll at the first floor side window had prudently withdrawn.

For my house, my parents had allotted me the principal Spare Room, because in the centre of it stood a very large dinner table, once to be found in the servants' hall of my Father's childhood home in Lincolnshire, but now the sole furniture our principal Spare Room contained. (The two lesser Spare Rooms were filled with cardboard boxes, which every now and then toppled in heart-arresting avalanches on still summer nights.) On the big table the driver and the shop boy set my house. It reached almost to the sides, so that those passing along the narrow walks would be in peril of tumbling into a gulf; but, the table being much longer than it was wide, the house was provided at front and back with splendid parterres of deal, embrocated with caustic until they glinted like fluorspar.

When I had settled upon the exact site for the house, so that the garden front would receive the sun from the two windows, and a longer parterre stretched at the front than at the back, where the columned entry faced the door of the room, I withdrew to a distant corner while the two males eased the edifice into exact alignment.

'Snug as a bug in a rug,' said Moon's driver when the perilous walks at the sides of the house had been made straight and equal.

'Snugger,' said Moon's boy.

I waited for their boots, mailed with crescent slivers of steel, to reach the bottom of our creaking, coconut-matted stair, then I tiptoed to the landing, looked, and listened. The sun had gone in just before the lorry arrived, and down the passage the motes had ceased to dance. It was three o'clock, my Mother was still at one of her schools, my Father was at the rifle range. I heard the men shut the back door. The principal Spare Room had never before been occupied, so that the key was outside. In a second, I transferred it to the inside, and shut and locked myself in.

As before in the shop, I walked slowly round my house, but this time round all four sides of it. Then, with the knuckles of my thin white forefinger, I tapped gently at the front door. It seemed not to have been secured, because it opened, both leaves of it, as I touched it. I pried in, first with one eye, then with the other. The lights from various of the pointed windows blotched the walls and floor of the miniature Entrance Hall. None of the dolls was visible.

It was not one of those dolls' houses of commerce from which sides can be lifted in their entirety. To learn about my house, it would be necessary, albeit impolite, to stare through the windows, one at a time. I decided first to take the ground floor. I started in a clockwise direction from the front portico. The front door was still open, but I could not see how to shut it from the outside.

There was a room to the right of the hall, leading into two other rooms along the right side of the house, of which, again, one led into the other. All the rooms were decorated and furnished in a Mrs Fitzherbert-ish style; with handsomely striped wallpapers, botanical carpets, and chairs with legs like sticks of brittle golden sweetmeat. There were a number of pictures. I knew just what they were: family portraits. I named the room next the Hall, the Occasional Room, and the room beyond it, the Morning Room. The third room was very small: striking out confidently, I named it the Canton Cabinet, although it contained neither porcelain nor fans. I knew what the rooms in a great house should be called, because my Mother used to show me the pictures in large, once fashionable volumes on the subject which my Father had bought for their bulk at junk shops.

Then came the Long Drawing Room, which stretched across the entire garden front of the house, and contained the principal concourse of dolls. It had four pointed French windows, all made to open, though now sealed with dust and rust; above which were bulbous triangles of coloured glass, in tiny snow-flake panes. The apartment itself played at being a cloister in a Horace Walpole convent; lierne vaulting ramified across the arched ceiling, and the spidery gothic pilasters were tricked out in medieval patchwork, as in a Puseyite church. On the stout golden wallpaper were decent Swiss pastels of indeterminate subjects. There was a grand piano, very black, scrolly, and, no doubt, resounding; four shapely chandeliers; a baronial fireplace with a mythical blazon above the mantel; and eight dolls, all of them female, dotted about on chairs and ottomans with their backs to me. I hardly dared to breathe as I regarded their woolly heads, and noted the colours of their hair: two black, two nondescript, one grey, one a discoloured silver beneath the dust, one blonde, and one a dyed-looking red. They wore woollen Victorian clothes, of a period later, I should say, than that when the house was built, and certainly too warm for the present season; in varied colours, all of them dull. Happy people, I felt even then, would not wear these variants of rust, indigo, and greenwood.

I crept onwards; to the Dining Room. It occupied half its side of the house, and was dark and oppressive. Perhaps it might look more inviting when the chandelier blazed, and the table candles, each with a tiny purple shade, were lighted. There was no cloth on the table, and no food or drink. Over the fireplace was a big portrait of a furious old man: his white hair was a spiky aureole round his distorted face, beetroot-red with rage; the mouth was open, and even the heavy lips were drawn back to show the savage, strong teeth; he was brandishing a very thick walking stick which seemed to leap from the picture and stun the beholder. He was dressed neutrally, and the painter had not provided him with a background: there was only the aggressive figure menacing the room. I was frightened.

Two rooms on the ground floor remained before I once more reached the front door. In the first of them a lady was writing with her back to the light and therefore to me. She frightened me also; because her grey hair was disordered and of uneven length, and descended in matted plaits, like snakes escaping from a basket, to the shoulders of her coarse grey dress. Of course, being a doll, she did not move, but the back of her head looked mad. Her presence prevented me from regarding at all closely the furnishings of the Writing Room.

Back at the North Front, as I resolved to call it, perhaps superseding the compass rather than leading it, there was a cold-looking room, with a carpetless stone floor and white walls, upon which were the mounted heads and horns of many animals. They were all the room contained, but they covered the walls from floor to ceiling. I felt sure that the ferocious old man in the Dining Room had killed all these creatures, and I hated him for it. But I knew what the room would be called: it would be the Trophy Room.

Then I realised that there was no kitchen. It could hardly be upstairs. I had never heard of such a thing. But I looked.

It wasn't there. All the rooms on the first floor were bedrooms. There were six of them, and they so resembled one another, all with dark ochreous wallpaper and narrow brass bedsteads corroded with neglect, that I found it impracticable to distinguish them other than by numbers, at least for the present. Ultimately I might know the house better. Bedrooms 2, 3 and 6 contained two beds each. I recalled that at least nine people lived in the house. In one room the dark walls, the dark floor, the bed linen, and even the glass in the window were splashed, smeared, and further darkened with ink: it seemed apparent who slept there.

I sat on an orange box and looked. My house needed painting and dusting and scrubbing and polishing and renewing; but on the whole I was relieved that things were not worse. I had felt that the house had stood in the dark corner of the shop for no one knew how long, but this, I now saw, could hardly have been true. I wondered about the lady who had needed to get rid of it. Despite that need, she must have kept things up pretty thoroughly. How did she do it? How did she get in? I resolved to ask my Mother's advice. I determined to be a good landlord, although, like most who so resolve, my resources were nil. We simply lacked the money to regild my Long Drawing Room in proper gold leaf. But I would bring life to the nine dolls now drooping with boredom and neglect. . . .

Then I recalled something. What had become of the doll who had been sagging from the window? I thought she must have been jolted out, and felt myself a murderess. But none of the windows was open. The sash might easily have descended with the shaking; but more probably the poor doll lay inside on the floor of her room. I again went round from room to room, this time on tiptoe, but it was impossible to see the areas of floor just below the dark windows. . . . It was not merely sunless outside, but heavily overcast. I unlocked the door of our principal Spare Room, and descended pensively to await my Mother's return and tea.

Wormwood Grange, my Father called my house, with penological associations still on his mind. (After he was run over, I realised for the first time that there might be a reason for this, and for his inability to find work worthy of him.) My Mother had made the most careful inspection on my behalf, but had been unable to suggest any way of making an entry, or at least of passing beyond the Hall, to which the front doors still lay open. There seemed no question of whole walls lifting off, of the roof being removable, or even of a window being opened, including, mysteriously, on the first floor.

'I don't think it's meant for children, Liebchen,' said my Mother, smiling her lovely smile. 'We shall have to consult the Victoria and Albert Museum.'

'Of course it's not meant for children,' I replied. 'That's why I wanted it. I'm going to receive, like La Belle Otero.'

Next morning, after my Mother had gone to work, my Father came up, and wrenched and prodded with his unskilful hands.

'I'll get a chisel,' he said. 'We'll prise it open at each corner, and when we've got the fronts off, I'll go over to Woolworths and buy some hinges and screws. I expect they'll have some.'

At that I struck my Father in the chest with my fist. He seized my wrists, and I screamed that he was not to lay a finger on my beautiful house, that he would be sure to spoil it, that force never got anyone anywhere. I knew my Father: when he took an idea for using tools into his head, the only hope for one's property lay in a scene, and in the implication of tears without end in the future, if the idea were not dropped.

While I was screaming and raving, Constantin appeared from the room below, where he worked at his books.

'Give us a chance, Sis,' he said. 'How can I keep it all in my head about the Thirty Years War when you haven't learnt to control your tantrums?'

Although two years younger than I, Constantin should have known that I was past the age for screaming except of set purpose.

'You wait until he tries to rebind all your books, you silly sneak,' I yelled at him.

My Father released my wrists.

'Wormwood Grange can keep,' he said. 'I'll think of something else to go over to Woolworths for.' He sauntered off.

Constantin nodded gravely. 'I understand,' he said. 'I understand what you mean. I'll go back to my work. Here, try this.' He gave me a small, chipped nail file.

I spent most of the morning fiddling very cautiously with the imperfect jemmy, and trying to make up my mind about the doll at the window.

I failed to get into my house, and I refused to let my parents give me any effective aid. Perhaps by now I did not really want to get in, although the dirt and disrepair, and the apathy of the dolls, who so badly needed plumping up and dispersing, continued to cause me distress. Certainly I spent as long trying to shut the front door as trying to open a window or find a concealed spring (that idea was Constantin's). In the end I wedged the two halves of the front door with two halves of match; but I felt that the arrangement was makeshift and undignified. I refused everyone access to the principal Spare Room until something more appropriate could be evolved. My plans for routs and orgies had to be deferred: one could hardly riot among dust and cobwebs.

Then I began to have dreams about my house, and about its occupants.

One of the oddest dreams was the first. It was three or four days after I entered into possession. During that time it had remained cloudy and oppressive, so that my Father took to leaving off his knitted waistcoat; then suddenly it thundered. It was long, slow, distant, intermittent thunder; and it continued all the evening, until, when it was quite dark, my bedtime and Constantin's could no longer be deferred.

'Your ears will get accustomed to the noise,' said my Father. 'Just try to take no notice of it.'

Constantin looked dubious; but I was tired of the slow, rumbling hours, and ready for the different dimension of dreams.

I slept almost immediately, although the thunder was rolling round my big, rather empty bedroom, round the four walls, across the floor, and under the ceiling, weighting the black air as with a smoky vapour. Occasionally, the lightning glinted, pink and green. It was still the long drawn out preliminary to a storm; the tedious, imperfect dispersal of the accumulated energy of the summer. The rollings and rumblings entered my dreams, which flickered, changed, were gone as soon as come, failed, like the lightning, to concentrate or strike home, were as difficult to profit by as the events of an average day.

After exhausting hours of phantasmagoria, anticipating so many later nights in my life, I found myself in a black wood, with huge, dense trees. I was following a path, but reeled from tree to tree, bruising and cutting myself on their hardness and roughness. There seemed no end to the wood or to the night; but suddenly, in the thick of both, I came upon my house. It stood solid, immense, hemmed in, with a single light, little more, it seemed, than a night-light, burning in every upstairs window (as often in dreams, I could see all four sides of the house at once), and illuminating two wooden wedges, jagged and swollen, which held tight the front doors. The vast trees dipped and swayed their elephantine boughs over the roof; the wind peeked and creaked through the black battlements. Then there was a blaze of whitest lightning, proclaiming the storm itself. In the second it endured, I saw my two wedges fly through the air, and the double front door burst open.

For the hundredth time, the scene changed, and now I was back in my room, though still asleep or half-asleep, still dragged from vision to vision. Now the thunder was coming in immense, calculated bombardments; the lightning ceaseless and searing the face of the earth. From being a weariness the storm had become an ecstasy. It seemed as if the whole world would be in dissolution before the thunder had spent its impersonal, unregarding strength. But, as I say, I must still have been at least half asleep, because between the fortissimi and the lustre I still from time to time saw scenes, meaningless or nightmarish, which could not be found in the wakeful world; still, between and through the volleys, heard impossible sounds.

I do not know whether I was asleep or awake when the storm rippled into tranquillity. I certainly did not feel that the air had been cleared; but this may have been because, surprisingly, I heard a quick soft step passing along the passage outside my room, a passage uncarpeted through our poverty. I well knew all the footsteps in the house, and this was none of them.

Always one to meet trouble half-way, I dashed in my night-gown to open the door. I looked out. The dawn was seeping, without effort or momentum, through every cranny, and showed shadowy the back of a retreating figure, the size of my Mother but with woolly red hair and long rust-coloured dress. The padding feet seemed actually to start soft echoes amid all that naked woodwork, I had no need to consider who she was or whither she was bound. I burst into the purposeless tears I so despised.

In the morning, and before deciding upon what to impart, I took Constantin with me to look at the house. I more than half expected big changes; but none was to be seen. The sections of match-stick were still in position, and the dolls as inactive and diminutive as ever, sitting with their backs to me on chairs and sofas in the Long Drawing Room; their hair dusty, possibly even mothy. Constantin looked at me curiously, but I imparted nothing.

Other dreams followed; though at considerable intervals. Many children have recurring nightmares of oppressive realism and terrifying content; and I realised from past experience that I must outgrow the habit or lose my house—my house at least. It is true that my house now frightened me, but I felt that I must not be foolish and should strive to take a grown-up view of painted woodwork and nine understuffed dolls. Still it was bad when I began to hear them in the darkness; some tapping, some stumping, some creeping, and therefore not one, but many, or all; and worse when I began not to sleep for fear of the mad doll (as I was sure she was) doing something mad, although I refused to think what. I never dared again to look; but when something happened, which, as I say, was only at intervals (and to me, being young, they seemed long intervals), I lay taut and straining among the forgotten sheets. Moreover, the steps themselves were never quite constant, certainly too inconstant to report to others; and I am not sure that I should have heard anything significant if I had not once seen. But now I locked the door of our principal Spare Room on the outside, and altogether ceased to visit my beautiful, impregnable mansion.

I noticed that my Mother made no comment. But one day my Father complained of my ingratitude in never playing with my handsome birthday present. I said I was occupied with my holiday task: *Moby Dick*. This was an approved answer, and even, as far as it went, a true one, though I found the book pointless in the extreme, and horribly cruel.

'I told you the Grange was the wrong thing to buy,' said my Father. 'Morbid sort of object for a toy.'

'None of us can learn except by experience,' said my Mother.

My Father said 'Not at all,' and bristled.

All this, naturally, was in the holidays. I was going at the time to one of my Mother's schools, where I should stay until I could begin to train as a dancer, upon which I was conventionally but entirely resolved. Constantin went to another, a highly cerebral co-educational place, where he would remain until, inevitably, he won a scholarship to a University, perhaps a foreign one. Despite our years, we went our different ways dangerously on small dingy bicycles. We reached home at assorted hours, mine being the longer journey.

One day I returned to find our dining-room table littered with peculiarly uninteresting printed drawings. I could make nothing of them whatever (they did not seem even to belong to the kind of geometry I was—regretfully—used to); and they curled up on themselves when one tried to examine them, and bit one's finger. My Father had a week or two before taking one of his infrequent jobs; night work of some kind a long way off, to which he had now departed in our car. Obviously the drawings were connected with Constantin, but he was not there.

I went upstairs, and saw that the principal Spare Room door was open. Constantin was inside. There had, of course, been no question of the key to the room being removed. It was only necessary to turn it.

'Hallo, Lene,' Constantin said in his matter of fact way. 'We've been doing axonometric projection, and I'm projecting your house.' He was making one of the drawings; on a sheet of thick white paper. 'It's for home-work. It'll knock out all the others. They've got to do their real houses.'

It must not be supposed that I did not like Constantin, although often he annoyed me with his placidity and precision. It was weeks since I had seen my house, and it looked unexpectedly interesting. A curious thing happened: nor was it the last time in my life that I experienced it. Temporarily I became a different person; confident, practical, simple. The clear evening sun of autumn may have contributed.

'I'll help,' I said. 'Tell me what to do.'

'It's a bore I can't get in to take measurements. Although we haven't got to. In fact, the Clot told us not. Just a general impression, he said. It's to give us the *concept* of axonometry. But, golly, it would be simpler with feet and inches.'

To judge by the amount of white paper he had covered in what could only have been a short time, Constantin seemed to me to be doing very well, but he was one never to be content with less than perfection.

'Tell me,' I said, 'what to do, and I'll do it.'

'Thanks,' he replied, sharpening his pencil with a special instrument. 'But it's a one-man job this. In the nature of the case. Later, I'll show you how to do it, and you can do some other building if you like.'

I remained, looking at my house and fingering it, until Constantin made it clearer that I was a distraction. I went away, changed my shoes, and put on the kettle against my Mother's arrival, and our High Tea.

When Constantin came down (my Mother had called for him three times, but that was not unusual), he said, 'I say, Sis, here's a rum thing.'

My Mother said: 'Don't use slang, and don't call your sister, Sis.'

He said, as he always did when reproved by her, 'I'm sorry, Mother.' Then he thrust the drawing paper at me. 'Look, there's a bit missing. See what I mean?' He was showing me with his stub of emerald pencil, pocked with toothmarks.

Of course, I didn't see. I didn't understand a thing about it.

'After Tea,' said my Mother. She gave to such familiar words not a maternal but an imperial decisiveness.

'But Mum—' pleaded Constantin.

'Mother,' said my Mother.

Constantin started dipping for sauerkraut.

Silently we ate ourselves into tranquillity; or, for me, into the appearance of it. My alternative personality, though it had survived Constantin's refusal of my assistance, was now beginning to ebb.

'What is all this that you are doing?' enquired my Mother in the end. 'It resembles the Stone of Rosetta.'

'I'm taking an axonometric cast of Lene's birthday house.'

'And so?'

But Constantin was not now going to expound immediately. He put in his mouth a finger of rye bread smeared with homemade cheese. Then he said quietly: 'I got down a rough idea of the house, but the rooms don't fit. At least, they don't on the bottom floor. It's all right, I think, on the top floor. In fact that's the rummest thing of all. Sorry Mother.' He had been speaking with his mouth full, and now filled it fuller.

'What nonsense is this?' To me it seemed that my Mother was glaring at him in a way most unlike her.

'It's not nonsense, Mother. Of course, I haven't measured the place, because you can't. But I haven't done axonometry for nothing. There's a part of the bottom floor I can't get at. A secret room or something.'

'Show me.'

'Very well, Mother.' Constantin put down his remnant of bread and cheese. He rose, looking a little pale. He took the drawing round the table to my Mother.

'Not that thing. I can't understand it, and I don't believe you can understand it either.' Only sometimes to my Father did my Mother speak like that. 'Show me in the house.'

I rose too.

'You stay here, Lene. Put some more water in the kettle and boil it.'

'But it's my house. I have a right to know.'

My Mother's expression changed to one more familiar. 'Yes, Lene,' she said, 'you have a right. But please not now. I ask you.'

I smiled at her and picked up the kettle.

'Come, Constantin.'

I lingered by the kettle in the kitchen, not wishing to give an impression of eavesdropping or even undue eagerness, which I knew would distress my Mother. I never wished to learn things that my Mother wished to keep from me; and I never questioned her implication of 'All in good time'.

But they were not gone long, for well before the kettle had begun even to grunt, my Mother's beautiful voice was summoning me back.

'Constantin is quite right,' she said, when I had presented myself at the dining-room table, 'and it was wrong of me to doubt it. The house is built in a funny sort of way. But what does it matter?'

Constantin was not eating.

'I am glad that you are studying well, and learning such useful things,' said my Mother.

She wished the subject to be dropped, and we dropped it.

Indeed, it was difficult to think what more could be said. But I waited for a moment in which I was alone with Constantin. My Father's unhabitual absence made this difficult, and it was completely dark before the moment came.

And when, as was only to be expected, Constantin had nothing to add, I felt, most unreasonably, that he was joined with my Mother in keeping something from me.

'But what *happened*?' I pressed him. 'What happened when you were in the room with her?'

'What do you think happened?' replied Constantin, wishing, I thought, that my Mother would re-enter. 'Mother realised that I was right. Nothing more. What does it matter anyway?'

That final query confirmed my doubts.

'Constantin,' I said. 'Is there anything I ought to do?'

'Better hack the place open,' he answered, almost irritably.

But a most unexpected thing happened, that, had I even considered adopting Constantin's idea, would have saved me the trouble. When next day I returned from school, my house was gone.

Constantin was sitting in his usual corner, this time absorbing Greek paradigms. Without speaking to him (nothing unusual in that when he was working), I went straight to the principal Spare Room. The vast deal table, less scrubbed than once, was bare. The place where my house had stood was very visible, as if indeed a palace had been swept off by a djinn. But I could see no other sign of its passing: no scratched woodwork, or marks of boots, or disjoined fragments.

Constantin seemed genuinely astonished at the news. But I doubted him.

'You knew,' I said.

'Of course I didn't know.'

Still, he understood what I was thinking.

He said again: 'I didn't know.'

Unlike me on occasion, he always spoke the truth.

I gathered myself together and blurted out: 'Have they done it themselves?' Inevitably I was frightened, but in a way I was also relieved.

'Who do you mean?'

'They.'

I was inviting ridicule, but Constantin was kind.

He said: 'I know who I think has done it, but you mustn't let on. I think Mother's done it.'

I did not again enquire uselessly into how much more he knew than I. I said: 'But *how*?'

Constantin shrugged. It was a habit he had assimilated with so much else.

'Mother left the house with us this morning and she isn't back yet.'

'She must have put Father up to it.'

'But there are no marks.'

'Father might have got help.' There was a pause. Then Constantin said: 'Are you sorry?'

'In a way,' I replied. Constantin with precocious wisdom left it at that.

When my Mother returned, she simply said that my Father had already lost his new job, so that we had had to sell things.

'I hope you will forgive your Father and me,' she said. 'We've had to sell one of my watches also. Father will soon be back to Tea.'

She too was one I had never known to lie; but now I began to perceive how relative and instrumental truth could be.

I need not say: not in those terms. Such clear concepts, with all they offer of gain and loss, come later, if they come at all. In fact, I need not say that the whole of what goes before is so heavily filtered through later experience as to be of little evidential value. But I am scarcely putting forward evidence. There is so little. All I can do is to tell something of what happened, as it now seems to me to have been.

I remember sulking at my Mother's news, and her explaining to me that really I no longer liked the house and that something better would be bought for me in replacement when our funds permitted.

I did ask my Father when he returned to our evening meal, whistling and falsely jaunty about the lost job, how much he had been paid for my house.

'A trifle more than I gave for it. That's only business.'

'Where is it now?'

'Never you mind.'

'Tell her,' said Constantin. 'She wants to know.'

'Eat your herring,' said my Father very sharply. 'And mind your own business.'

And, thus, before long my house was forgotten, my occasional nightmares returned to earlier themes.

It was, as I say, for two or three months in 1921 that I owned the house and from time to time dreamed that creatures I supposed to be its occupants had somehow invaded my home. The next thirty years, more or less, can be disposed of quickly: it was the period when I tried conclusions with the outer world.

I really became a dancer; and, although the upper reaches alike of the art and of the profession notably eluded me, yet I managed to maintain myself for several years, no small achievement. I retired, as they say, upon marriage. My husband aroused physical passion in me for the first time, but diminished and deadened much else. He was reported missing in the late misguided war. Certainly he did not return to me. I at least still miss him, though often I despise myself for doing so.

My Father died in a street accident when I was fifteen: it happened on the day I received a special commendation from the sallow Frenchwoman who taught me to dance. After his death my beloved Mother always wanted to return to Germany. Before long I was spiritually self-sufficient enough, or said I was, to make that possible. Unfailingly, she wrote to me twice a week, although to find words in which to reply was often difficult for me. Sometimes I visited her, while the conditions in her country became more and more uncongenial to me. She had a fair position teaching English Language and Literature at a small university; and she seemed increasingly to be infected by the new notions and emotions raging around her. I must acknowledge that sometimes their tumult and intoxication unsteadied my own mental gait, although I was a foreigner and by no means of sanguine temperament. It is a mistake to think that all professional dancers are gay.

Despite what appeared to be increasing sympathies with the new régime, my Mother disappeared. She was the first of the two people who mattered to me in such very different ways, and who so unreasonably vanished. For a time I was ill, and of course I love her still more than anybody. If she had remained with me, I am sure I should never have married. Without involving myself in psychology, which I detest, I shall simply say that the thought and recollection of my Mother lay, I believe, behind the self-absorption my husband complained of so bitterly and so justly. It was not really myself in which I was absorbed but the memory of perfection. It is the plain truth that such beauty, and goodness, and depth, and capacity for love were my Mother's alone.

Constantin abandoned all his versatile reading and became a priest, in fact a member of the Society of Jesus. He seems exalted (possibly too much so for his colleagues and superiors), but I can no longer speak to him or bear his presence. He frightens me. Poor Constantin!

On the other hand, I, always dubious, have become a complete unbeliever. I cannot see that Constantin is doing anything but listen to his own inner voice (which has changed its tone since we were children); and mine speaks a different language. In the long run, I doubt whether there is much to be desired but death; or whether there is endurance in anything but suffering. I no longer see myself feasting crowned heads on quails.

So much for biographical intermission. I proceed to the circumstances of my second and recent experience of land-lordism.

In the first place, I did something thoroughly stupid. Instead of
following the road marked on the map, I took a short cut. It is
true that the short cut was shown on the map also, but the
region was much too unfrequented for a wandering footpath to
be in any way dependable, especially in this generation which
has ceased to walk beyond the garage or the bus stop. It was one
of the least populated districts in the whole country, and,
moreover, the slow autumn dusk was already perceptible when I
pushed at the first, dilapidated gate.

To begin with, the path trickled and flickered across a
sequence of small damp meadows, bearing neither cattle nor
crop. When it came to the third or fourth of these meadows, the
way had all but vanished in the increasing sogginess, and could
be continued only by looking for the stile or gate in the unkempt
hedge ahead. This was not especially difficult as long as the
fields remained small; but after a time I reached a depressing
expanse which could hardly be termed a field at all, but was
rather a large marsh. It was at this point that I should have
returned and set about tramping the winding road.

But a path of some kind again continued before me, and I
perceived that the escapade had already consumed twenty
minutes. So I risked it, although soon I was striding laboriously
from tussock to brown tussock in order not to sink above my
shoes into the surrounding quagmire. It is quite extraordinary
how far one can stray from a straight or determined course
when thus preoccupied with elementary comfort. The hedge on
the far side of the marsh was still a long way ahead, and the
tussocks themselves were becoming both less frequent and less
dense, so that too often I was sinking through them into the

mire. I realised that the marsh sloped slightly downwards in the direction I was following, so that before I reached the hedge, I might have to cross a river. In the event, it was not so much a river, as an indeterminately bounded augmentation of the softness, and moistness, and ooziness: I struggled across, jerking from false foothold to palpable pitfall, and before long despairing even of the attempt to step securely. Both my feet were now soaked to well above the ankles, and the visibility had become less than was entirely convenient.

When I reached what I had taken for a hedge, it proved to be the boundary of an extensive thicket. Autumn had infected much of the greenery with blotched and dropping senility; so that bare brown briars arched and tousled, and purple thorns tilted at all possible angles for blood. To go further would demand an axe. Either I must retraverse the dreary bog in the perceptibly waning light, or I must skirt the edge and seek an opening in the thicket. Undecided, I looked back. I realised that I had lost the gate through which I had entered upon the marsh on the other side. There was nothing to do but creep as best I could upon the still treacherous ground along the barrier of dead dogroses, mildewed blackberries, and rampant nettles.

But it was not long before I reached a considerable gap, from which through the tangled vegetation seemed to lead a substantial track, although by no means a straight one. The track wound on unimpeded for a considerable distance, even becoming firmer underfoot; until I realised that the thicket had become an entirely indisputable wood. The brambles clutching maliciously from the sides had become watching branches above my head. I could not recall that the map had showed a wood. If, indeed, it had done so, I should not have entered upon the footpath, because the only previous occasion in my life when I had been truly lost, in the sense of being unable to find the way back as well as being unable to go on, had been when my Father had once so effectively lost us in a wood that I have never again felt the same about woods. The fear I had felt for perhaps an hour and a half on that occasion, though told to no one, and swiftly evaporating from consciousness upon our emergence, had been the veritable fear of death. Now I drew the map from where it lay against my thigh in the big pocket of my dress. It was not until I tried to read it that I realised how near I was to night. Until it came to print, the problems of the route had given me cat's eyes.

I peered, and there was no wood, no green patch on the map, but only the wavering line of dots advancing across contoured whiteness to the neck of yellow road where the short cut ended. But I did not reach any foolish conclusion. I simply guessed that I had strayed very badly: the map was spattered with green marks in places where I had no wish to be; and the only question was in which of those many thickets I now was. I could think of no way to find out. I was nearly lost, and this time I could not blame my Father.

The track I had been following still stretched ahead, as yet not too indistinct; and I continued to follow it. As the trees around me became yet bigger and thicker, fear came upon me; though not the death fear of that previous occasion, I felt now that I knew what was going to happen next; or, rather, I felt I knew one thing that was going to happen next, a thing which was but a small and far from central part of an obscure, inapprehensible totality. As one does on such occasions, I felt more than half outside my body. If I continued much further, I might change into somebody else.

But what happened was not what I expected. Suddenly I saw a flicker of light. It seemed to emerge from the left, to weave momentarily among the trees, and to disappear to the right. It was not what I expected, but it was scarcely reassuring. I wondered if it could be a will o' the wisp, a thing I had never seen, but which I understood to be connected with marshes. Next a still more prosaic possibility occurred to me, one positively hopeful: the headlights of a motor car turning a corner. It seemed the likely answer, but my uneasiness did not perceptibly diminish.

I struggled on, and the light came again: a little stronger, and twisting through the trees around me. Of course another car at the same corner of the road was not an impossibility, even though it was an unpeopled area. Then, after a period of soft but not comforting dusk, it came a third time; and, soon, a fourth. There was no sound of an engine: and it seemed to me that the transit of the light was too swift and fleeting for any car.

And then what I had been awaiting, happened. I came suddenly upon a huge square house. I had known it was coming, but still it struck at my heart.

It is not every day that one finds a dream come true; and, scared though I was, I noticed details: for example, that there did not seem to be those single lights burning in every upstairs window. Doubtless dreams, like poems, demand a certain licence; and, for the matter of that, I could not see all four sides of the house at once, as I had dreamed I had. But that perhaps was the worst of it: I was plainly not dreaming now.

A sudden greeny-pink radiance illuminated around me a morass of weed and neglect; and then seemed to hide itself among the trees on my right. The explanation of the darting lights was that a storm approached. But it was unlike other lightning I had encountered: being slower, more silent, more regular.

There seemed nothing to do but run away, though even then it seemed sensible not to run back into the wood. In the last memories of daylight, I began to wade through the dead knee-high grass of the lost lawn. It was still possible to see that the wood continued, opaque as ever, in a long line to my left; I felt my way along it, in order to keep as far as possible from the house. I noticed, as I passed, the great portico, facing the direction from which I had emerged. Then, keeping my distance, I crept along the grey east front with its two tiers of pointed windows, all shut and one or two broken; and reached the southern parterre, visibly vaster, even in the storm-charged gloom, than the northern, but no less ravaged. Ahead, and at the side of the parterre far off to my right, ranged the encircling woodland. If no path manifested, my state would be hazardous indeed; and there seemed little reason for a path, as the approach to the house was provided by that along which I had come from the marsh.

As I struggled onwards, the whole scene was transformed: in a moment the sky became charged with roaring thunder, the earth with tumultuous rain. I tried to shelter in the adjacent wood, but instantly found myself enmeshed in bines and suckers, lacerated by invisible spears. In a minute I should be drenched. I plunged through the wet weeds towards the spreading portico.

Before the big doors I waited for several minutes, watching the lightning, and listening. The rain leapt up where it fell, as if the earth hurt it. A rising chill made the old grass shiver. It seemed unlikely that anyone could live in a house so dark; but suddenly I heard one of the doors behind me scrape open. I turned. A dark head protruded between the portals, like Punch from the side of his booth.

'Oh.' The shrill voice was of course surprised to see me.

I turned. 'May I please wait until the rain stops?'

'You can't come inside.'

I drew back; so far back that a heavy drip fell on the back of my neck from the edge of the portico. With absurd melodrama, there was a loud roll of thunder.

'I shouldn't think of it,' I said. 'I must be on my way the moment the rain lets me.' I could still see only the round head sticking out between the leaves of the door.

'In the old days we often had visitors.' This statement was made in the tone of a Cheltenham lady remarking that when a child she often spoke to gypsies. 'I only peeped out to see the thunder.'

Now, within the house, I heard another, lower voice, although I could not hear what it said. Through the long crack between the doors, a light slid out across the flagstones of the porch and down the darkening steps.

'She's waiting for the rain to stop,' said the shrill voice.

'Tell her to come in,' said the deep voice. 'Really, Emerald, you forget your manners after all this time.'

'I *have* told her,' said Emerald very petulantly, and withdrawing her head. 'She won't do it.'

'Nonsense,' said the other. 'You're just telling lies.' I got the idea that thus she always spoke to Emerald.

Then the doors opened, and I could see the two of them silhouetted in the light of a lamp which stood on a table behind them; one much the taller, but both with round heads, and both wearing long, unshapely garments. I wanted very much to escape, and failed to do so only because there seemed nowhere to go.

'Please come in at once,' said the taller figure, 'and let us take off your wet clothes.'

'Yes, yes,' squeaked Emerald, unreasonably jubilant.

'Thank you. But my clothes are not at all wet.'

'None the less, please come in. We shall take it as a discourtesy if you refuse.'

Another roar of thunder emphasised the impracticability of continuing to refuse much longer. If this was a dream, doubtless, and to judge by experience, I should awake.

And a dream it must be, because there at the front door were two big wooden wedges; and there to the right of the Hall, shadowed in the lamplight, was the Trophy Room; although now the animal heads on the walls were shoddy, fungoid ruins, their sawdust spilled and clotted on the cracked and uneven flagstones of the floor.

'You must forgive us,' said my tall hostess. 'Our landlord neglects us sadly, and we are far gone in wrack and ruin. In fact, I do not know what we should do were it not for our own resources.' At this Emerald cackled. Then she came up to me, and began fingering my clothes.

The tall one shut the door.

'Don't touch,' she shouted at Emerald, in her deep, rather grinding voice. 'Keep your fingers off.'

She picked up the large oil lamp. Her hair was a discoloured white in its beams.

'I apologise for my sister,' she said. 'We have all been so neglected that some of us have quite forgotten how to behave. Come, Emerald.'

Pushing Emerald before her, she led the way.

In the Occasional Room and the Morning Room, the gilt had flaked from the gingerbread furniture, the family portraits started from their heavy frames, and the striped wallpaper drooped in the lamplight like an assembly of sodden, half-inflated balloons.

At the door of the Canton Cabinet, my hostess turned. 'I am taking you to meet my sisters,' she said.

'I look forward to doing so,' I replied, regardless of truth, as in childhood.

She nodded slightly, and proceeded. 'Take care,' she said. 'The floor has weak places.'

In the little Canton Cabinet, the floor had, in fact, largely given way, and been plainly converted into a hospice for rats. And then, there they all were, the remaining six of them, thinly illumined by what must surely be rushlights in the four shapely chandeliers. But now, of course, I could see their faces.

'We are all named after our birthstones,' said my hostess. 'Emerald you know. I am Opal. Here are Diamond and Garnet, Cornelian and Chrysolite. The one with the grey hair is Sardonyx, and the beautiful one is Turquoise.'

They all stood up. During the ceremony of introduction, they made odd little noises.

'Emerald and I are the eldest, and Turquoise of course is the youngest.'

Emerald stood in the corner before me, rolling her dyed red head. The Long Drawing Room was raddled with decay. The cobwebs gleamed like steel filigree in the beam of the lamp, and the sisters seemed to have been seated in cocoons of them, like cushions of gossamer.

'There is one other sister, Topaz. But she is busy writing.'

'Writing all our diaries,' said Emerald.

'Keeping the record,' said my hostess.

A silence followed.

'Let us sit down,' said my hostess. 'Let us make our visitor welcome.'

The six of them gently creaked and subsided into their former places. Emerald and my hostess remained standing.

'Sit down, Emerald. Our visitor shall have *my* chair as it is the best.' I realised that inevitably there was no extra seat.

'Of course not,' I said. 'I can only stay for a minute. I am waiting for the rain to stop,' I explained feebly to the rest of them.

'I insist,' said my hostess.

I looked at the chair to which she was pointing. The padding was burst and rotten, the woodwork bleached and crumbling to collapse. All of them were watching me with round, vague eyes in their flat faces.

'Really,' I said, 'no, thank you. It's kind of you, but I must go.' All the same, the surrounding wood, and the dark marsh beyond it loomed scarcely less appalling than the house itself and its inmates.

'We should have more to offer, more and better in every way, were it not for our landlord.' She spoke with bitterness, and it seemed to me that on all the faces the expression changed. Emerald came towards me out of her corner, and again began to finger my clothes. But this time her sister did not correct her; and when I stepped away, she stepped after me and went on as before.

'She has failed in the barest duty of sustentation.'

I could not prevent myself starting at the pronoun. At once, Emerald caught hold of my dress, and held it tightly.

'But there is one place she cannot spoil for us. One place where we can entertain in our own way.'

'Please,' I cried. 'Nothing more. I am going now.'

Emerald's pygmy grip tautened.

'It is the room where we eat.'

All the watching eyes lighted up, and became something they had not been before.

'I may almost say where we feast.'

The six of them began again to rise from their spidery bowers.

'Because *she* cannot go there.'

The sisters clapped their hands, like a rustle of leaves.

'There we can be what we really are.'

The eight of them were now grouped round me. I noticed that the one pointed out as the youngest was passing her dry, pointed tongue over her lower lip.

'Nothing unladylike, of course.'

'Of course not,' I agreed.

'But firm,' broke in Emerald, dragging at my dress as she spoke. 'Father said that must always come first.'

'Our father was a man of measureless wrath against a slight,' said my hostess. 'It is his continuing presence about the house which largely upholds us.'

'Shall I show her?' asked Emerald.

'Since you wish to,' said her sister disdainfully.

From somewhere in her musty garments Emerald produced a scrap of card, which she held out to me.

'Take it in your hand. I'll allow you to hold it.'

It was a photograph, obscurely damaged.

'Hold up the lamp,' squealed Emerald. With an aloof gesture her sister raised it.

It was a photograph of myself when a child, bobbed and waistless. And through my heart was a tiny brown needle.

'We've all got things like it,' said Emerald jubilantly. 'Wouldn't you think her heart would have rusted away by now?'

'She never had a heart,' said the elder sister scornfully, putting down the light.

'She might not have been able to help what she did,' I cried.

I could hear the sisters catch their fragile breath.

'It's what you do that counts,' said my hostess regarding the discoloured floor, 'not what you feel about it afterwards. Our father always insisted on that. It's obvious.'

'Give it back to me,' said Emerald staring into my eyes.

For a moment I hesitated.

'Give it back to her,' said my hostess in her contemptuous way. 'It makes no difference now. Everyone but Emerald can see that the work is done.'

I returned the card, and Emerald let go of me as she stuffed it away.

'And now will you join us?' asked my hostess. 'In the inner room?' As far as was possible, her manner was almost casual.

'I am sure the rain has stopped,' I replied. 'I must be on my way.'

'Our father would never have let you go so easily, but I think we have done what we can with you.'

I inclined my head.

'Do not trouble with adieux,' she said. 'My sisters no longer expect them.' She picked up the lamp. 'Follow me. And take care. The floor has weak places.'

'Goodbye,' squealed Emerald.

'Take no notice, unless you wish,' said my hostess.

I followed her through the mouldering rooms and across the rotten floors in silence. She opened both the outer doors and stood waiting for me to pass through. Beyond, the moon was shining, and she stood dark and shapeless in the silver flood.

On the threshold, or somewhere on the far side of it, I spoke.

'I did nothing,' I said. 'Nothing.'

So far from replying, she dissolved into the darkness and silently shut the door.

I took up my painful, lost, and forgotten way through the wood, across the dreary marsh, and back to the little yellow road.

NEVER VISIT VENICE

> Travel is a good thing; it stimulates the imagination. Everything else is a snare and a delusion. Our own journey is entirely imaginative. Therein lies its strength.
>
> *Louis-Ferdinand Celine*

I

HENRY FERN was neither successful in the world's eyes, nor unsuccessful; partly because he lived in a world society in which to be either requires considerable craft. Fern was not good at material scheming. His job stood far below his theoretical capacities, but he had a very clear idea of his own defects, and was inclined inwardly to believe that but for one or two strokes of sheer good fortune, he would have been a mere social derelict. He did not sufficiently understand that it has been made almost impossible to be a social derelict.

Not that Fern was adapted to that status any better than to the status of tycoon. Like most introverts, he was very dependent upon small, minute-to-minute comforts, no matter whence they came. Fern's gaze upon life was very decisively inwards. He read much. He reflected much. One of his purest pleasures was an entire day in bed; all by himself, in excellent health. He lived in a quite pleasant suburban flat, with a view over a park. Unfortunately, the park, for the most part, was more beautiful when Fern was not there; because when he was there, it tended to fill with raucous loiterers and tiny piercing radios.

Fern was an only child. His parents were far off and in poorer circumstances than when he had been a boy. He had much difficulty, not perhaps in making friends, but in keeping up an interest in them. There seemed to be something in him which made him different from most of the people he encountered in the office or in the train or in the park or at the houses of others. He could not succeed in defining what this difference was, and he simultaneously congratulated and despised himself for having it. He would sincerely have liked to be rid of it, but at the same time was pretty sure it was the best thing about him. If only others were interested in the best!

One thing it plainly did was hold Fern back in what people called his career. Here it did damage in several different ways. That it disconnected him from the network of favour and promotion was only the most obvious. Much worse was that it made favour and promotion seem to Fern doubtfully worth while. Worse still was that it made him see through the work he had to do; see that, like so much that is called work, it was little more than protective colouration: but see also that the blank disclosure of this fact would destroy not merely the work itself and his own income, but the hopes of the many who were committed to at least a half-belief in its importance, even when they chafed against it. Worst of all probably was the simple fact that this passionate division inside him ate up his energy and sent it to waste. Fern would have liked to be an artist, but seemed to himself to have little creative talent. He soon realised that it has become a difficult world for those who possibly are artists only in living. There is so little scope for practice and rehearsal.

Nor could Fern find a woman who seemed to feel in the least as he did. Having heard and read often that it is useless to seek for one's ideal woman, that the very fancy of an ideal woman is an absurdity, he at first made up his mind to concentrate upon the good qualities that were actually to be found, which were undoubtedly many, at least by accepted standards. He even became engaged to be married on two occasions; but the more he saw of each fiancée, despite her beauty and charm of character, the more he felt himself an alien and an imposter. Unable to dissemble any more, he had himself broken off the engagement. He had felt much anguish, but it was not, he felt, anguish of the right kind. Even in that he seemed isolated. The women must have realised something of the truth, because though both, when he spoke, expressed aggressive dismay, since marriage is so much sought after for itself, they soon went quietly, and were heard of by Fern no more. Now he was nearing forty: not, he thought, unhappy, when all was considered; but he could not do so much considering every day, and often he felt puzzled and sadly lonely. Things could be so very much worse, and that very easily, as none knew better than Fern; but this reflection, well justified though it was, did not prevent Fern from thinking, not infrequently, of suicide, or from letting the back of his mind dwell pleasurably and recurrently upon the thought of Death's warm, white, and loving arms.

One thing about which Fern felt true anguish was the problem of travel, or, as others put it, his 'holidays'.

Here the shortage of money really mattered. 'Why do I not go out for more?' he asked himself.

He had no difficulty in answering himself. Apart from the obvious doubt as to whether it was a good bargain to sell himself further into slavery in order to receive in return perhaps seven more days each year for travel and enough extra money to travel a little (a very little) more comfortably, he saw well that even these rewards might be vitiated by the extra care that would probably travel with the recipient of them. He realised early that, except for a few natural bohemians, travel can be of value only when based upon private resources: hence the almost universal adulteration of travel into organised tourism, an art into a science, so that the shrinking surface of the earth, in its physical aspect as in its way of life, becomes a single place, not worth leaving home to see. Fern saw this very clearly, but it was considerably too wide and theoretical a consideration to deter one so truly a traveller but who had yet travelled so little as Fern. What really held Fern back from travel, as from much else, was the lack of a fellow-traveller; remembering always that this fellow-traveller had to comply pretty nearly with an ideal which Fern could by no means define, but could only sense and serve, present or (as almost always) absent beyond reasonable hope.

He had shared a holiday with both his fiancées—one holiday in each case. Much the same things had happened each time; doubtless because men notoriously involve themselves (even when they do it half-heartedly) with the same woman in different shapes, or, perhaps, as Lord Chesterfield says, because women are so much more alike than are men. On each occasion, it had been two or three weeks of differing objectives, conscious and unconscious, at all levels, and, especially, of utterly different responses to everything encountered; but a matter also of determined and scrupulous effort on both sides not only to understand but to act upon and make allowances for the other's point of view. All these things had made of the holiday a repro-duction or extension of common life, which was not at all what

Fern had in mind. Both parties had, in the American formula, 'worked at' the relationship, worked as hard as slaves under an overseer; but the product was unmarketable. 'You're too soulful about everything,' complained one of the girls. She spoke quite affectionately, and truly for his own good, as the world goes, and as Fern perceived. None the less, he came to surmise that for him travel might be a mystical undertaking. He had some time read of Renan's concept that for each man there is an individual 'means to salvation': for some the ascent to Monsalvat, for some alcohol or laudanum, for some wenching and whoring, for some even the common business of day-to-day life. For Fern salvation might lie in travel; but surely not in solitary travel. And how much more difficult than ever this new consideration would make finding a companion! Almost, how impossible! Fern felt his soul (as the girl had called it) shrink when he first clearly sensed the hopeless conflict between deepest need and inevitable absence of response; the conflict which makes even men and women who are capable of better things, live as they do. He and the girl were on a public seat in Bruges at the time; among the trees along the Dyver, looking at the swans on the canal.

At least politeness had been maintained on these trips; from first to last. It was something by no means to be despised. Moreover, when Fern had travelled with others, with a man friend, or with a party, he had fared considerably worse. Then there had been little in the way of manners and no obligation even to essay mutuality. In the longer run, therefore, Fern had travelled little and enjoyed less. This in no way modified his unworldly attitude to travel. He knew that few people do enjoy it, despite the ever-increasing number who set forth; and resented the fact that actual experience of travel had seemed, for practical purposes, to put him among the majority, of them, but not with them, as usual. Nor could he see even the possibility of a solution. Not enough money. Not enough time. And no intimates, let alone initiates. It had been quite bad enough even when he had only been twenty-five.

Fern began to have a dream. Foreshadowings or intimations came to him first; thereafter, at irregular intervals, the whole experience (in so far as it could be described as a whole), or bits or scraps of it, portions or distortions. There seemed to be no system in its total or partial recurrence. As far as Fern was concerned, it merely did not come often enough. He felt that it would be unlucky (by which he meant destructive) to note too precisely the dates of the dream's reappearances. But Fern was soon musing about the content of the dream during waking hours; sometimes even by policy and on purpose. To the infrequent dream of the night, he added an increasing habit of deliberate daydreaming; a pastime so disapproved of by the experts.

Fern's dream, though glowing, was simple.

He dreamed that he was in Venice, where he had never been. He was drifting in a gondola across an expanse of water he had read about, called the Lagoon. Lying in his embrace at the bottom of the boat was a woman in evening dress or party dress or gay dress of some kind. He did not know how he had met her: whether in Venice or in London. Conceivably, even, he knew her already, outside the dream; had long known her, or at least set eyes on her. When he awoke, he could never remember her face with sufficient clarity; or perhaps could remember only for a moment or two after waking, in the manner of dreams. It was a serious frustration, because the woman was very desirable, and because between Fern and her, and between them only as far as Fern was concerned, was understanding and affinity. Such understanding could not last, Fern realised even in the dream: it might not last beyond that one night; or it might last as long as six or seven days. Fern could always remember the woman's dress: but it was not always the same dress; it was sometimes white, sometimes black, sometimes crimson, sometimes mottled like a fish. Above the boat, were always stars, and always the sky was a peculiarly deep lilac, which lingered with Fern and which he had never seen in the world exterior to the dream. There was never a moon, but behind the gondola, along some kind of waterfront, sparkled the raffish, immemorial, and evocative lights of Fern's hypothetical Venice. Ahead, in contrast, lay a long, dark reef, with occasional and solitary lights only. There were tiny waves lapping round the gondola, and Fern was in some way aware of bigger waves beating slowly on the far side of the reef. He never knew where the two of them were going, but they were going somewhere, because journeys without destination are as work without product: the product may disappoint, but is indispensable and has to be borne. Fern wished that he could enter the dream at an earlier point, so that he might have some idea of how he had met the woman, but always when awareness began, the pair of them were a long way out across the water with the string of gaudy lights far behind. For some reason, Fern had an idea that he had met the woman by eager but slightly furtive arrangement, outside an enormous hotel, very fashionable and luxurious. The gondolier was always vague: Fern had read and been told that, since the advent of powered craft gondoliers were costly and difficult. (None the less, this one seemed, whatever the explanation, to be devoted and amenable.)

The beginning and the end of the dream were lost in the lilac night. The beginning, Fern thought, the beginning of the whole, wonderful experience, might have been only a few hours earlier. The end he hesitated to speculate about. Nor could he ever, upon waking, remember anything that he and the woman had said to one another. A curious, disembodied feeling came back with him, however, and remained with him until the demands of the day ahead dragged him within minutes into full consciousness. He felt that his personal identity had been in partial dissolution, and that in some measure he had been also the night, the gondola, and even the woman with him. This sense of disembodiment he could even sometimes recapture in his daydreams, when circumstances permitted sufficient concentration. Above all, the dream, possibly more tender than passionate, brought a boundless feeling of plain and simple relief. Fern could not conceive of the world's cares ever diminishing to permit so intense a relief in waking life.

By day, more and more often, Fern saw himself in Venice. By night—on *those* nights—he was in Venice.

It had begun happening years ago, and he had still never been to Venice. The impact of Fern's dream upon waking existence seemed confined to the fact that when men and women spoke of their goals in life, as men and women occasionally do, referring to a Sales Managership or a partnership or a nice little cottage in the country or a family of four boys and four girls, Fern at once saw that lilac sky, heard the lapping of those tiny waves, felt a deep, obscure pain, and sensed an even greater isolation than usual.

He supposed that the dream was fragile. If thought about too practically, if analysed too closely, it might well cease to recur. The dream was probably best left in the back of the mind, at the edges of the mind; within that mental area which comes into its own between waking and sleeping—and, less happily, between sleeping and waking.

Possibly, therefore, the dream had the effect of actually deterring Fern from looking out much more practical knowledge

80

about Venice. All he knew about the place was scrappy, uncoordinated stuff ingathered from before the time when the dream had first visited him: for example, he had read a steam-rollered abridgement of Arthur Machen's Casanova translation, and, long before that, a costumed legend of Venice in the Renaissance by Rafael Sabatini, which belonged to his mother. Fern fully realised that, even geographically, the real Venice could hardly be much like his dream. And it scarcely needs adding that the woman in the dream seemed outside the bounds of possibility, let alone the money to pay for her and the gondola. Just as the real Venice could not resemble the dream Venice, so real life could not resemble life in the dream.

For years, then, Fern teetered along the tightrope between content and discontent; between mild self-congratulation and black frustration; between the gritty disillusionments of human intimacy and travel (for Fern the two became more and more inseparable), and the truth and power of his dream. It might be a twilight tightrope, but twilight was not an hour which Fern despised.

So when trouble was added unto Fern in the end, he failed for a long time to be aware of it. Then one spring day, and what was more, in the office, he suddenly realised that his dream had not returned for a long time. He thought that it must have been months since it had last visited him; perhaps more than a year. And, in consequence, he perceived that the dream of the day, always so much paler, of course, but normally, and given even reasonably right circumstances, almost summonable at will, had become totally bloodless and faintly hysterical. Instead of advancing to meet him half-way when he felt the need of it, it was more and more requiring to be conjured, even compelled. It had become much like an aspirin: an anodyne strictly exterior, and so a deceiver. Fern soon came to see that for months he had been standing naked against life's stones and spears without knowing it.

Even though it was the spring, always the most difficult season of the year, he looked himself over, confirmed that he was surviving, and seemed to inaugurate an inner change. This was perhaps the moment, which comes to so many, when Fern simultaneously matured and withered. He became more practical, as people call it; less demanding of life.

He was sincerely astonished when during that same summer he was given significant promotion in his work. In due course, he was equally surprised to find that the additional responsibilities of his new position by no means outweighed the advantage of the greater pay, as he had always supposed they would; the truth being that the tendency is for all to carry the same responsibility, so that soon all will receive the same reward, if reward will any longer be the word. People felt vaguely but approvingly that Fern had taken more of a grip on himself. Fern, cheated of his dream, sometimes even felt something of the kind himself. Two or three years passed, while the land steadily receded beneath Fern's tightrope.

When the dream snapped off (as seemed to Fern to have happened, so abrupt had been his discovery), its place was taken in the back and at the edges of Fern's mind by the sentiment of death. 'God!' he had thought earlier, feeling pierced by a sword through the stomach, as, at that moment, we all do; 'God! I am going to have to die': but in those days, with the rest of us, he had thought of it only occasionally. Now the thought was no longer an infrequent, stabbing shock. It was a soft-footed, never-absent familiar; neither quite an enemy to him nor quite a friend. The thought was steadily making Fern dusty, mangy, less visible; all in the midst of his perceptibly greater successfulness.

And it was almost as if it were these two things in conjunction, the new practicality and the faint, ever-spinning sentiment of death, that brought about Fern's ultimate decision actually to see Venice; as if he had abruptly said out loud 'After all, a man should visit Venice before he dies.' With departure in sight, and upon the advice of an older man, he read the Prince of Lampedusa's *Gatto pardo* in an English paperback. 'It happens to be about Sicily,' observed Fern's friend, 'but it applies to the whole of Italy, and it's concerned with the only thing that matters there, unless you're an actual archaeologist.' Fern gathered that the only thing which mattered was that Italy had undergone a great change.

II

Despite his ruminations and his hopes, Fern had never before travelled beyond France, the Low Countries, and Scandinavia, to all of which regions he considered himself comparatively acclimatised and much attached. By the time he found himself, as will shortly be seen, thinking once more about his dream, he had been in and around Venice for seventeen days, and they had been days of surprise, horror, fantasy, and conflict.

He could find kinship with no one. There was something terrifyingly insane about the total breakdown of the place: the utter discrepancy between the majesty and mystery of the monuments and the tininess of all who dwelt around them or came supposedly to gaze upon them. Fern looked upon these mighty works and despaired. Now he sat on an eighteenth-century stone bollard at the tip of the Punta di Salute, and summed it all up.

Many times Fern had read or been told that the great

trouble with Venice was the swarm of visitors. You could hardly see the real people, he had always been informed. Indeed, the real people were often said to be dying out.

But by now it was the visitors who seemed to him a mere mist: a flutter of small, anxious sparrows, endlessly twittering, whether rich or poor, about 'currency' (Fern could fully understand only those who twittered in English); endlessly pecked and gashed by the local hawks; endlessly keeping up with neighbours at home, who were as unqualified to visit Venice as themselves. All the visitors had at once too little time and too much. As he wandered down a calle or through a palazzo, he perceived that very few indeed of the visitors visited anything beyond the cathedral and the seat of the former rulers; or saw much even of these, if only because of the crowd inside and the shouting of the guides, as mechanical and stereotyped as the swift mutterings of the priests.

The visitors sat about the Piazza San Marco, proclaimed, by so many wise voices, as the world's most beautiful work of man (though infested with pigeons, shot or mutilated elsewhere in Italy), in a constant stew, rich or poor, about the prices: a preoccupation which was thoroughly justified. The women took off their shoes because they had walked a few hundred yards. They stuck out their poor legs, and, to do them justice, endeavoured intermittently but with pathetic unproficiency, to catch at life as it passed, to utter the right cries. If life, their faces enquired, could not be caught in Venice, where could it be caught? For a few, right back at home, Fern felt; for the majority, no longer anywhere. Of the men, most were past even making the attempt. They sat looking foolish, fretful, bored, insufficiently occupied, and, above all, out of place. Nor could Fern but agree it was hard that one could not buy an aniseed or a cup of coffee in a place so beautiful without the beauty being tarnished by the price—a price probably unavoidable from the caterer's point of view, because of forces as uncontrollable by him as by Fern. . . . And, of course, there were other visitors, mainly English, who despised the great and ancient monuments, structures on so different a scale from themselves, and spent their time poking their noses into what they conceived to be the 'real living and working conditions' of the Venetians.

It was not so much the visitors, with their fleeting passage, their phantom foreign money, that startled Fern, but these same Venetians. So far from the place being half empty, as he had been led to expect, it was swarming from edge to edge; and it swarmed with sentimental, self-satisfied philistines, more identical and mass-produced than he would have thought possible, inescapable except inside the faded, ill-kept palazzi, where one had to pay to enter. Those among the Venetians who were not leeching on the visitors seemed to be industrial workers from the vast plants lined up across the water at Mestre; labour force to the war machines of a new invader holding the city under siege of modernity and required merely to await the inevitable self-induced collapse, much as the Turks waited for Byzantium to destroy itself.

The human din in Venice cancelled the quiet which might have been expected from the absence of Motor Moloch. It continued throughout the twenty-four hours, merely becoming after midnight more sinister, shrill, and unpredictable. Every night gangs of youths screamed their way through the alleys. Folding iron shutters crashed like cannon through the early watches. Altercations, sexual or political, continued fortissimi in male voices for fifty minutes at a time. Fern, in his pension attic, would look at his watch and see it was two o'clock, three o'clock, four o'clock. The noise would diminish, he would fall asleep, and then there would be more screaming boys, more clanging shutters. It was a highly traditional uproar perhaps; but Venice seemed to have an unhappy aptitude for combining only the worst of past society with the society of today. What might once have been falcons, had become hawks, and were now carrion crows.

Fern went to hear *Rigoletto* at the Fenice, and to hear a concert with a famous conductor and a famous soloist: both occasions were more than half empty, and such people as were there, were either elderly Americans doing their duty by a dead ideal (often at the behest of their hotel porters) and intermittently slumbering, or dubious Italian youths, palpably with free seats and very concerned to make clear that fact to the fools who had paid. The performances in themselves seemed to Fern good, but that only made it worse. They seemed to be provided for a bygone generation; a bygone species of man, a world that had been laughed out of life and replaced by nothing.

Fern wandered through the shouting, pushing crowds, more and more sick at heart. As, at the concert, the beauty of the performance had only made more poignant the entire absence of a real audience, so, in the city at large, the incomparable splendour and grace of the structures only made more dispiriting the entire absence of these qualities in the beholders. The stripped palaces, indifferently maintained even when a few rooms were 'open to the public', failed even to evoke their past. They would appeal only to those ultimate playboys who positively prefer their roses or their canals to be dead.

Fern found only one place that satisfied when regarded even as a ghost; and as thus offering life of a kind and in a degree. This was a suite of comparatively small bedrooms and dressing rooms and powder rooms high up in one of the remoter palaces; all fragile woodwork in faded green, red, and gold, with elaborate Murano looking-glasses, tender, canopied beds, and flowery dressing tables. These small, fastidious, flirtatious rooms, alone in all Venice, vouchsafed that frisson which is history. Obviously few came near them, other than an occasional perfunctory cleaner, from year's end to year's end. This might spare the delightful rooms for their proper wraiths, but it also pointed to an insoluble dilemma.

In most of the palazzi Fern could spend a morning or afternoon and see only a handful of his kind in the whole building, and all of them rushing through in twenty minutes. Nor could this be sensibly objected to: with the destruction of their owners the palazzi had been destroyed also. It was offensive to pretend that these corpses still lived; odious to seek profit from their corruption.

Between the beauty of Venice and the people there was no link: not even of ignorant awe; perhaps that least of all. Much as the folk had pillaged the Roman villas, so Venice was being pillaged now; and Fern sensed that the very fact of the pillage being often called preservation, implied that total dissolution was in sight. Venice was rotted with the world's new littleness. To many her beauty was actually antagonistic, as imposing upon them a demand to which they were unable to rise. Soon the Lagoon would be 'reclaimed' and the Venetian dream submitted to a new law of values; a puritan law antithetical to the law of pleasure that had prevailed there for so long: the terrain applied to the uses of the post-Garibaldian mass, existing only in its own expansion. Mestre and multiplication would compel unconditional surrender. The state of affairs that Fern now looked upon was more of a pretence, more of a masquerade, than anything even in Venice's past. It was perhaps proper that Venice should end with a divertissement, but Fern felt that the fires of dawn were visible through the holes in the scenery; the decapitation overdue.

Sub Rosa

The Venetian dream?

Perched on his bollard, Fern realised with a start that he had been in Venice seventeen days, and not given a thought to his own dream.

During those seventeen days, he had not spoken to a single person except in the ways of triviality and cross-purposes. He never struck up acquaintance easily, but the conflictual impact of Venice, at once so lovely and so appalling, had transfixed him into even more of a trance than usual. He had wandered with a set stare; lost in a dream of another kind, a seemingly impersonal dream in which the dreamer had been the shadow. Big ships were passing quite frequently along the Canale della Giudecca to his left, into and out from the docks renewed by Mussolini. Unlike so much else, the ships were beautiful and alive at the same time. The scale of things contracted to the problems of one dreamer. Fern felt very lonely.

A manifest Englishman landed with an Italian youth from the traghetto at Fern's rear. He was bald and barrel-shaped. His large moustache and fringe of hair were ginger. He wore a brown tweed jacket buttoned across his stomach, dingy grey trousers, and an untidy shirt with a club tie. One might see him presiding knowledgeably over a weekend rally of motor cars in Surrey or Hampshire.

He walked out to the end of the stone promontory, dragging the Italian boy (in open white shirt and tight, bright trousers) by the hand. The Italian boy was making a girlish show of reluctance. The Englishman, a few feet away from Fern's bollard, pointed with his free hand to some object in the distance; something about which it was inconceivable to him that no one else should care, let alone a person for whom he himself cared so much. All the same, the boy did not care at all. He was no longer going through the motions of petulance, but

stood quite still, looking blank, bored, resistant of new knowledge, and professionally handsome.

'God damn it!' said the Englishman. 'You might show some
interest.'

The boy said nothing. An expression of dreadful disap-
pointment and wild rage transfigured the Englishman's
unremarkable face. He said something in Italian which Fern
took to be at once bitter and obscene. At the same time, he
threw away the boy's hand as if it had turned glutinous in his
grasp. He then strutted off by himself towards the Zattere.

The Italian still stood looking fixedly at the paving stones.
Then he thrust one hand into the back pocket of his trousers
and produced a neat pocketbook: possibly a gift from the
Englishman. After examining the contents with almost comic
care, he returned the pocketbook to its place and strolled off. In
pursuit, Fern imagined; though he did not turn round to see.
Judging from many experiences since his arrival, he thought that
were he to do so, the next approach might be to him. He had
found it a situation that put him at a loss in all its aspects. He
simply could not live up to what was expected of a lone
Englishman in Italy.

By now he felt so alone that he almost wished that he could.
Hitherto in Venice he had been neither happy nor unhappy but
simply amazed; on occasion aghast. Now the recollection of his
dream had coincided with the rapid dissolution of the peram-
bulating philosopher in him. Acclimatisation to Venice had set
in with a rush. The September breeze blew gently up the Canale
di San Marco in Fern's face; sweet and cool, as it sighed for the
slow sickness of Venice's stifling summer. The flashy motorboats
cackled and yelped around him, driving the gondolas to their
death. Fern, thrust back upon his own life, passed his hand over
his legs, his arms, his shoulders. He felt a pain he had almost

forgotten during the years he had walked his tightrope.

What could Venice do for him but sadden him further? Fern decided to go home next day; if the owner of the pension would permit him to depart ahead of his time. He rose, extended and contracted his legs, stumped up and down a bit, gazed for the last time upon one particularly incomparable Venetian prospect, and felt quite equal to weeping, had it not been for the self-consciousness of solitude in a foreign land.

He walked away.

III

That evening, Fern pushed his way along the Molo. He wanted no more unsettled business in his heart.

The owner of the pension had indicated that for a room in modern Venice, as for so much else, there is always a queue. He tried to charge Fern up to the end of the week, but did not try to keep him. Fern had already suspected that in the campaign between the visitors and the Venetians there are few clear-cut victories on either side.

Fern had even an excuse for his promenade. It was to be his last night in Venice, and, as he might have put it in his manly and practical aspect: 'You can't leave Venice without ever having been in a gondola.' Gondolas may not last much longer, nor may people. But gondolas, being no longer very functional, are not much good without someone to love on the journey.

On the Molo, Americans stood about, japing one another uneasily or over-confidently; wondering how to fill in before flying on to Athens or back to Paris the next morning; questing for highballs or local vintages on the rocks. Uncontrolled Italian children and their plump, doting parents effortlessly dominated the prospect. Away to the south, over towards Chioggia, single lights gleamed romantically. The sky was turning to deep lilac and filling with festive, silvery stars.

Fern turned leftwards up an alley, where it was quieter, then wound about through dark courts and passages, like a beetle through a tome. Immediately he was alone, or almost so, among the great dark buildings, his mind returned to those small, elegant bedrooms and boudoirs at the top of the palazzo he had visited. The recollection of them made him shiver with the pathos of something so hopelessly irrecoverable that was still so hopelessly necessary. Thinking about them, feeling still the intensity of their atmosphere, he could smell the perfume of the Venetian decadence; that long century when the lion drowsed, awaiting Napoleon, the city fell irrevocably to pieces, and all the fashionable wore curious, enveloping masks, so that they looked partly like strange animals, partly like comedians, and partly like ravishers and ravished.

There was such a figure standing before him; dark and motionless against the rail along the side of a canal, which edged the small piazzetta Fern had entered; neither quite in the light from the one lamp in the piazzetta, nor quite out of it. Fern slipped into a shadowy doorway and stared, silent and listening to his heartbeat.

On the other side of the canal loomed a formless stone structure, from all the windows of which seemed to shine an even, pale light, something between pink and blue; and Fern, whose hearing was at all times excessively acute, thought he could detect the faint echo of music and revelry seeping through the thick walls and closed casements. Then he realised that the pale light was the reflection of the late evening sky on the glass, and that the sound was no more than the general cry of Venice. He drew himself together.

Almost in silence down the canal came a gondola. Fern, however sharp his ears, could hear only the softest plash, plash, plash. Then the ferro came into view, and the gondola stopped by the figure against the railing. The gondolier seemed to be dressed in black. But Fern's attention was concentrated upon the equally dark passenger; the person for whom the gondola had come.

At first, and in the most curious way, nothing more seemed to happen. The gondola just lay there in the faintly coloured dusk; with the gondolier almost invisible, and the presumed passenger still apparently waiting for someone or something, certainly making no motion to step aboard, indeed making no motion of any kind. Two middle-aged men, both dressed in light colours, crossed the piazzetta from the opposite corner, and proceeded in the direction from which Fern had come. They were talking loudly and simultaneously, in the usual way, and gave no sign of noticing the gondola and the figure by the railing. Of course, there was no reason why they should notice them. All the same, Fern felt that two or three minutes must have passed, while the group remained motionless in dim outline against the vast stone building on the other side of the canal.

At least that length of time passed before it occurred to Fern that it might be for him they waited. He had set forth to destroy his dream (even though he had not expressed it quite like that) and thereby, as so often, might have wound up the mechanism for making it come true; because life goes ever crabwise, as that great Venetian, Baron Corvo, constantly proclaimed. Fern shrank back into his dark doorway. He feared lest the whiteness of his face give him away.

The strange set piece lingered for a few more moments. Then Fern realised that the figure which had been standing by the railing was now somehow in the gondola, and that the gondola was once more coming towards him. It glided down the side of the piazzetta, making only the ghost of a sound: the plash, plash, plash of the paddle might have been the wings of a night bird, or the trembling of Fern's own heart muscles. Five or six gay little children ran across the piazzetta in the line of the two men in grey. They were heavily preoccupied with abusing and hitting one another.

Peeping out, Fern saw that the passenger was still standing in the gondola, somewhat towards the bow. The whole course of events was too fanciful, so that Fern's only resolution was to withdraw. He was waiting until the disappearance of the gondola should make this possible. The gondola could hardly have taken more than a minute to pass, but before it had departed from Fern's view, as he hid in his doorway, the standing passenger made a slight movement: from within the dark hooded cloak a woman looked straight into Fern's pale face, and seemed to smile in welcome. In an instant, the gondola was gone.

A narrow fondamenta continued alongside the canal from out of the piazzetta. Fern ran to the corner and hastened after the vanishing boat, which seemed now to be travelling very much faster. As he sped on, his shoes clattering on the stones, he wondered if insidious Venice had promoted an insanity in him, a mad confusion between dream and dread. He was pretty sure that, if he should run at all, he should by rights run in the opposite direction. But having started to run, having begun such a disturbance of the night, he had to run on. He nearly managed to overtake the boat just as it was passing under the next bridge. One would have been convinced that the gondolier at least must have heard him and seen him, but the gondola slid on unde-flected. Fern realised that beyond the bridge the fondamenta did not continue. He stood on the crest of the arch and watched. He did not care, had no title, to call after. The stones of Venice closed softly over the departing shadow.

And then, only twenty or thirty minutes later, something happened which explained these small but singular events.

Deep in thought, and troubled in soul, Fern strolled back to the wide promenade which faces the Canale di San Marco and is the principal waterfront of the city. The distance from the piazzetta of the odd events was not great, but in Venice, for better or for worse, one can seldom walk straight ahead and unobstructed for more than a few paces, and Fern, his mind in any case on other things, lost himself in a small way at least twice. In the end, he emerged on the Riva. Everything was brightly illuminated, the sky was perfect, and Fern reflected that, after all, Venice did look rather festive, even a trifle exalted, as she should do. But his mind was on his own loneliness, and on his dream: if, at this late hour, he had, after all, made a tiny concession to Venice, he wanted someone with whom to join hands on it, wanted that person badly. Even so, he stood still, uncertain whether to turn leftwards where it would be quieter, or rightwards where adventure was more likely. Now that the chance had gone, he very positively wished that he had spoken to the woman in the piazzetta. It could hardly have been a matter of life or death. Fern trembled slightly. He was indeed an irresolute creature. By now, reason told him, it could hardly matter less which way he turned.

He simply lacked the heart, the energy, the curiosity to wander off towards the darker area to the left; to take a brisk solitary constitutional along the front, safe except perhaps from cutpurses, as his father would certainly do, and think nothing of it, indeed be all the better for it. Fern turned towards Danieli's (a line of American women leaned like beautiful wasting candles over the rail of the roof-garden, high above); towards the Piazza; towards life, in the commercial or Thomas Cook connotation of the word.

Within a minute or two, he thought he saw again the woman whose face he had seen so momentarily in the gondola.

She was standing by herself in much the same way at the edge of the canal, though this time it was the Canale di San Marco, almost the sea. She was still wearing the hooded black cloak, as in a picture by one of the Longhis, but was no longer so muffled in it. It looked to Fern that beneath it she was wearing a spreading, period dress. Despite the crowd, which had by no means ceased to push and bawl in his ears, he was really frightened. He did not put the thought into words within his head, but his thought was that this was an apparition, and that he was having a breakdown. The figure stood there so motionless, so detached from all those vulgar people, so spectrally apparelled; and, of course, so recurrent. As in the piazzetta, he stood and stared; not unlike a ghost himself. Everything faded but that single figure.

Then she walked steadily towards him, twenty or twenty-five yards, and spoke.

'English?'

She really was dressed in an eighteenth-century style, and beneath her hood Fern could see piled-up hair.

'Yes,' said Fern. 'English.'

'The city of Venice would like to invite you for a gondola trip.'

Here indeed was an explanation: at least within limits. She was connected with 'publicity' and was merely dressing the part. It was an explanation all too consistent with what Fern had seen of the place. He laughed a little too brashly, a little too brusquely.

But no doubt she was accustomed professionally to all gradations of oafishness.

'Complimentary, of course,' she said.

That, thought Fern, was less like the Venice he had so far seen.

The woman was an Italian, and did not speak words such as 'complimentary' with ease.

'Are you alone?' asked the woman.

'Yes,' said Fern. 'Quite alone. You must invite someone else. I don't qualify.'

'But you do qualify,' said the woman. 'The city of Venice wants to help lonely visitors.'

It sounded ghastly, but the woman spoke with an aspect of sincerity that at least made it possible to reply with reasonable self-respect.

'Tell me more,' said Fern.

'We go in a gondola,' explained the woman, speaking carefully, in the way of professional guides, as if to a backward child, 'along the Grand Canal and across the lagoon.'

It was not the manner in which Fern had visualised the realisation of his dream, but no doubt it was the dream which controlled the situation, and not he. Just then he could hardly be expected to think it all out.

'We?' enquired Fern. 'How many will there be?'

'Just you and I.' She said it with the dignity that certain Italian women can bring to statements that many other women can utter only with a blush and giggle or excessive explanation.

'And, of course, the gondolier,' she added with a beautiful smile.

'I shall be very pleased,' said Fern. 'Thank you.' He managed to accept with some degree of the same simplicity.

'There you are,' she said, using perhaps not quite the right idiom, and pointing to a gondola. Fern, even though apprehen-sive of capsizing the unknown craft, managed to hand her in as if to the manner born. They settled side by side on the cushions. Her cloak and wide skirt beneath spread themselves over his legs. She had neither spoken to the gondolier nor, as far as Fern had noticed, even looked at him. He cast off in silence, and they were out on the canal, with the other side, the Isola di San Giorgio Maggiore, looking disproportionately nearer almost on the instant. Fern tried to squint backwards in order to examine the gondolier, but it was difficult to see more than his shoes.

Fern squinted backwards a second time. They were not shoes. They were bare black feet.

But now there was nothing to worry about: indeed, when things were rightly conceived, there never had been anything to worry about. 'I think I saw you earlier this evening,' said Fern conversationally. 'On one of the narrower canals.'

'People often see me, but it is only a few that I can call,' she replied in her not quite perfect idiom.

She began to describe the sights they were passing. Fern knew most of them already, and more about them than the very basic information deemed appropriate for Anglo-Saxon visitors. All the same, he liked listening to her deep voice and was often charmed by the way she put things. The effect of her simple tale was quite different when one was alone with her, he felt, than it would have been if she had been speaking to a crowd of tourists. They entered the Canal Grande. Just visible across the water to the left was the bollard on which that same afternoon Fern had summed up his conflictual condemnation; had sentenced Venice to depart from his life the next morning.

Fern continued listening respectfully, but by now he could feel the warmth of her body, and the spreading of her stiff skirt over his legs was delightful. It was difficult to listen indefinitely to such topographical platitudes when there was so much else that might be said, and doubtless a limit on the time.

He must have conveyed something of discontent to her because it seemed to him that her flow of facts (not all of them facts either, he rather thought) began to falter. As they were traversing the few seconds of darkness under the Ponte dell' Accademia, she said 'Perhaps you know Venice as well as I do?' Her tone was not peevish but friendly and solicitous, and Fern decided, at once, that it was a most unusual thing for a professional guide to say in that way, especially an Italian professional guide, always fearful of losing all justification for existence if any real knowledge on the part of the visitor is admitted. Fern's heart warmed to her further.

'I'm sure not,' he said. 'I've been here just over two weeks. Just long enough to know that two months are needed, or perhaps two years.'

'If I go beyond the obvious things, I get into what you call deep waters.'

'I can well imagine,' replied Fern, not necessarily imagining very clearly. 'Let's stick to the obvious things.'

Fern, when he thought about it, could see and hear that the Canal Grande, most beautiful thoroughfare in the world (as so many have said), was its usual horrible self, loaded with roaring power-craft, congested with idiot tourists, lined with darkened palaces that should have been alive with lights; but he found that for once he was hardly thinking about it at all. He even reflected that he was glad the power-craft made his own progress slower; though it was, as ever in modern Venice, hard on the black gondolier.

'It was all so beautiful once.'

Fern could hardly believe his ears. He had so far found it a point of honour among Venetians not to admit that things had ever been better than they were now. He believed, indeed, that most of them were quite sincerely unaware of the fact.

Fern took his companion's hand. It seemed a very soft and unprofessional hand, and she let it lay in his undisturbed.

She spoke again. 'There is a rich American woman further back who has collected all the ugliest things in the world. You could never believe how ugly and how many. She keeps them in a half-built palazzo, which she never finishes. I could not bring myself to spoil so nice an evening by pointing to it.'

'I know about her,' smiled Fern. 'I've been there.'

'Can such a woman be capable of love?'

They were slowly passing the Palazzo Rezzonico.

'Never the time and the place and the one capable of love,' said the English poet.' Fern was rather surprised by himself.

A speed boat full of white-shirted youths whizzed across their bows, almost capsizing them.

'It will be better out on the lagoon,' said Fern's companion, drawing up her feet. 'Less interference and more real danger.'

Fern could not be sure what exactly she meant, but she seemed to find the prospect pleasurable, because her eyes gleamed for a second inside her hood as she spoke.

'Why danger?'

'At night there is always some danger out on the lagoon.' She said it placidly, perhaps with a faint potentiality of contempt. Fern did not risk making the potential actual.

However curious Fern was about her, he asked no personal questions. He probably felt that they could elicit only inappropriate answers, but more important was the fact that he found the relationship easy and delightful, just as it was. Particularly unwise would have been any reference to the many others with whom she must have made this excursion; 'lonely people': Fern knew it was an odious cliché. It had never before occurred to

Fern as possible that what was, after all, companionship on a business basis could so touch his real feelings. Least of all was it the way in which he had dreamed it.

But now she seemed to have shrunk away into the blackness. Fern still held her hand, but he felt that the racket around them, the emptiness of the palaces, spread a paralysing infection of disillusionment. He too began to long for the lagoon.

He decided that sincerity was best.

'I really didn't mean to stop you talking. I was enjoying it.'

'I have nothing to tell which you do not know already.' Her voice was muffled by the black garment into which she had withdrawn.

'I used to have a dream,' said Fern in something of a rush. 'For years I dreamt that I was doing exactly what I am doing now.'

'Venice is everyone's dream,' she replied. 'Venice *is* a dream.'

'With no reality?'

'The reality is what you call a nightmare.'

They were within two or three hundred yards of the Rialto bridge, high and wide with the marble bowers of ancient jewellers and poison-sellers. Here the scene on both sides of the canal was more animated: people sat at waterside café tables; a barge ploughed up and down bearing massed singers of 'O Sole Mio' and 'Torna a Surriento'. Many people were at least attempting to enjoy themselves.

'The city fathers would hardly approve of your calling Venice a nightmare,' said Fern, pressing her hand.

'The city fathers as you call them are all dead. Everyone in Venice is dead. It is a dead city. Do you need to be told?'

Then Fern got it out; put it into words. 'I need you to love me.'

Amid the glare of the café lights, and the booming of the drum, he lifted himself on to his elbow and looked down at her elusive face, cased in its dark hood.

She said nothing.

'Make my dream come true. Love me.'

She still did not speak. Now they were actually abreast of the man with the vast drum. He shouted something light-hearted and scatological as the gondola toiled past in the broken water. Boom, boom, boom, boom.

'Make my life worth while. Redeem me.'

From the depths of her black cloak she looked into his eyes.

'You said you dreamed no longer. Do you know why?'

'I think I began to despair of the dream coming true.'

'The dream stopped when you decided to visit Venice. Never visit Venice.'

She stirred, withdrew her hand, and kissed him softly with cool lips.

'Set me free,' said Fern. 'Give me peace.'

In the long darkness beneath the Ponte di Rialto, he put his hand on the tight bodice over her breast. When they emerged, his arms were so fast around her that nothing could ever part them. The sorters in the Post Office on the Fondamenta dei Tedeschi perceived this and called shrilly. It was rare to see anyone in a gondola except the elderly and exhausted, with death making a busy third at the paddle.

There was no more for Fern to say except endearments. On and up past the dark palaces went the gondola, ploughing and labouring, tilting and rocking, as powered craft, large and small, shot past like squibs and rockets. The very extremity and eccentricity of the consequent, artificial motion added to the isolation as Fern made love on the deep, velvety cushions. Their black gondolier must have had the tirelessness of a demiurge, so regular and relentless was their advance.

'You are the moon and the stars,' said Fern. 'You are the apples on the tree, the gold of the morning, the desire of the evening. You are good, you are lovely, you are life. You are my heart's delight.'

The Palazzo Vendramin-Calergi came into sight.

'Isolde!' said Fern tenderly.

He had found a travelling companion.

'Tristan!' she replied, entering into the spirit of it.

'Perhaps that was when Venice died?' suggested Fern. 'When *Tristan and Isolde* was composed here.'

'If Venice ever really lived!' she retorted.

But the gondolier changed the subject for them by turning off the Grand Canal on to the Rio di San Felice. They were bound for the wide waters of the lagoon.

In the Sacca della Misericordia, the almost rectangular bay on the Venetian north shore, all was silent. There are no footways and in the buildings was only an occasional dim light, suggesting a rogue tenant, even now up to no good.

'Is this where the danger begins?' asked Fern.

She made no reply, but drew even closer. Beneath the dim, lilac amphora of the sky, she was all black or white, like Pierrot. The gondolier, with strokes as strong and regular as if he were swinging a scythe, swept them forward to their consummation.

Here, to the north of Venice, the lagoon was incandescent. It seemed to Fern, who had never seen it like this before, a nearer word than phosphorescent, because the light which gleamed from the water, faintly around the gondola, but in distant patches quite brightly, was multi-coloured, blue, green, white, yellow, pink; and always with lilac in it too, from the infusion of the sky. There were small glittering waves, and vast, indefinite areas of coloured froth or scum, like torn lace.

Already it was a little colder.

They approached an island. Fern saw the white shape of a Renaissance church, and extending from it along the entire shore, a high wall, as of a prison or asylum. Ranged in the small piazzetta before the church door, was a line of figures, indistinct in respect of age, sex, or costume, but each bearing a lighted Venetian lantern, a decorated light on a decorated pole, a device, here, now, and always one of the distinctive splendours of Venice. The figures seemed to agitate the lanterns almost frenziedly, in welcome to Fern and his companion, but from the group Fern could hear no sound, though by now they were less than a hundred yards away, and the whiteness of the church behind them was luminous as a leper's face.

'Isn't it San Michele?' whispered Fern. 'The cemetery island, where at night no one stays?'

'The dead stay. By this time, no one knows how many of them. All who permit themselves to be taken from their beds, dressed in the sheets, and buried.' She pressed her soft cool lips on his to dismiss the thought.

When Fern looked up once more, they were almost past the island. The line of figures with the gorgeous lanterns lay far astern, though the lanterns were still tilting at odd, wild angles. It occurred to Fern that the figures were not expecting the gondola to stop, but had come out in order to speed it on its way, as it might be if it were the barge of Bianca Capello. He saw that the lights were now higher in the air, as the poles were lifted joyously to their full length. But there was still no sound beyond the sounds of night and the sea.

Out here, while the small, scattered navigation lights flickered and bickered, Fern could see that, in places, the water was not merely faintly radiant but transparent right down to the wrack and garbage settled on the bottom from earliest times. In other places, it was opaque, sometimes as if great volumes of powder had been dissolved in it, and sometimes as if it were effervescent and gaseous. Every now and then Fern could see bones, human or animal, arranged in dead seaweed, or a hideous pile of discarded domesticities, or a small, vague underwater mountain, not quite mineral, not quite vegetable, not quite animal, but riddled and crawling with life of a kind, notwithstanding. Big lumpy fish and pale grey or pale pink serpentine creatures, elaborately devious in structure, glided in and out of the clear patches, sometimes seeming almost to gambol round the gondola, occasionally breaking surface for a second, with a gasp and croak. Everywhere was an entanglement of seadrift, rotted but constantly self-renewing. The north shore of Venice, always the dark side of the city, was now a necklace of single lamps round the throat of the night: the different floors of the buildings were levelled off by distance and amalgamated with the public lamp posts of the Fondamenta Nuove. Over on the left of the gondola, the ancient glassworks of Murano, working day and night to produce brittle joys for visitors, thrust quick swords of fire into the encroaching blackness.

Further than Murano it seemed impossible for even this gondolier to continue with so much power; but there was no sign of flagging.

'He is a strong man,' said Fern.

'Here there is a current,' replied his companion. 'Here the struggle ends.'

Fern perceived that they had indeed changed direction. Ahead lay a long dark shore, as in his dream. But he knew quite well what it was. It was the Litorale; the long, narrow, reef strengthened and sustained through the ages to prevent the high seas of the Adriatic from entering the lagoon and eroding Venice; a reef penetrated by three gaps or Porti, through which shipping passed, one of which, Fern knew, must be somewhere ahead, the Porto di Lido, standing at the north of that notorious wilderness of pleasure. He realised now where their journeying would end. Where else could an official tour of Venice terminate but at Lido?

'We leave the Laguna Morta and enter the Laguna Viva,' said his guide.

Fern was not sure that this was exactly accurate; but it did not really matter, because the next thing she said was 'This is the moment of love,' and because that, for some little time, was what it proved to be.

After so many mortal years, Fern's dream was proving more than true. Fern was proving himself right and the rest of the world wrong.

Now the sky was at last completely black, the stars gave little light, and the effulgent lagoon was becoming the sombre sea. Upon all the black gondolier must have looked down, with more time to stare, now that his work was lighter, but about him it did not seem to Fern the moment to concern himself. To Fern, life had become an affair of moments only; a present without past, without future.

How long had passed by the hands of Fern's watch, he never knew, because when, somewhat later, he looked at his watch, he found that it had stopped.

IV

When first he stirred, he realised that a fairly stiff breeze was blowing round the little craft. The gondola was tossing and plunging quite seriously.

Fern drew himself up and looked round. There were biggish

waves, and the scanty lighting at the northern, garrison end of Lido, instead of lying ahead, was distinctly to the rightward, the garish glow of the pleasure grounds completely out of sight: to all intents and purposes, Fern realised with a shock, the lights of the Lido pleasure area were *behind* them. It was somewhere in this watery region that on the Festa de Sensa the Doge at the prow of the *Bucentaur*, loveliest vessel in the world, each year married the sea. It startled him that his own strange marriage had found its culmination just there. This was when Fern looked at his watch.

Then he twisted right round, for the first time since he had entered the boat, and, kneeling on the keel, looked straight back at the gondolier. Then he had his third and greatest shock. There was no one there at all. The gondola was merely being swept out to sea on the current. It came to Fern that, even though there are said to be but small tides or no tides in the Mediterranean, yet the very expression, 'Laguna Morta', referred to areas 'under water only at high tides'; and that now the lagoon was emptying, pouring out through the relatively narrow breach ahead.

When Fern first roused himself after the moment of love, he had left his companion remuffled in her black cloak, soft, small, and silent. Now he turned to where she lay beside him. He could not decide what first to say. It seemed terrible to speak at once of the mere practical circumstances, and worse if the circumstances were of danger, as he could not doubt they were. He was appalled by the surmise that the gondolier, strong as he was, had been somehow swept from the boat, while the two of them had been lost in passion and the spell of the night. Gently, he put out his hand and drew away the black hood. Then, in the solitude of the sea and against the rising wind, Fern screamed out loud. Inside the black hood was a white skull; and an instantaneous throwing back of the entire black cloak, revealed inside it only an entire white skeleton.

V

At the Porto di Lido, the main entrance to the harbour of Venice, two very long stone breakwaters run far out to sea. There was no question for Fern of a storm having arisen, or of any serious change at all in the weather. The change was merely that brought about by leaving a more or less still and dead pool for the living, unpredictable ocean. Even the wind which so alarmed Fern, was little more than the breeze encountered in almost all regions when one embarks seriously upon open waters. Between the Porto di Lido breakwaters, therefore, vessels passed in and out in fair numbers, hardly sentient of the racing ebb which for a single gondola was so formidable.

Fern, in fact, passed no fewer than four incoming ships; and two others overtook him. Some of them came far too close to his uncontrolled cockleshell, but his wild shouting and waving reached never a soul aboard any of them, so black was the night, so black his craft, in accordance with the decree of 1562. Between the long breakwaters, the passing ships were the obvious danger: it was certainly not rough, though it was reasonably unpleasant for a man pitching about in a vessel so small as a gondola. The possibility of the gondola, instead of being run down, sinking beneath him, did not, therefore, seriously occur to him until the real sea was drawing quite near.

He shrank forward to the peak of the vessel, so as to separate himself from his now terrible companion, and squatted before the tall iron ferro, only a few inches ahead. The ferro would surely drag the boat down all the faster when the moment came.

At the very end of the leftward or San Erasmo breakwater, the shorter of the two, Fern could just make out a large inscription daubed by supporters of the previous Italian regime, and never obliterated owing to difficulty of access—and perhaps other things. It was to the effect that a single hour as a lion is to be preferred to a lifetime as an ass.

And now there was only the Lido breakwater and, afterwards, the turbulent, nocturnal Adriatic. The gondola sped on like a black leaf on a millstream.

Fern had proved his resolution to leave Venice before the morrow night.

THE UNSETTLED DUST

DURING THE period of my work as Special Duties Officer for the Historic Structures Fund, I have inevitably come upon many strange and unexpected things in all fields; but only three times that I can recollect have I so far encountered anything that might be thought to involve an element of the paranormal.

Since interest in paranormal phenomena appears to be growing steadily, partly no doubt as an escape from a way of life that seems every day to grow more uniform, regulated, and unambitious, I have thought for some time that it might be worth while to set out at least one of these cases, the most striking, I think, of the three, in an orderly though completely frank narrative; separated from the many other documents connected with my employment. It is not a matter of struggling for half-lost memories, since for the most part the task consists in adapting extracts from my Diary for the period of time concerned. I have now been Special Duties Officer for just over ten years, and I think the moment has come to set about the task.

It so happens that it has been during those ten years that the Fund has set up a Psychic and Occult Research Committee. As is well known, the Council hesitated for many years before taking this step, having in mind the extreme undesirability of the Fund involving itself in controversy of any kind, and also the constant danger of its being charged with crankiness or reaction; but in the end the pressure became so great that a response could no longer be avoided. I think it was inevitable. The link between an interest in old buildings (often ruinous and sometimes ecclesiastical), and an interest in what are popularly called 'ghosts', is obvious. Also the Fund, like most established voluntary societies, is supported mainly by the elderly. A Psychic Committee was and is as inescapable as the Animals Committee that has been with us almost from the start.

The P. and O. Research Committee has undoubtedly done much good work, but I have hesitated to deliver to them a report of my own, despite the fact that I am possibly in a position to deliver three. The Fund is a very conservative organisation (not in the party sense, of course), and my dilemma is that of the civil servant. If a civil servant takes an initiative and things go right with it, he cannot, in the nature of his employment, look for much in the way of reward; whereas if his initiative goes wrong, he can expect all kinds of trouble, everything from a reprimand to blocked promotion, and a permanent black mark against his name in the files. It is accepted, therefore, that the way to advance in the civil service, or in any field where civil service conditions prevail, is never to take an initiative and never to support anyone else's. It is inevitable that this should be so, as long as we base all our administration on the bureaucratic model. The Fund is not as hard a master as the civil service, of course, if only because no one had to answer to Parliament for its actions; but caution is compelled upon it by its sheer size, and by its obligation to offend no one, if this can possibly be avoided, not even its direct critics. A report, even if carefully edited, delivered by me to the P. and O. people on any one of my three cases could, in my judgement, lead to contention, to unpopularity in various quarters for the author, and conceivably even to a libel action in which the Fund would be involved. There are few subjects on which people are more touchy than the 'supernatural', as they call it. It is the measure of the importance they attach to it, even if few of them care to admit it. The delivery of such a report would hardly be construed by the Council as lying within my duties, if trouble resulted. One can but speculate upon the mass of important information which never sees the light of day for similar reasons. I have thought it best to confine the circulation of my narrative to a few selected people, binding them in advance to the strictest confidence; and to place a copy for posterity in my small archives.

The position of Special Duties Officer, of which I have so far been the only incumbent, was created when the growth of the Fund, and the number and variety of its properties, conjured up a miscellany of tasks, often urgent, but all outside the scope of any member of a staff which had been recruited almost solely for duties connected with preservation in the strictest sense—and which, as was freely admitted at the time, was often by then advanced in service. My ploys have varied from setting up a large bequest of sculpture in a once ducal park, to organising a sailing-boat harbour on an island off the Welsh coast; from a frustrating six months devoted to relaying an ornamental paving, to an even longer period spent in promoting an open-air season of fertility plays with singing and dancing. Most of my work has been done in the open air, trying to dodge the British climate, the local authority philistines, and the Fund's own members, so many of whom have ideas of their own and think they have bought the entire staff with their own small subscriptions. Well, not *all* perhaps. Some of the members are very nice people, and eager to offer their hospitality. I have had my moments of cynicism, when I have felt that all that has mattered of the Fund's work has rested on my single shoulders, but that was mere self-pity and I really know quite well that I have done much better as a Fund officer than I could expect to do in any other job. I fell right on my feet when the Fund engaged me.

The events I am about to describe took place at Clamber Court in Bedfordshire, a seat of the Brakespear family, the family of which one branch is said to have provided the only Englishman ever to be Pope; who was also the Pope with the greatest physical strength of all the Popes. The Clamber Court branch was represented by two unmarried sisters. Their father, the last Lord St Adrian, had died years before, and their mother was said to have been a little queer ever since. At least that was the gossip around the Fund office. In the end, the girls had settled Clamber on the Fund, but remained there themselves as Fund tenants. The same office gossip said that the girls had lived very wildly at one time, having no one to control them, and had got through a lot of money. Explanations like that might have been true in former times, but there is seldom much in them nowadays. It is far more likely that the Brakespears were orphans of the social storm like most of the Fund's clients.

My sojourn in the house had nothing to do with the building itself or the surrounding property, as I shall explain in a moment, but it so happens that I had paid Clamber one previous visit. It had not been in the course of my duties, which do not include any kind of regular round. I went there as an ordinary Fund member, without disclosing anything more. In those early days, I often found it instructive to do this and to note how my colleagues were faring in their endless struggle with the different buildings, often near to collapse even when offered to the Fund; and with the odd and recalcitrant people who lived in them. In those days, the Fund's aged President frequently described the staff as an extra-large family, and it was by no means only a cliché: one felt the presence of the Fund wherever one went, watching how one behaved, and difficult to get away from. Of course I felt much more at home in a year or two, much more sure of my ground. When it came to my going to places like Clamber Court, it should also be remembered that I had worked at one time in architecture, though I never qualified; and so had an interest in buildings for their own sake. Naturally that is true of many of the Fund's staff.

Clamber Court proved to be a square, four-storeyed, brick pile, with, on each side, a square, two-storeyed, smaller brick pavilion. The pavilions had slate roofs coming to points, and pilasters on three sides. They were linked to the main block by lengthy one-storey passages, with big, circular-topped windows. This branch of the large Brakespear family had become rich at the time of the Hanoverian succession, and had then entered upon a new period of importance, drifting so far from the other branches that ultimately no heir could be found to the title. A conspicuous feature of the property was two very long drives. The first one led from the front of the house, dead straight down a two-mile avenue of fine old trees to a noble, ornamental gateway on the main road. The other ran, less straight, but at no less length, from a pretty lodge at the east to a related lodge at the west (also on the main road). The drives crossed at about a quarter of a mile from the house-front. At the point of intersection was a baroque fountain, with an heroic male figure about to drive a spear into a fat boar. I found it an uncomfortable group, but redeemed by the all too unusual excellence of its condition and maintenance. In modern Europe, most estate fountains are broken, sordid, and regarded with indifference even by their owners. This one shimmered, and, supreme marvel, actually spouted water, quite probably at the proper force. I had already noted that the drive down which I had driven my Mini (the transverse drive) was clean and weeded; the gate painted; the gateman respectful. I now observed that every pane of glass in the two long corridors from the main house to the pavilions appeared to be in place, and gleaming in the spring sun. The Fund cannot always afford perfections of that kind. Almost certainly, the Brakespears must have had something left in the kitty.

The interior of the house confirmed this. Not only did it contain many objects of real excellence, but it was painted, tended, and polished. There were no sagging wallpaper and no holes in the ceiling. On the other hand, I could not say that the house was dusted. This was curious. One might have written names in the deposit on the gleaming surfaces, as Rembrandt did in Korda's film. Indeed, I did write 'Historic Structures Fund' on the top of a dining-room table, and the words stood out quite clearly in the light of a sunbeam. The odd thing was that one of the house employees, a tall, grey woman in a grey nylon wrapper, just watched me do it from the other side of the room, and said nothing at all, though she was presumably stationed to keep an eye on the behaviour of the public. I particularly noticed that she didn't even smile at what I had done. I was so surprised by the dust in the house and by the indifference shown to it that the next day I sent a memo to the Fund's Regional Representative. I suggested that there might be a cement works in the district, an idea that had occurred to me during the night; and that the Fund should possibly require all the house windows to be kept shut.

That was nine years ago. Two years later, I was required to stay in the house for (as my Diary confirms) eighteen days. The reason was the need to superintend one of the maddest schemes in which the Fund ever entangled itself—indeed, the maddest of all, as I said at the time, when anyone asked me, and as events

114

have since confirmed, to my very sincere regret: the so-called recovery of the River Bovil. For years, there had been complaints in various quarters (none of them, of course, in full possession of the facts) that the Fund was too conservationist and backward-looking; too little prepared to enter the field and do battle. The worst consequence of this uninformed agitation was that the Fund found itself saddled with the project for cleaning out the weeds and mud from this small, local river that no one had ever heard of (not even the people who lived in the district, as I soon found), and patching up the broken-down locks. The view that I (and others) expressed was the obvious one that if there was any real demand for the river, then the proper public authorities could be depended upon to attend to it. The matter was simply nothing to do with the objectives of the Fund. But there was the usual group of hot-heads, with not enough work to do in the world, as one could not but feel; and they had interested one of the local landowners in putting up a little money, though only one landowner and nothing like *enough* money. They said that most of the work could be done by volunteers, and that the public would find the rest of the finance. Needless to say, neither claim proved to be true, and the whole business committed the Fund to endless travail, by no means ended yet, nor likely to be. The Fund is simply not equipped for struggle, argument, and publicity. Nor has my own experience disposed me in favour of what are called 'voluntary workers'. In practice much more is always achieved by regular, salaried staff, keeping themselves out of the limelight. And so it has proved in the case of the Bovil project. But if I say more on that topic, I shall be suspected of disloyalty to the Fund Council, which would be quite wrong. It is more a case of loyalty being often best shown by preventing mistakes being made.

After (in my view) insufficient discussion, the Bovil project was agreed to and the hottest and most thrusting of the hotheads put in charge of the actual works, a man named Hand. I myself didn't think he was altogether an Englishman, but it was obvious that he was very young for the degree of responsibility in which he had involved himself, so I was asked to look after him during the first stages of the work, as I was twenty or more years older and had gained experience from a wide variety of different jobs. Hamish Haythorn, the National Secretary of the Fund, wrote to Miss Agnes Brakespear, reputedly the more businesslike sister, to ask if I could stay at Clamber Court while I was launching the scheme. The Fund expects people whose properties have been accepted, to help in this way, as the need may arise; though sometimes Fund employees find themselves offered only an attic and very simple fare. This had by then happened to me several times, and I was quite prepared for it at Clamber Court. (Nowadays, of course, in my case it hardly ever happens, because I have learned to enter into the different foibles of the Fund's tenants.) I remember that Miss Brakespear took a long time to answer at all, and all the while the Bovil scheme was held up; but we heard from her in the end, and off I went that very afternoon. I arrived in good time for dinner, though that, as I have just said, might not have meant very much.

There was a long tradition that the great gates on the main road were opened only for family weddings, family funerals, and visits of the Sovereign, and the smaller gate further up the same road, had been padlocked by the Fund's Regional Representative, because it had proved impossible to find a tenant for the adjoining lodge, owing to the noise of the traffic; so that I wound my way in my Mini through the lanes leading to the eastern entry, as I had done two years before. It had perhaps been not quite as much as that, because now it was earlier in the spring, with not yet a leaf on any of the big, old trees: in fact, not yet officially spring at all. This time, the man at the gate was wearing a hat, which he touched when opening for me.

My spirits rose as I saw that the long, winding drive was as spruce as before. All the hedges within view had been properly laid and many of the farm gates had been renewed. The hero huntsman when at length I reached him, was enshrined among complex traceries of water, and the doomed quarry adrip with it. The house, I thought, as I completed the finishing stretch up to the wide parterre of rectangular stones before the double stair case, looked immaculate but unfunctional, like a vast Staffordshire model. When I stopped my engine and stepped out, the complete silence contributed to the illusion. I stood for a moment looking down the slow descent to the great gates, and watching big, black rooks wheel like sheets of burnt newspaper between the bare trees, the only life there was.

'Hullo,' said a casual voice from above. 'Come in.'

Standing with her hands on the balustrade at the top of the two flights of steps was a woman; plainly one of my two hostesses, though I had never then knowingly seen either. I wavered, as one does, between ascending the right-hand steps or the left, but she said nothing and just watched me.

'I'm Olive Brakespear,' she said as I arrived, and held out her hand. I should have expected the hand to be cold, as it was one of those fine March days, which often seem the chilliest of the year. But it was not. 'You're my landlord.' In my experience, the tenants always either said something like that or, alternatively, did everything to pretend that the relationship was the other way round.

Miss Brakespear, however, was an unusual figure. She was well above average height for a woman (and six or eight inches

117

above mine), and remarkably slender and well-shaped, though tough and wiry looking. The last impression was reinforced by the fact that she was wearing worn brown riding breeches, worn brown riding boots, and a dark-blue shirt, open at the neck and with the sleeves rolled up. Her face, neck, and forearms were all tanned and brown, even though it was the end of the winter. Her face was striking because she had strong, prominent bones, large, melancholy eyes, and a big, rectangular mouth, but some might have said that her head was too long, her cheeks too sunken. She had straight reddish-brown hair, starting rather far back on the brow. It was glossy and well-kept, like the mane of a racehorse, but worn shoulder-length and curled outwards at the ends, after the fashion which prevailed during the Second World War. It was very difficult to guess how old she was. Her physical style was one which is eminently durable.

'I was watching the rooks,' she said. 'Sometimes when the trees are bare and the light beginning to go, I do it for an hour at a time.' Looking at her in her blue shirt, I am sure I must have shivered. 'Come on in, or you'll get cold,' said Miss Brakespear.

The big, oblong, pillared hall contained only formal furniture, though I was pleased to observe a heap of the Fund's official, blue-covered, guidebook to the house. The wide door had lain open while Miss Brakespear stood outside, so that the cavernous room was cold and echoey, especially as there was no fire. It was also dim, as evening was descending, and Miss Brakespear had not turned on the light.

She went before me up the dark main staircase, taking two steps at a time with her swinging stride. Impeded by my bundle, I followed her much less gracefully.

We turned leftwards along a high, wide passage which traversed the first floor of the house, with big white doors opening into silent rooms on either side. I had not previously been upstairs, because the rooms open to the public were all below. Miss Brakespear's step in her riding boots was sharp and swift, whereas I am sure that I merely shuffled. At the eastern end of the passage, Miss Brakespear opened the door of my room. At least I had not been relegated to one of those designed for occupation by the servants.

It was a big, square, dark red room, with a heavy dado, two windows looking down the long avenue, a modern double bed, and a general look of having been furnished by a good contractor in, perhaps, 1910.

'Turn on the light, if you like,' said Miss Brakespear; 'unless you prefer the dusk, as I do. There's a bathroom opposite. It's all for you, because nowadays there's never anyone else on this side of the house. My sister and I sleep at the other end. Elizabeth Craw, our housekeeper, sleeps upstairs, and the two girls in the village. You'll find the whole house quiet for your work until the open season begins at Easter. Come down for a drink when you're ready. In the music room to the left of the hall.'

She strode away down the dark passage, leaving my bedroom door open. She had a rich and liquid voice, really rather beautiful; and a casual inflection which one felt never varied, no matter what she was saying or to whom. I noticed that she had not mentioned her mother, who was supposed to live somewhere in the house also.

I shut the door and stood in the middle of the room waiting. I might well have been waiting for the twilight to become more like darkness, so that, even by Miss Brakespear's standard, I could turn on the light with a good conscience. Then I realised how absurd this was, and pressed the switch. The result was disappointing. The only light in the room came from three rather faint bulbs attached to a brass frame which the 1910 contractor had suspended from the plaster rose in the centre of the coffered ceiling. They would effectively illumine neither a reader in bed nor a maker-up or report-writer at the heavy dressing table. I felt that from the park my room must look little more luminous than in the year the house was built.

I unpacked a few things and stowed them away. I set my book hopefully by the side of the bed (Christopher Hussey's *The Picturesque*, I see in my Diary that it was). I cased the room for heat of any kind. There was none. I wondered if I should change into something darker, but decided that I could decide while taking my drink, as it was still early enough to change after it, if that seemed appropriate. I crossed the passage to the bathroom.

Here the electric light seemed a little stronger. I looked at my hands as one does after a journey, to see how travel-stained they are. They were filthy. I was astonished, and as I turned the tap of the washbasin (of course, there was nothing like that in my bedroom), I worried about having shaken hands with Miss Brakespear. Then I realised that the grime had spread from darker patches at the tips of my fingers, and that I had probably picked it up in my bedroom. And only then did I remember about the dust I had noticed on my previous visit to the house. The matter had not lately been in my mind. I remembered also about the memo on the subject which I had sent to old Blantyre, the impoverished country gentleman who acted as the Fund's Regional Representative in that area. Thinking about it now, I was almost sure that Blantyre had never even sent an acknowledgement; so that, almost certainly, he had taken no action whatever. I let the water run and run, but it never ran hot.

I remembered the beautiful music room quite well. As I stood in the dark hall outside the thick, closed door, I could just hear the sound of a piano within. Real music in the music room of a British mansion is today so rare that at first I took it for granted that the wireless had been turned on, but when I opened the door and entered, I saw that Miss Brakespear was herself playing. She did not stop when I walked in, but merely indicated with a movement of her head that I should sit down. The gesture seemed quite friendly but she did not smile. I suspected that Miss Brakespear smiled seldom. In here a big log fire burnt: the supply of logs, rough and knotty, being piled high in a vast, circular bin of chased brass, itself gleaming like a yellow furnace. I know nothing about music but it seemed to me that Miss Brakespear played the piano much as she talked; beautifully, but with a casualness that was not so much indifference as the reflection of melancholy and resignation. There was no music before her, and no light by which she could have read it: quite possibly she was improvising, though she seemed to my ignorance to be doing it with depth and fluency. I daresay this was nonsense on my part, but as she played on and on, I found that I was pleased to warm myself right through at rather long last, and to listen to her and watch her dim shape by the light of the fire. I could see that she was still wearing her riding clothes, with the tips of her boots on the pedals.

I am not sure how much time passed in this way; but certainly it was quite dark outside the uncurtained windows, when the door opened and a third person stood there. It was another woman. I could not see her at all clearly, but I could see the shape of her dress and the outline of her hair. She stood for a while with the door still open behind her. Miss Brakespear went on playing, as if in a trance with herself. Then the newcomer shut the door and turned on the light: more effective lighting than in the rooms above. At once, Miss Brakespear broke off.

'Dreaming?' asked the newcomer; none too agreeably, I thought.

Miss Brakespear made no direct reply. 'Agnes,' she said, 'this is Mr Oxenhope, at once our landlord and our guest. Mr Oxenhope, let me introduce my sister, Agnes.'

The other Miss Brakespear (hereafter I must call them Olive and Agnes, though I do not find it comes very naturally) seemed little interested. 'How do you do?' she said in an off-hand way from the door.

'How do you do?' I replied.

Now that the lights were on, I glanced about for dust.

'You really are a fool,' said Agnes to her sister, and walked over to the fire. One could have said she spoke in affectionate derision, as is the way within a family (the alternative commonly being silence); but I might rather have called it habitual derision, accepted derision.

Olive closed the piano and got up. At that exact distance from me, and by fairly strong artificial light, her neck, inside the open collar of her dark shirt, looked more withered and less shapely than I had thought. 'How did the meeting go?' she asked quietly.

'Exactly as expected,' replied Agnes, standing before the blaze, her feet slightly apart, her hands behind her back. She was of an entirely different physical type from her sister: a squarish, fattish woman of about my height, with a thickening face and neck, dark eyes and abundant dark hair in a style more fashionable than her sister's. She wore a plain dress in thick, purple wool, and black, high-heeled shoes. She might have been described by an enemy as too heavily made up, but that is a difficult problem for a woman of her build and period of life: even though I should not have cared to assess her exact age within a range of perhaps twenty years. As will be gathered, she seemed very much more the customary Englishwoman than her sister; and she had something of the frustration and suppressed, long-lost feeling that goes with the customary Englishwoman, however banal the customary manifestation of it. When one spends one's time going round the different properties of the Historic Structures Fund, one grows to learn the essential characteristics of the customary Englishwoman.

Olive had unlocked an ebony and ivory cabinet and was getting us drinks. There was no further reference to the meeting that had been mentioned. Indeed, there was silence. I knew that it was for me to help things along, but I could think of nothing to say. Agnes saved me the trouble.

'What are you feeling for?' she asked.

It seemed appallingly observant of her.

'I thought I'd dropped my handkerchief,' I improvised, perhaps more readily than convincingly.

'Mr Oxenhope's visit has nothing to do with the house,' said Olive conciliatingly. It was excellently intended, no doubt, but the form of words suggested that she too had cottoned on. Because I had, of course, been feeling (as Agnes had put it) for dust. And, what was more, I had been doing it without being aware of it. Needless to say, it was very discourteous of me, socially speaking.

'And his gropings have nothing to do with his handkerchief,' said Agnes drily. 'With *either* of his handkerchiefs the one in his sleeve or the pretty one in his breast pocket. Do you carry three handkerchiefs, Mr Oxenhope?'

'No,' I replied calmly. 'We were sitting here in the dark and I thought the handkerchief had fallen out of my sleeve.'

'I believe you, Mr Oxenhope. Sitting in the dark is the only thing my sister really likes doing.'

'Not altogether,' said Olive. 'As you might guess, I like riding too. Do you ride?'

'I'm afraid I don't.' As a matter of fact, I had thought of

trying to take it up when I began to realise what my work with the Fund would be like, but Hamish Haythorn had strongly advised me against it, saying that it was a mistake to meet the tenants on their own ground. I have since wondered whether Haythorn's view was not affected by the fact that he could neither ride himself nor be conceived as capable of it. But no doubt this was mere malice on my part.

'Just as well for you,' said Agnes. 'Going riding with my sister is an act of desperation.'

'I'm sorry all the same,' I said, looking at Olive as I spoke, and trying to meet her eyes, because, self-sufficient though she seemed, I was growing sorry for her, as well as for myself.

'Sherry?' asked Olive, either avoiding my glance or being unaware of my intention. 'Or gin? Or pascado? Pascado is an aperitif that Agnes brings back from one of her committees. It is Elizabethan and based on quince juice. Or would you prefer a whisky?'

I thought that I had better make some effort to appease Agnes, so volunteered for the pascado.

'Very few people like it,' said Agnes.

The evening continued to be uneasy.

The sisters were, at the least, utterly bored with one another. Such communication as they attempted was confined to jibing and belittlement. As at the start, most of the attacking seemed to come from Agnes; but I thought this might have been partly because Olive gave the impression of having years ago said all she had to say, and of by now preferring to sit in silence. Later that evening it seemed to me, however, that Olive on several occasions struck home on her own; though Agnes each time behaved as if she were too stupid to understand. It might have been the fact of the matter, but I doubted it. The sisters had obviously been committed to this form of exercise for years, and every sentence and every small action had overtones and undertones soaring and sinking beyond the apprehension of any outsider. I, of course, attempted intermittently to make 'general conversation', but Agnes was antagonistic, and Olive, though perfectly polite, was indifferent and world-weary. One might have said that Olive knew it all already, but I doubted whether she really did. I suspected that she fought off knowing, and that it was really Agnes who knew much more. One often finds this with women of Agnes's type. I perhaps make it all sound as if I was having a dreadful time, and it is certainly true that I was not enjoying myself; but by then I was surprisingly accustomed to such family sessions in the houses I visited. I had found them to be common: perhaps as patrician standards merge with plebeian ones, and there is less opportunity for the graces of entertainment as distinct from the utilities. The new conditions take different people in different ways, but are seldom to the advantage of guests.

There seemed to be no question of any clothes being changed for dinner. When we entered the dining-room, the big, polished table was as dusty, beneath the shaded candles, as it had been when I saw it two years earlier in the sunlight; and the tall, grey woman who stood there waiting for us, was recognisably she who had watched my writing on it with my finger. Supposing that Agnes would be observing me, I tried to avoid all reaction.

Dinner was good and the wine excellent, but conversation there was almost none. The presence of the grey servant (still, by the way, in a grey nylon wrapper) seemed to prevent the sisters even from bickering. I felt that very little ever went into the house: not even ordinary news, let alone what are called ideas. It would be very difficult for the Brakespear sisters to have many friends. Apart from foodstuffs and practicalities, I felt that

125

almost nothing and nobody entered but the public visitors in
summer: by definition aloof and alien; merely staring in through
the bars, and, even then, uncomprehending of everything that
mattered, even when (occasionally) qualified to discriminate
between Meissen and Nymphenburg.

And, as I had seen for myself, the visitors to Clamber Court,
though, according to Haythorn, increasing slightly in number,
were powerless to dispel the dust. On the dining-room table it
was so thick it marked my cuffs. I observed circles left in it by
platters or glasses that had been removed, became inconspicuous
within minutes, and by the time the meal was finished, had
almost vanished, though not quite, when one carried the exact
spot in one's mind and looked keenly. But the fare was fine. In
very few of the Fund houses, if any, had I been offered such
wine (let alone anywhere else). I knew this even though I was by
no means a connoisseur; little more than of music.

Back in the music room after dinner, a wry discussion
started about the ethics of coursing. I could contribute little. The
sisters disagreed about reafforestation, and later about the
flowers that were being planted for the benefit of the summer
visitors. My views were hardly sought. I imagine that Agnes
would have despised them and Olive pitied them. Ultimately,
Agnes said she must get on with the accounts, and sat by the fire
making entries in a black book, with a pile of bills and receipts
on the floor at her feet. 'You won't mind being treated as one of
the family,' she had said to me before starting this labour.

Olive suggested that I might care to look for a book in the
library. It was well known to be a very fine library, largely
assembled by a Lord St Adrian of the early eighteenth century
and hardly disturbed since. But I said that I was in the middle of
a book I had brought with me, and that I might fetch it down
from my bedroom in a moment. I made no further move,

because I always have difficulty in reading when in the company of others, let alone the company of strangers. Instead, I turned over the pages of *Country Life* and *Field*, dusty back numbers of which lay about the room, looking almost unopened. They would have to be burnt or stacked before the public season opened.

Olive merely sat in front of the fire, with her long legs stretched towards it. Her eyes remained open, but almost expressionless; too resigned, I thought, even to look sad. I was sure that she would have returned to the piano, if Agnes had not been there. Olive was by no means in her first youth, but there was something appealing about her, and, though it may not be a suitable comment for even this confidential record, I thought, by no means for the first time in such surroundings, what an odd way it was for people of opposite sexes to spend the evening, when, after all, there was nothing ahead that any of us could be sure of but infirmity, illness, and death. It is strange that people train themselves so carefully to go to waste so prematurely.

Every now and then, Agnes wondered sharply whether I would mind adding something up or working something out for her; and surprisingly bristly some of these small tasks of hers proved to be. Olive never even sighed. In the end, the grey servant appeared (the sisters addressed her as 'Elizabeth') and brought in a large bowl of fruit.

'What time would you like breakfast?' Agnes asked me.

'What time would suit you best?' I responded politely.

'Elizabeth will bring it to your room,' said Agnes. 'We go our own ways.'

I suggested a time and the grey servant departed.

'I understand that you'll be fully occupied throughout the day?' asked Agnes.

'Very fully,' I replied, remembering what I was there for and in for.

'Then we shall see you as tonight?'

I expressed assent and gratification.

Over oranges and apples, the evening ended. Agnes ate nothing, but, as well as an apple, I accepted from Olive a whisky, and she herself consumed a noticeably stronger one. Already, on our first evening together, we were running out of generalities.

'More whisky?' asked Olive after a munching silence.

I accepted, though it was unlike me. She refilled my glass to the same strength as her own. The curious dust lay all around me in the warm light.

There was some clattering with bolts and chains, some checking of locks and hasps: all Agnes's work.

'Don't wait,' she said, but we did, and all ascended the stairs together.

The sisters turned to the right, where I turned to the left, but I had not even shut the door of my imperfectly lighted room when I heard familiar steps approaching along the passage, and Olive stood in the doorway.

'I just came to say I'm sorry we're so dull.' She spoke in her usual non-committal voice, but softly; perhaps so that Agnes could have no chance of overhearing.

'I'm sorry I don't ride,' I said; and I still think it was clever of me to think of it so quickly.

'Yes,' said Olive. 'It's a pity. Especially when we can do so little to entertain you. The company of two middle-aged sisters who don't get on, isn't much fun.'

'I don't see you as middle-aged at all,' I replied. Whether I did or not, I saw Olive as most attractive, especially at that moment, when she stood slender and poetical in my doorway, and both of us were about to go to bed.

But she made no response. She did not even smile. There was merely a moment's silence between us.

Then she said 'I apologise for us. Goodnight,' and walked quickly away.

I found myself thinking of her for a long time, and being kept from sleep by the thought.

My breakfast arrived at the exact moment I had named. The grey factotum woke me when she knocked. Having fallen asleep belatedly, I had then slept deeply. It seemed very cold. Without thinking about it, I swept the dust off the polished bedside table with my pyjama sleeve. Then I realised that the grey Elizabeth, who was putting down my tray on the table, might take my action as a slight.

'The dust seems to blow in again as soon as it's swept away,' I said, shivering in my unheated bedroom, and in the tone of one making an excuse for another. 'There must be some dusty new industry near the house.'

'It blows in off the drives,' said Elizabeth. 'The drives are always dusty.'

'If that's what it is, I think something might be done. I'll have a word with Mr Blantyre about it. He might arrange to have the drives tarmacked—anyway, near the house. The dust is really rather terrible.' After all, I was one who had some indirect responsibility in the matter.

'Terrible, as you say,' said Elizabeth non-committally. 'But please don't bother. There's nothing to be done about it.' She spoke with surprising authoritativeness; as if she, and not the Brakespear sisters, were the Fund's tenant—or, rather, perhaps, still the landowner.

To argue would naturally have been a mistake, so, continuing to shiver in the cold of the morning, I asserted that the coffee on the tray would suit me well and that there was no need to change it, as she had suggested, for tea.

I found it hard to accept Elizabeth's explanation of the omnipresent dust. It was true that the drives were dusty, noticeably so, quite like what I imagine country roads to have been in the early days of motoring, when veils and goggles had to be worn, and the back of the neck thickly muffled; but there was so much dust in the house, and with so many of the windows shut, at least during the winter. For example, I had not opened mine on going to bed the previous evening, though this was contrary to a rule of health from which I seldom depart. I drew on, over my pyjamas, the heavy sweater I had brought against the river winds; poured out excellent hot coffee with a shaking hand; chewed scrambled egg and toast; and resolved to pay Blantyre a visit, even though it meant driving more than forty miles each way, to discover why still no action seemed to have been taken on my memo of two years before.

I put on all my thickest garments, descended, looked in the cold state rooms for the sisters, failed to find them, and decided simply to depart as had been agreed the previous night. As I drove away in my Mini, I observed my wake of dust with more conscious care. There certainly was a cloud of it, a rare sight nowadays in Britain, but I still found it hard to believe that all the self-renewing, perennial dust of Clamber Court came from the two drives, long though they were.

I noticed that the water in the bowl of the huntsman fountain was patched with ice, though the jets still spurted frigidly upwards and sideways. The immaculate fountain was a symbol of the whole property: cold but kempt, as one might say. And one could only suppose that the responsibility and burden lay upon Miss Agnes Brakespear. Nobody who lacks direct knowledge of such a task can know how heavy it is in the conditions of today. I, with my increasing professional experience in such concerns, thought I could understand how irritating Olive Brakespear's attitude might be to Agnes Brakespear. Olive still behaved, however diminished her force, as if Clamber Court maintained itself; still took the house, in however reduced a degree, at its own valuation when built. The struggle lay with Agnes; and no doubt the better part of the nation owed her a debt, and others like her. All the same, I knew which of the sisters was the one to whom my greatest debt was owed. I thought sophistically that there would be little purpose in keeping up Clamber Court unless someone had at least an inkling of the style associated with dwelling there. It was a sentiment of a kind often to be discovered in the Fund's own literature. Olive Brakespear also served. Still, it seemed hard that dedicated Agnes should be additionally encumbered with so much dust. The cold wind blew it around me. It penetrated cracks in the bodywork, however shut the windows.

I drove towards the little house which young Hand had leased beside one of the broken-down locks. It had been unoccupied for years, having neither gas nor electricity, neither water, except from the river, nor a road; so that Hand did not have to pay very much for it, which was just as well, as the Fund was all too heavily committed in other directions on his behalf. I had to leave my car by the roadside and cross two freezing fields by a muddy path. Hand and a group of six or eight other youthful enthusiasts were frying bacon on a primus stove while the wind whistled through the broken windows. A row of Hounsfield beds, all unmade after having been slept in, was almost the only approach to furniture. The party seemed to be dressed entirely in garments from those places known as 'surplus stores'. In every way, it was an odd background for a project under the auspices of the Historic Structures Fund, though no doubt it had a certain pioneering value in its own way.

Unfortunately, I arrived considerably later than the hour we had agreed; though this did not surprise me, as I had always said that the time insisted on by Hand was far too early, especially as it was still winter—officially and in every other way. They were sarcastic about my lateness, and they were hardly of the type to appreciate my concern with the worrying problem of the dust; which, therefore, I did not even mention.

I shall say little more of the Bovil Restoration Project: partly because most of the details are already well known (at least among those likely to be interested in them), and have been the subject of an exhaustive Report, edited by Hand himself (though I myself think an independent editor would have been better); and more because it is my sojourn at Clamber Court that I am describing, upon which the Project impinged hardly at all. The two parts of my life at that time were almost in watertight compartments, to use the obvious but apt metaphor.

After that rather terrible first day on the river, freezing cold (and, later, raining as well), muddy everywhere, and spent mainly (as it now seems) in pushing through endless thickets of dead bramble and dogrose, with insufficiently defined authority over Hand's rough-mannered group, I returned to Clamber Court and a first-class dinner with much relief. The second evening with the Brakespear sisters, a replica of the first, presented the oddest contrast to my day with Hand and his noisy friends, as can easily be imagined. A really bitter wind was getting up, as it often does towards the end of March; but though it made the house creak a little, it did nothing to disturb the dust. At one point, I had proposed to mention the dust to Olive Brakespear, if I could find myself long enough alone with her; having at least made a start with the grey Elizabeth. But no possible moment seemed to arise that evening. Perhaps I was too exhausted with the river, to embark gratuitously upon new uncertainties. Probably I thought that I should wait until I knew the Brakespears better: if one ever could.

Only when back in my room for the night did it clearly strike me that Agnes might deliberately have prevented my being alone for more than a minute or two with Olive. Thinking back over the evening that had just passed, I could recall more than one moment when Agnes had obviously been about to fetch something or do something, and when, instead, she had remained. The reasons for leaving us had been tiny, and many people might have been dissuaded by mere inertia; but hardly, I felt, Agnes. She had sat on, though she had been fretful and under-occupied from the start; and was then all the more fretful, no doubt, if she felt tied by the task of never taking her eyes from two people she did not trust. Could it relate to her immediate suspicion of me concerning the dust, when first she saw me? Did she imagine that Olive and I were becoming affectionate? Was it merely that she did not believe in allowing Olive any unnecessary peace? Or had I altogether deceived myself?

One of the moments which I found to be oddest in this generally odd way of life, was the moment when I returned to the house after my day on the river. It was always evening and always I seemed quite alone in the world, or at least in the big park. There was not even a light in the house, because Olive never turned one on unless compelled, and Agnes came back an hour or so later from undertakings which were apparently demanding, apparently unsatisfying, but never quite defined (and one could hardly enquire). Everything was silent. I had to mount the curving stone steps, and disturb the silence by pressing the little bellpush at the centre of the long façade, stretching through the evening from pavilion to pavilion. The illusion of the house being a vast, empty model always returned to me at this time. That there should be any living person in the huge, dark, noiseless interior seemed either absurd or sinister.

But I never had to ring more than once. The grey Elizabeth always appeared after the same short interval and let me in. She never put on a light for me, and I never did it for myself. I suppose we both held back out of regard for Olive. I myself found Olive's day-after-day passivity as unfathomable as Agnes's day-after-day agitation. Three or four of these days passed, and I never saw Olive on a horse, though all the time she wore the same worn riding breeches and boots. It was true that I had always left fairly early and returned fairly late, and that Olive might have tended to these clothes because she looked her best in them, as many women do. All the same, I might by now have been invited to visit the stables, at least in principle. Elsewhere, it had usually happened during my first luncheon; with the time unchallengeably fixed for immediately after it: at houses where the stables still functioned, of course, and had not been let off as a mushroom farm or school of art.

Up the dark staircase I went on my fourth evening (as I see it was from my Diary), while Elizabeth trailed back across the almost empty hall to the kitchen at the rear. I walked leftwards from the landing along the dark passage to my room.

Then something absolutely unexpected took place. I opened the door and I saw the back of a man standing before one of the two windows; the window not fronted by the big dressing table. He was looking out into the dark park: dark, but not yet completely dark, and, of course, less dark than the interior of the house. I could see perhaps a little more than just his black silhouette.

The Unsettled Dust

I know exactly what happened next, because I wrote it down the next morning. First, I stood there for a quite perceptible time, in plain shock and uncertainty. The man must have heard me approaching and opening the door, but he made no move. I then switched on the three poor lights, though far from sure what I ought to do next. The man did then turn and I got a quite good view of him. He was taller than I was, young and handsome, with a prominent nose and a quantity of dark hair which curled effectively on his brow. This description makes his aspect sound like that of an artist, but, in fact, it was more like that of an athlete, and perhaps most of all like that of a soldier. I cite these misleading popular types only to give some idea of the impression he left upon me during the seconds I looked at him. Undoubtedly, he was very well dressed in a conventional, unostentatious way. He might have been a visitor to the house, who, in the dusk, had strayed into the wrong room. What he next did, however, made an idea of that kind unlikely (though not impossible): he simply walked with a quick step towards me as I stood by the door, looked straight into my eyes (of that, naturally, I am certain), and then, without a word, strode past me into the passage outside. I do not think I was more than normally upset (I noted down the next morning that I was not), but, none the less, I could find nothing to say, even though silence made me look a fool. He departed down the passage and vanished in the darkness. I made no note of how far I could hear his steps if at all. I imagine that waiting for him to speak took all my attention. And now, of course, I have no recollection.

From every point of view, I should, I suppose, have followed him, but, instead, I shut the door, and walked over to the window where he had been standing. The floor boards were thick with dust, but there was no mark of his feet. It was when I saw this that real fear began to rise in me: the explanation that

135

the dust had already covered the marks, though not, in its own way, impossible, to judge by what I had noticed elsewhere in the house, was by now hardly less unsettling than the notion of there being something queer about the man himself.

I went through my drawers and I accounted for all objects that I could remember to have left lying about. Nothing seemed missing. I was almost sorry.

I returned to the window and looked out on the darkening park. And then something really frightening took place. It was now dark enough for my ill-lighted room to reflect itself in the glass and appear in even more ill-lighted reproduction outside; but not dark enough for the room to be *all* I could see beyond the window. Through the reflection of the back wall of the room, the wall behind me as I stood, I could still see the shadows of trees and the whiteness of the intersecting drives. The outline of the huntsman fountain was clear enough quite to catch my attention. As I stared at it, I saw, or thought I saw, the figure of the man I had seen, standing on the drive a short distance to my left of it. There really was not enough light to distinguish one person from another, and certainly not at anything like that distance; but I had no doubt that this figure was he. Moreover, I had never before looked from my window and seen anyone on the drive. It was a very isolated and, one would have thought, undermanned establishment. The moment I set eyes on the figure standing on the drive, I was carried away by terror, so that I may not be completely reliable about what happened next. I did not seem to see the figure move, but within moments, instead of being on the drive, it was somehow within the four walls of the room that was reflected immediately before me. The reflection of the room was mis-shaped, as such reflections always are, and the walls were still transparent, but it was impossible to doubt where the figure now stood. Staring out petrified, I made absolutely certain, as a child might; checking in the reflected room the different objects which I knew were in the real room behind me: and among them the figure stood.

I know, as will be seen, that at this point, I cried out. Those who deem this either weak of me or incredible, are invited to find themselves in a like situation. But I did manage to turn myself round, to confront the intruder: perhaps because it was even worse to suppose he was standing out of my sight.

I found I was alone in the room. I stared at its emptiness to make quite sure; and then looked back at the reflected room. That was now empty also, apart from my own vaguely reflected shape in the foreground. I fell into an armchair.

There was a knock at my door; and I thought that the manner of it was familiar.

'Come in.'

It was the grey Elizabeth, who had knocked as when she brought my breakfasts.

I rose to my feet. I don't quite know why.

'Miss Brakespear says she heard something and asked me to find out whether anything was wrong.'

On the instant, I decided to plunge.

'When I came in here a few minutes ago, a man was standing by the window looking out.'

'Yes, sir,' was all the grey Elizabeth said.

'What do you mean by that? Who was he?'

'Other people have supposed they saw him.'

Annoyance rose in me to drive out fear.

'Are you saying that I've been given some kind of haunted room?'

'Certainly not, sir. People have seen him in many different rooms. But you won't see him again. No one has ever seen him more than once.'

'Have *you* seen him?'

'No, sir.'

'Who is he?'

'That's not for me to know.' She looked and spoke as if I had asked her something improper.

'Then I shall ask one of the Miss Brakespears.'

'Please don't do that, sir. The tale upsets the Miss Brakespears very much. Let's just keep it to ourselves, sir. I'll tell Miss Brakespear that you cried out because you'd cut yourself.'

It sounded utterly absurd. It reminded me of the suggestion that the dust in the house came from the drives.

'But I haven't cut myself.'

'Yes you have, sir. Look.'

It was not the least astonishing thing. There was a quite bad gash on the soft part of my left hand, the area between the little finger and the wrist. Half my hand was greasily wet with blood. I did not know how I had done it, and I never learned. Possibly it had happened while I was blundering about the room a few minutes earlier.

'Let me get the first-aid box,' said the grey Elizabeth. It was scarcely practicable to object. She departed and soon came back with it. The Fund's rules require that at least one box of this kind be kept at every property, because the public visitors manage to do the most extraordinary things to themselves.

The grey Elizabeth bound me up quite skilfully; so skilfully that I had to congratulate her.

'Miss Brakespear taught me,' she said. 'She's a qualified, trained nurse.'

It was obvious that the grey Elizabeth admired Agnes. I had noticed it before.

'And now, sir,' said Elizabeth, finishing me off, 'if I promise that you'll see nothing ever again, will you please promise me that you'll not speak about what you've seen to the Miss Brake-spears?'

It seemed to me an excessive request.

'They shouldn't have people to stay in a haunted house without warning them.'

'They seldom do, sir. With respect, sir, you'll recall that you were not invited by either Miss Brakespear.'

It could hardly be denied.

'And therefore, sir, I'm sure you'll agree that it would be better to leave private things unspoken.'

This exceedingly plain hint brought back to me that at other properties of the Fund I had sometimes stumbled upon privacies that I should have preferred to be ignorant of; and that, occasionally, small difficulties had ensued.

'You'll know better than I do, sir, that in houses where things such as we're talking about are supposed to happen, the owners often don't care for them to be spoken of.'

That too I did know; and the Fund's Psychic and Occult Committee has since been much impeded by it.

But I was still doubtful, as was only natural.

'How can I be sure that nothing more will happen?'

'Those to whom anything happens, find that it happens only once. In this house, anyway,' replied the grey Elizabeth, with the most convincing confidence.

'I might be an exception.'

'Even if you are, sir, you wouldn't wish to do a hurt to the two ladies.'

The truth was that by now I knew in my bones that it was not a thing to talk about with the sisters. I could not even imagine how I could possibly begin.

'All right,' I said to the grey Elizabeth. 'All right, if nothing more happens.'

Suddenly Agnes Brakespear appeared in the doorway, wearing one of her dark dresses.

'Whatever is going on? Elizabeth, why didn't you come back to tell me? Mr Oxenhope, are you hurt?'

'I foolishly managed to cut myself, and Elizabeth has been binding me up.'

So that evening passed like the three previous ones.

When the time came for bed, I certainly cannot say that I was easy in my mind, but I thought that I could rely upon the grey Elizabeth. I had gone through an exhausting day in the open with Hand and his intolerable gang, and I soon fell asleep.

When Elizabeth brought me breakfast, I felt that we were parties to a bargain, and took advantage of this to make some new, exploratory remark about the dust.

'Old houses are always full of dust,' she replied, calmly avoiding my eye; 'do what you will. A gentleman in your position must know that better than I do.' And she went without asking me a question, as she usually did, about the contents of the tray being to my liking.

That day was Saturday, but Hand had pointed out that so far from the weekend being a holiday, it was the time when we could expect the number of volunteers to be doubled. This was obvious enough, but I must have looked put out, because Hand had gone on to say that he was sure they could manage on their own if I cared to miss the Saturday and Sunday. But I was certain that something appalling would happen in my absence, so did not avail myself of his suggestion.

For example, friction had already begun with the riverside farmers, as anyone could have foreseen, and Hand was only waiting his chance to deal with them forcefully, so that the name of the Fund would quite probably have been dragged into the national press. For weeks the local paper had contained little but correspondence about the scheme, and 'statements' concerning it from Mayors, Chairmen of Councils, and business-men: the great majority adverse, as could well be understood. The editor had also published two long letters from Hand himself, but both so aggressive and so clever in the wrong way that they could only have done more harm than good. Hand was never able to understand the kind of objections that normal, reasonable people feel to operations that directly forward none of their interests. The majority like to confine any idealism they may have to approved outlets, and not let it enter their immediate environments and working lives. This may or may not be sensible and admirable, but it is a fact of life. Hand could never really grasp it.

At weekends on the river, there were even girl volunteers, or, more probably, girls who followed boys who had volunteered; so the chaos and confusion were worse than ever. Some of the volunteers showed qualities that were, doubtless, in many ways excellent, even though ill-adapted to the world of today, when everything at all serious is settled by agreement, manifestly or behind the scenes. I should not necessarily have been opposed even to the scheme itself, provided that the Fund had not been required to assist with it, let alone I personally. The central mistake was in the commitment of the Fund to anything so harebrained and explosive . . . All the same, I ploughed on through a welter of mud and a continuous bitter wind; doing my best among people with whom I had little in common, if only because I was older and had seen so much more of the world than they had.

And every evening I returned to the vast, dusky, silent house; ascended to the room where I had made that strange encounter; hung my clothes out to dry; scraped the worst of the mud off my boots on to a sheet of local newspaper; lay on my bed for half an hour; and then went down to Olive playing out her endless dreams on the music room piano. She sometimes spoke, but never stopped playing or offered me a drink until Agnes's step could he heard in the stone-paved hall. Where I left my car at the front of the house, Agnes left hers at the back, and entered through the kitchen quarters. When she came into the music room, she was always the first to speak, and seldom much more agreeably than on my first evening. It was plain that Olive's habitual silence irritated her in itself, and one could understand how this might be, when Agnes had to live with Olive year after year. Nor could I doubt that there were other things than silence about Olive that irritated Agnes. Agnes always wore one of the woollen dresses I have mentioned. I saw three or four of them in all. I imagine that, unlike Olive, she, to this extent, changed for dinner. I had not so far set eyes on her at any other time of the day. Agnes usually made some formal enquiry about the progress of the river project, to which I made a formal reply; and nothing more was ever said on the subject, somewhat to my relief. We talked about Agnes's local preoccupations, with Olive sometimes breaking her silence to be sarcastic, though only mildly and gently so. We discussed topics in which no one of us succeeded in interesting any of the others for a moment. Agnes produced a large embroidery frame and decussated away the hours, without, to my mind, producing anything very beautiful. The work was for presentation at Christmas to the meeting place of a women's organisation in a nearby town.

One evening, I remember, we talked about the Fund itself. Agnes was not very cordial.

'Since the property was settled on the Fund,' she asserted, 'we haven't been able to call our souls our own.'

I had heard something of the kind from other tenants, so

cannot say that I was exactly shocked.

'The Fund has the ungrateful task of having to meet the requirements of the State,' I replied. 'It does all it can to soften the wind to the shorn lamb.'

'By this time it could do more to stop the wind blowing,' said Agnes.

This, for me, was too much after the style of Hand. I had been listening to such tiresome talk all day.

'The Fund has to keep out of all controversy,' I said, with such deliberate firmness as I could achieve. 'If it didn't, it wouldn't be permitted to hold property, and your house might have been pulled down by now, or become an institution.'

'*Our* house!' exclaimed Agnes, with bitterness. The tenants all feel the same, and I suppose one cannot blame them.

'Since the Fund took over, we've been living here on sufferance, almost on charity. Our lives have ceased to be our own. We are unpaid curators. The nobility in Poland who have had their estates stolen, are sometimes permitted to go on curating a few rooms in their former houses. Though in England it is dressed up, that is our position, and nothing more. At least it is my position. I can't speak for Olive.'

Olive was lying back in her usual chair before the fire, her legs stretched out, her hands beneath her head.

'Oh, I agree,' she said. 'We are simply waiting. Soon it will all be gone.'

'The Fund,' I pointed out, 'likes to keep members of the family living in the house. The public doesn't take to museums, and very few of them know or care anything about architecture or pictures. What appeals to them is getting into someone else's home, and having the right to poke about inside it. It is only on that basis that the Fund keeps going. It may or may not be sensible and admirable, but it's a fact of life, and we all have to do our best to accept it, even though I quite see it's often not easy.'

'You can't *live* in a house you no longer own,' said Agnes. 'The choices, the decisions, the responsibilities are no longer yours. You are at the best a housekeeper; at the worst, a dummy. Not that people in any way cease to hate and envy you. Often they hate and envy you more, because they've seen more. The difference is that you're tied down, and deprived of any redress against them. I hope you'll agree from what you've seen that I'm an efficient housekeeper, but I spend as little time in the house as possible. I get away as much as I can, even if what goes on outside the walls is often frustrating too.'

'It won't last,' said Olive. 'It can't last. Not even in Poland.'

'My job is to see that it does last,' I said, smiling. 'Or at least it is the job of my colleagues.'

'We should have fought harder for ourselves,' said Agnes. 'We should have put up more of a struggle.' She spoke as one merely placing an opinion on record; not even attempting to convince, not expecting in the least to be agreed with. Here she differed from Hand, who would have begun to make immediate plans, however impracticable.

An irritation of our age is the collapse of the rules concerning names. My hostesses had still not begun to address me as 'Nugent', no doubt owing to my invidious position, of which, like many of the other tenants, they were so excessively conscious. And, in that same position, it was hardly for me to begin calling them 'Agnes' and 'Olive'. On the other hand, the old fashioned formalities would have seemed strained; would have caused the very embarrassments they were designed to eliminate. We never altogether reached a settlement of this problem. No doubt that was symbolical. It was a house in which the rules lingered, because a house in which it was otherwise impossible to live with decency; but the rules, like Olive Brakespear, now lacked force, let alone fire.

Often I thought about Olive; about her square mouth, her slenderness, her lovely hands, her air of poetical mystery: but though there had seemed to be a certain understanding between us from the start, she took care to add not one twig to the tiny flame, one brick to the rudimentary fabric. Probably she no longer had twigs or bricks in her store.

I found that Agnes was beginning to talk much more to me, even though it was most of the time at me. 'This whole thing about us and the Fund is grotesque,' she would exclaim. 'Don't you think so?' Or she would suddenly make a wide and difficult enquiry: 'What do you think of Dutch barns? The Fund must have more experience of them than I have'; or 'Are there any *really good people* working for the Fund? Is there even one?' Once she suddenly asked: 'What is your own candid view of my sister Olive?', and this with Olive sitting there as usual, silent and indifferent unless directly addressed.

At least it all tended to ward off sheer dullness. And the food and drink continued as good as the general maintenance. And the dust remained. By then, snatching thirty minutes here and thirty minutes there, I had prowled half across five parishes looking for a cement works, but had failed to find one.

And next came the incident of the dust-cloud at dawn.

Each night, worn with the burden of communication, we went to bed rather early. I was usually quite ready for it; so hard was my life on the river—in a way, I suppose, so healthy, albeit unenjoyable. I used to fall asleep immediately, and every night thought less of the intruder I had seen; but I found that on most mornings, I awoke early. The truth was that, as in many country houses, far too long was officially set aside for slumber. I would awake, and in the cold, grey light see by the ticking French clock that it was only six, or even earlier; whereas Elizabeth could not be expected to arrive with my breakfast until half past seven. Sometimes I climbed out of bed and walked several times up and down the room in my pyjamas, deliberately chilling myself; having learned from experience elsewhere that the change from cold air to warm sheets and blankets often sends one more quickly back to sleep than anything else.

At that hour, the fountain huntsman looked both more alive and more mythological than when he stood transfixed and obsolete in the rushing world. One felt that he was the single living man in square miles of farm-haunted landscape. As I stumped about looking for new sleep, I glanced out at him, even when I had to scrub the frost off the panes to see him.

On one of these early mornings, I saw something else. The park was greyly lit, lightly frosted, and, as far as I could see and hear, perfectly unpopulated and still: an excellent world, in fact, for a stone man to hunt in. As I looked out, excited, I admit, by the cold, quiet beauty of the scene, I saw a cloud of dust bowling along the white drive from among the trees on the left; a *globe* of dust might better describe it. It was possibly ten or twelve feet high, and quite dense; and though more or less spherical, dragged a dusty train behind it, like a messy comet. The dust looked almost black in the faint dawn light, but I was sure it was really grey—the perfectly ordinary grey one would expect. It rolled along quite steadily towards the fountain; and, in the apparent absence of any wind, I thought at once that it must be raised by some small, heavy vehicle—or, anyway, moving object—at the invisible centre of it. The invisibility was especially odd, however: one would expect to have seen something of such a vehicle, probably the front of it, butting out from the cloud that followed it. I was so carried away that I actually opened one of the heavy sash windows with their thick glazing bars, and listened for the noise of an engine. I could hear nothing at all: not even awakening rooks and hedge-hoppers.

Leaning further out, I saw the dust-cloud roll on until it reached the intersection of drives at the fountain; and then the episode ended in total anticlimax: somehow the cloud was not there at all. It could not really have blown away, because there was no wind; and that quite apart from the question of there having presumably been some solid object to cause it, though still none was visible. I could not even say that I had seen the cloud disperse. It was more as if I had been so concentrated on the movement and character of the cloud that I had been half-asleep to the particulars of its dissolution, to a development so unanticipated. Anyway, there was now neither cloud nor cause for cloud: nothing but the cold, still morning with the stone huntsman perched half-iced at the centre of it.

I shut the window, shivered a little, and returned to bed, though not to sleep. In fact, it was this seeming freak of nature that I have described, which really propelled me to Blantyre. That same morning, I drove round to Hand's lock cottage; told the assembled volunteers that other Fund business, coming unexpectedly, would compel me to be missing from the river that day; made no reference to the rather obvious looks of relief which followed my words; and drove off to Bagglesham, where Blantyre, the Fund's Regional Representative, operated from his crumbling, half-timbered house in a side street. It had once belonged to a family of pargeters, and legend said one could still smell the dung that went into their special kind of plaster; but that was a paranormal manifestation that never came my way.

Basil Blantyre, who has since, unfortunately, died (still in harness), was already nearer to eighty than to seventy, and sensibly reluctant to leave the warm fire in March weather; but he welcomed me in most cordially, though I had not been able to tell him I was coming. There was a telephone at Clamber Court, but I had never heard it in use, and I thought that a call to the Fund's local luminary could, if overheard, cause only trouble. Blantyre most kindly made me a cup of instant coffee with his own hands. He lived quite alone, his wife having never fully recovered (as I had been given by Hamish Haythorn to understand) from the shock of the bankruptcy and the compulsion to leave the house where the Blantyre family had lived, reputedly, since the Middle Ages. To Blantyre, as to me (and others), the Fund had proved a welcome haven from life's storm.

'I want the lowdown on Clamber Court and the Brakespear sisters,' I said, pushing back the scum on the hot coffee.

'There was a lot of sadness in the family. I speak of the time before Clamber was settled on the Fund.'

'There hasn't been much happiness since, judging by what I've seen and heard.'

'What can you expect, Oxenhope? People don't like losing their houses and still living on in them. That at least Millicent and I were spared.'

Quite possibly this was a form of sour grapes, as the Blantyre house had been much too far gone for any decision but demolition.

'There may be more to it than that,' I said. 'What splendid coffee! There seem to me some very odd goings-on at Clamber Court.'

'So I have heard,' said Blantyre, looking away from me and into the blazing logs.

'To start with, the Brakespear girls appear to have no visitors. Apart, of course, from the public.'

'Poor old dears!' exclaimed Blantyre vaguely.

'They're not as old as that. I acknowledge that I myself find one of them quite attractive.'

'So-ho!' exclaimed Blantyre in the same vague way. It was manifest that he had long ago lost all touch with the Clamber situation.

'And then,' I said, 'the house is full of dust.'

'Yes,' said Blantyre. 'I know. That's just it.'

'That's just what?' I asked, putting down my cup. The second half of the contents was thick and muddy.

Blantyre did not answer. After a pause, he answered with another question.

'Did you see anything else? Or hear?'

'See,' I said, lowering my voice, as one does; even though it was still the middle of the morning. 'Not hear.'

'You saw *him*?' asked Blantyre.

'I think so,' I said. 'I suppose so.'

'And *it*? You perhaps saw *it* as well?'

'Yes,' I said. 'This very morning, as a matter of fact.'

'You don't say so.' Blantyre turned back towards me.

'If what I saw was the same it.'

'I have no doubt of it,' replied Blantyre.

'I first saw the dust, the ordinary dust, when I visited the house two years ago. I went incognito, you know.'

'You should never do that,' said Blantyre very seriously.

Coming from a man almost twice my age, I let the reproof go.

'At the time I sent you a memo on the dust,' I said.

'I don't wonder. Many people do.'

'You mean that there's nothing to be done about it?'

'What do *you* think about that?' asked Blantyre. 'Now that you've had more experience.'

'The servant says it blows in off the long drives.'

'So it does,' said Blantyre. 'In a way.' Here he started coughing rather alarmingly, as if the dust had entered his own lungs.

'Can't I get you something?' I asked.

'No, thank you,' Blantyre wheezed. 'Just give me a minute or two. You haven't finished your coffee.'

I swallowed a little more, and then sat looking into the fire, as Blantyre had done. Before long, his breath seemed to be coming more easily.

'Will you please tell me the story?' I asked, still staring at the logs. 'All within the four walls of the Fund, of course.'

'You mean that I shan't last long? That I ought to pass it on before I go?'

'Of course not. I never thought of such a thing. After all, the Brakespear girls must know, and almost certainly, Elizabeth, and doubtless others.'

'Not many others,' said Blantyre. 'Or only village tales. If the Fund has to have official knowledge of the story, it is my successor I should tell, but I don't know who he'll be and I daresay I shall never meet him, so I'm prepared to tell you. You've been *staying* in the house, I believe? Spending nights there?'

'Yes,' I said. 'And still am. All thanks to young Mr Hand.'

'There's a good lad,' said Blantyre unexpectedly. 'It's a bad thing for England that they're not more like him.'

'Who knows if you're not right, but you can be glad you don't have to work with him.'

'Men of the best type are seldom easy to work with. Being easy to work with is a talent that often doesn't call for any other talents in support of it.'

I said nothing: again remembering Blantyre's age. This time the gulf between the generations positively yawned at my feet.

'If you're called upon to live in the house,' said Blantyre, 'you've possibly a claim to the story. Not that I've heard of actual harm coming to anyone. Not physical harm, anyway. Only to Tony Tilbury, who was killed. But he was just run over.'

'I don't follow,' I said.

'The one certain fact is that Tony Tilbury was run down and killed early one morning by a car which Agnes Brakespear was driving.'

'Oh,' I said, feeling a little sick.

'Olive Brakespear saw it happen from one of the windows. That's another fact: at least, I suppose so. There is considerable doubt as to how far her account of the details can be relied on.'

'I shouldn't have thought it was an easy place to have an accident of that kind; especially with nothing else about.'

'You're not the only person to have thought that, and, in fact, if it hadn't been for Olive's evidence, Agnes would have been in serious trouble. A manslaughter charge, at least. Even murder, perhaps.'

'Who *was* Tony Tilbury?'

'He was a fine-looking young chap; descended from one of Queen Elizabeth's admirals. I met him myself several times, when we were still in the old place. But then I think you may have seen for yourself what he looked like. If we understood one another just now. The thing was that Tilbury and Olive Brakespear were in love—very much in love, people say—and Agnes objected.'

'You mean she was in love with him herself?'

'Perhaps,' said Blantyre. 'That's one of the many things that no one knows, or can be expected to know, unless one of the sisters speaks up, and I should say that's pretty unlikely by this time. But there's no doubt at all about the rows it all caused between them. There were plenty of people who were quite prepared, or said they were, to swear to having seen Agnes setting about Olive, and even threatening to kill her.'

'That seems an unlikely thing to threaten before witnesses.'

'It's what people said. Whether they would really have taken an oath on it when it came to the point, is, needless to say, another matter. It never did come to a point of that kind, because Olive swore at the inquest that she had seen the whole thing from one of the windows and that the car had quite obviously got out of control. She swore that she saw Agnes struggling with it and doing all she could be expected to do. Even so, there were a lot of unanswered questions, when it had come to running down a solitary man in all that open space. And, apparently, Olive at one point half-admitted that she couldn't *really* see, because of all the dust which the car had stirred up. Agnes made a big thing of the dust too, in her own evidence. She put a lot of the blame on it. In the end the Coroner gave Agnes the benefit of the doubt, and the jury brought in Accidental Death. I daresay the dust was pretty decisive, however you look at it. It can get into people's eyes, like smoke. That's not the only dusty verdict I've known to come from a coroner's jury. Inquests often take place in rather a rush, oddly enough; though I didn't attend the one on Tony Tilbury.'

'Why did people suppose he was standing about all by himself at that hour of a winter morning?'

'It wasn't winter,' said Blantyre. 'It was pretty near midsummer. Hence all the dust.'

'Oh,' I said. 'I hadn't realised.' Blantyre waited for me to go on. 'At Clamber there seems dust enough at any time. Even so, what was Tilbury doing?'

'Agnes and Olive told a story about Tilbury sleeping badly and often going out in the early hours to walk about the park. I daresay it was more or less true. But what people said was something different. They said that on the morning in question, Tilbury was about to elope with Olive. A far-fetched thing to do, in all the circumstances, but the two of them were said to have been driven to it by Agnes's behaviour. The idea seems to me to leave a lot of unanswered questions also. And I don't know that there's any real evidence for it at all. Tilbury's own car—a racing sort of thing—was found in the background along the drive, but there was nothing very remarkable about that. As a matter of fact, I'm not sure that the whole business, queer though it was, would have started so many tales, or at least kept the tales going for so long, had it not been for one or two other things.'

'What were they?' I asked.

'In the first place, Olive had a complete breakdown after the inquest—or so, once again, it was said: I suppose one can't be certain even of that. All that is certain is that she was missing for more than a year. And when she came back, she had changed. She had intended to be a professional pianist, as you possibly know: perhaps before she met Tony Tilbury. Even that was odd: the effect that Tilbury appears to have had on her. Tilbury was an agreeable young chap, and good-looking, of course, but perfectly ordinary, as far as I could ever see; and it was hard to imagine why a sensitive, artistic creature like Olive should be so gone on *him* in particular. Because I think she really was gone on him. I don't think there's much doubt about that. I'm told they behaved quite absurdly together, even in public. Anyway, when she came back, after more than a year, from wherever it had been, she'd given up music and gone nuts on riding; and not the usual sort of riding either, but endless treks all by herself. She still does it, or did, the last I heard. But you'll probably know more about that than I do.'

'Olive still plays the piano as well,' I said. 'Whenever Agnes lets her.'

'I see,' said Blantyre, looking me in the eye. 'Well, there you are. I mean as to the relationship between them. You've summed it up from your own observation.'

'I'd believe almost anything about their relationship. But what's the next reason why people still talk?'

'Do you have to ask? You're not the only one to have seen things and heard things—or to have *said* they'd seen and heard them. Not that I wish to reflect any doubt upon you personally, you understand.'

'Elizabeth told me that no one sees anything more than once. At least, she said that no one sees what I now take to have been Tilbury's figure more than once?'

'Did she now? That's a new superstition to me. But it follows a familiar line, of course, and when things like that are alive at all, they always grow. Also I haven't been to Clamber for some time, though that's probably something I shouldn't admit. I just don't like the place, and, between ourselves, I don't go out much more than I can help in any case, unless it happens to be set fair weather.'

'Elizabeth implied that people have seen him in many different rooms in the house.'

'I suspect,' replied Blantyre, 'that he's just in the whole place, and that the people who see him, do so when they happen to be in the right mood. What exactly that means, I have no idea, but none of the theories that are supposed to explain these things, goes very far, as you may have noticed. "All telepathy", people say, for example. What does it mean? Whether it's true or not? It gets one almost no distance at all, though it may perhaps just be worth saying. I claim no more for what I have just suggested about Tony Tilbury at Clamber.'

'And, from what you say, we know no more about what those three people were doing all up and about so early in the morning?'

'Not a thing. Nor ever shall, in all probability. Of course the father had died years before. As a matter of fact, he killed himself: so much seems certain, though they succeeded in hushing it up, and I've never come upon so much as a rumour as to his reasons. The older people who knew him, just say he always seemed depressed or always seemed aloof, or some such word. All in all, they're not a lucky family. The mother went queer after her husband's death, though she's still alive.'

'I was told in the Fund offices that she lived in the house.'

'I don't think so,' said Blantyre, smiling a little. 'It's the sort of thing that I should be notified about officially, wouldn't you say? I suspect it's another example of the growth that takes place in the absence of facts. Or have you heard the old thing screaming in the night above your head?'

'Never,' I replied.

'Well, I hope you don't. It's not a pleasant sound, I assure you.'

Blantyre spoke as if it were one with which he was thoroughly familiar.

'And that reminds me,' he went on. 'I shouldn't be frightened of Clamber, if I were you, or let it get me down. I mention this because that might be the tendency of some of the things I've said. I think it is quite unnecessary. It's true that I don't like the place, but it's far more true that no one was ever hurt by a ghost yet, unless he made use of the ghost to hurt himself. Ghosts don't hit you over the head: you do it yourself when you're not thinking about it, and blame them for it because you can't understand yourself. A homely illustration, but all the records confirm the truth of it. It's only in fiction that there's

155

anything *really* dangerous. And of course old houses do tend to dust up when their families no longer own them: though that's not a line of thought we are permitted to pursue. So now let me make you another cup of coffee.'

Despite Blantyre's reassurances, I was thereafter really afraid not only of Clamber Court, but of the two sisters as well. Fortunately, I had only four more nights to stay there; because my nights had become as forbidding as my days.

Driving back from seeing Blantyre, I actually came upon Olive on her horse, visibly now a rather elderly animal, though once, I had no doubt, a nice roan. Despite all the references to riding, I had never seen her mounted before, probably because I had always before driven about the countryside either too early or too late. The horse was stepping out slowly towards me, along a very minor road. The reins were quite loose in Olive's hand. There seemed little chance of the desperate galloping and charging that Agnes had implied was Olive's manner of equitation; though I could well believe that Olive was entirely capable of such things, perhaps even longed for them. Possibly it was what once she did, but did no more. The weather was as bleak as ever, with a bitter wind getting up under a cold sky, but Olive wore a sand-coloured shirt, open at the neck, and so old that, when I came up with her, I saw little tears in it. When first I saw her, she was looking up at the grey, almost white, heavens, while the horse found his own way. There was no reason why she should have taken any notice of my car, nowadays one of so many in the lanes, had I not slowed almost to a stop, because of the horse and because it was Olive. She met my eyes through the windscreen, even smiled a little, and raised her left hand in greeting, like a female centaur. She made no sign of stopping or speaking, but rode slowly on. I watched her for a few seconds through my rear window: noticing the small tears in her shirt, noticing and admiring the straightness of her back, the sleekness of her hair, the perfection of her posture.

Although I had stayed for a simple lunch with Blantyre, because he seemed lonely and pressed it upon me, and because it hardly seemed worth visiting the river for a short spell of failing light, I arrived back at Clamber Court much earlier than usual. Naturally, the grey Elizabeth looked surprised.

'I've been visiting Mr Blantyre, our local Representative,' I said.

It was an explanation that was unlikely to be well received, and Elizabeth's surprise duly changed to hostility and suspicion.

'Aren't we doing what they want?' she asked.

'Of course you are. I was only passing the time of day with him.'

But I cannot deny that, going along the familiar passage to my room, I felt very quavery. I even hesitated before opening my door. The room, however, was merely much lighter than it usually was when I came back to it.

An indefensible thought struck me. For the first time, I was more or less alone in the house and it was still daylight. I resolved to look about, starting with the room next to my own. Or at least to try the door. It was better, I thought, to know than not to know.

Still in my overcoat, I tiptoed back into the passage. There were little cold draughts, and I pushed back my own door as far as it would go. I did not want it to slam and bring upstairs the grey Elizabeth. I did not want it to make a noise of any kind or to shut me out.

The door of the next room was locked. It was only to be expected. I did something even more indefensible. I removed the key from the lock of my own door and tried it in the lock of the next door. My thought was that when the house had been built, an operation of this kind would have had small chance of success, but that the 1910 contractor who had plainly made big changes, might well have installed new locks that were not merely standard but identical. I was right. The lock stuck a bit, but I made the key turn. I did not just peek in, but threw the door wide open, though, at the same time, I did it as quietly as I could.

The room was entirely empty of furniture, but the air was charged with moving dust. It was almost as thick as the snow in those snowstorm glasses one used to buy from pedlars in Oxford Street. Moreover, it seemed to move in the same, slow, dreary swirl as moves the toy snow when the glass is reversed and the fall begins. There was a bitter wind outside the house, as I have said, and draughts inside it, but the room was fusty and stuffy, and I could not see how the March wind could explain everything.

Not that it mattered: at least to begin with; for through the wheeling dust I could see that at the window of the empty room a figure stood with its back to me, looking out towards the park.

It was Agnes, dressed in her day clothes; and I could see another key of the room lying on the window sill. She had locked herself in. I had been wrong in taking it for granted that at that hour she would every day be occupied with her committees and public works.

So much time passed while I just gazed through the terrifying dust at Agnes's motionless back that I really thought I might succeed in shutting the door and getting away. But exactly as I was nerving myself to move, and to move quietly, Agnes turned and looked at me.

'I know it's no longer our house, my sister's and mine,' she said, 'but still you are our guest, Mr Oxenhope, even if only in a sense.'

'I apologise,' I said. 'I had no idea the room was not empty. I have been seeing Mr Blantyre today. Unfortunately, he's not very well, and there are one or two things I thought I should check on his behalf, before the house opens to the public.'

'Of course it is what we expect and have become accustomed to. I am not complaining. What else would you like to see? The key of your room doesn't open every door.'

'I don't think any of the other little items will involve keys,' I replied, 'though thank you very much. As for this room, I only wanted to make sure it was empty, because we should like to store a few things in it.'

'There are other empty rooms in the house,' said Agnes, 'and I am sure we can spare this one.'

'All the same, I do apologise again for not speaking to you first. It was simply that I had a little time on my hands, as today I haven't visited the river.'

'It is no longer our house,' said Agnes, 'so that, strictly speaking, there is no obligation on you to ask us about anything. Has Mr Blantyre any criticisms of my housekeeping?'

'None,' I assured her. 'We agreed that it is one of the best maintained of all the Fund's many properties.'

And, interestingly enough, the dust had by then ceased to swirl, though I am sure it still lay thick on the room floor, the floors of the other rooms, the passages, the stairs, the furniture, and all our hearts.

THE HOUSES OF THE RUSSIANS

> One day, when the Blessed Seraphim was a child, his mother took him to the top of a bell-tower which was under construction. The child slipped and fell a hundred and fifty feet to the cobblestones below. His distracted mother rushed down expecting to see his mangled body, but, to her astonishment and joy, he was standing up apparently unhurt. Later in life he was several times in mortal danger and each time was saved by a miracle.
>
> *Prince Felix Youssoupoff*

'MAY I BUY you a drink, sir?' Dyson asked the old man politely. 'You look as if you had seen a ghost.'

The old man was indeed very pale and he clung a little to the bar, but he smiled slightly at Dyson's way of putting it. 'In my mind's eye perhaps,' he replied. 'Thank you. May I make it a small whisky?'

'I'd say it's a miracle you're here at all, let alone safe and sound,' said the man behind the bar, who had been staring out of the window at the back, and had seen what had happened. 'There've been many of our customers who weren't. Most dangerous road in the west country that is now. There's even been talk of closing the house before some lorry knocks into it and closes it for us.'

' 'Bout time the whole village was redeveloped,' said Rort, 'judging by some of the places we've seen.' It was not a tactful remark, but Rort was far from consciousness of offence. He always assumed that his standards were shared by the vast majority, had they the honesty to admit it.

Before picking up the whisky Dyson had bought him, the old man did something most unexpected: one might say that he crossed himself, but he did it in a queer, backwards way that I had never seen before. He then downed the whisky in one gulp.

Not being myself a Catholic, or an authority on ritual, I might have thought that I was deceived about the old man's gesture, but Gamble, who was always the most observant among us of what was said or done, asked the old man a question: 'Does that exorcise the ghost in your mind's eye?'

'Ghosts,' said the old man quietly but amiably. 'Ghosts in the plural. But I have no wish to exorcise them, even if exorcism were possible or relevant. Whereas it is neither.'

'Tell us about exorcism,' said Dyson.

'Exorcism may only be attempted upon licence from an Archbishop, and in any case is applicable only when a person is believed to be possessed by a devil. That is not my case. There was nothing diabolical about my escape, I assure you.'

'But there was something supernatural?' responded Gamble; often a little too much the cross-examining barrister when all the circumstances were considered.

'Yes,' said the old man in his quiet and simple way. 'At least *I* think so. It was connected with this.' He put his fingers in his bottom left waistcoat pocket and produced a coin or medal. It was dull rather than bright as it lay on his palm in the dim light of the bar; and a fraction smaller, I should say, than a penny.

The barman got in first. 'Can I hold it?'

'Certainly,' said the old man, passing it over. 'But it has no intrinsic value.'

'Just a lucky charm?' asked the barman.

'More a token. The visible symbol of an invisible grace.'

'My mother has one. Given her when she married my father, by my gran, who got it from the gypsies. I suppose these marks are the Romany?'

'No,' said the old man. 'That's Russian.'

'Have another drink,' said Gamble, 'and tell us about Russia.'

'Tell us the whole story,' said Dyson.

We were really all there to learn about fisheries: agricultural and icthyological students, prospective economists and sociologists, one or two sportsmen and aspirants to tweedy journalism, all male and all young; plus the one old man, retired, and representative of a type often to be found on such courses, often, I fear, regarded by the rest as more or less a nuisance. We were all boarded out on the villagers. After our substantial teas, we assembled together every evening at this battered little pub because the competitive establishment was flashy and perceptibly dearer. It was now our third night. Hitherto, the old man had spoken hardly at all. His years had cast a certain constraint upon us, but he had arrived late and left soon, and, in any case, most of us were so brimming with fish-talk and career-talk that his presence inhibited us little. I myself had supposed that he seemed genuinely pleased just to listen to us. The men who ran the course did not fraternise with us in the evenings. In any case, most of them were housed with the flashy competitor.

One reason for the old man's near-accident had been the failing light. As he went on talking, darkness fell and the night wind off the sea began to creep under the door and across the stone flags. Infrequently, a solitary villager appeared, quietly ordered his drink, and settled to listening with us. One suspected that the presence of our group in the bar every evening was tending to keep out the regulars.

'Not Russia,' said the old man. 'I've never been there, though I've known Russians—in a way. It was in Finland that I knew them.' He was looking at his recovered token.

'Surely Russians are rather unpopular in Finland?' asked Gamble.

Rort was about to speak, probably in dialectical contradiction, but the old man began his story, ignoring Gamble.

'Until I retired I was an estate agent and surveyor. At the time I am talking about, I was little more than a clerk, working for a firm called Purvis and Co. I was supposed to be learning the business, and Mr Purvis was very keen that I should, because he knew my father and because he had no sons of his own. He did everything he could for me; then and for a long time afterwards. I owe Mr Purvis a great deal. When he died prematurely in 1933, I inherited most of his business. Of course, I was a qualified surveyor by then, and quite competent to handle everything that arose. Ten years earlier, I knew nothing.

'In 1923, Purvis and Co. had a client with an interest in a Finnish timber plantation. He was in the trade in a big way, with large offices down in the east end of London, but he wanted his son to have experience of all sides of the business, and for this reason proposed to lease a house in Finland for six months and actually move over there with his wife and the boy. I should mention that the wife was Finnish herself. The man's name was Danziger, so his own forebears may all have come from the Baltic also. I never set eyes on the elder Danzigers because Mr Purvis used to go to see them instead of them coming to see him, but I met the son several times. Later it struck me that he had all the wildness and toughness I saw in the Finns, but none of the steadiness and application. He might have done better as a militiaman in the Winter War than as a merchant. But of course the Winter War came much later than the time I am talking about, and as a matter of fact young Danziger was already dead before it happened.

'The nearest town to the particular timber plantation was a place called Unilinna. Mr Purvis had been asked to go there himself, have a look round for a suitable house, and, if he found one, try to get hold of it. He asked me if I would like to come with him, but said that the firm could not afford to pay my fare, especially as I was such a junior. I was so pleased that I talked my father into paying for me, and, as a matter of fact, I think that this was just the main reason why Mr Purvis had chosen me. He knew that my father could manage it, where the fathers of some of the other juniors probably couldn't. Mr Purvis knew better than most that shrewd economies like that often make all the difference to the success of a business. He needed someone amenable in Finland to take notes and hold the tape. Later, it might have been different. I grew very much into Mr Purvis's confidence, and I am sure that he would have picked me anyway.

'I had never before been abroad at all. This may seem strange to you, when nowadays students spend so much of their time travelling on grants, but you may recall that the First World War was not long over, and that travelling had become enormously more difficult than it had been before the war started, when you didn't need so much as a passport. The change put off people like my father from even making the attempt. Besides, I think they were afraid of the alterations they might see.

'Mr Purvis and I took the two-funnelled Swedish-Lloyd

steamer from Tilbury to Gothenburg, with him all alone in a first-class cabin, and me in with a young Swedish missioner, as he called himself, who prayed out loud for most of the two nights, wore dark grey vests and pants, and tried to convert me by catching hold of both my shoulders and speaking to me very slowly and gravely about hell and repentance. He also left a tract in English under my pillow or in my shoes every time I went outside.

'In Gothenburg, Mr Purvis took me to the beautiful amusement park called Liseberg, where I saw a different aspect of Swedish life. Oddly enough, Mr Purvis liked places like that, and would sit for hours staring at the lovely Swedish girls, and commenting to me on their points, as if they had been horse-flesh. We did exactly the same in Stockholm. We went to the Gröna Lunds, where conditions were distinctly less elegant and refined than at Liseberg, but Mr Purvis didn't mind in the least. I daresay he enjoyed it all the more. I was amused to see that he was quite the Englishman abroad. I should have preferred to go off on my own a bit, but Mr Purvis seemed to like my company so much that it would obviously have been a mistake.

'After a night in Gothenburg and a night in Stockholm, we took the Finnish steamer across the Baltic from Nortälje to Turku. We sailed through the Åland Islands, hundreds of them, mostly uninhabited, which had been captured from the Bolsheviks by the Finns marching scores of miles across the winter ice in 1918. From the harbour at Turku we went on by the boat train to Helsinki, where we spent our fifth night. We arrived very late and had to leave early the next morning, so I didn't see much of Helsinki, but it is astonishing what you can do with even an hour or two if you really want to, and I shall never forget the shape of the Great Church against the starry sky, or the view from the Kauppatori across the straits to the fortified island on the other side. There was a kind of mystery about them I have never met anywhere else. It was July or August, and in Finland never quite dark; which added to the beauty of it, even though I had no particular wish for the full midnight sun. I fancy that daylight all the time would be worse than darkness all the time. Staring out across the sea from the Kauppatori at midnight wasn't so much Mr Purvis's kind of thing, but he was very good about it all the same, recognising that I was travelling abroad for the first time, and bought us both a Finnish liqueur called Mesimarja.

'The next morning we set off for Unilinna, where we arrived about lunch-time. We passed four nights there in all. It is not a very large town and as we spent most of our time moving about it to look at various houses, I got to know it quite well. It was a beautiful place. It lay, like so many Finnish towns, on the narrows between two lakes, but it also spread over several lake islands all connected by bridges, so that it was often difficult to recollect whether you were on the mainland, so to speak, or on an island. In Finland the difference between mainland and island is often indistinct. There are supposed to be tens of thousands of lakes, many of them linked together, as at Unilinna, and there are rivers also, even canals. The sea-coast is broken up into islands in just the same way. The main impression I had of Finland was of life being mingled with the water in every direction. In between the lakes are ridges of rocky hills, mostly a hundred feet or two hundred feet high, and all covered with conifers. They look right there, of course, even if they look wrong and ugly round here. I gathered that most of the conifers I saw round Unilinna belonged to the firm in which Mr Danziger had an interest. Every autumn they were floated down to the sea in rafts for export.

'Unilinna was very much a watering place for holidaymakers. It had a gay front with flags, as if it had been the seaside. The steamers lined up along it, going to different spots on the lake, some of them taking all day to reach. The steamers burnt only wood and gave off a wonderful smell, which sometimes you noticed all over the town. At one end of the front was an enormous ruined castle. It was the single proper tourist attraction I had time to see. The outside was magnificent, but I discovered that the outside was about all there was to it, as far as I was concerned. The inside was given up to open air plays, and they weren't much use when you couldn't speak more than a few words of Finnish. Yes, I did manage to pick up just a little, but long plays in verse were something different. Nor, of course, were they right for Mr Purvis either. He liked to sit outside a café passing the girls in review. They were every bit as gorgeous as the Swedish girls, but not so elegantly dressed. Looking at them was as near as ever I got to them.

'There were gypsies too; real opera gypsies with dark faces, flashing eyes, and brightly coloured clothes. They were to be met with all over the town, but especially in the market, which, as far as I could see, spread all the way along the waterfront every morning, but seemed to disappear almost completely after about midday. The gypsies would half come up to you and half speak, but draw quickly away, almost vanish into the air, when they realised you couldn't speak their language, any of their languages. For I was given to understand that many of them were Russian gypsies, fled since 1917 from the Bolsheviks. If this was true, they were in fact the first Russians I ever knowingly met. If, of course, gypsies can properly be described as Russians. Perhaps not. In any case, it is always a problem about Russians: when you go into it, they are so often something else: Ukrainians, Georgians, Asiatics, and, since 1939, Lithuanians, Latvians, and Estonians, in so far as any have survived. You can look out from Helsinki over the sea to Estonia, but since 1939, you haven't been able to go there, not just for the trip.'

'Of course you can go there,' muttered Rort.

Again the old man ignored him.

'All the time we were in Unilinna the sun shone by day and it was very hot, but in the evening a quite thick mist would rise, so that the temperature changed completely. The visitors would say it came off the lakes and look suspicious, but of course that wasn't the point. The mist would have been there even if there had been no lakes. It meant that next day the sun was likely to shine again. It was elementary meteorology.

'Mr Purvis had some kind of an introduction to a man in Unilinna who was the equivalent of an estate agent. We went to see him as soon as we had moved into an hotel and had lunch. His name was Mr Kirkontorni. He was quite a young man and he spoke English remarkably well. I remember wondering both how he had learnt so much and why. I couldn't believe that he met more than two or three Englishmen a year, and the Americans had not then discovered Finland at all. He knew the Danziger family quite well and he had a list of properties for us to visit, with particulars all written out in his own English, including many comments that an English estate agent would have hesitated to put in writing. Not derogatory comments, just plain-spoken and unconventional.

'We spent that afternoon looking at various places, and a large part of the following days, but all that won't interest you. Mr Kirkontorni apologised for being unable to come with us himself. He offered us a junior to go round with us, someone rather like me, but Mr Purvis refused. The lad couldn't really speak English, and Mr Purvis always disliked the company of strangers on a job like this. We found our way about on a plan of the town which Mr Kirkontorni lent to us. Mr Purvis was vain about maps and insisted on keeping this one entirely to himself, though, having other things on his mind, he would have done better to have left the path-finding to me.

'Where the lad might have helped would have been with the people who occupied the various properties. Fortunately, Mr Kirkontorni had been able to warn most of them that an English agent (as he put it) was coming, but there were still some who had heard nothing, or had not grasped the message, and we had several comic experiences. But the usual trouble was that the lady of the house had cleaned the whole place up especially for us, and even laid out a large meal on the table, with a clean, white tablecloth. There was a limit to what the two of us could eat and drink, especially as the lady often just stood or sat and watched us do it, and still more of a limit to the time we had, but of course we couldn't be rude, and we fell more and more behind schedule, especially as not many of our hostesses had much English, though they all seemed to have a few phrases, like 'Sit down' and 'Help yourself' and 'Very good', which they said pointing to cakes and bottles. Another difficulty was that Mr Kirkontorni had spoken of only one visitor, so that everywhere I came as a surprise. The main effect of that was to waste still more time. But we managed to get round most of the places on our list, even though we didn't examine all of them as well as we might have done. At the end of the first afternoon, Mr Purvis said that at least we should not have to spend much on dinner; and that couldn't be denied.'

The old man chuckled a little, and Dyson took the opportunity to buy him another drink.

'Did you discover anything suitable?' asked Jay, who had not said much earlier.

'Oh, yes,' said the old man, 'and the Danzigers moved in and everything went so well that old Danziger wrote a special letter to Mr Purvis at the end of it, and said how pleased he was. Mr Purvis even managed to get a sort of bonus out of him on top of the usual commission and expenses. A trinkgeld he called it. But, do you know, I've quite forgotten which place it was we settled on. There were so many we saw, and so many people, all perfectly charming, in so far as we could understand them. But there was one place I know it wasn't. It was a place that only I saw, and that Mr Purvis didn't.'

The old man paused; probably choosing his words, rejecting the spontaneous ones, having reached a point in his tale where persuasiveness might be required, and, therefore, artifice.

'What was Mr Purvis doing at the time?' asked Gamble, encouragingly and because someone had to say something, but still perceptibly the examining barrister.

'Mr Purvis was asleep,' said the old man, in a new tone of voice, 'or at least lying down in his room.

'It was the day after we arrived. We'd spent hours and hours walking round the town in the sun, and, as I say, we'd had a lot of mixed stuff to eat and drink. Mr Purvis said he wanted to put his feet up. I wouldn't have minded doing the same myself, but it was the first chance I'd had on the whole trip to get away on my own for a little, and I couldn't let it go. We agreed a time for me to come back and see how Mr Purvis was doing, and I wandered off to the north side of the town, where till then I had hardly been, the southern end of the northern-most of the two lakes, if you follow me. The reason why we hadn't been there much was that Mr Kirkontorni had said it was out of the sun and rather a run-down area. Of course a southern aspect does matter considerably in Finland, especially to a rich man with local connections, like Mr Danziger.

'The evening mist that I have spoken of was rising quite thickly, but in patches. In places it was really dense, but other places were still open, with the mist all round at a little distance, like clearings in a forest. Also, a breeze was getting up, so that the mist was beginning to swirl a bit. It was quite a queer effect altogether; with the sun still shining through at the same time. I felt hot and cold all at once.

'I strolled down to the waterfront of the northern lake, where I had never been before, though I had seen the water at the ends of streets sloping that way. Most of the town was built on the two sides of one of the ridges I've mentioned. To go from one lake to the other, you had to go up and then down. This made the two sides of the town look different. The ridge also sloped downwards to the west, until it faded away altogether, and you came to the passage from one lake to the other. The steamers on the northern lake all went through this passage, or straits as you might say, and moored at the piers on the south side of the town. I remember all this quite clearly. Unilinna was a town of the size you could take in as a whole, at least if you were being trained in surveying. And you can get a very clear impression of a place if you are walking about it steadily for four days.

'The northern waterfront really was rather a mangy place. There was a lakeside roadway of a kind, but it was narrow and very rough. The houses were either cut up into tenements or just standing empty. There were warehouses too, but not much look of trade. There was an odd feel about the area. I thought it was mainly that there were no kids playing in the streets, as you would have expected there to be. In fact, there was hardly anyone about at all. The whole place made me remember how little I knew about foreign countries. Also I had learnt from various things that had been said, about the terrible civil war in Finland, which had ended only a few years earlier.

'But much the most interesting thing was the view out across the lake. About a third of a mile from the waterfront was a wooded island, and there was a wooden footbridge right across to it, starting from about a couple of hundred yards to the left of where I stood. I suppose the island was about half a mile long, or a little more. When I say it was a wooded island, I mean that, as far as I could see through the patches of mist, it appeared to be all thick trees from end to end. Not conifers either, but big, spreading trees that must have been planted for some particular reason. I thought at first that it might be a nature reservation, but I then noticed signs of more and more houses among the trees, chimney-stacks and ridges of roofs sticking out, and sometimes bits of the façades, where the sun caught them. There were also the remains of jetties for boats, so little left of them that you didn't notice them at first. And, as far as I could see, certainly no boats, although in most parts of Finland you see boats all along any shore where there are houses. I set off to investigate further.

'There was no one on the long footbridge, and it was in very bad repair. It was about six feet wide, with thick transverse planks and a stout wooden double railing on either side, but, even so, it struck me as quite dangerous to cross, because many of the planks were missing and many others loose or broken, and because long sections of handrail would obviously collapse under any kind of pressure. It didn't matter much about the handrail, which would have come in only if there had been a crowd, and that seemed unlikely; but the planks really quite scared me, especially as there were patches of thick mist on the bridge, and a nasty current running underneath it towards the narrows over on my left where the ships went through. There was no question, by the way, of a ship going through where I was, because the bridge was only three or four feet above the water. When there had been boats at the little jetties, they must have been prevented by it from sailing right round the island. It struck me that the footbridge might often be under water, and that this could hardly have been good for it. The whole arrangement seemed rather inefficient, but a higher bridge would of course have cost much more and no doubt the island wasn't thought worth it. All the same, I wondered how the people got on without bridge or boats, even though they were so close to the town.

'Having dropped the nature reserve idea, I thought that the island might be a private housing estate and that at the far end of the bridge might be a locked gate or at least a notice that I shouldn't understand. But there was nothing of that kind. From the end of the bridge three rough tracks led away, one round the southern shore of the island which I had been looking at, one round the northern shore, and one up on to the usual low but steep ridge which was the island's backbone. There was no one about and no sound at all, probably because sound was muffled by the mist which seemed to be thicker now that I had reached the island, than it looked from the far shore, and very much colder. The mist had either descended on the district more heavily than on the previous evening, or else there was something about the island which made it cling there particularly. I thought it might be something to do with the thick trees. I looked back over the bridge and found that I could not see the other side, not even in patches. The mist was becoming a real fog. I even wondered whether I ought not to go back, but there seemed no sensible reason. I had left Mr Purvis only twenty or thirty minutes before, and though I did not much like crossing the bridge, I did not seriously doubt that I could do it, and by now there seemed no reason why going back at once should be any more pleasant than going back after I had walked round the island. There was no question of night coming on as soon as that.

'I picked the path which went up on to the ridge. I suppose I thought that the mist would lie heavier round the shores of the lake, and that I would get a better general idea of the island's layout from the higher ground. Not that it was all that higher, only the usual hundred feet or less. Nor did it make any difference to the big heavy trees. They grew so thickly along the ridge that when I got there, I found I could see very little. And they were all absolutely still in the cold mist.

'I scrambled up the slope—it was only a mud-track, and it must have been terrible after rain—and when I reached the top, came almost at once upon a house, looking in the mist much bulkier than it probably was. It was built of wood, but was much more elaborate and fanciful than any of the houses I had so far seen in Finland. It was of a fanciful shape and plan, to begin with. It had been painted in several different colours. It had huge, carved barge-boards along the edges of the roof, and carvings in many other places too. Some of them struck me as rather quaint. But I didn't have time to look at them properly. The whole house was badly out of repair. I doubted if it had been painted since before the war—the *first* war, you know, and the enormous bargeboards were crumbling away, quite dangerously, I thought. The garden was completely gone to ruin.

'Normally I should have supposed the house to be empty, but that was not so. There was a fence round the garden, a heavy wooden paling, something with the weight and solidity of the wooden railing across the footbridge. Even so, there were gaps in it, and there was also a gate, which was lower than the rest of the fence. I had been creeping along the fence looking through the gaps, but it was across the top of the gate that I saw a woman sitting among the long grass and in all that mist. She was not a young girl, but she had very fair hair, tied up at the back of the head. She wore a loose brown dress and she was doing something with a machine of some kind, not spinning but possibly weaving, or possibly something quite different. I don't know what it was, but it seemed to me a very odd time and place to do it. I had only one quick look, because the woman caught my eye on the instant, as if she had been waiting for me to come into view, and stared back at me. I could see quite plainly that her eyes were a very bright blue, and that was just about all I did see with any certainty. I could have sworn that she was frightened, and I suppose it was fairly reasonable that she should be, especially if she had heard me shuffling along her fence. I wanted, above all, not to get into a scene, because of course of the language. So I got away as quickly as I could without actually running. I hesitated even to glance back, because I thought the woman might have come to the gate or be looking over it, but in the end I did, and there was nothing; only the high black paling, and the falling-down house looking huger and vaguer than ever in the mist.

'Then I came upon another house. Like the first one, it was on the south side of the ridge walk, but the trees were so thick that it could have made little difference in either case from a prospect point of view. This second house was quite different from the first, something unusual in Finland to start with, because in Finland the houses are much more alike than they are here. It is the same in many foreign countries, as you will all know. This house was a neat, classical affair, built in white stone, with a columned portico like a Greek temple. It was all on one storey, but it occupied quite an area, and was no mere bungalow in the usual sense. The only trouble was that it was in the same state of ruin. The garden couldn't have been attended to in any way for years; some of the stones in the house walls had big splits in them, which suggested something wrong with the builder in the first place; and at least one of the portico columns had fallen right over, as if it really had been an old temple in Greece. As something to come upon in all that mist and quietness, it really was depressing.

'But there appeared to be some who did not necessarily think so. Because in several of the windows there were faint lights, so that once again the house was occupied. They had probably lighted up against the mist rather than against the night, so had not bothered to draw the curtains, as people don't at such times. If, of course, it was ever necessary to draw the curtains in that place. If, for that matter, there were curtains to be drawn, with, obviously, so little money around. I could easily have investigated further, as this time there was no wooden paling, but a low iron fence, now unpainted, rusty, and broken down, but very special and ornamental when it was first put up. But I didn't investigate further. I walked on. I daresay I should again have thought about walking back if it had not been that I feared to pass the woman who was working the machine in her garden. And it was not only because of the language difficulty that I feared it. The whole business was really very queer. So I continued ahead.

'Again there was quite a gap between the houses, which seemed to have been dotted about the tracks in the woodland wherever the fancy struck, but before long I came to the third one. This was a tall brick affair with Italian details; rather the kind of thing you can still see in places like Sydenham and Stoke Newington—"gentlemen's villas", they used to be called, rather handsome and often very well built. I suppose the style began in the Italian countryside, but nowadays we connect it with cities, and it seemed very out of place among all those forest trees. They were actually growing in through the upper windows. This house, I thought, really was empty. I could see no sign of life about it at all and it was even farther gone than the others. As a matter of fact, I didn't care for it; looming up half-ruined in the mist, with the branches of the trees breaking through the upper windows. It made you think of squelchy, white creatures scudding about the rotten floors, and brightly coloured funguses sprouting on the walls. But I was held as well as frightened, and hung about for a bit wondering whether I dared take a closer look. The front door was at the top of a flight of steps, just like Sydenham, and I could see the remains of a paved path leading to the broken-down gate where I stood. As I shifted around outside, I realised that once again the house was not empty at all. It couldn't be, because someone had come out of the front door. There was what I might call a big, tall, black figure standing on the top step.

'I hadn't heard the door open, or heard anything else for that matter, but the mist seemed to kill all sound, as I've said, and I was growing quite accustomed to not hearing much. Nor had I seen the figure appear. I had been gazing around at the whole scene, noting this and that, and there was quite a lot to gaze at, and to think about. I'd seen the last of the sun when I crossed the bridge, but, all the same, there was still plenty of light in a misty sort of way, and I could see the black figure at the top of the steps really quite clearly. Properly, the dusk had hardly even begun. I call it a black figure: not only was it black from top to bottom, but it seemed to me both taller and wider than an average figure—considerably taller and considerably wider. All the same, it *was* a human figure (lest you be thinking something else): I could see the big white face.

'But that was just about all I did see. This time I took to my heels and I'm not ashamed to say so. Each one of you would have done the same, believe me.'

177

The old man paused. He must have been right about us too, because, rather curiously, I thought, no one said a word. Even the man behind the bar leaned across it like a trick waxwork, his chin propped on his forearm. The old man continued.

'I ran on, past more houses, I don't know how many, which I didn't stop to examine, but which certainly gave no obvious sign of life. Running and walking fast, I reached the other end of the ridge and slithered down the lumpy mud slope to the lake shore at the far side of the island. At this point it struck me to wonder why the tracks through the woodland were not completely overgrown, with so few people about. This gave me a new fright. When you get into that frame of mind, almost everything in the world can seem frightening.'

Dyson interrupted. 'I expect the Finlanders went across at weekends and ploughed the place up.'

'No,' said the old man. 'The Finns didn't. I don't to this day know what the answer was.'

'Please go on, sir,' said Dyson.

'It was much the same at that end of the island as it had been at the footbridge end. There were simply the other ends of the same three tracks: the one along the ridge, and the one along each shore. By now I had more or less confirmed that there was no other way off the island than the footbridge. It was true that I hadn't seen the north shore, but I knew that it faced the open lake, whole square miles of water. There couldn't be a bridge there. I had to go back.

'I chose the southern shore. I couldn't return along the ridge, and I had lost the taste for exploration. I already had some idea what the south side of the island was like, because I had seen quite a lot of it through the mist from the mainland, and with the sun shining on it too. Mostly trees and broken-down landing places, as you'll recall. I admit that about the north shore a thought in my mind was that no one lived close opposite it on the mainland, so that no one could see at all easily what went on there. I daresay it was an absurd thing to think. I'm sure it was. But of course the island had got on my nerves.

'As I walked along the lakeside, stepping out pretty fast, I saw that the same big houses continued here too, all set back among the trees, so that they hardly made the most of their position, which was really a very fine one, especially if the sun should come out. The houses here were all locked up, but did not seem to be quite so neglected as the houses on the ridge. Pretty clearly, they had been designed as summer residences, and yet it was summer now, more or less, and there was no one about. Of course, it was hard to be certain, in the light of my experiences, that there was no one inside any of the houses, but I had no intention of trying to make sure. At the best of times, to pass by a lot of empty houses is a sad proceeding. It makes you think all the wrong thoughts. Especially when you're young, and not used to such thoughts. And most of all when the empty houses are set in a beautiful spot. That's the worst thing of all.

'Curiously enough, however, it was just about then, when I was feeling lower and lower, that the idea came to me: why might not one of these houses suit Mr Danziger? By which I mean I thought that buying the whole island for development might appeal to Mr Danziger, with a nice house for himself thrown in, a house with a lot of character, quiet, yet near the town and the timber plantation, if only the bridge was repaired, which could easily have been done, or so it seemed to me. I knew that Mr Danziger had gone in for several developments of this kind in different countries. I was quite cheered up by my own cleverness, quite carried away by the idea. I thought there might be something in it for me personally. It was my own discovery, and nothing to do with Mr Kirkontorni or Mr Purvis.

The whole run-down island seemed to offer the possibility of an outstanding speculation . . . No doubt I thought also that it would enable me to get my own back on the island. I daresay that was my real motive all the time. I am sorry that it should have been so.'

'At that stage it was rather understandable,' observed Dyson.

'At that stage perhaps it was,' acknowledged the old man. 'And yet no one and nothing on the island had done me any harm. I was no more than a raw lad trespassing; not perhaps in the full legal sense, but assuredly pushing in where I wasn't wanted. Trespassing, and not equipped to understand. What right of complaint had I?'

'What happened next?' asked Jay.

'I was striding along, all but forgetting the things that had upset me, and working out a lot of nonsense about putting up small, modern houses on the island and what I could hope to get out of it for myself, when I came upon a house where there was a crowd of folk at home, and, what was more, and to judge by the noise, giving some kind of a party. There were lights on inside the house, though they looked yellow and rather dim, as room lights always do when seen from the daylight outside, but I stared in, and could see quite a mass of people bobbing about and enjoying themselves. I suppose they were twenty or thirty yards away, down the length of the garden in front of the house. The garden was completely gone to seed like all the others. The party looked pretty peculiar too. You know how it is when you see a lot of strangers enjoying themselves inside a room at a little distance, when they don't know you're looking in at them. And, of course, this lot were foreigners as well. They were wearing all kinds of gay clothes in very bright colours, and really seemed to be beating it up. They were too far away for me to hear very much, especially as all the windows were tight shut, as they usually are abroad. I rather imagine that they were double windows too; to keep out the winter snow and cold. That was quite the usual thing in Finland. One thing I wondered about was the light; whether gas or electricity could be laid on to the island. It might be useful to know. I craned about but couldn't see. I was too far away, and the lights themselves seemed to be out of my line of vision.

'That jolly party took a further small weight off my mind, as you may be able to imagine, but what was my surprise to find that the next house was giving a party too, and the next after that. I looked in at both of them but couldn't see any more than in the first house, in fact rather less, because these two houses were set even further back among the trees, and further away from the path I was on. Every time there seemed to be a good-sized crowd, and of all ages, including plenty of children. It was just like Christmas, especially with all that mist, and now with dusk coming down in a big way. It occurred to me that it must really be some kind of national celebration. I wouldn't have expected to know what.

'The next three or four of the houses were locked up and empty, or looked like it, and I walked down to have a closer look at the jetties I've mentioned. It was the usual story. In the first place, they had been very heavily built of wood, like the bridge and many of the fences, but all of them seemed fallen to pieces, and really pretty dangerous, anyway with children around, as there were. There was nothing to stop anyone going out on to them, and there was the swift current sweeping past to the narrows. In England, the local authority would have compelled them to be cleared away and the waterside fenced. And I had been right in what I thought when I looked across from the other side: there wasn't a boat in sight, not even a sunken boat, as far as I could see. Probably the current was enough to carry away a small boat that had been neglected, especially as there were probably floods after the winter snows.

'And then I came upon a wooden house painted in faded blue, where there was still another of those parties. I was getting used to them by now, and didn't suppose there was much more I could learn by just staring in from a distance through the front windows. But I stopped and looked for a moment all the same.

'I saw at once that this time there was a face looking back at me. It was a small, round, white face, which was peeking out watching the darkness fall. At the other houses everyone had been too busy with the festivities to do a thing like that. They had all been looking inwards.

'It was a child, which had somehow detached itself from the general goings-on. And this time there were rather special goings-on. The child caught my eye and waved to me through the glass with its little white hand. It was wearing some kind of dark tunic, buttoned right up. I waved back.

'As far as I was concerned, the things happening behind the child were very interesting. Believe it or not, in the room was another of those figures that I had seen come out of the house on the ridge above; very tall, very wide, all black, just the same; but this time I had some idea of the answer: it was an Orthodox priest, in his black robe and high black headdress. I had seen pictures of them, but I had never seen one in real life, and if you had asked me before that moment, I should have answered for sure that they had died out long ago. As I realised what it was, I felt better once more. The figure I had seen coming out of the house on the ridge had upset me badly.

'This man was occupying himself in handing something out. All the people at the party seemed to be getting one of these things. The last comers were formed up in a queue. Every time the priest handed out, the recipient, whether a man or woman, gave a kind of bob and passed on. I saw it happen about three times before the child at the window waved to me again. I presumed that he had already received his object. I imagined that the children might have come first, as there seemed to be none of them in the queue. On the other hand, there were no other children near the window either. I could not be sure whether the child who waved, was a boy or a girl, but I thought it waved like a boy.

'Again I waved back, and then thought it was time to move on. I was very interested in the priest and the distribution, but it would have been rude to go on peering. When the child realised that I was going, it made the most violent gestures inviting me into the house instead. You know how vividly children can do it. In this case, it was just as well from one point of view, because we were unlikely to be able to communicate in any other way.

'All the same, I shook my head. It was hopeless to think of going in and probably being unable to speak to a soul, especially as I should have had to begin by explaining what I was doing there, with that handout going on. I might have been in real trouble and taken for a thief.

'Still I found it difficult to proceed on my way and disappoint the child so badly. There was a kind of urgency about the little lad which made one care. And there was the foreign factor too. I didn't want to make some social blunder.

'I smiled as broadly as I could manage, pointed to my watch, moved my shoulders as if I had to hurry off to an engagement, and tried to look sorry. I must have done it fairly well because the next thing that happened was that the child jumped down from whatever it was kneeling on at the window and came running out down the garden towards me. It was indeed a boy, about ten I should say, dressed not in shorts but in breeches, which little girls didn't wear in those days. He also wore boots up to his knees. I was a trifle concerned about what was likely to happen next.

'The boy somehow got through the gate, though it looked both heavy and collapsed, and at once proceeded to offer me something. Yes, it was the medal you've seen. That was what the priest had been giving out. Blessed medals: I mean medals that had been blessed. The boy gabbled at me, but of course I couldn't understand a word. "English", I said, rather hopelessly, and of course wouldn't take his medal from him.

'He snatched hold of my hand to prevent my getting away, and went in for more dumb show. I can't tell you how good he was at it. He made me understand quite clearly the blessing that went with the medal, the luck if you like. He imitated all sorts of things going wrong, and how the medal would save me and make things go right again. The only thing I had to do was have the medal always with me and cross myself at the moment of need with it in my hand. He had let go of me because he saw that now I shouldn't just walk off. He showed me again and again. And all without a single further word. He made me feel it was a matter of life or death. Which of course it was, as you have all seen for yourselves.'

'We have that,' said the barman reverentially.

I saw a flash of impatience pass across Rort's face, but he did not comment.

'Not that I believed anything of the sort at the time,' continued the old man. 'Naturally. All the same, I was terribly struck by the boy's cleverness and his sincerity. What reason had he to care about *me*, like that?

'In the end, I took the medal, supposing that he could always get another one for himself, and did everything I could to say thank you. He just stood there with his boots close together on the mud track and smiled at me, like the boy scout

184

on the poster who has just done his good deed. And yet more than that: the boy had his own way of smiling. I daresay it was just that he was a foreigner.

'I wondered if there was anything further. Apparently there wasn't. So I then went through the same kind of pantomime to say goodbye. I felt that just an ordinary casual goodbye would hardly do. But I didn't have to worry. Goodbye, the actual English goodbye, was an expression the boy knew.

'Before walking off, I looked back at the house. The priest in his high black hat and long black robe had come out and stood all by himself under the porch, looking at us down the length of the weedy garden path. I now saw that he had masses of white beard. It covered his entire face, so that you could see only his sunken eyes. As you probably know, Orthodox priests do not disfigure the image of their Maker. The priest stood quite still, and I had no idea as to whether there was something I ought to do. But I couldn't think what, so I smiled feebly and just shuffled off. The boy didn't stop to watch me. Immediately I turned, I heard him dash back into the house. I did look behind me through the mist after a minute or two, but I could see nothing of the festivities, not even the lights, owing to the house being set back among the trees. Nor were there any more houses with parties. All the rest of them that I saw, were shut up like tombs.

'Although the mist was at its thickest on the bridge, and although it was almost night anyway, I had no trouble at all in getting across. I just walked steadily on until I reached the other side and didn't worry about the loose planks and the holes. Only when I arrived safely did it pass through my mind for a moment that I had had my medal to protect me. But the crossing was not really dangerous if you used reasonable care, as you will have gathered: so I gave no further thought to the notion.

'When I got back to our hotel I realised that I was actually ahead of the time I had settled with Mr Purvis, though so much had happened to me that this seemed incredible. When the moment came, I knocked him up (he was flat out with his boots off), and we had something to eat, despite all the eating we had done already, but I said nothing about my adventures. Mr Purvis, fine man though he was, wouldn't have taken much stock in things like that. I merely told him I'd been for a longish walk; which helped to explain how I had managed to get up another appetite.

'Inevitably, Mr Purvis asked me whether I had seen any likely houses. Young and ignorant though I was, I had by now begun to feel rather differently about the idea of Mr Danziger buying up my island, with me getting a cut. I don't think I could have said *why* I felt different about it, but I knew very well that I did. All the same, I told Mr Purvis *something* of what I had found: not laying it on at all, and not making it sound extra attractive.

' "Mr Danziger wouldn't care for a place like that," said Mr Purvis.

'He spoke to settle the matter. I can almost hear him now. He went on to say that Mr Danziger wasn't looking for an investment: that when an investment was among the things he was looking for, he never failed to indicate that fact to Mr Purvis. I felt, even then, that Mr Danziger, if he was the successful businessman everyone took him to be, would probably be glad to be put in the way of a promising investment at any time, even when he wasn't expecting it. But Mr Purvis had not brought me to Finland in order to argue with him, and, in any case, I was really relieved that the island would remain undisturbed, as far as my influence went. Nor am I saying that Mr Purvis was necessarily mistaken in his view of Mr Danziger.

The Houses of the Russians

Probably he was quite right. In any case, he seemed pleased with me, because he ended our meal by buying me a Finnish liqueur called Lakka. They make these different liqueurs out of berries picked in the Arctic, and very good they are. I've never met with better liqueurs anywhere.'

'Can you get them in England?' asked Gamble.

'No, no. Like many good things, they don't travel,' replied the old man.

We waited for him to resume.

'Curiously enough, in view of how firm he had been with me the night before, it was Mr Purvis who raised the question of my island and the houses on it, the next morning with Mr Kirkontorni. I should not myself have mentioned the matter again, however much I thought about it.

'Mr Kirkontorni knew at once what Mr Purvis was talking about, and didn't have to ask me for details.

' "They're the houses of the Russians," he said.

' "How's that?" asked Mr Purvis.

' "In the days before the war," said Mr Kirkontorni, "Finland was very popular with the Russians in summer. They used to build villas on the coast and on the lakes, and Unilinna was one of the places they liked best. The families spent the summer here, and a very gay time they made of it. I can remember them myself. Though I was only a child at the time, I've never seen or heard the like of their great dinners, and musical parties, and dances. Unilinna has never been quite the same place since they left; either for the money they brought or for the fun either. We had mixed thoughts about them at the time, but most of us have missed them badly since they went. All day they scattered gold and all night they sang. Not that what I've said is popular everywhere politically. And people are right there too: at politics the Russians have never been good."

187

' "I suppose there are none of them left now?" asked Mr Purvis. I had not told him one way or the other, but only about the island itself and the empty houses, so you can imagine how I waited for Mr Kirkontorni's answer.

' "There are supposed to be a few," said Mr Kirkontorni; "but we don't have anything to do with them any more. Politics again. Finland used to be a kind of Russian colony, as you know, and we didn't like that, though most of us had nothing against the Russians personally. And since then we've had our civil war, when we starved, and they tried to enforce Bolshevism here and would have done if we hadn't had assistance from the Germans. Today most people want to hear no more of the Russians than they can help. In fact, their houses are supposed to be unlucky, and no one goes near them. If anyone did, he wouldn't be very popular either."

' "Who owns the houses now?" asked Mr Purvis.

' "I really couldn't tell you. I should think it's a matter for international law, by this time. No one's ever bought them from the Russians: first because it wouldn't be thought right; second because there've been no Russians to buy from. Very much not, as we all know."

' "It makes you think," said Mr Purvis.

' "It's another reason why our people say the houses are unlucky."

' "You can't wonder at it," said Mr Purvis.

' "*Miehen on mela kädessä, Jumala venettä viepi*," said Mr Kirkontorni. That's a Finnish proverb, meaning man holds the paddle, but God does the steering. I heard it several times on our way home, when we idled about for a few days, and visited several Finnish townships.

'They said no more on the subject of the houses, and a little later Mr Purvis and I were tramping round Unilinna again in the full heat of the sun, eating a lot, drinking a lot, sweating a lot, and stumbling over the language, to say nothing of the map, which Mr Purvis would keep for himself. I have an idea it was on that day that we found the place Mr Purvis recommended to Mr Danziger, and that Mr Danziger liked so much. It must have been, because by the evening Mr Purvis was so done up that he kept me hanging around him, fetching the waiter up to his room and the chambermaid, and on the final day we took it very much easier. On that third evening, the one I'm speaking of, I couldn't get out at all. When Mr Purvis wasn't wanting things from the hotel staff, with me acting as intermediary, especially with the language, then he was dictating notes to me about the places we had seen, while he soaked his feet in a footbath, that had to be just the right size not to get cold, and even then had to have more hot water added to it about every five minutes, and more funny salts too, that the hotel had advised and that I'd had to scour the town to find. Mr Purvis kept changing his mind about the notes, and particularly about what was suitable for Mr Danziger to hear about. Mr Purvis always said that manner of presentation to the client was quite as important as what was presented, and often more so: and of course he was quite right. When it came to the matter of the hotel, he was a proper traveller of the old school, who knew his rights, and expected to get value for his money. Altogether I had my hands full that evening. I was not left under the impression that I was travelling only for pleasure.

'The next day, as I've said, wasn't very serious. If we'd happened to come upon Windsor Castle offered for a song, I doubt whether Mr Danziger would have heard much about it. Mr Purvis made a point of always knowing his own mind, and I'm sure he'd made it up by then. At one point, during the hot afternoon, he even suggested that I take him to have a look at the houses on the island, just for the jaunt and I suppose for the breeze off the lake, but I told him about the dangerous bridge and what a long walk it all was, and he settled for a short steamer-trip instead. We crossed to a tiny lakeside village, all set around with conifers and red rocks, and there, in the small, stone church, we saw a Finnish wedding, with the bridal couple in national dress and the dark building as full of lighted candles as a grotto. We didn't go in, but watched from outside the west door, which they'd left open, as it was so sunny, though the sun hardly entered the church at all. I noticed that the officiating pastor, who stood behind the altar rails, was not in any way like the black figures I had seen on my island. This gave me a surprise; but of course I said nothing about it to Mr Purvis.

'When we got back, Mr Purvis was all smiles, and suggested that I have a further look round on my own for a bit, while he took a rest. "You're only young once," he said, as if I'd been holding back. I arranged to call for him later, as I'd done two nights earlier.

'Of course I went down at once to have another look at my island. Mr Kirkontorni had said it was an unpopular thing to do, but I could hardly worry much about that, as I didn't live in Unilinna or even in Finland. I was still frightened of the island, but I had an idea that a return visit would clear various things up, and that Mr Kirkontorni's information would enable me to look at it with new eyes, and add some queer items to my small stock of knowledge. But, given the chance, I couldn't have kept away from the island anyway. What I did hope was that I shouldn't meet one of these black priests. I had realised of course that they were probably quite the usual thing in Russia, and the thought of them was not as bad as it had been, but I still did not care for them at all.

'I had also realised that the peculiar writing on the medal I had been given, must be Russian. It was only a guess, because until then I hadn't known that Russian was written in a different script. I remember taking the medal out of my pocket and looking at it as I walked down the empty street to the northern waterfront. It was not very encouraging to think that apparently people didn't like living even where they could *see* the island. It was a different thought from the one which had struck me on the island itself, as you may remember.

'I can't say there was anything remarkable this time about the way I crossed the bridge. I just went carefully and watched where I put my feet. I was earlier than on my previous visit, and the late afternoon mist was only beginning to rise. The island looked very beautiful, with its huge trees, and the fanciful houses sticking out here and there. From the bridge you couldn't see how badly they needed painting. The faded paint probably made them look prettier, as it often does from a distance.

'My idea was to start out along the southern path, where I'd seen those parties going on among the few Russians that Mr Kirkontorni had said were still left. I wasn't at all keen about the big houses on the ridge, and what I really wanted was to have another look at the Russians themselves, especially as I seemed to be the only person who cared about them.

'From the moment I started along that path, I felt a great sadness all about me. It was not the kind of feeling I was used to—not at that age. Naturally I put it down to the fact that now I knew about the houses, and couldn't see them any more as mere property going to waste. Not that property going to waste is ever a cheerful sight in itself. I told myself that it must be the sad story I'd heard about the Russians, even though Mr Purvis and I had been left to fill in the details, which, at that time, I knew no more about than any other ordinary English boy.

Whatever I told myself, I felt worse and worse with every step I took. I felt as if a great pit was opening wider and wider, that previously I'd known nothing about; and that pretty well the whole world was sinking into it, so that soon it would be as if I were alone at the North Pole or on the moon, with no one even to cry out to. You may think that's a bit far-fetched after all these years, but it's exactly how it was. It was the feeling of being completely cut off and helpless that was the worst part; and the fact that on the face of it this was nonsense, because I could always run back across the bridge, only made it worse. I felt there was some explanation, something I didn't know about, which was the real cause of the trouble. All the same, I was determined not to run away just because I was in a blue funk.

'In the middle of it all, I remembered my medal. I pulled it out and held it clenched in my hand. Whatever I thought it might do, it didn't do. I went on feeling exactly the same. But I continued clutching hold of the medal, as I ploughed forward. And this time, the sun was shining all the while, as I've said.

'I reached the wooden house painted blue where I'd talked with the Russian lad, seen the priest giving out the medals, and all the rest of it. There was no one about and everything was quite silent, but the house was not locked up, like the houses between it and the bridge. On the contrary, the door where I had seen the priest watching me from behind his huge, fluffy beard, stood wide open.

'I can't tell you how, but I knew at once that there was no one inside.

'The house had an utterly unoccupied look, but that didn't always mean much on the island, and I think it was the wide open door itself which told me there was no one there. I thought I could risk taking a look.

The Houses of the Russians

'I struggled with the gate. It was even heavier and more jammed than I had supposed when I first saw it, and I couldn't think how the Russian boy had managed it so well. But I shoved it back and pushed my way up the garden path through the long grass and weeds. Believe it or not, I walked straight in. All things considered, I think it was plucky as well as cheeky, but I still didn't suppose that anything was *really* wrong. How could I? I knew nothing.'

At this point, a couple of locals who had drifted into the bar, and had been seated in the background intermittently muttering short, slow sentences to one another, drifted out again.

'There was nothing inside but blood,' said the old man. 'Blood everywhere. Big blotches on the peeling walls, with darker centres, where the blood had started its spurting. Blood splashed about the grey ceiling, as if kids had been in there with squirts that had got out of control. Blood heavy on the floorboards, dusty and rotten though they were. I could see the shapes of bodies, as they had lain there; many bodies, because it was a big room, thirty or thirty-five feet long I daresay, and perhaps twenty-five feet wide, and these shapes were right across the floor. After that, I have never doubted the marks that are said to be on the Holy Shroud at Turin: at least I have never doubted that they could have been made by a human body. The blood leaves an extraordinarily definite outline. In that room, the marks suggested that several of the bodies had lain across one another. There was even blood on the windows, including the window where the little boy had waved to me. The sunshine shone through it like stained glass, and made the room redder still. It was like the Holy Grail, all glowing, and yet the room was filthy and dusty too. And the blood smelt. I can smell it now, when I think about it. At the time I all but fainted with the smell of it.

'But I didn't faint. I think it was partly because I still didn't fully understand. I got out and tore off to the bridge as fast as my young legs would carry me.

'Or rather *towards* the bridge. Because on the way I met the first person I'd seen on the island that day. He was a scruffy specimen too, dressed in little better than rags. If he hadn't been in the very middle of the mud road, I'd have run right past him.

'He said something to me in what I took to be Russian, and for some reason I stopped. His hair was going grey, and he had straggling grey wisps on his face and chin; not a proper beard, but just about the last word in neglect and untidiness. Of course I must have been looking very peculiar myself at that moment.

'I made my usual answer: "English." I imagine I was pretty well gasping.

' "What are you holding in your hand?" he said: just like that, and quite comprehensibly.

'I unfolded my hand and showed him my medal lying on the palm of it. I was past caring if he snatched it.

' "Do you know what that means?" he asked, pointing to the words.

'I shook my head.

' "The Feast of the Sleep of the Theotokos," he said. "It is a privilege to possess such a medal. Only at the Feast are they given. They bear a blessing."

'In the light of what I had just seen, it had become a little hard to believe in that blessing.

' "But to participate, you have each time to cross yourself. Like this." He showed me, as the boy had done. The Greeks do it differently from the Latins, as I expect some of you know. I had forgotten that part of it until he reminded me.

' "I am a hermit," he said, "having been long a pilgrim. I am now the only Christian soul resident on this island, where once there were so many."

'I could only bow my head. Raw though I was.

' "Remember and live," he said. "Remember and live long." '

'Then he passed by me without a smile, and I walked quite slowly to and across the bridge, feeling much calmer.'

The old man stopped.

We had not expected an end just there, and were taken by surprise.

'What's the Feast of the Sleep of the whatever-it-was?' asked Gamble, somewhat ineffectively.

'It's an annual celebration in the Orthodox Church,' replied the old man, 'but the details you'll have to discover for yourself.'

'And the charm has worked ever since?' enquired the bar-man.

'According to my belief, it has worked on several occasions, even though I was raised in a faith which has no part in such things. Plainly I cannot expect it to work for all time.'

'In a sense perhaps you can,' said Dyson, quite quietly.

'Anyway it worked tonight right enough,' said the barman, still awed by the evidence of his own eyes.

Of course we were all shying away from the core of the experience, as people do. And it seemed inappropriate just to thank the narrator and compliment his tale, as mere courtesy suggested. We all seemed painfully short of any right things to say. This may help to excuse a certain discordancy in a question which Rort put at this point.

'The suggestion is that the people died in the civil war?'

'No,' said the old man. 'The civil war began only in 1918, and all the Russians had gone back to their own country long before that. It was in Russia that they died, not in Finland.'

195

Rort smiled, too polite to express doubt. One could tell from his face that he thought the tale too preposterous to be worth powder and shot. 'I expect they'd most of them done the same kind of thing to their serfs and servants in their time,' he said, entering, as he saw it, into the spirit of the narrative.

'I don't know about that,' said the old man. 'All I know is that, speaking for myself, I wouldn't have much truck with the people responsible for what I saw until they at least repudiate what they did then.'

'If we followed that line of thought, we'd have a third world war,' said Rort.

But the old man said nothing further; nor, after Dyson had thanked him (quite adroitly) on behalf of us all, did he or we return to the subject during the remainder of the course.

NO STRONGER THAN A FLOWER

Beauty, whose action is no stronger than a flower.
William Shakespeare

'NATURALLY *I* DON'T care, because I love you,' said Curtis. 'I'm thinking entirely of you.'

Nesta had always been given to believe that, whatever they might say to one, it was a woman's appearance that men really cared about; and indeed she thought that she well understood their point of view. So understanding had she been, in fact, that she had long regarded herself as truly resigned to the wintry consequences in her own case. She would not, therefore, ever have accepted Curtis's proposal of marriage, had she not greatly, though as yet briefly, loved him. She had a temperamental distaste for extreme measures.

This trait of Nesta's, and her inexperience of men, had prevented her discerning that Curtis was a far more desperate character. Having in his early twenties loved a woman of great beauty, he considered that he had learnt his lesson: beauty, although it had its place, was not to be lived with. He took it for granted that there were other values. He was horrified, therefore, to find himself now preoccupied, almost unconsciously at

197

the start, with a stealthy campaign to persuade Nesta to do something about her looks. The campaign, he perceived, was being planned even before he proposed to her. This present suggestion was a climax.

'I don't really believe in it,' said Nesta.

'But, darling, how can you tell if you don't put it to the test?'

Of course this was old stuff between them.

Nesta said nothing.

'I don't see that you have anything actually to *lose*,' said Curtis.

'I suppose I might lose you.'

'Darling, please don't be silly. I keep saying it's *you* I'm thinking about.'

'I wonder how I've managed until now?'

'You've had no one to look after you.'

If she could have accepted that at anything like its face value, she would doubtless have at least tried to do what Curtis wanted. As it was (although she did not doubt that Curtis loved her in his own way), she did nothing. A date had been fixed for the marriage, and Nesta was afraid that if she took the step demanded of her, and it did not end in reasonable success, then Curtis would jilt her.

After the marriage, it became suddenly clear to Nesta that to the generally accepted rule about men Curtis was no exception. Curtis had gone about his plan cleverly enough to confuse her at a time when she so much wanted to be confused; but marriage cleared her mind like a rocket piercing a cloud and releasing a downpour. Possibly the worst symptom was that from the nuptial day Curtis had never referred to the matter. Apparently he had decided to accept her as she was. And since, having been long self-occluded, she was greatly wishful of change and adventure, she could not welcome his decision.

One trouble with Curtis's previous attitude had always been its practical vagueness. As often with men in difficult and embarrassing contexts, he had urged action upon her with a persistency which indicated, she now saw, that latterly the subject was always in the front of his thoughts about her; but never making any very precise or feasible proposition. He would generalise about the importance and efficiency of beauty culture, and even, more than once, hint at plastic surgery; but at the smallest demur by Nesta would fall back upon an aloof irritability which she took to imply that naturally the details must be left to her. There was about him a suggestion that it was the least she could contribute. Why? Because she was a woman, she supposed. It was also the reason why she loved him.

One thing which marriage did for Nesta was to stoke up a romantic sensitivity which previously she had banked down with daily loads of dust and ashes. She acquired an impersonal dissatisfaction with a way of life which a year before she would have thought ecstatic if it were not that she would then have altogether excluded it from her thoughts as impossible. Curtis's passion might be somewhat guarded, but it was neither infrequent nor frightening; his general consideration for her was admirable; and he provided her, starved as she was of affectionate outlet, with continuous opportunities to assist and look after him. Only he no longer suggested that she should seek advice about her appearance; no longer remarked that every woman did so or wasn't a woman.

Eight or nine months after she was married, Nesta for the first time gave the problem exact and businesslike consideration. As commonly happens after a long period of irresolution, an apparent answer, a seeming first step, stared her in the face immediately she started seriously to look for it. She went to the library of her mother's club, where she read through the flowing advertisement columns of the fashion papers for women, papers which she would not have about the flat, lest Curtis misunderstand, and perhaps pity, her interest in them; and in one which was new to her (it was entitled 'Flame'), she found a relevant intimation. Restrained, sensitive, civilised, promising nothing and alluding only to a consultation without obligation, it bespoke as much as could be hoped for, Nesta thought, in such a case, although placed somewhat unnoticeably in a corner of the penultimate page. There was an address to which enquirers were invited to write for an appointment. No telephone number was given, but it was not a matter about which Nesta would have telephoned.

The reply to Nesta's letter was elegantly typed on thick paper, bearing at the top a representation, embossed in red, of a sleek, slightly formalised head and neck (a desirable looking creature, Nesta admitted, rubbing the raised surface with her finger); but the address was in a street, and indeed a part of the town, which were outside her restricted topography. The suggested appointment was for that morning. There was no need to confirm it, stated the letter; apparently in no doubt that Nesta would haste to attend. Nesta put the letter in her handbag. She decided in favour of a taxi.

It was a long journey and a disappointing landfall. They were high terrace houses of that kind which while apparently built for single families, and certainly very inconvenient to operate on any other basis, yet give the impression of never having been so occupied. Now, in this particular street, they appeared largely to be let out in single rooms for habitation by the elderly and disappointed. The presence of children playing on the pavement manifested both life's renascence and the street's continued social descent.

The house Nesta sought was in the middle of the row. Its knocker and letter box flap were polished and the lace curtains at its windows clean and lusciously draped; but the general effect was somehow still so cheerless that Nesta upon beholding it as she stepped out of the taxi, immediately decided to go home.

She hesitated for a moment, trying to assemble an explanation.

'Don't yer like the look of it?' enquired the driver.

Nesta turned to him. 'No,' she said, and regarded him seriously.

It seemed all that was needed.

' 'Op in. I'll soon 'ave yer back 'ome.'

Nesta nodded.

But already the moment was gone. The front door of the house was open, and a woman advancing down the short strip of garden. Nesta was unequipped with the ruthlessness which might have enabled her to act on her impulse and bolt.

'It was you who wrote to me?'

Again Nesta nodded. The woman was staring at her.

'Make up your mind,' enjoined the taxi-driver. He seemed to disapprove of the latest development. But Nesta was looking in her handbag.

'I'm Mrs de Milo. You made an appointment with me.' It was a statement of fact.

'Yes,' said Nesta. 'I think I'm in time.' She had found the fare, but the taximan still seemed doubtful.

Mrs de Milo made no reply, but stood staring at Nesta, as if minutely considering whether she for her part would take matters further. Mrs de Milo was an ageless woman with a white smooth face, Grecian nose, and large but well shaped breasts. She wore an elegant white overall of medical aspect, gleaming with starch. Her black hair, very thick and glistening, was parted in the middle and drawn into a carefully composed bun.

'Come in,' said Mrs de Milo, her mind apparently made up. 'We can't talk in the street.'

The taxi began to move off.

The effect that evening on Curtis was interesting. His expression when Peggy let him into the flat and he first saw Nesta was one which Nesta found it difficult to decide about, wrought up though she was to observe him minutely. Then he spoke.

'Darling!'

She would not smile.

'Darling, I thought for one moment—'

Still she left him to define.

'All the same . . . You do *look* different?'

She perceived. Curtis's initial response had been nothing less than complete non-recognition. Although she had been standing in shadow it was startlingly more than she had reckoned upon.

She did not go to him, but rather drew back a step.

'I've altered my hair style.'

'I'll say you have.' He was almost peering at her. 'Why?'

'I wanted a change.'

His face lightened somewhat.

'Anything you want, darling.'

Peggy asked if she should bring in soup. It was amusing that Peggy had never seemed even to notice the innovation.

'Give me a minute of time to change,' said Curtis, as he always did. When alone with Nesta, he dined in one of his older suits.

Nesta turned and, full in the light, looked at herself yet again in the expensive, but not very beautiful hanging glass which had been her father-in-law's wedding present.

Nine days later (Nesta had begun to keep a diary) Curtis, without explanation or precedent, suddenly, in the middle of dinner, began to make a scene.

They had been eating for some time in silence, when Curtis, his fish unfinished, crashed down his knife and fork and bawled out: 'What the hell's the matter with you, Nesta?'

One change in Nesta seemed to be that her nerves were growing stronger, so that she no longer trembled before the unexpected, as she had hitherto tended to do. Now she looked Curtis in the eyes. 'Nothing is the matter with me that I know of.' Her look changed as she added, 'I'm sorry the dinner isn't better. You know it's Peggy's night out.'

'You're a better cook than Peggy any day.' It was hard to believe, notwithstanding, that indifferently cooked fish was responsible for Curtis's remarkable wrath.

'I expect I didn't stick closely enough to the directions.'

'Why have you messed up your hands like that?'

It was, in fact, the first time she had worn brightly coloured nail varnish.

'Do you like it?' She stretched out her hands across the table. It was true that they now looked unlike the hands of a capable cook.

'It makes me sick.'

Nesta slowly withdrew her hands and placed them in her lap.

'It's hideous. Besides, it's vulgar. Never do it again.'

None the less, now that the cause of his fury was exposed, the fury was ebbing, the more quickly for its violence.

'After all they're my hands.'

Curtis was stricken by her placidity.

'Don't do it again, there's a good girl.'

'I think it's nice.'

'Oh darling, it's not. It's horrible.'

Nesta remembered having read in some cynical book that although a woman's appearance is what a man most cares about, yet, too often, the more she does about it the less he cares for the result and for her.

Curtis had assumed that Nesta would discontinue the notion. When he proved wrong, the thing became a small obsession with him. By bed and by board, Nesta's painted hands seemed to be deflecting him, warding him off. He had assuredly never realised that he cared so very much about carmine finger nails.

It was in his behaviour to Nesta, in acts of omission, that his distaste found expression; for after the first outburst, he seldom returned to the subject in words. He was ashamed and uncomprehending; and felt compelled secretly to agree with Nesta that her hands were her own. Also he felt that he lost status by his concern with something so unimportant. He apprehended hostility to Nesta creeping into and about him like a snake; and was dismayed.

For Nesta, in her insensitiveness to his needs and impulses, it seemed to him that the manicuring of her nails had become a main business of her life. Every evening she seemed to be plying a battery of small instruments infinitely sharp, and unpleasantly surgical in aspect; or, in the alternative, endlessly filing. The distinctive gritty sound of Nesta filing her nails became to his nerves in their emotional aspect what the dentist's drill was in their physical aspect. Once he found words to suggest that, instead of in the evening, she tend her nails during the day when he was out of the house; but later he divined that already she had been tending them by day also. Even apart from his antipathy to coloured nails, it was a disquieting revelation. It disgusted him in itself, as if Nesta had acquired a pathological obsession.

As sounds unheard can, it is said, be sweeter than those heard, hostility unacknowledged can be bitterer than open warfare. To her preoccupation with her hands, Nesta shortly began to add the extravagant and wasteful buying of clothes. Previously she had seemed content with exactly the type and size of wardrobe favoured by other married women of her age and income level and district. Now she was buying recklessly; and, what Curtis found, if possible, even more disturbing, was dressing more and more oddly. As far as he could see, her eccentric but costly garb lacked even the justification of being in the mode.

There was one evening when he arrived to escort her to a bridge party. The invitation was of long standing, and the date agreed for weeks.

'Darling, I'm sorry but you simply can't show yourself at the Foxtons like that.'

'Does it become me?'

'That's not the point. You know what the Foxtons are like. The *Foxtons*,' he repeated with desperate emphasis.

'Should I surprise them?'

'Put on something else quickly, darling. We're forty minutes late already. More.'

'*You're* late. I've been dressed for hours.' She picked up a tiny scalpel-like object, and began to bore with it at her nails. She brought to the task a curiously profound concentration, slowly moving her bare elbows as she made the minute movements. She resembled a subaqueous tree, gently rippling in the movement of the water.

'You're spending far too much on clothes anyway,' said

Curtis, his nerves flaring, as always, at the sight of her occupation. 'I can't keep up with you.'

'Keep up with me?'

'Pay the bills,' Curtis said bitterly, although he was neither poor nor ungenerous.

'Have you been asked to pay any bills? Extra bills?' Not for a moment did she look up from her work.

'I almost wish you would ask me. I don't want them all to descend on me at once.'

She made no reply to that, but simply said 'What about the Foxtons?'

'I'll ring up, while you change.'

'I'm not going to change for the Foxtons.'

He was sincerely shocked. The Foxtons were among their best friends.

'Darling, we'll have no friends left.'

It was hard not to think so; because even when Nesta did go out, he noticed that she seemed no longer to enjoy her former quiet popularity, and fancied that thereby he himself became suspect also for the shadowy change in her.

Although he had been married less than a year, Curtis came to dread his return home in the evening. Not only was Nesta apparently losing all taste for the small dinner parties and little gatherings with their friends which he so much enjoyed, but she seemed also to be losing her interest in him. It was not that the housekeeping appeared to be neglected: on the contrary, Curtis thought he now discerned a new and conscious punctiliousness over every detail. But the effect was of a household in the charge not, as is desirable, of benevolent and invisible fairies, but rather of recent graduates from a College of Domestic Science. Nesta seemed to manage her home more and more impersonally; and she carried this impression into every aspect of their joint life. Fundamentally Curtis had married neither for passion nor even for a well-kept home, but for sentiment: so that Nesta's changed behaviour particularly distressed him. She herself seemed neither happy nor unhappy; but to find an obscure contentment in sitting always by herself, impelling Peggy to correct every deviation from formal domestic perfection, wearing ornate clothes, and endlessly employing her elaborate manicure case and green taffeta covered beauty box. From the latter, when open, rose a vapour of invisible but choking face-powder and a mêlée of headachy perfumes.

A very upsetting development was when Nesta began to wear hats with veils. It was now that Curtis seriously wondered what to do about her. He thought of mentioning the course of events to a doctor, but there was really nothing to be said which would not sound impossibly foolish. Nesta, although unsympathetic, was perfectly rational in her dealings with him, and was running the house more efficiently than ever. Her body was, of course, her own, to adorn as she wished. She acquired what appeared to be a large number of new hats, many of them evening hats, in the French manner, and an equally large number of veils, varying in colour, opacity, and pattern; and before long was never to be seen by Curtis without one. Because it was at this point that she began to keep strictly to her own room at nights. For reasons unacknowledged by either, they had occupied separate rooms from the start; but the rooms had a communicating door which until now had never once been locked. Nesta met Curtis's questions with simple statements that she wished to sleep alone 'for the present'; and when he became more pressing, with quiet defiance.

The new hats were all in what Curtis took to be more or less the fashion, although he did not move in circles where those

207

fashions obtained in their full purity; and the veils were at all times elegantly, even coquettishly adjusted. Sometimes the mesh was large, and Curtis thought that he could see her face almost as well as if the veil were not there; but, on the whole, and as time passed, his idea of Nesta's features fell into steadily increasing indistinctness and even distortion. The only exception was her mouth, which she exposed in order to eat, dexterously twisting the veil above her upper lip. To Curtis, in his isolation from her, Nesta's mouth seemed newly and poignantly desirable. Its image lingered in his thoughts, growing more and more sensual as he brooded upon it. Before long he wanted merely to kiss her mouth, more than once he had wanted entirely to possess her. But he considered that to kiss her would be undignified while she continued to use him so disparagingly. Even more, he doubted whether she would welcome his kiss. He held back from a conflict which might have to be final.

One day, between morning and evening, she seemed to have changed all the furniture in the flat, installing many new objects, moving into new positions most of the things which were there already, and undoubtedly casting a number of pieces away. Into the drawing room Nesta had brought a full-length looking-glass, tall and wide, stately and heavy, and bordered with a tumbling riot of gilt fauns and maenads. It might have come from a Venetian palazzo which had been redecorated in a late period. She had altered the lighting in the room, so that at night all of it bore upon the new looking-glass; which, indeed, was now almost the only object left in the room. The flat, however, was a large one, and Curtis through his inner storm of protest and bewilderment felt an intimation that Nesta had transformed something commonplace into something exciting and dramatic. Unfortunately Curtis had married neither for excitement nor for drama.

No Stronger Than a Flower

Now they dined by the light of candles stuck in writhing silver candelabra. One night Nesta was wearing a misty dress, entirely white but not in the least bridal; and over her head a silky white veil, against which her mouth as she ate showed red as a new wound. To Curtis, Nesta's mouth seemed miraculously to have changed its shape: it was impossible that it could ever have been so desirable. He forced himself to eat and to complain. He took up the theme which worried him almost as much as the change in Nesta herself.

'If you go on spending money like this, you'll compel me to disclaim responsibility for your debts.' Even the spoon with which he was eating his soup was new and sweetly chased.

'You have no responsibility for my debts.'

Nesta had a small income of her own, but Curtis well knew that it could come nowhere near to meeting her present almost daily orgies of expenditure. He considered that her implication to the contrary was insulting to his intelligence.

'I hope you'll explain that to the lawyers. The law says that a husband is responsible for his wife's debts,' said Curtis wearily and bitterly. He had no expectation of making any impression on her.

'You're paying for nothing more than you ever did.'

Curtis put down his beautiful alien soup spoon. He knew that many months had now passed since all this began, and indeed there had been no bills for any of it.

'Who is paying then?'

'I am paying. You are getting the benefit without paying.'

'You can't be paying. You haven't got the money.' His need to cover her lovely mouth with kisses made him foolish. 'There's someone else. All this nonsense is for someone else.'

Nesta laughed.

'It's for someone else,' Curtis repeated.

'No. It's for me.' She spoke with a significance he was too irate to grasp.

'I should have stopped it once and for all long ago.'

'How?'

'Had you locked up, if necessary.' At this moment indeed he would have done worse things than that.

'How could you stop it? You started it.'

Curtis changed colour in the candlelight. He remembered the saying that what you fear is true.

'It wasn't even for your own sake. You were thinking entirely of me.'

'Nesta!' he cried. 'Tell me what is happening to you?'

But without replying, she produced a tiny shining implement and began to file her nails. The absorption which always accompanied this process was around her like a screen.

Feeling fear and shame and pity, he went to her. He pulled up a chair and put his arm round her shoulders.

'Nesta,' he said. 'Let's be as we used to be.'

He tried to kiss her. Before his lips touched hers, he was conscious of a sharp pain. He raised his other hand to his cheek. It was smeared with blood.

'Get back,' cried Nesta. 'Mind my dress.'

Now he was holding his handkerchief to his cheek with both hands. The blood seemed to be spurting out. Already Curtis felt that everything about him was discoloured with it.

Nesta had risen and was standing in the corner of the room gazing at him. He could see her eyes bright through the white silk veil.

Even with the pain of the injury and the discomfort of the blood, he also saw something else. He had supposed that Nesta, even though it seemed inconceivable, had struck at him with the small sharp file. But as she stood, the light fell on her hands, and he saw that every one of her painted nails had been sharpened to a deadly point.

'So that's what your manicuring amounts to.'

'It's time you noticed.' Nesta still spoke quietly. Curtis had seated himself at the far side of the table, on which he placed his elbows as he held his soaking handkerchief to his face. 'This is the way they grow. I keep trying to blunt them.'

Curtis looked at her.

'To file them down and to make them look socially acceptable. The way you want them.'

'It's the most horrible thing I ever heard of.' Of course she was mad.

'It's getting more difficult all the time. The more I file them, the sharper they get. I don't know why I go on bothering!'

Curtis was trying to collect himself. 'Look, darling,' he said to her across the table. 'Look, darling, you're ill. You're saying so yourself. If you'll give me a minute of time to clean up, I'll go and rout out Nicolson. I'm sure he'll come round.' Nicolson was their doctor.

'I'm not out of my mind, if that's what you mean.' She said it so calmly that Curtis, who had risen to his feet, stopped and sat down again. 'Out of my body perhaps. Not my mind. I don't suppose Nicolson can do more about the one thing than he can about the other.' She put her hands on the table, interlocking the fingers. 'Have you any further suggestions?'

'There must be something for us to do.' He thought wildly of psychiatric clinics, marriage guidance centres, and other such outposts in the jungle. The whole territory was one into which he had never thought he would have to enter.

'Perhaps what I need is an ugliness salon. You don't happen to know of one?'

'I've never seen you look so beautiful.' He had ceased to play his appointed part, and spoke his thought.

'But you don't want me all the same? Not now? Not really?'

'Of course I want you. You're my wife. If only things could be as they were. That's what I want.'

She picked up an exquisite decanter, one of their new acquisitions, and filled a delicate wineglass. 'You know I had no idea,' she said, 'how deep it goes. Most people know nothing. Nothing. It goes to the very bottom of life.' She drained the glass. A drop of the red wine hung on her mouth. She licked her lip.

'What does? I don't understand you.'

Regarding her, and trying to puzzle out what he felt to be her insults, he was for a moment far from sure that really she looked any different from the way she had looked on the day he married her. As far as one could see: and behind her white veil. Apart from her hands, of course.

'As you don't understand me, you can't want me,' said Nesta.

'But I do want you,' cried Curtis. 'I tried to kiss you and you wouldn't let me.'

She was standing with the tips of her fingers resting on the white table cloth. Curtis was reminded of a clawed goddess with a beautiful immemorial face which he had once seen in company with that earlier woman in his life. Nesta's bright eyes were again fixed upon him. 'You say you want to kiss me,' she said. 'How long is it since you've even seen my face? Do you think you'd still recognise me?'

She began to unwind her veil. Then she picked up one of the heavy candlesticks and slowly moved it towards her face. Except that she was now elaborately made up, Curtis was still unable to define the change in her.

'Well?' She was pressing for a response.

Curtis did not move, but sat, one hand still to his cheek, staring at her familiar face as Odysseus stared at Circe.

'I never gave you a likeness of me, but I had one taken all the same.' Putting down the candles, she opened her bag and passed a half-plate photograph across the table.

Curtis did not look at it.

'It's wonderful what make-up will do when you have a good photograph to copy,' said Nesta. 'Do you think it's like me?'

Curtis snatched at the photograph and without glancing at it, tore it into confetti.

'It doesn't matter now,' said Nesta, 'although it seems to be the only print left. It's become so difficult to make myself like it that I should have to stop trying anyway. There are limits even to make-up, you know. Besides, why should I? So look your last. There'll be only your memory left.'

She was blowing out the candles one by one. Curtis had sunk his torn face in his hands.

When the last candle was out, she spoke again.

'Kiss me goodbye.'

Curtis could hear her moving towards him through the blackness, thick with the smell of wax. He crouched into himself, but now she was beside him. Her warm lips softly and gently touched the invisible back of his neck. Her hair was newly and wonderfully fragrant.

He heard her pass onwards to the door. In the next room, the drawing room, her steps paused for many seconds, and he realised that she was looking at herself in the tall and stately glass which seemed to have come from some Italian palace. Then the steps resumed, more slowly he thought, as doubtless she drew on her furs; and soon he knew that he would never see or hear her again.

THE CICERONES

JOHN TRANT entered the Cathedral of Saint Bavon at almost exactly 11.30.

An unexpected week's holiday having come his way, he was spending it in Belgium, because Belgium was near and it was late in the season, and because he had never been there. Trant, who was unmarried (though one day he intended to marry), was travelling alone, but he seldom felt lonely at such times because he believed that his solitude was optional and regarded it rather as freedom. He was thirty-two and saw himself as quite ordinary, except perhaps in this very matter of travel, which he thought he took more seriously and systematically than most. The hour at which he entered the Cathedral was important, because he had been inconvenienced in other towns by the irritating continental habit of shutting tourist buildings between 12.00 and 2.00, even big churches. In fact, he had been in two minds as to whether to visit the Cathedral at all with so little time in hand. One could not even count upon the full half-hour, because the driving out of visitors usually began well before the moment of actual closure. It was a still morning, very still, but overcast. Men were beginning to wait, one might say, for the year finally to die.

The Cicerones

The thing that struck Trant most as he entered the vast building was how silent it seemed to be within; how empty. Other Belgian cathedrals had contained twenty or thirty scattered people praying, or anyway kneeling; priests importantly on the move, followed by acolytes; and, of course, Americans. There had always been dingy hustle, ritual action, and neck-craning. Here there seemed to be no one, other, doubtless, than the people in the tombs. Trant again wondered whether the informed did not know that it was already too late to go in.

He leant against a column at the west end of the nave as he always did, and read the history of the Cathedral in his Blue Guide. He chose this position in order that when he came to the next section to be perused, the architectural summary, he could look about him to the best advantage. He usually found, none the less, that he soon had to move if he were to follow what the guide book had to say, as the architecture of few cathedrals can be apprehended, even in outline, by a newcomer from a single point. So it was now: Trant found that he was losing the thread, and decided he would have to take up the guide book's trail. Before doing so, he looked around him for a moment. The Cathedral seemed still to be quite empty. It was odd, but a very pleasant change. Trant set out along the south aisle of the nave, holding the guide book like a breviary. 'Carved oak pulpit,' said the guide book, 'with marble figures, all by Laurent Delvaux.' Trant had observed it vaguely from afar, but as, looking up from the book, he began consciously to think about it, he saw something extraordinary. Surely there was a figure in the pulpit, not standing erect, but slumped forward over the preacher's cushion? Trant could see the top of a small, bald head with a deep fringe, almost a halo, of white hair; and, on each side, widespread arms, with floppy hands. Not that it appeared to be a priest: the figure was wearing neither white nor black, but on

215

the contrary, bright colours, several of them. Though considerably unnerved, Trant went forward, passed the next column in the arcade between the nave and the aisle, and looked again, through the next bay. He saw at once that there was nothing: at least there was only a litter of minor vestments and scripts in coloured bindings.

Trant heard a laugh. He turned. Behind him stood a slender, brown-haired young man in a grey suit.

'Excuse me,' said the young man. 'I saw it myself so don't be frightened.' He spoke quite clearly, but had a vague foreign accent.

'It was terrifying,' said Trant. 'Out of this world.'

'Yes. Out of this world, as you say. Did you notice the hair?'

'I did indeed.' The young man had picked on the very detail which had perturbed Trant the most. 'What did you make of it?'

'Holy, holy, holy,' said the young man in his foreign accent; then smiled and sauntered off westwards. Trant was *almost* sure that this was what he had said. The hair of the illusory figure in the pulpit had, at the time, reminded Trant of the way in which nimbuses are shown in certain old paintings; with wide bars or strips of light linking an outer misty ring with the sacred head. The figure's white hair had seemed to project in just such spikes.

Trant pulled himself together and reached the south transept, hung high with hatchments. He sought out 'Christ among the Doctors'. 'The masterpiece of Frans Pourbus the Elder,' as the guide book remarked, and set himself to identifying the famous people said to be depicted in it, including the Duke of Alva, Vigilius ab Ayatta, and even the Emperor Charles V himself.

In the adjoining chapel, 'The Martyrdom of St Barbara' by De Crayer proved to be covered with a cloth, another irritating continental habit, as Trant had previously discovered. As there seemed to be no one about, Trant lifted a corner of the cloth, which was brown and dusty, like so many things in Belgian cathedrals, and peered beneath. It was difficult to make out very much, especially as the light was so poor.

'Let me help,' said a transatlantic voice at Trant's back. 'Let me take it right off, and then you'll see something, believe me.'

Again it was a young man, but this time a red-haired cheerful looking youth in a green windcheater.

The youth not only removed the cloth, but turned on an electric light.

'Thank you,' said Trant.

'Now have a good look.'

Trant looked. It was an extremely horrible scene. 'Oh boy.'

Trant had no desire to look any longer. 'Thank you all the same,' he said, apologising for his repulsion.

'What a circus those old saints were,' commented the transatlantic youth, as he replaced the worn cloth.

'I suppose they received their reward in heaven,' suggested Trant.

'You bet they did,' said the youth, with a fervour that Trant couldn't quite fathom. He turned off the light. 'Be seeing you.'

'I expect so,' said Trant smiling.

The youth said no more, but put his hands in his pockets, and departed whistling towards the south door. Trant himself would not have cared to whistle so loudly in a foreign church.

As all the world knows, the most important work of art in the Cathedral of St Bavon is the 'Adoration' by the mysterious van Eyck or van Eycks, singular or plural. Nowadays the picture is hung in a small, curtained-off chapel leading from the south choir ambulatory; and most strangers must pay to see it When Trant reached the chapel, he saw the notice at the door, but, hearing nothing, as elsewhere, supposed the place to be empty. Resenting wildly the demand for a fee, as Protestants do, he took the initiative and gently lifted the dark red curtain.

The chapel, though still silent, was not empty at all. On the contrary, it was so full that Trant could have gone no further inside, even had he dared.

There were two kinds of people in the chapel. In front were several rows of men in black. They knelt shoulder to shoulder, heads dropped, hip-bone against hip-bone, in what Trant took to be silent worship. Behind them, packed in even more tightly, was a group, even a small crowd, of funny old Belgian women, fat, ugly, sexless, and bossy, such as Trant had often seen in other places both devotional and secular. The old women were not kneeling, but sitting. All the same, they seemed eerily rapt. Strangest of all was their motionless silence. Trant had seen such groups everywhere in Belgium, but never, never silent, very far from it. Not a single one of this present group seemed even to be aware that he was there: something equally unusual with a people so given to curiosity.

And in this odd setting not the least strange thing was the famous picture itself, with its enigmatic monsters, sybils, and walking allegories, and its curiously bright, other-world colours: a totality doubtless, interpretable in terms of Freud, but, all the same, as dense as an oriental carpet, and older than Adam and Eve, who stand beside. Trant found the picture all too cognate to the disconcerting devotees.

He let fall the curtain and went on his way, distinctly upset.

Two chapels further round, he came upon the 'Virgin Glorified' by Liemakere. Here a choir-boy in a red cassock was polishing the crucifix on the altar. Already, he had thin black hair and a grey, watchful face.

'Onze lieve Vrouw,' said the choir-boy, explaining the picture to Trant.

'Yes,' said Trant. 'Thank you.'

It occurred to him that polishing was odd work for a choir-boy. Perhaps this was not a choir-boy at all, but some other kind of young servitor. The idea of being shortly ejected from the building returned to Trant's mind. He looked at his watch. It had stopped. It still showed 11.28.

Trant shook the watch against his ear, but there were no recovering ticks. He saw that the polishing boy (he was at work on the pierced feet) wore a watch also, on a narrow black strap, Trant gesticulated again. The boy only shook his head more violently. Trant could not decide whether the boy's own watch was broken, or whether, conceivably, he thought that Trant was trying to take it from him. Then, all in seconds, it struck Trant that, whatever else there was about the boy, he certainly did not appear alarmed. Far from it. He seemed as aloof as if he were already a priest, and to be refusing to tell Trant the time on principle; almost implying, as priests presume to do, that he was refusing for the other's good. Trant departed from the chapel containing Liemakere's masterpiece rather quickly.

How much time had he left?

In the next chapel was Rubens's vast altar piece of St Bavon distributing all his goods among the poor.

In the next was the terrifying 'Martyrdom of Saint Livinus' by Seghers.

After one more chapel, Trant had reached the junction of the north transept and the choir. The choir was surrounded by a heavy and impenetrable screen of black marble, like a cage for the imperial lions. The guide book recommended the four tombs of past bishops which were said to be inside; but Trant, peering through the stone bars, could hardly see even outlines. He shifted from end to end of the choir steps seeking a viewpoint where the light might be better. It was useless. In the end, he tried the handle of the choir gate. The gate had given every appearance of being locked, but in fact it opened at once when Trant made the attempt. He tiptoed into the dark enclosure and thought he had better shut the gate behind him. He was not sure that he was going to see very much of the four tombs even now; but there they were, huge boxes flanking the high altar, like dens for the lions.

He stood at the steps of the altar itself leaning across the marble rails, the final barricade, trying to read one of the Latin inscriptions. In such an exercise Trant made it a matter of principle not lightly to admit defeat. He craned his neck and screwed up his eyes until he was half-dazed; capturing the antique words one at a time, and trying to construe them. The matter of the cathedral shutting withdrew temporarily to the back of his mind. Then something horrible seemed to happen; or rather two things, one after the other. Trant thought first that the stone panel he was staring at so hard, seemed somehow to move; and then that a hand had appeared round one upper corner of it. It seemed to Trant a curiously small hand.

Trant decided, almost calmly, to see it out. There must obviously be an explanation, and anything like flight would make him look ridiculous, as well as leaving the mystery unsolved. An explanation there was; the stone opened further, and from within emerged a small, fair-haired child.

'Hullo,' said the child, looking at Trant across the black marble barrier and smiling.

'Hullo,' said Trant. 'You speak very good English.'

'I *am* English,' said the child. It was wearing a dark brown garment open at the neck, and dark brown trousers, but Trant could not quite decide whether it was a boy or a girl. From the escapade a boy seemed likelier, but there was something about the child which was more like a girl, Trant thought.

'Should you have been in there?'

'I always go in.'

'Aren't you afraid?'

'No one could be afraid of Bishop Triest. He gave us those candlesticks.' The child pointed to four tall copper objects, which seemed to Trant to offer no particular confirmation of the child's logic.

'Would *you* like to go in?' enquired the child politely.

'No, thank you,' said Trant.

'Then I'll just shut up.' The child heaved the big stone slab into place. It was a feat of strength all the more remarkable in that Trant noticed that the child seemed to limp.

'Do you live here?' asked Trant.

'Yes,' said the child, and, child-like, said no more.

It limped forward, climbed the altar rail, and stood beside Trant, looking up at him. Trant found it difficult to assess how old it was.

'Would you like to see one of the other bishops?'

'No thank you,' said Trant.

'I think you ought to see a bishop,' said the child quite gravely.

'I'd rather not,' said Trant smiling.

'There may not be another chance.'

'I expect not,' said Trant, still smiling. He felt it was best to converse with the child at its own level, and make no attempt at adult standards of flat questioning and conventionalised reference.

'Then I'll take you to the crypt,' said the child.

The crypt was the concluding item in the guide book. Entered from just by the north-western corner of the choir, it was, like the 'Adoration', a speciality, involving payment. Trant had rather assumed that he would not get round to it.

'Shall I have time?' he asked, looking instinctively at his stopped watch, still showing 11.28.

'Yes,' said the child, as before.

The child limped ahead, opened the choir-gate and held it for Trant, his inscriptions unread, to pass through. The child closed the gate, and led the way to the crypt entry, looking over its shoulder to see that Trant was following. In the rather better light outside the choir, Trant saw that its hair was a wonderful mass of silky gold; its face almost white, with the promise of fine bones; its lips unusually red.

'This is called the crossing,' said the child informatively. Trant knew that the term was sometimes applied to the inter-section of nave and transepts.

'Or the narthex, I believe,' he said, plunging in order to show who was the grown-up.

The child, not unnaturally, looked merely puzzled.

There was still no one else visible in the cathedral.

They began to descend the crypt stairs, the child holding on to the iron handrail because of its infirmity. There was a table at the top, obviously for the collection of the fee, but deserted. Trant did not feel called upon to comment.

In the crypt, slightly to his surprise, many of the lights were on. Probably the custodian had forgotten to turn them off when he or she had hurried forth to eat.

The guide book described the crypt as 'large', but it was much larger than Trant had expected. The stairs entered at one corner, and columns seemed to stretch away like trees into the distance. They were built in stones of different colours, maroon, purple, green, grey, gold; and they often bore remains of paint-ing as well, which also spread over areas of the vaulted stone roof and weighty walls. In the soft patchy light, the place was mysterious and beautiful; and all the more so because the whole area could not be seen simultaneously. With the tide of centuries the stone-paved floor had become rolling and uneven, but agreeably so. There were occasional showcases and objects on pedestals, and there was a gentle perfume of incense. As Trant entered, all was silence. He even felt for a moment that there was something queer about the silence; that only sounds of another realm moved in it, and that the noises of this world, of his own arrival for example, were in a different dimension and irrelevant. He stood, a little awed, and listened for a moment to the nothingness.

The child stood too, or rather rested against a pillar. It was smiling again, though very slightly. Perhaps it smiled like this all the time, as if always happy.

Trant thought more than ever that it might be a girl. By this time it was rather absurd not to be sure, but by this time it was more than before difficult to ask.

'Bishop Triest's clothes,' said the child, pointing. They were heavy vestments, hanging, enormously embroidered, in a glass cabinet.

'Saint Livinus's ornament,' said the child, and crossed itself. Trant did not know quite what to make of the ornament.

'Animals,' said the child. It was an early book of natural history written by a monk, and even the opened page showed some very strange ones.

The child was now beginning positively to dart about in its eagerness, pointing out item after item.

'Shrine of Saint Maracarius,' said the child, not crossing itself, presumably because the relic was absent.

'Abbot Hughenois's clothes.' They were vestments again, and very like Triest's vestments, Trant thought.

'What's that?' asked Trant, taking the initiative and point-ing. Right on the other side of the crypt, as it seemed, and now visible to Trant for the first time through the forest of coloured columns, was something which appeared to be winking and gleaming with light.

'That's at the end,' replied the child. 'You'll be there soon.'

Soon indeed, at this hour, thought Trant: if in fact we're not thrown out first.

'Via Dolorosa,' said the child, pointing to a picture. It was a gruesome scene, painted very realistically, as if the artist had been a bystander at the time; and it was followed by another which was even more gruesome and at least equally realistic.

'Calvary,' explained the child.

They rounded a corner with the stone wall on the left, the forest of columns on the right. The two parts of a diptych came into view, of which Trant had before seen only the discoloured reverse.

'The blessed and the lost,' said the child, indicating, super-fluously, which was which.

Trant thought that the pictures and frescoes were becoming more and more morbid, but supposed that this feeling was probably the result of their cumulative impact. In any case, there could not be much more.

But there were still many things to be seen. In due course they came to a group of pictures hanging together.

'The sacrifice of three blessed martyrs,' said the child. Each of the martyrs had died in a different way: by roasting on a very elaborate gridiron; by disembowelling; and by some process involving a huge wheel. The painting, unlike some of the others, was extraordinarily well preserved. The third of the martyrs was a young woman. She had been martyred naked and was of great and still living beauty. Next to her hung a further small picture,

224

showing a saint carrying his own skin. Among the columns to the right, was an enormous black cross. At a little distance, the impaled figure looked lifelike in the extreme.

The child was still skipping in front, making so light of its disability that Trant could not but be touched. They turned another corner. At the end of the ambulatory ahead was the gleaming, flashing object that Trant had noticed from the other side of the crypt. The child almost ran on, ignoring the intervening sights, and stood by the object, waiting for Trant to catch up. The child's head was sunk, but Trant could see that it was looking at him from under its fair, silky eyelashes.

This time the child said nothing, and Trant could only stare.

The object was a very elaborate, jewelled reliquary of the Renaissance. It was presumably the jewels which had seemed to give off the flashing lights, because Trant could see no lights now. At the centre of the reliquary was a transparent vertical tube or cylinder. It was only about an inch high, and probably made of crystal. Just visible inside it was a black thread, almost like the mercury in a minute thermometer; and at the bottom of the tube was, Trant noticed, a marked discolouration.

The child was still standing in the same odd position; now glancing sideways at Trant, now glancing away. It was perhaps smiling a little more broadly, but its head was sunk so low that Trant could not really see. Its whole posture and behaviour suggested that there was something about the reliquary which Trant should be able to see for himself. It was almost as if the child were timing him, to see how long he took.

Time, thought Trant, yet again; and now with a start. The reliquary was so fascinating that he had managed somehow almost to forget about time. He looked away and along the final ambulatory, which ran to the foot of the staircase by which he had come down. While he had been examining the reliquary, someone else had appeared in the crypt. A man stood in the centre of the passage, a short distance away from Trant. Or not exactly a man: it was, Trant realised, the acolyte in the red cassock, the boy who had been polishing the brass feet. Trant had no doubt that he had come to hurry him out.

Trant bustled off, full of unreasonable guilt, without ever properly thanking his child guide. But when he reached the boy in the cassock, the boy stretched out his arms to their full length and seemed, on the contrary, to bar his passage.

It was rather absurd; and especially as one could so readily turn right and weave a way out through the Gothic columns.

Trant, in fact, turned his head in that direction, simply upon instinct. But in the bay to his right, stood the youth from across the Atlantic in the green windcheater. He had the strangest of expressions (unlike the boy in the cassock, who seemed the same dull peasant as before); and as soon as Trant caught his eye, he too raised his arms to their full extent, as the boy had done.

There was still one more free bay. Trant retreated a step or two, but then saw among the shadows within (which seemed to be deepening) the man in the grey suit with the vague foreign accent. His arms were going up even as Trant sighted him, but when their eyes met (though Trant could not see his face very well) he did something the others had not done. He laughed.

And in the entrance to the other ambulatory, through which Trant had just come and down which the child had almost run, bravely casting aside its affliction, stood that same child, now gazing upwards again and indeed looking quite radiant, as it spread its arms almost as a bird taking flight.

Trant heard the great clock of the Cathedral strike twelve. In the crypt, the tone of the bell was lost: there was little more to be distinguished than twelve great thuds, almost as if cannon were being discharged. The twelve strokes of the hour took a surprisingly long time to complete.

In the meantime, and just beside the reliquary, a small door had opened, in the very angle of the crypt. Above it was a small but exquisite and well preserved alabaster keystone showing a soul being dragged away on a hook by a demon. Trant had hardly noticed the door before, as people commonly overlook the working details of a place which is on show, the same details that those who work the place look to first.

In the door, quite filling it, was the man Trant had believed himself to have seen in the pulpit soon after he had first entered the great building. The man looked much bigger now, but there was the same bald head, the same resigned hands, the same multicoloured garments. It was undoubtedly the very person, but in some way enlarged or magnified; and the curious fringe of hair seemed more luminous than ever.

'The cathedral closes now,' said the man. 'Follow me.'

The fair figures encircling Trant began to shut in on him until their extended finger-tips were almost touching.

His questions went quite unanswered, his protests quite unheard; especially after everyone started singing.

INTO THE WOOD

> At night those unfortunates who suffered from insomnia
> or nightmare used to wander about in the fields or the
> woods, trying to reach a pitch of exhaustion that would
> give them back the power of sleep. Among the afflicted
> creatures were people from the upper classes, well-
> educated women—why, there was even a parish priest!
>
> *August Strindberg* ('*Inferno*')

THESE AREAS ARE not uncommon if you know how (or are
compelled) to look for them. As men and women work more
and more against nature, nature works more and more against
men and women. All the same, a few of the areas are of long
acceptance; dating back to the earliest memory of man, as the
international lawyers put it. Some of them, in the beginning,
were probably holy places of the pre-Christians; of whom a few
even now survive on our continent, if, once more, you know
how (or are driven) to look for them. Sometimes one is amazed
to discover how little that is real or true ever finds its way into
general knowledge: in so far, of course, as general knowledge is
still an expression with meaning.

'Harry and Molly Sawyer' was what they had printed on their
Christmas Cards; with an address in a Cheshire town that was

hardly a town any more, but a sprawling and sleeping area for Manchester. Harry Sawyer's business card indicated that he was an 'Earth Mover', though when one met him he seemed to have neither the back muscles of Atlas nor the mental leverage of Archimedes, nor yet the power to shake the world of Marx or Hitler; and when one saw his yellow, space-fiction machines on the move, each with SAWYER painted in black capitals on all four sides, each able to pulp a platoon of soldiers at a swing of the beam, one wondered how long he could possibly hope to keep them under control.

Margaret Sawyer saw as little of the yellow monsters as she could, and, with the other well-to-do Manchester wives, strove for domestic realisation among an ever-growing assembly of lesser monsters, all whirring, spinning, and chopping, in kitchen, washroom, and lounge. Among other things, the gadgets ('gad-flies', she once thought) were supposed to give her more time for her children, two girls and a boy; but it seldom worked that way. Margaret could hardly hope to be happier than the other Manchester wives; but until one night in Sweden, she would have rejected the idea that she was positively unhappy. Nor was she: until that night she was insufficiently grown for happiness or unhappiness; might well have been among those who express doubt as to whether the words mean very much.

Sawyer had to visit Sovastad, on the eastern side of central Sweden; where a big, wide, dangerous, costly road was being built across the mountains into Norway. As he would have to stay there at least a week, the Swedes, hospitable as ever, had suggested that he bring Margaret with him. Those of the Swed-ish wives who were not pursuing careers of their own, would be able to look after her during the day, and see that she had a good time. Margaret had acquiesced: one could not use a stronger word.

And so, on the whole, it had worked out. Margaret had never been so thoroughly and efficiently looked after in all her previous life; never had so concentrated a good time. There was a high-powered, unflagging, day-and-night cordiality among the richer Swedes, to which she was totally unaccustomed, and which by the end of the week, she found very exhausting, though she would have hesitated to say so, even to herself, because, back in Cheshire, she had supposed it to be the very thing she wanted. Harry also grew quieter and quieter. He admitted to her that he found Swedish businessmen and business methods very hard going. 'Particularly the younger men,' he said. 'They're so keen and sharp, they take the skin off your hands, and then they turn round and deliver a lecture about British Imperialism and what's wrong with our hospitals. You can't tell where you stand at all.'

Nor, despite the social whirlwind, did Margaret find Sovastad a jocund town. It straggled along the shore of a vast, black lake, described as one of the biggest not only in Sweden but in Europe; and the high mountains to the west cut off the sun halfway through the day, darkened the streets, and made the water look like tar. The lake was said to be so deep as never to have been fathomed, and, as often in such cases, to harbour a creature of enormous bulk, terrifying aspect, species unknown to zoology, and origin unknown to all. There were many representations of this beast in the conscientious provincial museum, round which Margaret was conscientiously conducted by three Swedish ladies, all better dressed than she was and better preserved also, all erudite about the exhibits, in a manner unimaginable in Manchester. In late medieval woodcuts, the creature appeared with protuberant eyes, a forked tongue, and a thick circle of whiskers like seaweed. In eighteenth-century guides to natural philosophy, it had quietened down into the likeness of a baroque ceiling embellishment. A century later, with the advance of the scientific attitude, the most barbaric devices had been constructed by the locals to trap and kill it. They were all faithfully exhibited, and the Swedish ladies explained in detail how they would have worked. Margaret was glad that there had been no occasion.

'So the creature's still in the lake?' she asked. She could not pronounce the Swedish name for the monster.

'The children think so,' replied the Swedish ladies.

The lake was, in fact, named after it, they explained: 'Lake Orm', meaning 'serpent'. It was one of the few Swedish words Margaret felt able more or less to manage. The high tessitura in which the language is spoken, the combination of breadth and altitude in the vowel sounds, were quite beyond her. All the same, a guidebook to the district which she came upon later, said that the name of the lake originated merely in its serpentine periphery, with long arms reaching into the mountains like tentacles.

Sovastad, Margaret decided, was a little too small for its pretensions. The Swedes made the very most of every urban feature, designing them splendidly, using them fully, but the population was not big enough to prevent the rocks struggling through in almost every street and prospect, and determining the prevailing ethos. By half past three in the afternoon, the feeling would set in that this was a community almost as involved in a ceaseless struggle with harsh natural forces as a colony of Esquimaux. There was every amenity, but they were a little like the comforts of an air force base with a bitter war on its hands. Not that Margaret could think of any better adaptation to the forbidding rocks and endless winter, to which much reference was made, jocular but surprisingly grim also. Beyond doubt, the Swedes had done wonders, but a feeling of strain was pervasive. Perhaps only a newcomer, a visitor from abroad, would be aware of it.

At the same time, there was always in Sovastad a faint mistiness, a clammy softness; or, when the sun was striking directly down, an expectation of it. It too seemed to pervade the communal life; in the hectic quality of which was something almost Russian. When the sun did strike, the faint, vague mist seemed to make it still hotter. Then, very quickly, the high mountains would cut off the radiance, and within a quarter of an hour, Margaret would feel as chilled as previously she had felt warmed. She would have liked to wear trousers, but Henry implied that it would diminish their status, already none too secure. When Margaret pointed out how many of the Swedish women wore them, he inevitably replied that this was one of the very reasons why she shouldn't.

Henry's attitude, and the possibility of consequent dissension between them, was the main reason, as far as Margaret was concerned, for their going on Sunday for a drive through the mountains by car, instead of for a trek on foot, which the Swedes had suggested in the first place. She could hardly, she felt, go mountaineering in a two-piece from Kendall, Milnes and frail, almost cocktail-time shoes; especially when so many continentals tended to adopt near-battledress for even an afternoon walk. The Swedes would laugh at her, and, however she dealt with the situation, Henry would sulk. It was remarkable how deeply men seemed to feel such things when their attitude to the whole question of clothes was almost always so entirely negative.

Therefore they went, six of them, by car, higher and higher, along roads very unlike the one which Henry was building to a scale that was not human. The conifers that cover so much of Sweden, the pools, quagmires, and small lakes that occupy so much of the land area, were sad, and, at the same time, slightly mysterious and equivocal, but Margaret became aware of a spell in the very monotony, even though she was seated in the back of the big Volvo with a married couple eager that she miss absolutely nothing. The spell lay perhaps in the monotony and the boundlessness combined: already she had seen much landscape like this on the way up from Stockholm, she knew that it extended all the way northwards to the commencement of the tundra, and she had become aware how different are Swedish distances from their aspect in the ordinary school atlas. There were no footpaths through the trees, such as still survive through most woodlands in England; no tracks; no apparent access to the woods at all except by struggle. It was not so much that these millions of conifers would be likely to conceal a huge, lost city or a race of pygmies, but rather that they might of themselves generate and diffuse forces quite outside their arboricultural aspects, forces which one might have to tramp far and long to sense, because it might take much time and distance to disengage oneself sufficiently from machines like Henry's, from life like that in the Cheshire subtopia.

They reached a high place. The car stopped and they got out. 'Don't leave the road,' said the Swedes. 'You'll sink above your ankles.' Margaret thought it was an exaggeration, but it was still odd that women were required to array themselves primarily as erotic objects, even on the most unsuitable occasions, even when they had passed forty, even when the last thing that men like Henry seemed to think of was eroticism, anyway where his wife was concerned. Moreover, there was a wind blowing with a filter of ice behind it, to which Margaret was unaccustomed in England.

Still she gazed around, conscious of the spell. From this height, there were dark green trees to the edges of the earth.

Directly below, like a big, irregular rent in the greenery, spread the Orm, all of it visible at once; the square miles of black pool beside which stood the puny town; the winding, octopus arms stretching towards her. Sovastad looked like a cluster of limpets on the hard rock; or like the first town that men had built. The line of the new road made another tear in the woodlands, but outside Sovastad there was hardly a building to be seen in the entire panorama.

When, however, in a few steps they reached the top of the ridge, with a similar vast expanse of green to the west, Margaret saw that on this side a single structure rose fairly near at hand from the trees on the westward side of the mountains. It was a sizeable, wooden edifice, painted white, and with a slate roof.

'Who lives there?' asked Margaret, making conversation.

'It is the Kurhus. A sanatorium,' said one of the Swedish wives.

'It is not only for the sick,' explained the other Swedish wife. 'It is a place where people stay, but where there is treatment too, if you want it.'

'What you call a rest cure,' added one of the Swedish husbands.

From what Margaret had seen of Swedish life, she was not surprised.

'It has fallen out of fashion,' observed the second Swedish husband. 'People have no time for rest cures today.'

'Your country has the reputation of having more welfare than anywhere else,' Margaret could not help observing.

'Welfare is not rest,' replied the Swede; speaking quite severely.

'The Kurhus would do better to move with the times and become a motel,' said the other Swede. 'Businessmen today often prefer to sleep outside the city, provided there is a good road.'

'It must have a wonderful view, and the afternoon sun and the sunset too,' remarked Margaret. In Sovastad, there were no sunsets.

'That is true,' said one of the Swedish women seriously. 'The Kurhus sees the sinking sun. It is appropriate.'

No more was said on the subject, but, after they had gone for a little walk along the ridge (Margaret would gladly have continued much further), they drove a short distance along the western flank of the mountain before returning to Sovastad, and actually passed the Kurhus portal. Flowers hung from baskets and a number of people were sitting about at tables on a terrace. To Margaret, it did not look in the least out of fashion or unsuccessful. Indeed, she liked the look of it very much: especially the contrast between the small but elegant sophistications of decor and the immense wild prospect extending north, south, and west under the warm sun. The new road had not yet reached this side of the mountains, and Margaret had no idea whether it ever would. Since they had come to Sweden, Henry seemed to experience such difficulty in holding on to the various rights and duties of his position that he had never found breathing-space to go into such geographical particulars with her.

Two days later, in fact, things rose to a crisis. In the middle of the morning, Henry routed Margaret out of a Konditori, where she was consuming successive cups of excellent but expensive coffee, and told her that he would have to go back for the next two nights to Stockholm, and that their departure for England would have to be postponed until at least two days after that. 'I shall be obliged to come back here again, dammit,' said Henry. 'I must make sure that they really understand what Stockholm has decided.'

'What a pest for you!' said Margaret.

'Will you come to Stockholm with me, or would you prefer to stay here till I come back? I'm sure the Larssons and the Falkenbergs will give you a good time.'

'I don't want much more good time just for the present. May I go and stay at the Kurhus?'

Henry looked doubtful. 'They said it wasn't up to much.'

'That might mean it's quiet. Of course, I mustn't keep the room in the hotel here at the same time, but I'm sure you can arrange something.'

'Never mind about that,' said Henry generously. 'If you want a change, of course you must have it.'

'If you're not going to be here,' said Margaret, 'I want some more of the sun. If you'll tell me when you'll be back, I'll be here again waiting for you.'

'A completely new girl,' said Henry, and kissed her.

At the Kurhus next midday, Margaret was given the most beautiful room: large, with a view from the windows extending for miles, charmingly furnished, and with no fewer than three long rows of assorted books in at least four languages. Margaret, who read books, looked at this small library with considerable curiosity. As far as she could tell, the volumes seemed even to have been chosen with care, and to be by no means mere left-behinds or the bedtime reading one might expect—if one could in an hotel expect anything of that kind at all. But immediately it had occurred to Margaret that these were not books of the sort that most people would read to induce slumber, she observed that the next work on the shelf was a substantial tome named *Die Schlaflosigkeit*, which she suspected might mean 'Insomnia'. She put it back in a hurry. Margaret made a point of sleeping like a top and believed that insomnia was largely a matter of suggestion. She wanted to know nothing about it. The next book was Daudet's *Sapho*. If she had been there to improve her French instead of to have a rest, that might have been well worth struggling with.

After she had said goodbye to Henry, and before leaving Sovastad, Margaret had braved the language barrier in order to buy herself a pair of sober green trousers, dark as the conifers; a coffee-coloured shirt, a lighter green anorak, and a pair of tough shoes. Into this costume she now changed. Probably she was too old for it, at least by British standards; but she intended her standard, for these two days, to be that of the woods and rocks and mountains, rather than that of the neighbours at home. Feeling almost a girl again, she fell on the huge double bed and, splaying out her legs, wrote a joyful postcard to each of her three children at their respective boarding schools. Then, to her intense surprise, she found that in the full flood of the mountain sun she was falling uncontrollably asleep.

When she woke up, she had, to say the least of it, missed luncheon. It was really rather queer. She had slept the night before, as long and as well as she always did, even though in the next bed Henry had probably tossed and turned as usual. She could not remember when last she had fallen asleep in the middle of the day: hardly, she thought, since she had been made to have a daily rest as a child. As far as she could recall, she had not dreamed. It was simply as if two hours or more of her proper life had been stolen from her, arbitrarily cancelled. 'It's the relaxation,' she thought; not quite daring to think, 'It's the relief' . . . 'It's the beautiful big bed.' (Henry always insisted on single beds, because he slept so badly; and it was a long time since she had slept in—or even on—anything else.) 'It's my new clothes' . . . 'It's the sun, the mountain air.'

She was not exactly hungry, but felt that if she didn't eat *something* at this accustomed hour, she would regret it. Also she had to buy some stamps. She drew up the zip of her anorak, arranged her shirt collar outside it, put on some lipstick, and descended, feeling strange in every way, but not unpleasantly so. Architecturally, the hotel really was rather fine in its period manner: a wide staircase, with brass wood-nymphs holding up the baluster, wood-nymphs that were half trees; a square hall with tall, thin, Gothic windows, and more wood-nymphs in the stained glass.

From experience of other continental hotels, Margaret had rather expected that someone would enquire solicitously, or pester (according as one saw it), about her lunch—for which she (or Henry) would be, in any case, paying, in accordance with Henry's usual rule. But no one did. In fact, there was no one about at all; not even behind the hotel desk. Nor was there a sound; not even of birds without. The big front door stood wide open and the hall was like a temple into which sunlight streamed through every aperture, strewing the stained glass nymphs across the white-tiled floor. Margaret reflected that even if she had been set on lunch, she would hardly have got it. At the thought, she felt quite empty.

She imagined that people would be sitting about on the terrace, as she had seen them when she had driven past; but there proved to be no one. She stood by the balustrade, enthralled, though a little oppressed also, by the immensity of sunlit green. The sun was almost directly overhead and really hot. Margaret took off her anorak, and sat down on one of the brightly-coloured terrace chairs, uncertain what to do next. She noticed that almost every window in the hotel seemed to be wide open; possibly a consequence of the hotel's sanatorium function. She noticed also that below the terrace on this side, the opposite side from the road (itself a minor one), ran a path. It emerged from the woodland on her right and entered the woodland on her left.

For some reason, it made her think of the track along which the figures pass when a medieval cathedral clock strikes the hour. She expected to see a red-eyed dragon emerge from one of the green tunnels, with a jewelled St George in pursuit; and disappear into the other tunnel, eternally unconquered, though hourly beset. Or perhaps it might be a procession of twelve wise virgins; or of six pilgrims and six temptations. She herself sat at a higher level, observant of all, like the Madonna. It was along tracks such as the one below that all creation ran from darkness to darkness, everything from the stars to the rabbits in the corner of an altarpiece; until Copernicus, and Kepler, and Brahe, and Galileo began upsetting things. One of the hospitable Swedes had shown her a big illustrated book about Brahe, translating all the captions into better English than the English speak. The Swedish family had not appeared to doubt that Brahe and his kind were advantageous.

Out of the forest, as Margaret sat in the hot sun, came not St George, but a bustling grey-haired woman in a red dress and carrying illustrated papers. Obviously a hotel resident, she ascended the steps to the terrace.

'Good afternoon,' she said to Margaret, staring at her clothes. 'You are a newcomer.' The woman could not have been anything but a lady from England. 'It is unfortunate that I cannot in all honesty wish you a happy stay.' Margaret supposed that she was a trifle eccentric, as the English abroad are so often said to be.

'I'm only here for two nights,' she said smiling.

'Really!' exclaimed the English lady, apparently much surprised. 'A casual. We get very few casuals nowadays. So much the worse, perhaps. But it's connected with changing tastes.

There's nothing to do here, you know. Absolutely nothing. What made you come here?'

'I drove past with some Swedish friends and liked the look of it.'

'A pity your Swedish friends didn't tell you that this is not an ordinary hotel. Some of them must have known perfectly well. Most people in Sweden know, and a good many elsewhere too.' She was standing with her hand on the back of the chair on the other side of the table from the chair on which Margaret was seated.

'But my friends did tell me,' said Margaret patiently. 'They warned me it was partly a sanatorium. As a matter of fact, they more or less advised me against coming here. I just didn't think their reasons were very good. As far as I was concerned anyway. I wanted the sun and I wanted not to have to wear my best clothes all the time. That was all. I wanted a rest. For two days, you know.'

'I see,' said the English lady.

'But won't you sit down?'

'Thank you,' said the English lady. 'I had better introduce myself. I am Sandy Slater. At least that is what I have always been called. No one has ever called me Alexandra. *Mrs* Slater, by the way; though my marriage was little more than a formality. I was born a Brock-Vere.'

'I am Margaret Sawyer. I have usually been called Molly, but I like it less than I did. Mrs, too. My husband is concerned with building the new road.'

'I understand that the new road will make little difference to the Jamblichus Kurhus. The authorities have taken care to keep us at a distance.'

'Is that a good thing? I imagine that the owners mightn't think so. One of my Swedish friends actually said that the

Kurhus ought to go in more for attracting motorists.'

'He must have been a very ignorant man,' said Mrs Slater firmly. 'I notice that many of the Swedes are nowadays. If you will forgive my saying so about a friend of yours.'

'Oh, that's all right,' said Margaret. 'They're friends of my husband's really. Or not even that. More business acquaintances. Not that they haven't been very kind to us. They've been quite fantastic. Though that reminds me,' she continued. 'For some reason I fell asleep almost immediately I arrived here, which is something I never normally do, and in consequence I missed lunch, though it seems a silly thing to say. I'm beginning to feel rather hungry. Is it possible to attract some service?'

'Not until four o'clock,' said Mrs Slater.

'But it's not yet three!' exclaimed Margaret. 'This is as bad as England. I shall be *paying* for lunch too, or at least my husband will. He *will* book everything, though I should often prefer to be less tied down.'

'Clearly,' said Mrs Slater in a calm voice, 'you have no idea what this place is. Why do you suppose it is called the *Jamblichus* Kurhus?'

'I didn't know it was until you just mentioned it. It doesn't seem to be put up anywhere. I suppose he was some nineteenth-century German doctor who invented a patent treatment? So many of them seem to have done it.'

'Jamblichus was the one among the seven sleepers who after they had slept for two centuries, went down into the town in order to buy food, tendered the obsolete coins, and found himself arrested. Don't you remember your Gibbon?' enquired Mrs Slater, even more unexpectedly.

'You mean the *Decline and Fall*? I'm afraid I've never had time for it. I have three children to look after, you know.'

Mrs Slater gazed at her. 'It's different here,' she said

241

weightily. 'But I knew about Jamblichus before I came here. He's the only one of the seven sleepers whom most people can name. Anyway, places like this used often to be called Jamblichus Groves; even by the unsophisticated. This, my dear Mrs Sawyer (how odd that our husbands' names should be so alike), is an establishment for insomniacs. One can hardly call it an hotel, because hotels are primarily places to sleep in. Still less can one call it a cure, because there is no cure.'

'I noticed a book in my room—' began Margaret, then reflected. 'How terrible! Do you mean that you suffer from it?'

'Not as badly as some—including some who are here. I usually get a few hours in the course of a week. Some of the people here haven't slept for years.'

'But that's impossible!' cried Margaret. She recollected herself. 'But you mean that they haven't slept *regularly* for years?'

'I mean that for years they have not slept at all. Not at all. Never.' Mrs Slater seemed still to be speaking quite calmly.

'But surely,' enquired Margaret timidly, 'surely you can't *live* without *any* sleep?'

'You can,' replied Mrs Slater. 'In a way. You can live here.'

'What is there special about here, and why do people who have difficulty in sleeping have to live with other people who have difficulty in sleeping? I know very little about it, I'm afraid, because I seem always to have slept rather well, but I should have thought that living all together would be the very worst thing for them.'

'When the trouble passes a certain point—a point far short of never sleeping at all, I assure you—the victim is driven out. Sleepers cannot live for long with an insomniac. It is like living with something supernatural: people who are normal, come to feel it as a shadow on their own lives. And they come to feel it quite soon. I speak from knowledge. I told you that my marriage was little more than a formality. I am sure you thought that I was born to be an old maid, as so many Englishwomen are, in spite of all the pretences and defences. Whether I am one of that kind or not, it was my inability to sleep that ended my marriage. Marriage—anyway the usual kind of marriage—is one of the things that insomnia makes impossible. One of the many and important things.'

'I suppose I can imagine that,' said Margaret, 'or begin to imagine. But I still find it unbelievable. I'm glad to say I've always been a good sleeper myself—though, as a matter of fact, always a little afraid of not being—yet I've naturally known people who aren't. It's awful for them, as I quite see, but it doesn't have to be quite as bad as you say. I'm sure it doesn't.'

'That is the usual reaction,' replied Mrs Slater, still quite calmly. 'At least, the usual first reaction. The answer is that the people you have known aren't real insomniacs at all. They are just people who from time to time have difficulty in sleeping as much as they would like to, or think they ought to. It may be a matter of personal psychology, or temporary stress, or even digestion. But, in the very great majority of such cases, it is simply a matter of the person not really needing anything like as much sleep as he supposes—or, more usually, wants. People *want* sleep, just as they want love, or want what they call distractions, or even want death. In purely biological terms, most people sleep far more than they need to. Twice as much, or even more.'

Margaret felt that she herself was incriminated by her admissions and by Mrs Slater's didactic stare.

'The quantity of sleep required to eliminate the poisons from the blood stream is much less than people like to think,' continued Mrs Slater. She broke off. 'You do *know* that that is the physiological function of sleep?' she asked.

'I think I learnt it at school,' said Margaret, caring less and less for the conversation, feeling more and more aware of a threat, but unable to stop listening, or even asking, however empty her inside.

'As I say, much less sleep is required physiologically than people choose to think. In fact, it is perfectly possible to eliminate the poisons without sleeping at all. Some people, a few people, are built like that.'

Margaret, secure in her steady sleepiness and in all it stood for, had given so little conscious thought to the biology of it that she was in no position to argue.

'That,' said Mrs Slater, 'is the plight of the true insomniac. He is one who has little need for sleep at any time; or none.'

'I suppose there might be certain *advantages*,' said Margaret.

'That is often the second reaction,' said Mrs Slater. 'There are no advantages; or at least not by the standard of the world outside. The man or woman who in the true sense cannot sleep is a kind of troll, as they call it here. Life is so made that without sleep only a troll can endure it. The sleepers have no alternative to driving us out.'

'I've heard the word, but I've never quite known what a troll is.'

'Those who are kept out. The unearthly and mysterious, as people say,' replied Mrs Slater. She seemed to speak with some slight relish.

'Is lack of sleep as disastrous as *that*?'

'Even the most normal people teeter all their lives along a narrow line between good and evil; between impulse and judgement, as we may say. Sleep does two things for the normal person. It gives him constant, long periods of respite from the conflict. It also enables his impulses to find a certain fulfilment

244

in dreams, especially his most lawless impulses. You doubtless have dreams of that kind, Mrs Sawyer?'

'Sometimes,' said Margaret.

'Think for yourself what life must be like for one who has neither dreams nor tranquillity. Such a life is unendurable, and those condemned to it must become trolls, as I just said.'

Margaret produced a packet of cigarettes from the pocket of her trousers and offered one to Mrs Slater.

'No thank you,' said Mrs Slater. 'When we cannot sleep, the narcotics soon cease to have power over us. All of us here have to live with reality for twenty-four hours out of twenty-four . . . This is not a place for a holiday, Mrs Sawyer; still less for a rest. None the less, I so much hope you won't go.'

The smoke from Margaret's cigarette rose perpendicularly in the still, warm air. Through it, she had been quietly inspecting the aspect of Mrs Slater. Margaret could see neither horns nor tip of tail, neither exceptional wrinkles nor even unusually tragic eyes. Mrs Slater's eyes were not happy eyes, but her total appearance, eyes included, was unreservedly typical of her age, type, and station. She might have been the Acting Vice-Chairman of a Women's Institute in East Sussex.

'What is everyone doing now?' Margaret asked.

'They are resting,' said Mrs Slater. 'At night the insomniac is at his most active. No kind of repose is possible. But much rest is needed when you do not sleep, however hard it is to find. In the afternoon most of us can at least stop moving about. Some persuade themselves that this cessation of movement even amounts to a kind of sleep.'

'What about you?' asked Margaret. 'I'm not keeping you from your rest, am I?'

'No, Mrs Sawyer. I was restless this afternoon in any case. In so far as the idea of rest has any meaning for people like me, I have been restless all day.' Whatever Mrs Slater's plight, Margaret was, among other things, beginning to find her continuous self-pity as jarring as her paradoxes were unconvincing. She had noticed before that a person's troubles, the pity the person has for those troubles, and the pity a second person feels for the first person, are all independent from one another. 'Perhaps I have been restless today,' continued Mrs Slater, 'because I knew that a stranger was coming.'

'I shouldn't think that's very likely,' said Margaret.

'Many of us here acquire such foresight,' said Mrs Slater. 'It is likely that we should, when you think about it. It's another of the reasons why people dislike and fear us, and drive us out. All the same they're not above sneaking back to us when they're in trouble themselves. They creep back during the night in search of our guidance. I have always thought that the Witch of Endor was one of us.'

While Mrs Slater had been speaking, an elderly couple had come out of the building and sat down in silence at a table on the other side of the terrace. They were followed almost immediately by another similar couple, who seated themselves at the next table but one to that occupied by Margaret and Mrs Slater.

Margaret could not help asking a question.

'These couples . . . Are *both* of them sufferers?'

'Yes,' replied Mrs Slater; 'but they are not couples in the usual sense.' She spoke in a lowered voice, as if she had been intercepted in the drawing room of a private hotel at Eastbourne. 'They are merely unhappy people who have found another unhappy person. Most of us remain alone. It makes little difference really. Though now, of course, Mrs Sawyer, *I* have found *you*.' Mrs Slater did not smile. Margaret wondered whether it would have been any better if she had smiled.

'Even to a lost soul like me, it still means something to find another English gentlewoman.' Mrs Slater glanced again at Margaret's somewhat ungentlewomanly costume. 'Most of the people here are, naturally, foreigners; people with whom one has merely this one, dreadful thing in common. The only other English at the moment are two very old women, so old that they are both more than a little dotty. As soon as it is four o'clock, you and I must have tea together, Mrs Sawyer.'

A young man in a black suit and wearing a black tie, had appeared; and then a dark, swarthy woman, who looked like a middle-aged stage gypsy. They had each taken up a table, so that five tables were now occupied, but in the manner of a continental café, there were still many more tables that were empty. Margaret noticed that none of the residents greeted any of the others—or, for that matter, acknowledged her own arrival. They all sat quite silent, and, it seemed to Margaret, almost motionless; though ideas of that sort, she at once reflected, were probably morbidity on her part.

'Thank you very much,' said Margaret to Mrs Slater. 'If you'll forgive me, I must first go and wash.' She rose and picked up her anorak.

'As you wish,' said Mrs Slater, in her tiresomely resigned way. 'I shall sit here and wait for you. It will be nice to talk about the London shops, which I shall never see again.'

'Actually, I live near Manchester.' It was doubtless silly to be unkind, but, whatever happened, Margaret did not intend her friendship with Mrs Slater to ripen.

Coming down the Kurhus steps was a girl who looked hardly more than a child. She was tiny and slender, with very pale, fair hair, hanging to her shoulders. She wore the simplest possible white cotton dress, without sleeves, and showing almost no figure. Her legs were bare, but white sandals were on her feet. As she descended, her eyes met Margaret's. They were exceedingly blue eyes, but singularly lifeless; more like screens than like pools. Margaret would have expected sleeplessness to manifest most of all in the eyes, but these were the first unusual eyes she had seen in the Kurhus, and it was inconceivable that this very young girl could be among Mrs Slater's insomniacs; even if all the other people were, about which Margaret felt considerable doubt.

Margaret fancied that self-pity might not be Mrs Slater's only aberration—or, to say the least, hyperbole; but she knew with certainty that the Kurhus was now spoiled for her, Margaret, and that she wanted to escape from it. She wanted not least to escape from Mrs Slater personally.

The big hall was quite full of people, who seemed to be converging from all directions, but still without speaking. There were many assorted ages, and various palpable indicia of different nationalities. All the same, it was a perfectly commonplace group; seemingly remarkable only for its silence. The silence, however, chilled Margaret's nerves. Escape she must. The crowd rambled forward to the sunny terrace.

'I've decided to follow your example,' said a voice in Margaret's ear: actually a voice; but, unfortunately, it was the voice of Mrs Slater. 'I'm going to spruce myself up before we have tea together.'

Margaret could only nod. Mrs Slater passed her and ascended the staircase between the wood-nymphs that were half trees.

There was now a young Swede behind the hotel desk. It was he who had booked her in and taken away her passport when she arrived. He had fair hair with tight curls, and looked like a boxer or a bison.

Margaret decided not to beat about the bush. She told the hotel clerk that though she had known the Kurhus was partly a sanatorium, she had not realised that so many of the inmates would be patients rather than guests, and that she wanted to go elsewhere. This would surely be understood, though it might not be popular. She thought she would just make off in a taxi; and, if she could devise nothing better, merely return to the hotel in Sovastad.

The first difficulty proved to be that the reception clerk seemed to have very little English, so that he was unable properly to understand her. Margaret had met few Swedes with whom she had been so unable to communicate. But she recognised that her message was unusual and her request arbitrary. So she concentrated on the essential: immediate departure.

'Your passport,' said the clerk. 'It has gone. It will not be back until tomorrow. I told you.'

It was true that he had. It was the kind of thing that often happened in continental hotels, and Margaret, knowing that she was booked in for two days, had not worried about it.

'Where is it?' she asked the clerk.

'Gone. It has gone. I told you.' The clerk stared at her, faintly pugilistic, faintly bovine.

Margaret knew from experience what a hopeless morass this sort of thing could be, even at the best of times; even when it was only that Henry's business compelled the two of them suddenly to go elsewhere.

'I'm not leaving Sweden. I'll come back in a taxi and collect my passport tomorrow. I want to go now just the same. I'm sorry about it, but all these sick people depress me. I quite understand that I shall have to pay. I am prepared to pay for the whole reservation now, if you'll get me a taxi.' She produced a wad of notes from her other trouser pocket. Suddenly her mountain costume, which for a brief time had meant so much to her, had become a middle-aged folly, and a conspicuous one. All the other, rather horrible people were dressed with utter conventionality.

'No taxi,' said the reception clerk, sulky but firm.

'What do you mean?' cried Margaret; less and less dignified, as she all too well knew.

'No taxi after four o'clock,' said the reception clerk.

'Why ever not?' cried Margaret; even while she knew it was not the way to put it if she wanted to get results.

'Not after four o'clock,' repeated the reception clerk.

Margaret began a foolish altercation; feeling all the time like an English innocent abroad in some banal farce. Quite protracted the dispute must have been, as well as foolish; because in the middle of it, Margaret realised, with something not far short of alarm, that Mrs Slater had reappeared on the staircase in a pink silk tea gown with polka dots; with too much rouge on her cheeks; and with her grey hair so frizzed up that it all but stood on end.

'Mrs Slater, please,' shouted the reception clerk. 'Please explain to this lady—'

But Margaret was saved from final public shame. At this moment, a senior personage appeared from a room behind the desk. He was, like his subordinate, a noticeably muscular looking man, but his thick black hair was greying, his face was still and worn.

'Forgive me, madam,' he said to Margaret, in more or less perfect English. 'I have been listening, and I have to give you my personal assurance that tonight nothing can be done.'

Mrs Slater had put her hand on Margaret's left elbow, and was standing expectantly. Margaret would not have hesitated to offend her, had there seemed any real prospect of departure from the Kurhus; but, as things were, she was rather glad that nothing the Manager had said, and that Mrs Slater could have heard, had been particularised.

'Come on and let's have our tea,' said Mrs Slater breezily.

Margaret could only turn away from the desk and follow her; quite unwashed.

Margaret had noticed on other occasions how differently one can feel about a group of people seated around a picturesque hotel terrace after one has come to learn a little more about them; after the hopeful, even happy, expectation one feels at first sight, has been tempered by some degree of real contact. Emerging down the Kurhus steps, with Mrs Slater's red hand pressed lightly against her forearm as if to guide her, Margaret recollected that these were the people who had looked so gay when three days before she had sped past in the superlatively hospitable Volvo.

Mrs Slater guided her back to the same table; which she had 'reserved' by leaving copies of *Vogue* and *The Lady* lying about.

'Please call me Sandy,' said Mrs Slater.

There *was* something queer about the look of the people sitting on the terrace, though it was nothing obvious. To a passerby, they would still be a perfectly average assembly of respectable citizens. Their oddity lay in their quietness and aloofness. By now, some of them were occasionally exchanging a few words, but the words were palpably functional, connected with the tea, the coffee, the fluffy, flaky cream cakes, or the heat of the afternoon: Margaret felt that they had long ago said absolutely everything they could possibly say. She had a frightening glimpse into how long they had probably had in which to say it. In any case, most of them were solitaries, as Mrs Slater had remarked: scattered about one at a table, often with head sunk, and in no case making any attempt at communication or affability. An unusual proportion of the whole group was, however, reading, including, in several cases, two at the same table; and reading, almost always, not mere glossy ephemerae, as in Mrs Slater's case, but heavy, austerely bound volumes with many hundreds of pages. That was only to be expected, Margaret supposed, recollecting the remarkable little library in her own bedroom. There was more and more evidence that Mrs Slater had not drawn as long a bow as Margaret had assumed and hoped.

'Please call me Sandy,' said Mrs Slater a second time.

Margaret supposed she had again been rude in making no specific response.

'If you wish,' she said, trying to sound neither too ungracious nor too gracious. 'So long as you don't call me Molly.'

'Oh but I want to do that,' said Mrs Slater. The tips of all her red fingers were on the edge of the white, wooden table.

'You may call me Margaret.' It sounded feeble, but the right note was so difficult to strike.

'I have ordered a real English tea for both of us, Margaret. I have one every day. The two old ladies used to do the same, and we all had tea together, summer and winter; but now they don't come down until nightfall. I don't think they eat during the day any more.'

'You make them sound like vampires,' said Margaret. Really Mrs Slater had to be regulated.

'You are quite right, Margaret,' replied Mrs Slater seriously. 'I have often thought that the origin of the vampire belief lies in the insomniacs. There is something not quite nice about us, as I have told you.' Mrs Slater actually giggled. It was a most unusual thing to do on the Kurhus terrace.

A young waiter in a linen jacket arrived with a double English tea on a heavy brass tray; including sandwiches, near-Dundee cake, and even hot scones in a silver calabash, from which the sun glinted and sparkled, like a tiny display of white fireworks.

'Shall I be mother?' enquired Mrs Slater; already, however, in the act of pouring. The fluid streaming from the long, thin, silver spout, looked very pale. Probably there were not enough tea-bags in the pot.

None of the others was consuming a meal like this, though most of them seemed to be consuming something. Margaret noticed that the small, slim girl in the white dress, was merely absorbing a proportionately small tumbler of water. At least, it was presumably water. She lay back at a table by herself, facing the sun; almost staring at it with her blue eyes. She was so very exiguous that her white dress looked as if inside it were merely a few pieces of straw and cardboard; leaving her head, legs, and arms as the only parts that were what they seemed. Two young men were sitting, each by himself, at tables quite near her. One would have expected them to show at least covert interest, but Margaret could see no sign of it. One was eating an äggöra and drinking coffee, but both seemed far gone in melancholy.

'That girl,' asked Margaret. 'Surely she is not here because she can't sleep?'

'That girl,' replied Mrs Slater, 'has never been asleep in her life.'

'I find it awfully hard to believe.'

'In England perhaps. Here they'd know at once what she was.'

Margaret looked up from her second scone.

'What do you mean by that? How would they know what?'

'They'd know that she doesn't sleep,' said Mrs Slater in her calm, conclusive way. 'There are more people like that here than there are in England, and of course the population's much smaller, so everyone gets to know the signs. It's how woods like

253

this began. But won't you take off your jacket again? You must be too hot, I'm sure.'

'No, I'm not too hot.'

'I expect you thought you were coming to some kind of ski-ing hotel?'

'Not exactly, in the middle of the summer.'

'I should be delighted to lend you a frock. We're much the same size and much the same age, so that the same style should suit us, and all my clothes come from England. We're quite a dressy party here at night.'

'Thank you very much, but I've got several dresses. I've been wearing them ever since I've been in Sweden,' Margaret added, unkindly once more. 'I hoped things up here would be more informal and that I should get two or three days of mountain walking.'

'Not days,' said Mrs Slater gently. 'It's by night that we walk the mountains here. We don't wear special clothes for it. It's our way of life, so to speak, our destiny. Nothing special about it for us. It's why the wood was put here in the first place.'

'What do you mean by "wood"?' asked Margaret. 'Which wood? There are trees as far as the eye can see, and almost all Sweden seems to be made up of them.'

'Round the Kurhus is a wood,' said Mrs Slater, 'with paths in it, paths everywhere, paths that have been there for hundreds of years. You saw me following one. It is a Jamblichus wood.'

'I'm sorry to be rude, but I think that name sounds like Alice in Wonderland.'

Mrs Slater smiled faintly. 'I always thought it was more like Edward Lear,' she said.

'How can you tell, with all these trees, where your particular wood begins and ends?'

Into the Wood

Mrs Slater looked down at the stone flooring of the terrace. 'If I were to suggest that, with all these trees, it perhaps has no beginning or ending—at least in your sense of the words—you wouldn't believe me.' Then Mrs Slater added softly, and as if interrogating her own heart: 'Would you?'

'It would mean an awful lot of walking, for some of these older people.'

'You are right,' said Mrs Slater, looking up at Margaret, and again speaking firmly. 'A time comes when people can go no further. In the end, the paths just lose themselves among the trees.'

Really it all *was* like the Alice books; the Alice books and no others. Margaret thought so more and more. It was one thought that helped to keep out other thoughts.

'I've eaten far too much tea.' Curiously enough, she had; despite everything. At least she had if life at the Jamblichus Kurhus (an unconvincing name in almost any language, she would have thought), if life at the Kurhus followed any sort of normal order. 'What time's dinner? I take it that there is dinner?'

'We follow the customary scheme of things. Perhaps we value it all the more,' said Mrs Slater, courageous to the last. 'Dinner is described as from eight, but most of us are very punctual. You are sure you have a frock? I hope you will share my table?'

'I should be delighted,' said Margaret. 'Thank you.'

Margaret wanted both to stretch her legs in the sunshine and mountain air and to examine for herself Mrs Slater's alleged wood, where she suspected she would find nothing very special. But she did not want Mrs Slater to come with her. In fact, a further thing she wanted very much, was simply to get away from Mrs Slater. She thought of escaping by going up to her room as an excuse, and then running off into the forest, but this might be made difficult by the fact that the only public exit from the Kurhus seemed to be that on to the terrace. Moreover, she felt in her bones that she would never evade Mrs Slater of all people, merely by dodging her round the bushes, as if they had been two schoolgirls. Mrs Slater would be the first to cry caught any day.

Mrs Slater insisted on showing Margaret some of the large dress illustrations in *Vogue*, making, on the different garments, comments which were detailed and long-winded, but which struck Margaret as academic, where Mrs Slater's own needs and circumstances were concerned, and as rather creepy when applied to her own supposed case.

'*You* would look *gorgeous* in *that*,' Mrs Slater would breathe out earnestly; pointing at something fleecy with her dark red forefinger and pushing the something almost into Margaret's face, while Margaret gazed out at the slopes of green descending from the terrace and ascending another mountain ridge, ten, twenty, or thirty miles off, it was hard to guess how many.

'If *I* lived *your* life, I'd always wear nice things,' said Mrs Slater. 'I have excellent taste.'

Margaret had often heard women of sixty or seventy talking for hours in just that way: weighing every detail; speculating, wistfully or cattily, about how this or that garment would suit this or that common acquaintance; at once identifying with and envying Margaret herself, when she happened to be at their disposal for the purpose. The half-dream, half-contest seemed to keep innumerable women not happy, but certainly alive, even through senility. It must serve a purpose, but Margaret did not find it even pathetic. She found it a spun-out makeshift (the very words were significant) which symbolised the worst aspect of being a woman. But everyone lived on makeshifts. Look at Henry, his lumbering toys and his social anxieties!

'What colour do you find suits you best?' asked Mrs Slater.

'This colour,' said Margaret, pointing to her legs. 'That colour': pointing to the wilderness of leaves.

The others on the terrace had stopped eating and drinking. In any other community, half of them would by now have fallen asleep.

'Forgive me, please,' said Margaret. 'I should like to wander about a little before dinner.' She rose. No one seemed to take any notice; even to glance at her.

'I'll show you round,' said Mrs Slater, scrambling together her papers. 'There are things that need to be explained.'

'It's very kind of you, but I'll take my chance.' Margaret had a bright idea. 'Like a famous Swede, I want to be alone.'

Mrs Slater was not to be silenced conclusively. 'Just as you like,' she said, 'but remember: it is not like going for a stroll in England.'

The differences, Margaret at first thought, were that here there were no litter, no structures, no advertisements, no noise of cars and aeroplanes and radios, and, above all, no people. Man had presumably planted these trees and tramped out these paths, but he had done nothing else. It was, indeed, very unlike a wood in Cheshire.

When Margaret had descended from the terrace, she had by instinct avoided the green tunnel from which Mrs Slater had originally emerged, and, crossing below the terrace, had entered the other one, which for a few yards ran beneath the wall of the Kurhus itself. Margaret could hear the swill and clatter of the kitchen; and as well as these things, the chatter of the staff, which harmonised with them. After the silent terrace, the cheerful sound came as a relief. But it was audible for only a minute or two; nor was the Kurhus building visible for longer than that through the forest.

And almost immediately, the fat, beaten path reached a nodule whence it unwound into a dozen or more rabbit runs among the trees. It was as if at this point the withdrawal of man had left small animals to continue his work. The paths, though very narrow, seemed definite, but it was impossible to know which to choose. All were compelled to wind continuously, as they pressed forward through the irregularly planted trees. Already, after only a few hundred yards from the terrace, there was a real danger of being lost. It struck Margaret as an ideal area for going round and round in a hopeless circle, as the lost are well known to do, owing (she had heard) to almost everybody having one leg shorter than the other. It was not at all the sort of situation she had contemplated as having perhaps lain behind Mrs Slater's rejected offer of guidance. She had visualised something far more fanciful.

She selected a path almost at random, and began to weave about among the trees. The path, however narrow, was unobstructed: there was no question of pressing through bushes, or pushing aside branches. Even the surface was comparatively smooth. It was almost as if the vegetation had been cut back, but Margaret saw that there was no sign of this. It seemed rather as if it had never grown across the path; just as weeds never take root in water that is constantly traversed by boats. Margaret perceived at once what this implied: the little paths must be in continuous use, as Mrs Slater had said. It was a further confirmation of Mrs Slater's entire improbable thesis about the insomniacs.

Margaret stopped. There was a steady, rustling, pulsation in the thick undergrowth between the trees; and a whirring and flapping among the leaves overhead that would rise and fall suddenly, like a very irregular line on a graph. To judge by the sounds, there might have been condors among the branches and anacondas among the bushes. Margaret, in fact, was unsure what might not really be there: were there not still wolves and bears in Sweden, and, probably, many more varieties of reptile than in Britain? The brush was here as high as her elbows and dense enough to conceal anything short of an elephant. It was a second situation that she had not thought of when dismissing Mrs Slater's offer.

She walked on. The narrow shafts of sun struck down like spotlights in a theatre, she being the principal actress; the wider cataracts descended like a benediction in an Italian painting, she being the saint. But in many places the trees were so thick that the sunlight penetrated only as a flickering radiance, suggesting a different and brighter world above. After a time, and quite suddenly, the underbrush almost ceased and the little tracks traversed dunes of pine needles.

Tracks, not track. Even through the underbrush had run several transverse tracks. Out here, many intersecting paths could be seen simultaneously, which was reassuring, because, at the worst, and if one knew one's direction, one could cross the open ground, but disconcerting too, as suggesting that the entire forest was a maze.

Margaret was in many ways enjoying herself, but she realised that she would have to go back. She regretted that she had so little equipment for pathfinding. She had been feeling regrets of that kind almost since she had first arrived in Sweden. But it was so difficult to know what one could do. All the possibilities seemed ridiculous. Her mother had not let her even be a Girl Guide.

Margaret felt, in any case, that woodland techniques, though important in themselves, were very secondary to something else

. . . She had words for it, she had long had them, though they were negative words: what was needed was the rejection of so many of the things that her husband, Henry, appeared to stand for. The thought had roamed about her brain and body for years, like a germ in the blood, always poisoning her content. In this Swedish forest, a far and lonely place by comparison with most other places she had known, the unrest flared up and momentarily put her off balance. She attempted to make her usual answer to herself: tried to enter into Henry's point of view, to make proper allowance for the fact that he was far from a free agent. He was hardly more a free agent than the people were at the Kurhus, according to Mrs Slater's tales, and according to the evidence of these teeming little rabbit-runs through the woods. All the same, she felt that it was up to a man to be more of a free agent than Henry was. It was not that she herself especially wanted to blaze trees and utter bird-calls. It was rather that the forest symbolised something that was outside life—certainly outside Henry's life and her own. And not part of Henry's inner life either, though it apparently was part of hers, if one could judge by what she felt now.

Margaret took a small pull on herself. Henry must be broadly right and she broadly wrong, or life would simply not continue as it did, and more and more the same everywhere. The common rejoinder to these feelings of rebellion was, as she knew well, that she needed a little more scope for living her own life, even (as a few Mancunians might dare to say) for self-expression. But that popular anodyne never, according to Margaret's observation of other couples, appeared in practice to work. Nor could she wonder. It reduced the self in one to the status and limits of a hobby. It offered one lampshade making, or so many hours a week helping the cripples and old folk, when what one truly needed was a revelation; was simultaneous self-expression and self-loss. And at the same time it corrupted marriage and cheapened the family. The rustling, sunny forest, empty but labyrinthine, hinted at some other answer; an answer beyond logic, beyond words, above all beyond connection with what Margaret and her Cheshire neighbours had come to regard as normal life. It was an answer different in kind. It was the very antithesis of a hobby, but not necessarily the antithesis of what marriage should be, though never was.

Margaret could again hear the sounds of the Kurhus kitchen. A girl there was singing. Margaret stopped and listened for a moment; which, as she reflected, she would probably not have done had she been able to understand the words. The song had some pure existence and beauty, which understanding of the words, while possibly bringing something else, would have destroyed. Listening to the talk in the intervals at Hallé concerts, Margaret had suspected that too much understanding of musical theory can be similarly destructive. And so often people said to her that when they travelled abroad they wanted really to meet and know the local population; in the same sort of way, as far as possible, as they met and knew their fellow English. They spent hard evenings learning languages for the purpose—or in the hope. Margaret realised that this was not her idea at all. The song of this girl was precisely akin to the song of the forest: if one worked at it, one would cease to hear it. In fact, now that Margaret came to think, she realised that she had been unconsciously disengaging the song from the loud clanging of pans in which, properly speaking, it was submerged. She had been hearing only the song, and nothing of the mechanism that, objectively, almost overwhelmed it; and assuredly put it in its place. So it had been in the forest. One had to lose the noise of the mechanism, not least the ever-deafening inner echoes of it. One had to dispel practicality. Then something else could be heard—if one was lucky, if the sun was shining, if the paths were well made, if one wore the right garments: and if one made no attempt at definition or popularisation.

Margaret perceived with surprise two practicalities: she had been walking for an hour and a half, far longer than she had supposed; and from the clear ground where the rabbit runs were all visible at once, she had returned without giving a thought to her route. Blazing trees could not be the only ciphering. Losing one's way was largely an act of intention.

All the same, Margaret had virtually to scamper into her dress with the velocity of a child. Not only was the terrace deserted, but there was the beginning of a crowd in the hall, as she hastened through. They were arrayed in half-festivity; the counterpart of half-mourning. As usual, Mrs Slater had spoken aright. What was more, Margaret observed that her huge bed had not been 'turned down'. It was the first hotel of that standing where she had encountered such an omission.

Margaret stood for a moment naked in the evening sunlight, finding her silhouette more pleasing than she had found it for some time; then scrambled into a stone-coloured garment in hard silk, the best she could do for Mrs Slater, whom there could be no hope of eliminating.

'Look,' said Mrs Slater. 'There are the other two English-women.'

Few could have told to what nation they belonged. They resembled two very ancient, long neglected, near-to-death bushes; which now put out each year only a few half-hearted leaves in the entire mass. One felt that at any moment, a branch might quietly drop off, or the entire bole split and subside.

'Mrs Total and Mrs Ascot,' expounded Mrs Slater. 'I used

to be able to play games with them, but no more. I do wish you were here for longer, Margaret. You can imagine how alone I am.'

'Is there really nowhere else you could go?'

'The other places are even worse.'

There was more conversation at dinner, in a variety of tongues; and more at the end than at the beginning. Undeniably it was as if they were all working up to something, even though they did it in a careful and hypochondriac way. None the less, those who had sat alone on the terrace, sat alone in the dining-room also. It was merely that some of them spoke from time to time across a void, and that certain of the couples appeared more in touch. Also there were more people in the dining-room than Margaret had until then seen in the Kurhus. Certainly the better spirits could not be attributed to liquor, because there was none. Margaret was accustomed to hotels where before one dined, one had several drinks at the bar, sometimes in advance of one's husband. Occasionally one met people there. Infrequently, they were quite interesting. She realised that here there was seldom anyone new to meet. She was surprised that no one other than Mrs Slater seemed concerned to meet *her*. Possibly it was the language difficulty.

'Drink is absolutely forbidden?' She feared that again she was tending merely to bait poor Mrs Slater.

'Nothing is *forbidden*,' replied Mrs Slater, in a very English way. 'If we don't smoke or drink, it's because we've all learnt better. When you can't sleep, the consequences of drinking are indescribable. You do know that the physiological function of alcohol is soporific? For us, it would be like an impotent man taking an aphrodisiac.'

Margaret especially disliked Mrs Slater's occasional shafts of modern frankness. Besides she had always understood that it was exactly what impotent men did do.

'Of course it's entirely different for you,' said Mrs Slater. 'I am sure that if you were to stay longer, something could be arranged with the doctors. I myself shouldn't mind your drinking all you wanted.'

'Doctors!' said Margaret. 'I hadn't realised that there were doctors.'

'Oh yes. Though of course they're no use to us. There's no cure for *our* condition.'

'Then why are they here?'

'Old People, like Mrs Total and Mrs Ascot, can't settle down unless there are doctors about. And I am sure it applies to the foreigners too. Don't you think it applies to most people today, whatever their age? They must all have doctors, be the cost what it may.'

'I suppose I should have expected doctors,' said Margaret. 'Where are they now? Have we seen one?'

'The surgery is on the very top floor. The kirurgi, as it's called in Swedish. There are two doctors on duty at all times, night and day, in case there's a crisis. You will help yourself to rödkål from the bowl?'

They were seated by a window, outside which summer night was falling.

'What sort of crisis is commonest?'

'I'm afraid our most frequent crises are sudden mania and sudden death. For this reason, the doctors have to be fairly young and strong. The same applies to the male staff in general, as you may have noticed. With insomnia, there is often a quick snap. The strain can be borne no longer. That is still another of the reasons why we have always been made to live apart. The provincial mental hospital finds many of its recruits here, but few of its so-called cures. You'd hardly believe it, but even *there* people like us don't sleep. And as for our dead, there is a special place for *them* in the wood: not easy to find unless you know where to look. Even after death, it's the same old story of exclusion. But I fear that all this is hardly the way to make you extend your visit. I know only too well that instead of arousing love and pity, as one might hope, the facts do just the opposite. We poor folk are doomed to eternal self-sufficiency, whether we like it or not. So eat up your mört, Margaret, and take no notice of all these gloomy thoughts.'

Margaret decided that, in fact, she did not feel as gloomy as she should have done. Mrs Slater still wallowed too much; and Margaret's main feeling about the Kurhus as a whole was acute and ever-growing curiosity, reprehensible though that might be. She felt mildly stimulated by a community so entirely novel and unpredictable, however unconvivial. Besides, her experience in what Mrs Slater called 'the wood', had perceptibly shifted the four points of her inner compass. Life's terms of reference had changed . . . Conceivably, she reflected, as Mrs Slater helped her to a crumbling wodge of efterrättstarta, the unaccustomed liberty and isolation would have gone a little to her head, wherever she had found herself; but the real wonder lay in taking only one short step and lighting upon an entire world so different. These people round her might, in a sense, be outcasts, as Mrs Slater said. Quite possibly, they suffered; looking at them, it was hard to be sure. What Margaret did know was that the Kurhus had already recharged the battery of her life, rewound the spring. After long inertia, she was again, mysteriously, on the move.

'Cream?' enquired Mrs Slater, holding high a silver boat. 'Or as the Swedes call it, grädde?'

On the move once more, and so soon after starting, Margaret could not be expected to think about how to stop.

'Why do you smile?' asked Mrs Slater.

'I'm so sorry,' said Margaret. 'It must have been something in my own thoughts.'

'No, there's no coffee,' said Mrs Slater. 'As everybody knows, the physiological consequence of coffee is wakefulness. But in your case it may this time be just as well that there is none. Because if I were you, I should go straight to bed.'

'But I don't feel in the least like sleep.' Margaret spoke without thinking. At the Kurhus, even new clichés were needed. 'Oh, I've said the wrong thing. I do apologise.'

Mrs Slater gazed back with fishy eyes.

'Even if you don't sleep, stay in your room.'

'Why?'

'At night we walk. After dinner, we begin; and many of us walk till dawn. It is not a thing for you to see.'

'Mrs Slater,' began Margaret.

'Sandy, if you don't mind.'

'Sandy, of course.' Again Margaret smiled. 'Sandy, if what you say is true, I'm very very sorry for you all, but you can't suppose that I could come here, and listen to what you've told me, and not want to see for myself? It may be wrong of me, but I just can't help it.'

'I suppose it's natural,' said Mrs Slater, 'and I've known it often. With the world what it is today, I imagine we're lucky that people aren't brought in buses to stare at us, like they used to stare at the lunatics in Bedlam. I expect it will come to that in the end, though they won't get the local people to drive the buses for them. We're unlucky, and on the unlucky is a curse. I warn you, Margaret. The local people know and are right.'

Margaret looked down at the gay table mats.

'Since you're warning me, please tell me exactly what

266

you're warning me of. What could happen to me?'

But Mrs Slater was entirely unspecific. 'Nothing good,' was all she said. 'Nothing that you would wish. I am speaking to you as a friend.'

It was very unconvincing. Margaret even wondered whether she was not being merely warned against making undesirable acquaintances. It was difficult to decide what to do.

The dining room was rapidly emptying. All seemed to be quiet once more. The diners were leaving in silence; almost stealthily, Margaret thought. It was nearly dark, but the air was still faintly crimson from reflections of the sunset.

'Tell me,' said Margaret, 'what happens in winter, when the snow is on the mountains? They talk a lot about that in Sovastad.'

'We suffer the more,' replied Mrs Slater. 'We sit all night and wait for the spring. What else could we do?'

'All right,' said Margaret. 'I'll stay in my room. And tomorrow I think I'd better go somewhere else.'

'Please don't go before you have to,' pleaded Mrs Slater. 'You'll be all right. You'll sleep since you've had no coffee. There is nothing to keep you awake. You'll have an excellent night.'

The big hall was lighted, though only rather faintly, by pretty lamps, in which the brass nymphs on both sides of the staircase gleamed and flickered. A well built elderly man whom Margaret had noticed dining by himself, stood in a far corner, apparently musing. There was no one else to be seen. Mrs Slater once more put her hand on Margaret's arm.

'I'll see you to the door of your room,' said Mrs Slater.

'No,' said Margaret. 'Let's part here.'

Mrs Slater paused.

'You won't forget your promise?'

'It wasn't a promise,' said Margaret. 'But I'll not forget.'

Mrs Slater withdrew her hand, then held it out as if to bind Margaret in a pledge. But all she said was, 'Then, good night.' Bravely she added, 'Sleep well.'

'See you in the morning,' said Margaret, wondering if she would, and if these were appropriate words. Was it possible that at this moment Mrs Slater was preparing to 'walk'?

A middle-aged woman, perhaps eight or ten years older than Margaret, but still noticeably beautiful, descended the staircase in a costly-looking fur coat, although the evening was very warm, tap-tapped across the white, tiled floor, and went out into the darkness.

Mrs Slater went up the staircase without once looking back at Margaret. She disappeared down a corridor which was not Margaret's corridor.

Margaret had intended herself to go up almost immediately, having delayed for a moment only from anxiety to avoid a bedroom colloquy with Mrs Slater; but on the instant she was alone, the elderly man in the corner of the hall advanced towards her and said, 'Forgive me, but I was bound to overhear what Mrs Slater, a dear friend of us all, was saying to you. There is little conversation here, and most that is said, is heard not by one alone. You would be mistaken altogether to accept Mrs Slater's sad view of our curious community. There is, I assure you, a different side to us. We are not sad all the time. You felt that yourself when you walked this evening in our wood.'

'Did you see me there?' asked Margaret. 'What you say is quite true.'

'Just as most of the things that are said to one are heard by many, so most of the things that each of us does, are known to all. Would you do me the honour of taking a cup of coffee with me?'

268

An elderly pair came down the stairs and went silently forth.

'Mrs Slater said there was no coffee. She also advised me against going out.'

'Mrs Slater, as you say in English, exaggerated, so let us then have coffee. You will see.'

He pressed a bell on the reception desk. One of the white-jacketed waiters appeared. The elderly man gave the order in the most usual way.

A man of about forty, who had not changed from his light suit for dinner, walked straight from the dining-room, across the hall, to the steps down to the terrace.

'Let me introduce myself. I am Colonel Adamski. You, I know, are Mrs Sawyer.'

For a member of a community that seemed so silent and so uninterested, it was amazing how much he knew.

They shook hands.

'The point that Mrs Slater overlooks is that only by great sacrifice can we poor human beings reach great truth.'

Margaret sat up straight. 'Yes,' she said. 'I understand. I really do.' She was astonished with herself.

'Of course you do,' said Colonel Adamski. 'The Italian man of the world, Casanova—if you'll forgive my mentioning such a scamp—remarks on the basis of unusually wide knowledge of the world that, in his observation, only one human being in a hundred, or some such proportion, ever experiences the jolt that sets the faculty for truth in motion. Casanova's faculty was set in motion by freemasonry—though that is something else that, as a good Catholic, I should not bring into the conversation, least of all with a charming lady. Nor is a jolt—a shock, a blow, a fatality—always necessary. I doubt whether you regard yourself as having suffered a jolt?'

'I think that what Mrs Slater had to say might have been a jolt,' said Margaret. 'This afternoon, I mean.'

'You are right to name the time,' said Colonel Adamski, lightly pouncing. 'Already you understand much: so much more than you know. For the reason why Mrs Slater is so sad and so uncomprehending is that she walks in the afternoon instead of at night.'

'Does she not walk at night as well?'

'Seldom.' The Colonel broke off. 'But here is our coffee. Will you please pour? Alas, my hand is not steady.'

'I'm so sorry.'

'It was that terrible war we fought, where the powers of darkness were almost equally strong on both sides. Not a righteous war, not a necessary war, not a war in which victory was for one moment possible. You can see at once, I would suppose, that I take an unusual view for a Polish officer. It was towards the end of that war that I stopped sleeping—stopped entirely; and it has been here that I have seen the truth of things. Great sacrifice: great truth. It is something that Mrs Slater, who walks in the afternoon as if she were on holiday at Royal Leamington Spa or Royal Tunbridge Wells, does not understand.'

'Colonel Adamski,' said Margaret. 'I have to ask you whether you take milk?'

'No milk. It is black coffee, pure but strong, that fortifies against the powers of darkness with which the world is filled.'

All the time, people were passing through the hall in ones and twos, more commonly the former; and the night, now utterly black when viewed from the lamplight, was swallowing them. Warm though it had been, and in the Kurhus still was, Margaret was becoming aware of a little icy gust every time the door opened.

'A long war,' said Colonel Adamski. 'Those so-called

concentration camps, of which we hear so much. A bad illness. A heartbreak that is without hope. The suffering that grows with religion. These are among the things that set the faculty for truth in motion. Or sleeplessness. Shakespeare complains often of not sleeping, but see how much he owes to it! Even the absurd local poet, Strindberg, would be still more grotesque if shafts of truth had not occasionally struck home as he lay wakeful; at one time in this very place. It would have been better by far if he had never left it. Then think of your own great statesman, Lord Rosebery: recognised by all as a man marked out, a man in a different mould from the pygmies who swarmed around his feet; though few of those who knew this, could say why. Some of them even wrote books to explain how unable they were to account for Lord Rosebery's obvious greatness. Did you know, Mrs Sawyer, that for many years Lord Rosebery hardly slept at all?'

'I'm afraid he was rather before my time,' said Margaret.

'He would have understood well that we who live here are at once cursed as Mrs Slater says, but chosen also. He had the blue eyes that are commonest among our kind.'

'It seems to me that most of you look very much like the rest of the world.'

'We have the commonplace aspect of monks. Remove the distinguishing clothing, and many monks resemble Mrs Slater. If you will pardon the paradox.'

The hall was now quite quiet.

'May I give you some more coffee, Colonel Adamski?'

'If you please.'

She refilled both cups, and then sat thinking.

'Are there boundaries?' she asked, after a while 'Or frontiers? To me it seemed that the wood, this special wood that you all speak of, was just part of the whole Swedish forest.'

'That is true,' said the Colonel. 'Every now and then one of us fails to return. Some find tracks into the further forest, and return never.'

'Perhaps they have merely decided to leave the Kurhus, and find that the simplest way of doing it? I can imagine that. I wanted to leave this afternoon, but it seemed almost impossible . . . I am glad now that I stayed,' she added smiling and unwrapping a lump of sugar from its paper.

The Colonel bowed gravely. 'They go,' he said, 'because they have reached their limit. For men and women there is to everything a limit, beyond which further striving, further thought, leads only to regression. And this is true even though most men and women never set out at all; possibly are not capable of setting out for those who do set out, the limit varies from individual to individual, and cannot be foreseen. Few ever reach it. Those who do reach it, are, I suspect, those who go off into the further forest.'

Margaret's eyes were shining. 'I know that you are right,' she cried. 'It is something I have long known, without finding the words.'

'We all know it,' said the Colonel. 'And we all fear it. Because beyond our limit, is nothing. It is a little like the Italian parable of the onion: skin after skin comes away, until in the end there is nothing—nothing but a perfume that lingers a little, as the dead linger here a little after death, perfuming the air, and then are gone. Or, more grandly, it is like Nirvana, no doubt; though Nirvana is something no European can understand. For me, it is like a particular moment in the war; a moment when, having no weapons, I had to fight hand to hand. It was not a moment I care to recall, even when I walk in the wood. It is far from true, Mrs Sawyer, that we soldiers are men of strength and blood. Few soldiers are like that in the least. But it was for me

272

the moment when I stopped sleeping, stopped dreaming. Dreams, Mrs Sawyer, are misleading, because they make life seem real. When it loses the support of dreams, life dissolves. But perhaps we have spoken enough of this funny little group to which I have found my way? Even I who am one of them, do not deceive myself that it is the whole world, and you are only a visitor among us, here today and gone tomorrow, as your idiom puts it?'

'I shall be sorry to be gone,' said Margaret matter-of-factly. She tilted the coffee pot, then lifted the lid. 'I'm afraid there's no more. In England the coffee's bad, but there's more of it. I expect that's symbolical too.'

The Colonel laughed politely.

'Should I enter the wood, Colonel Adamski? Now, I mean, when all of you are walking? Mrs Slater forbade me most strictly. What do you advise?'

'You will have realised by now that on many questions there is no one view amongst us. No more than in the rest of the world. No more than in a monastery, to return to that example. You might be surprised! I went to school with monks, and can assure you that they differ among themselves every bit as much as politicians or businessmen. Mrs Slater's view reflects Mrs Slater. When I was stationed for years in Britain with the Polish forces, waiting and learning, but mainly waiting, I learned that Britain's strength lay in women like Mrs Slater, cautious and unimpassioned. It would be wrong for me to argue with so excellent an example of your fellow-countrywomen.'

'But should I enter the wood, Colonel Adamski?'

'Why ever not, Mrs Sawyer, if you want to? Why ever not? Few of us night-walkers actually bite. And certainly we should never bite a lovely lady like you.'

He moved in his chair.

'Oh,' said Margaret, remembering. 'I do hope I haven't been keeping you?'

'But most agreeably.' The Colonel rose and faintly clicked his heels. 'Your husband is a fortunate man. I could only wish he didn't build roads.'

'Why?' asked Margaret.

The Colonel spread out his hands.

'The blood. The noise. The aggression and hostility. The devastation and emptiness. The means with no ends. The first roads, the first roads like that, were built by Hitler. The place of war is now taken in society by motoring. I, a soldier, tell you that my trade has changed its shape. But these are not things I should disclose to a roadbuilder's wife, who has done me the honour of taking coffee with me after dinner. I apologise, Mrs Sawyer. I go.' The Colonel again made the faintest possible click with his heels, and went off up the stairs, stepping very silently for so well-built a man.

It seemed likely that all who meant to go out, had now gone; possibly the entire guest-list, with the exceptions of Mrs Total and Mrs Ascot, Mrs Slater and Margaret herself. Margaret sat on in the silent hall with its scattered fairy lights, hardly in sum providing even illumination by which one wishing to, could read. In the end, a single late-departer descended the staircase. It was the small, slim girl, who earlier had worn a white dress. Now she wore a dark garment (there was not enough light for Margaret to discern the exact colour); which fitted as a skin and as tightly as a young one. She tripped down the stairs, swiftly but not hurriedly; not only as if to be last was her proper place, but perhaps even as if aware that she was expected and awaited. She looked skinnier and frailer than ever: her legs attenuated rather than slender, her breasts almost invisible in the darkness of the fabric that covered them. As she walked past, she glanced at Margaret directly, for the first time: her big blue eyes seemed to flash for a half-second, as a light caught them; and to Margaret it seemed that her tiny, almost wasted mouth smiled slightly, though whether in recognition it was impossible to say. In any case, she was past in a moment, and, in another, out through the door on to the terrace, where the blackness covered and absorbed her instantly.

Margaret found that, without volition, she had risen to her feet and was staring out towards the night beyond the glass panels in the door. She walked down the hall and followed the girl on to the terrace.

It was quite unexpectedly cold: she had forgotten the contrast in temperature between the Swedish daylight and the Swedish darkness. Later in the year, as she understood, there would be no darkness at any time during the twenty-four hours, but now it was thick and moonless and starless, thick and icy. Shaking all over in her dinner dress (though she could recall that many of the other guests had not looked particularly wrapped up when they went forth) and with her teeth already chattering so badly that her head felt like a skull, Margaret none the less groped her way slowly along the dark terrace, trying to dodge round the almost invisible tables and chairs, and guiding herself by the dim pale line of the stone balustrade to her left. In the end, she reached the few steps down to the transverse path along which Mrs Slater had so long before emerged; descended them with stress in her high-heeled shoes; and tottered off towards the wood she had entered that afternoon, the wood about which opinions seemed to differ so much, the wood where her own view of things had shifted perceptibly, as she knew quite well, and even though she had but dropped in as a foreign tripper, and but for a period of time to be counted more rationally in minutes than in hours, days, or years.

She went forward among the trees for perhaps fifty yards, then stopped. She had not even reached the nodule where the wider path untwined into the little rabbit runs. She realised that if she went further, she would lose even the edgeless oval of something less than darkness behind her. Now there was no sound from the Kurhus kitchen, nor a light, visible through the foliage, in any part of the structure. It struck Margaret that the staff might go away each night to sleep. For the staff—the staff, of course, *slept*; and might well find the indulgence easier when uncontrasted with universal wakefulness. To Margaret, the cold was the strangest thing. In only a few minutes her body had become so cold that she no longer even suffered from the chill. It felt like a body packed in a single block of ice; serene, and no longer any responsibility of hers. She wondered whether if one really were packed in a block of ice, one still spent a third of one's life with one's eyes closed, sleeping.

She had ceased to shiver or to chatter. She stood still and, there being nothing at all to see, listened. The steady, slight rustling of the afternoon was still to be heard. It could then have been the small creatures of the day. Margaret supposed it could now be the small creatures of the night; even more numerous, she understood. Still it seemed unlikely that small creatures would continue the same noise—and the same *degree* of noise (so that only when one stopped making an unnecessary noise oneself could one hear it)—in light and in darkness. Then Margaret realised that this might be a wood in which *nothing* slept; perhaps not even the trees.

The soft rustling went on and on. Occasionally a black bird swooped down invisibly. Outside and beyond the clear ice that enfolded her, Margaret suddenly began to be afraid lest in the darkness one of the perambulant Kurhus guests brush past her. She doubted whether she could face such an occurrence.

Into the Wood

Probably it was this comparatively trifling fear which tipped the scale. Probably everything in the world is decided by tiny last straws. Though she had no doubt that, for a little time to come, she would despise herself, Margaret resolved upon retreat, upon leaving it at that: she would return to the Kurhus at once; go to her room; rub the ice out of herself with the huge Swedish bath towel, have a hot bath, turn on the heater, if there was one; snuggle down, as the women's papers put it, in bed; aim to sleep, even pray to sleep, if she had to, though not once in her life hitherto had she found sleep to involve anything of the kind. And tomorrow, as would then be logical and necessary, she would return, having made herself as invisible as possible during the short remaining time at the Kurhus, to Sovastad, a day of her holiday lost, to say nothing of a day of Henry's money. Perhaps, she thought, she had reached her limit; considerably sooner than for a brief period that evening she had supposed, even taken for granted about herself.

As she picked her way out of the dark wood, she realised that she had begun to shiver again. Crossing the silent hall, she wondered whether it would all end merely in a bad cold. It would be an appropriate sequel to her surrender. She despised herself for not changing her clothes and returning to the wood. She had not even confirmed that the people who had gone out through the Kurhus hall were in the wood at all. She was only sure that even in her thickest clothes she would find the wood almost as icy as if she were wearing nothing.

She rubbed herself down. She sank into steaming water. She went to bed. She felt self-betrayed, that she had behaved as an average woman would do; she had reached a point where she could be told little more and beyond which, if she went on, she would have to go alone, frozen and undefended; but she soon slept, and with no special measures.

When she woke to the morning sun (as high as this on the mountains the sun could shine at any hour), she knew that she would have to go at once. If a taxi could not be got, she would make her way on foot down the mountain to Sovastad, leaving her small luggage for Henry to go after when he returned. At one point she would not have wished that Henry should visit the Kurhus, but now it did not matter. She put on the dress in which she had arrived.

There was no demur. The hall was empty of guests, as it so often was, but the young Swede who looked like a boxer, was behind his desk, produced Margaret's passport, and said he would ring up for a taxi at once. He did enquire whether Margaret wanted breakfast, but seemed unsurprised when she declined. Margaret wanted to meet neither Mrs Slater nor Colonel Adamski, and did not know which, in their very different ways, she wanted to meet the less. Perhaps she wanted least of all to meet the frail-looking girl with bright blue eyes; whose resistance to cold, even in thin black tights, seemed to be so much greater than her own. The young reception clerk did not offer to abate half of Henry's liability; or seem to think that the matter called for reference.

Surprisingly soon, the taxi arrived and Margaret directed it back to the familiar hotel in Sovastad. She hoped that she would not find it full. Her present reservation began, of course, only on the night of the next day, when Henry would be back. Looking out of the taxi's rear window, she saw the white tables scattered about the deserted terrace, the bright flowers in hanging baskets, the vast sweep of green descending the side of the mountain, of which the lower part had not yet caught the morning sun. Presumably the regular inmates of the Kurhus were, in their own way, resting after the night's peregrinations.

There was still so much that Margaret did not understand.

The hotel in Sovastad said it was already fully booked that night, and was none too polite about it either. Had it not been that she and Henry had just stayed in the establishment for a week, and had this not been emancipated Sweden, Margaret might have thought from the demeanour of the reception staff that a foreign woman travelling alone was not welcome as a guest. All three of them glowered at her, as if she were a complete stranger and an undesirable one. Moreover, the taxi-driver had brought her case into the hotel and was shifting about apparently almost as eager to be rid of her as were the hotel people.

'Can you recommend me somewhere else?'

'The Central.'

'You realise that I shall be returning here tomorrow?'

They simply stared back at her and said nothing. She imagined that they had not enough English to understand her.

The taxi-driver, with extreme grumpiness, took her to the Central.

The Central was apparently so fully booked that the elderly woman behind the desk did not even need to consult her record. In fact, she did not speak at all. She merely shook her head, on which the smooth grey hair surmounted the familiar Swedish bone structure. However, she shook it with great decisiveness.

'Can you recommend me somewhere else?'

This time Margaret seemed more or less to be understood.

'Krohn's.'

Sovastad was only a small town, despite its skilful graft of Scandinavian urbanity, and Margaret appreciated that as the quest continued, standards were bound to sink. Krohn's was a pension, basically, perhaps, for commercial travellers. None the less, it was clean, bright, and attractive.

It was also full up. This time the reception was in charge of a small boy, with a tousle of wild blond hair larger than his face, and curious, angular eyes. He wore an open white shirt, and a scarlet scarf round his neck. He could speak no English at all, so that it was useless even asking for a suggestion of somewhere else. Foreign visitors were unusual at Krohn's.

The boy stood behind a table (Krohn's did not rise to a formal reception desk) holding tight to the edge of it, and visibly wishing Margaret out of the place and far away. One might have thought he was quite frightened of her, and Margaret supposed it was only reasonable seeing that he was perhaps but ten or eleven, and with not a word he could share with her.

'Where now?' she asked the taxi-driver.

It was still only half-past ten, but the situation was becoming disturbing. Margaret wondered if the taxi-man would by this time suggest that she return for the night to the Kurhus. She began to wish that she was not alone in Sovastad. She supposed that she could have recourse to Henry's Swedish friends, but it was the last thing she wanted (short of returning to the Kurhus) and the last moment at which she would have wanted it. She would have such particularly difficult things to explain, and she was bound to be questioned with solicitous closeness, and probably reported back to Henry in the same spirit.

'Frälsningsarmen,' he said.

'What's that?'

'Frälsningsarmen,' he said again. 'It's all you'll get.'

This last could hardly be true, Margaret thought. Sovastad was not a large town, but she herself, during the previous week, had seen more than three places at which it seemed possible to stay. Possibly the taxi-driver knew that all were full. Possibly there was some big event in the town which had booked all the beds. She decided at least to have a look at the place the taxi-driver had suggested.

It proved to be a hostel of the Salvation Army.

'No, really,' said Margaret; but she was too late.

A woman officer had immediately appeared and was not so much welcoming her in, as drawing her in; pulling at her arm, gently but very firmly, as if already commencing the process of redemption, manifesting the iron goodness beneath the common flesh.

The place proved to look quite agreeable (as well as most astonishingly cheap, to judge from the prominently placed list of charges): more like a normal hotel, though simple and scrubbed, than like Margaret's idea of a Salvation Army hostel in England, concerning which *Major Barbara* was her most recent authority. Margaret's room contained a Bible, a book in Swedish expounding the Bible, a holy picture, and a selection of Swedish tracts; there seemed to be no reference to any more direct programme of observance in the establishment.

At one moment, however, when Margaret was lying down, there was a knock at the door, and the officer who had received her, handed her a tract in English. It was entitled 'Purification', and the woman passed it over unsmilingly. Margaret had realised already that the woman had very little English. Now Margaret got the impression that the English tract was the fruit of searching in cupboards and chests for something suitable to the visitor from abroad. She felt mildly appreciative of so much trouble on her behalf and smiled as gratefully as she could. The woman went silently away.

There seemed to be no further attempt at Margaret's conversion.

Indeed, she was perfectly free to go off into the town and eat there or go to the cinema. There was no real reason why she should not be, but she felt faintly surprised all the same. A more real difficulty was that she had already very much seen all there was to be seen in Sovastad, and also very much wanted not to meet at the moment anyone there whom she knew. She therefore read for much of the day and industriously washed things; lunched in the hotel or hostel or whatever it properly was (the food was primitive but good); and confined herself to sneaking out to dinner in a café she had not before entered. She did not read the tract on purification.

She found the café disappointing. She was hidden away in a corner and served with a rudeness and indifference she had not previously met with in Sweden—or perhaps elsewhere either. But Margaret had not travelled very much, and still less on her own. She knew that lone women were often said not to be popular with waiters, or even with restaurant managements. 'No wonder,' she thought, 'that, with one thing and another, women tend to retreat into their little nests.' Altogether, she reflected, her short period of time away from Henry might well, in one way and another, have been the most vivid and informative of her entire life. She tried to put away the thought. It might at all times be a mistake to know more than one's husband. She had never before noticed the Swedes as being so dour and unobliging, but that was doubtless something to be learnt too.

That night Margaret slept brokenly and badly. There was heavy traffic in the street outside. Margaret wondered how much worse it would be when Henry's road was completed; thought warmly of Colonel Adamski; and tried to deflect her mind, though, lying there awake, it was difficult. She explained to herself that she had, after all, consumed very little energy that day; done little but lie about and ruminate.

At some dark and unknown hour, there was a tap at the door. It actually woke Margaret up.

Into the Wood

The woman officer entered. Could this be another, Margaret instantly thought, who did not sleep? It seemed very unlikely, despite Adamski's emphasis upon the all-sorts-to-make-a-world theme.

The woman was carrying a candle. She walked towards the bed and, without preliminary, asked in her strong accent 'Would you like me to pray with you? I'm afraid I can pray only in Swedish.'

Margaret sat up, with a view to showing some kind of respect. Then she felt that the black nightdress which Henry liked, might here be a mistake.

'It's very kind of you,' she replied uncertainly.

'Do not despair,' said the woman. 'There is pardon for all. For all who seek it on their knees.'

'But if I could not understand you—' said Margaret, trying to cover her unsuitable apparel with her arms. It was neither a very ready nor a very gracious reply, but Margaret, newly awakened from scanty sleep, could think of nothing else.

The woman gazed at her from behind the candle in its cheap tin candlestick.

'We never force salvation upon any,' she said, after a longish pause. 'Those who are able to find it, seek it on their own.'

It did seem to Margaret that the woman, having decided to appear at all, could have been more cordial; but she thought she had heard that something of what the woman had said was an item of Salvation Army philosophy.

The woman turned and walked away, shielding the candle-flame with her left hand, and quietly closing the door. Margaret felt that she herself would have been obscurely glad of something further; but had to admit that she had offered little encouragement. She returned to her disturbed and scrappy slumbers. The night seemed very long as well as shockingly noisy;

283

and Margaret had troubled thoughts about the morrow.

In the morning, the woman officer was merely quiet and efficient, though still unsmiling, at least where Margaret was concerned. Margaret wished she could have eaten more of the pleasant breakfast, but found that her mind was too full of conflict. Henry was due to arrive before lunch, and in due course she set off for the railway station, this time carrying her own bag. The place where she had stayed seemed to think it the normal thing to do. They did not offer to send for a taxi, and Margaret felt one could hardly ask. Nor did she much care for the taxi-drivers of Sovastad. Perhaps her muscles had strengthened a little, as her vision, for better or for worse, had a little cleared.

'Had a good time?'

'Lovely.'

'You look a bit peeky.'

'I didn't sleep very well last night.'

'Missing me, I hope?'

'I expect so. How did you get on in Stockholm?'

'Bloody. These Swedes just aren't like us English.'

'Poor Henry.'

'In fact, I've got a problem on my hands. I'll tell you all about it over lunch.'

Which Henry did. Margaret could not complain that he was one of those husbands who keep from their wives everything that they themselves take seriously. And, immediately lunch was over, Henry had to dash off to a different conference with Larsson, and Falkenberg, and the other local ogres. Margaret did not have to consider further, as she had been considering now for more than twenty-four hours, how much she should tell Henry. It was unlikely that at any time she would have to tell him anything crucial about what had happened to her. 'You're still looking under the weather, old girl,' said Henry, as he tore off. 'Even the reception people and the waiter seemed to notice it. I saw them glancing at you. I don't know when I shall be back. I should go and get some sleep. Just trot upstairs and relax.'

He kissed her—really most affectionately.

Margaret did not feel at all like sleep; nor, for that matter, did she feel particularly out of sorts. None the less, she went to their room, took off her dress, and sprawled on the bed in her blue lambswool dressing-gown. It was quite reasonable, after last night's traffic, that she should be short of rest, and perhaps even show it. All the same, no sleep came; and Margaret faced again the problem that there was nothing more to do in Sovastad. Henry's solution to that would undoubtedly be a resumption of sociabilities with the Larssons and Falkenbergs and their kind; which, as he had already observed, would kill two birds with one stone, keep Margaret occupied while assisting business. One reason why Margaret felt unattracted was the time-limit on such associations: she could not, on the instant, become gay and intimate with strangers, and then, on the instant, cut it all off. And it was even worse when the time of cessation was so mobile and indefinite. Margaret could only give, or even take, when she had some consciousness of continuity. Probably, she thought gloomily, it was a serious limitation in the wife of a business-man.

In the end, she put on her dress once more, went out to buy three more postcards, and sent them off to her children. She continued to prevent her mind from dwelling upon all that had happened since the previous triptych of postcards to Dinah, Hazel, and Jeremy.

But it was not until well past midnight that she began to feel alarmed: to be precise, when she heard the tinkling church clock strike three, as she had heard it strike one and two.

Even then, she thought, it might have been simply the fact that once more she was sleeping with Henry in the room. Heaven knew that Henry slept noisily enough to keep anyone awake, especially one who a second time had exerted herself so little during the day. Henry rolled and squirmed. He groaned and snored and panted. Sometimes he cried out. Margaret had to admit that Henry was not (to use his own idiom) good publicity for the institution of slumber. Not that many would sympathise with his wife's predicament: it was too utterly ridiculous, and probably too familiar also. A good wife would take it in her stride; restricted though the stride of a good wife might be.

The tinkling clock struck four and five and six, and Margaret never slept at all. It also struck a single, delicate note at the intermediate half-hours. At some time after half-past-six, with heavy rain, which had begun to fall about an hour earlier, beating drearily against the bedroom window, Henry sat up, trained auxiliary to the day's commands.

At breakfast, he said that she still looked odd, and she noticed that he was watching for the Swedes to be eyeing her. She still did not feel anything out of the ordinary. She had said nothing to Henry about not sleeping. She remarked to herself that to miss one night's sleep was nothing at all by the standard of people who slept badly. Or, at least, by the proclaimed standard. She had been immensely exposed to the suggestion of insomnia; could hardly have been more exposed. Normality, her own possibly rather notable normality of somnolence, would probably be restored when she was returned to her own proper bed. On present evidence, that looked like being the day after tomorrow, but one never knew. The road ruled all.

'Hedvig Falkenberg was asking after you,' said Henry. 'Rather pointedly, I thought. Make some kind of contact, will you? I can't have a coolness with the Falkenbergs on my hands. On top of everything else. They can be damned sensitive, these foreigners.'

Margaret more or less promised, and meant to keep her word. She did not even have to tackle the terrifying Swedish telephone, as one would at home. She had merely to walk the half mile or so up to the Falkenberg's house on its low ridge above the town. Visitors seemed at all times to be not merely welcome but awaited. The walk would do her good. Even the steady rain might wake her up or make her sleep: it was striking how a single force could lead to antithetical results. But Margaret let the hours pass and did nothing. And when Henry returned that night, she did not even have to make an excuse.

'Everything's settled, Molly,' he cried, almost exuberantly. 'Thank God, we can go home tomorrow.'

Possibly it was owing to the lifting of the weight on his mind that, on this second night after his return from Stockholm, Henry slept much more quietly; much better, as people say. Margaret heard him purring gently and evenly as a child: hour after hour after hour, while the church clock chimed and the rain pattered. As this second sleepless night slowly passed, Margaret ceased finding explanations, making excuses, pretending to herself.

If only she could walk about! A few minutes after the stroke of five, she got out of bed, and, in almost total silence, drew on her shirt, trousers, and anorak. She stood for a long time looking out at the infinitely slow and laboured dawn. She would have liked to escape, but in this place the door would be locked, and a night porter, even if there was one, would shrink away from her and be beyond communication. She must still, for a spell, be reasonable.

She hid away her clothes and crept back into bed. Henry was still purring away, but as she drew near to him, he seemed to give a single, curious sigh, as of a man dreaming about the past which is always so much sweeter than the present.

'Henry,' said Margaret after breakfast. 'You have said several times that I'm not looking very well. As a matter of fact, I haven't been sleeping. And quite by chance, I've found a place where people from all over the world go when they don't sleep. Would you mind very much if I stayed behind for a while? Just for a short time, of course?'

The argument took every bit as long as she had expected, but Margaret was developing new resources now, even though she had little idea of what they were.

'I'll let you know immediately I get out of the wood,' she promised. 'It's one of those things you have to live through until you emerge the other side.'

NOTES BY THE AUTHOR

At Mr James Wade's Request[1]:
A Few Small Notes upon *Sub Rosa*

The dedicatee was Marina Mahler, grand-daughter of the composer.[2]

'The Unsettled Dust' is based upon a visit to Wimpole Hall, the residence of Mrs Bambridge, only daughter, and principal legatee, of Rudyard Kipling. In her will, Mrs Bambridge left the house to the National Trust. The dust in the story is authentic, when I visited the place; and its origin particularly mysterious in that the general maintenance was at the highest level. Other themes in the story derive from my own experience of the National Trust, and of the campaign for restoring derelict navigations; I being the founder of the Inland Waterways Association.

'The Houses of the Russians' (one of his best stories, in the author's opinion) is based upon the Finnish town of Savonlinna. The town is described fairly faithfully, and the deserted houses of the Russians will be found on their island by anyone who cares to look, and to cross the crumbling bridge. Perhaps the bridge is now repaired. Perhaps the houses are demolished. I was there in the mid-1960s.

289

About 'No Stronger than a Flower', written many years ago, Margaret Rawlings (eminent actress) remarked that, 'The moral is always stick to *Elizabeth Arden*'.

The cathedral in 'The Cicerones' (originally commissioned by August Derleth[3], and published by Arkham House) was at Antwerp, but the events described in the story happened to me so precisely (almost) that I moved the whole thing, including all the detail, to the cathedral at Ghent. I fear, therefore, that the student has to visit both cathedrals: not that he will regret doing so, or she.

There are such establishments as are described in 'Into the Wood', though the quotation by way of epigraph from Strindberg's *Inferno* is something of a cheat, because, though Strindberg was of course a Swede, the actual place he refers to in this passage was in Germany. The town referred to in the story is Östersund, which, in my opinion, is much as I describe it, and the lake is Lake Storsjön, complete with monster (visit the local museum for further details).

Everything in 'Ravissante' is topographically correct, and all the Belgian painters named, exist; their works being every bit as remarkable as is implied. This story led to a strange row, of shaking significance to all authors: a lady to whom I presented a copy of the book (thus surely establishing my innocence?) claimed that Madame A. was a caricature of her, and would never speak to me again. Authors beware! The unconscious does strange things, within both them and their readers.

'The Inner Room', which has been reprinted many times, and which was filmed by Universal[4], is based simply upon looking into the window of a toyshop in Hounslow when I can't have been more than five. I was in the company of my great uncle: see my autobiography, *The Attempted Rescue*. In the window were the wires described in the story, and the shop keeper refused to sell them to my great uncle on my behalf.

About 'Never Visit Venice' I can only remark that the 'large inscription daubed by supporters of the previous Italian regime' were still in the position described when I was there in about 1962. Much nonsense is talked about Venice, which is again hardly dealt with in my story, 'Pages from a Young Girl's Journal'; but, in fact, it is of course the most beautiful place in Europe, beyond all comparison, and a transcendental experience to visit, especially in Autumn. The point is that one has to go with the right person; and this is the point implicit in both my stories. If one does not, the city takes a curious revenge.

Robert Aickman
October 1978

Notes
1. James Wade (1930-1983) was known in the horror field for his short stories and weird poetry.
2. Gustav Mahler's granddaughter was 'Marina' (b.1943), suggesting that the dedication of *Sub Rosa* to 'Miranda' in 1968 may have been an error.
3. August Derleth (1909-1971) published 'The Cicerones' in *Travellers by Night* (1967).
4. Aickman may have been aware of interest in filming 'The Inner Room', but no such film is known to exist.